The

THE 4TH SECRET

R. D. SHAH

CANELO

First published in the United Kingdom in 2016 by Urban Fox Press

This edition published in the United Kingdom in 2020 by

Canelo Digital Publishing Limited
Third Floor, 20 Mortimer Street
London W1T 3JW
United Kingdom

A CIP catalogue record for this book is available from the British Library.

Print ISBN 978 1 78863 737 4
Ebook ISBN 978 1 911591 68 9

Look for more great books at www.canelo.co

Printed and bound in Great Britain by Clays Ltd, Elcograf S.p.A.

To the young lady who stole my heart
and the reason this book is so very late.

'Charlotte Isabella'

My beautiful daughter

Chapter 1

That blood-curdling growl echoed down the murky stone-walled corridor once again, as Father Danilo Baziak stumbled upon the soft uneven soil surface beneath him and fell face-first to the mud floor. The sharp pain barely registered as he looked down to see a jagged piece of stone protruding from the earth, which had dug deeply into his thigh. Immediately he scrambled to his feet and forcefully limped onwards even as a feeling of sheer terror engulfed him.

What in God's name were those things? Human beings or animals? And as for their teeth!

Baziak pushed the horrifying image of them from his mind and focused on the wooden ladder at the end of the passageway, just metres ahead. If he could only make it outside, his jeep was parked within a stone's throw. Those damn things might be fast but let them try and outrun a four-litre engine.

Baziak struggled to keep his injured leg moving forward, as the pain from the jab he had received began to stifle his senses, but a distant scuttling sound behind him now encouraged him to step up the pace.

They were getting closer.

Within seconds he had reached the steps and was already pulling himself up them as, somewhere below, the sounds of scuffling grew louder and louder. Reaching the top step, he threw back the trapdoor and pulled himself up onto the cold floor, before slamming the cover back down and locking it shut as, below, that *something* began to thump heavily against it.

The room around him was dark except for a few silver rays of moonlight shining through the two large shattered windows in the wall opposite, exposing the dilapidated interior of a small church. The wooden flooring was peppered with gaping holes through which an assortment of thistles and other weeds had sprung up, and chips of grubby white paint littered the ground like fallen snowflakes encountered on a cold winter's night.

Baziak was back on his feet in an instant, and racing over to the Church's only exit. But, as he reached the door something solid struck the other side of it with such force that the cleric was thrown right back across the room, and slamming hard against some desiccated wood panelling that gave way with a loud crack. As dust and splinters of fractured wood sprinkled all around him, Baziak struggled to focus his thoughts on the cause of the blow... though he realised he already knew. The impact had hit him pretty hard and his vision was blurred, but it wasn't what he saw but what he smelt that sent a fresh wave of fear coursing throughout his body. A blend of rotting flesh and pungent chemicals assaulted his nose like smelling salts, and out from the now open entrance doorway something moved. Something fast. *Something* big.

A bulky shadow swept across the wall and then came to a halt within inches of the strip of moonlight separating them. Baziak could feel his breathing quicken uncontrollably as his eyes tried to focus. He couldn't yet get a clear image; the force of the impact and the dust in his eyes having seen to that, but he didn't need one... for he knew what was there. That swaying shadowy outline was now joined by two others and the reflective glint from their teeth betrayed the true height of these things.

Father Baziak shakily got to his feet, but his wounded thigh immediately gave way and he crumpled back onto the floor with a thud. The heaving silhouettes began to encircle him whilst all the time staying just out of the moonlight, and expelling a series of scratchy low-level grunts. Baziak felt a stream of warm liquid trickle down inside his trouser leg as he lost control of his bladder, but the humiliating sensation seemed to bring some clarity to the priest's thoughts and he felt a sliver of strength return to his muscles. He immediately latched onto this resurgence and then closed both his eyes and pressed his hands together in prayer. 'Oh, my Lord, give me the strength to do your will and endure this evil...' He was only halfway through uttering his prayer when a warm and fetid breath brushed his cheek, the putrid and offensive smell of it now overpowering.

'I have a message for your masters,' a voice whispered, in a deep and husky tone, as the priest continued to mutter prayers, his eyes still tightly shut. 'And don't bother wasting your breath as it won't do you any good here, priest,' the voice then hissed angrily. 'Your soul now belongs to me.'

Chapter 2

'And welcome back to The Midnight Hour, where we're talking to the renowned archaeologist and Cambridge professor Alex Harker about the success he's enjoyed during the past year, and to try and dig a little deeper into his personal method for success.'

Alex Harker sat back deeper into his chair and forced a smile at this wholly unremarkable pun, with only one thought occupying his mind: *What the hell was he doing here on a late night show that catered to a mixture of drunken college students and the unemployable, even if it was being filmed during the afternoon.* Just off stage, the keen-looking and wide-eyed expression of Dean Thomas Lercher – or Doggie to his friends – instantly reminded him.

While being persuaded to participate, Harker was told: 'Look, I know this show's not your usual kind of thing but its youth demographic is off the chart, and that's who we primarily want to attract to Cambridge University; the best young minds of tomorrow.' The head dean of archaeology had continued. 'Besides there is no such thing as bad publicity, so do this one for me would you?'

Since Harker's recent discovery of the still-surviving Knights Templar, along with their sworn enemies, the secretive religious sect known as the Magi, he had been working hard to keep Doggie appeased. Even though the archaeology dean had learned only a fraction of the Secrets Harker himself had uncovered, keeping him off the subject of the relics they had both discovered had proved a considerable challenge. Harker had been forced to mollify the older man by agreeing to any piece of promotional activity that was asked of him and that had unfortunately included a toe-curling interview with none other than this star of late-night talk-show cheese, Vinnie McWhicker. Aggressive, unashamedly coarse and frankly just plain offensive, McWhicker had garnered a reputation for his on-air rants, most of which subsequently ended up littering the next day's tabloids.

3

From people with a fetish for plastic surgery to proponents of gay marriage, Vinnie hated them equally. That it was such a widely watched programme astounded Harker, but to his mind it probably had something to do with the majority of its audience at home on a Friday night being fairly drunk and killing off their last half hour of consciousness with this outrageous weekly spectacle of depravity. To be fair, the host had been taking it quite easy on Harker so far but that was probably more to do with the last guest – a prized poodle who could fart on command – that had taken a chunk out of Vinnie's hand when the host's wandering finger had got rather too close to the offending orifice and less to do with any respect the man might feel for Harker. With his greasy-quiff haircut, a bandage wrapped around his bitten digit and a truly revolting diamond-cut yellow blazer, McWhicker was rightly at the top of his game in the world of late-night sleaze, and Harker was just praying that he could get through this with as much of his dignity intact as possible.

'Right, so let's chuck away any notions of grandeur that come with your being a professor and get down to the nitty-gritty.' McWhicker began snidely. 'Many of our viewers may know you from your work in bringing the Dead Sea Scrolls to the UK blah, blah, blah. But I'm sure our viewers are more interested in your most recent discovery... Maybe not!' McWhicker let out a sarcastic laugh, and much to the amusement of his audience. 'No, but seriously, you've had a pretty good time of it lately and your newest find has made all the papers but, for anyone who's been living under a rock, why don't you tell our viewers exactly what you found and, more importantly, what's your secret to discovering these things?'

Harker ignored the host's attempt to goad him and, with a glance at Doggie offstage – who was drawing his fingers across his mouth in the shape of a smile so as to encourage him to be play nice – Harker moved straight into his answer. 'I'd like to claim that I had a secret but I would be merely lying. As archaeologists, we can spend our entire lives sifting through the earth while searching for clues to human history and ninety-nine percent of the time our discoveries are simply down to hard work, data analysis of digs and we pursue clues found in the history books, but rarely do we just simply stumble across artefacts by sheer luck. Yet in this case, that's exactly what happened.'

'Come on, Professor, you're being modest.' McWhicker butted in, and almost managed to sound sincere.

4

'Honestly, it's the truth. You see, about four months ago I was given permission to examine the archives of the British museum right here in London and hidden away in some of the dustier sections I came across a written tablet. The text had been written in Latin and must have been stored in there since God-knows-when. At first I just glanced over it and was about to move on, but something caught my eye. It was a word – *Caesar*. Even now I'm not sure why but I had a feeling it was important.'

'And you were right to be curious?' The TV host was now sounding genuinely intrigued by Harker's account.

'Yes, thankfully. Upon closer inspection, the tablet I had discovered proved to be an eye-witness account of Caesar's funeral. Now the body was cremated eventually, but this account stated that for three days the corpse was on exhibit for the masses to come and pay their last respects. What was really interesting, however, was the mention of a vault where Caesar's most personal effects were taken and stored. The tablet didn't mention the exact location, but it did include references to a few ancient sites around the city of Rome. With some further investigation these clues led my team and myself to a certain area on the outskirts of the city. After permission from the authorities, we formed a dig site, and within days we came across a hollow stone structure or vault. And it was inside it that we made this remarkable discovery.'

Behind Harker a large plasma screen burst into life, displaying the image of a ghostly-white face, the edges of which were lined with a mix of sparkling rubies, emeralds and diamonds.

'This is what we found: the death mask of Julius Tiberius Caesar.' Harker shifted in his seat so as to get a better view of the bright screen, while McWhicker also edged closer.

'That's fascinating, Professor, but don't we already know what Caesar looked like?' McWhicker said at last, clearly unimpressed by the discovery. 'Aren't there hundreds of sculptures and coins depicting the face of the Caesar?'

'You're correct that there are many *depictions* but they are exactly that,' Harker gestured towards the screen, 'simply depictions. This is a real-life snapshot, if you will, of Caesar at the very end of his life, and you can make out every feature – the wrinkles, the scars, everything.' Harker now returned his full attention to the monitor, which zoomed in closer to reveal the intricate details of the corpse's skin.

'Wow!' McWhicker offered, sounding even more sarcastic than usual. 'You can even make out the individual pores.'

Harker ignored the man's habitual flippancy and thankfully the audience did as well. 'Yes, it has to be the most accurate representation of Caesar's features that's ever been found. The find of a lifetime in itself but, more remarkably still, the vault was full of the great man's personal effects, including his sword and battle armour. They're still in excellent condition given that they're a few thousand years old.'

The screen faded into a gold breast-plate neatly displayed on a wooden mannequin, with a shiny sword propped underneath.

'That must be worth a fortune?' The McWhicker stammered, finally seeing something of sufficient interest to quell his continuous mockery.

'Absolutely priceless.' Harker affirmed, and momentarily glanced over towards Doggie, who looked ecstatic at this assessment of its worth.

'Very impressive, Professor,' McWhicker declared, before reverting back to his questioning stance. 'Will the public be able to view these items for themselves?'

'I'm happy to say yes. All the items we've recovered will be put on display at Cambridge University between the 1st and the 28th of next month, for anyone to see totally free of charge...' Harker paused briefly as he spotted Doggie rolling a finger at him, urging him to include a pre-prepared snippet. '... but we will of course welcome donations from the public, as funds are essential to carrying out this type of discovery.'

This suggestion brought a sly look to McWhicker's face. 'Well, you've got to make money out of it somehow, haven't you? OK we still have a few minutes, so let's take some questions from the audience.'

McWhicker scanned the various raised hands before his pointing finger settled on an attractive blonde in her twenties. 'Yes, you there in the purple tank-top.'

The girl stood up with her hands nervously clasped together. 'Professor Harker, you exhibited the Dead Sea Scrolls only last year, and now you've found this, too. Can we expect such a discovery to become a yearly event?'

The question was slightly tongue-in-cheek of course, and the sentiment was not lost on Harker as he casually slumped back in his chair. 'I really hope not, because I could use a holiday at some point.' The reaction of amusement he got was somewhat muted, so he immediately sat back upright and continued. 'Er, finds of this importance are rare but, as an archaeologist, it's what keeps me going and I can only hope that my luck holds out.' This answer was received with a bit more enthusiasm, and the woman sat back down with a smiling nod, even as McWhicker motioned for another member of the audience to stand up.

'You mention luck, Professor, but surely you must be the luckiest man alive to have achieved the success you've had just in the last year. Truthfully, what is your secret?'

Even as the man sat back down, Harker's thoughts began to wander. The fact was he had not found the tablet hidden away in the archives of British museum, as he had just announced, but actually in one of the Templar's highly guarded vaults that Sebastien Brulet had allowed him access to. At first the Templar Grandmaster had not exactly been bowled over by Harker's idea of using the collection of numerous artefacts in their possession to enable new archaeological discoveries but, after some convincing, Brulet had eventually allowed him admission to the less sensitive areas of the vault. The Templar's leader had delivered only three stipulations. The first was that Harker should not embark on any all-out crusade to unearth as many items as possible, one rapidly after the other, and thus incur a high level of suspicion regarding such finds. The second was that he was only to go after items of historical and not religious significance, and thirdly there was to be no suggestion of any connection with the Knights Templar and their organisation. This last was a no-brainer, of course, but as always Brulet had laid down the law and therefore it had to be said.

Harker, of course, agreed to all three demands and, after finding the ancient tablet referring to Caesar, he had smuggled the item into the British Museum in a satchel, and then placed it on one of the many rows of shelves, just waiting to be discovered. He had even scrawled a fake filing number in black crayon onto the side of the piece, to ensure that the curators would believe it had simply been misfiled, and therefore become lost amongst the thousands of artefacts stored there. The ploy had worked and the Museum's curators had been extremely grateful to Harker for making such an important discovery.

At the time Harker had felt like a bit of a scam artist, but how else could he bring such a wealth of discoveries to the world's attention without actually mentioning the Templars. A thought that reassured him was that the true crime would be to never let these treasures of history see the light of day. For they belonged to the people of the world and not just to a select few, and it was a sentiment that, thankfully, Brulet agreed with whole-heartedly.

'Lucky, yes, but, as I said I'm not sure I have a secret,' he eventually replied. 'I like to think that archaeological discoveries are born out of making connections. Linking pieces of a puzzle which in turn allow us to make an educated guess as where we should look next. Sometimes you find you're right, and sometimes you're wrong... This time I was right.'

This response drew a look of confusion from McWhicker. 'But I thought you said it was all pure dumb luck?'

'Well, I am not sure about the *dumb* part,' Harker replied stubbornly, 'but yes, in the case of this discovery, luck very much played its part, whereas all the other important discoveries I've made in my career have been a consequence of following clues – and sometimes you get lucky and at other times you're met with disappointment.'

'So you're more like a detective, really?'

This last comment by McWhicker was no doubt said to offer his guest a stroking of his ego, in the hopes that it might elicit a self-important response.

'You could say that,' Harker replied, feeling a bit self-conscious at the notion, 'but I don't carry an official badge or anything.' His remark extracted a laugh from the audience, much to the delight of McWhicker who gave an-over-the top bellow of mirth before turning back to his guests.

'Right, one more question.' McWhicker said and once again swivelled his hand across the seated audience before settling on a man in his late twenties wearing a T-shirt reading *Conspiracy Theorists Rule*. 'Yes, you, sir.'

'Professor Harker, isn't it true that you were involved in a cover-up of the highest level last year at the Vatican?'

The question caught Harker totally by surprise and, after a brief stunned pause, he regained his composure and addressed the man, who was now glaring at him. 'I'm not sure I follow you?'

'I mean,' the young man continued smugly, 'that you were directly involved in the disappearance of Pope Adrian VII, and in the stories circulated in the media regarding his disclosure to world leaders that the second coming is upon us and that Jesus once more walks the earth?'

Usually when someone voices an outlandish statement, others will immediately take it upon themselves to laugh or shake their heads, but as Harker watched the audience in front of him, he detected not even an ounce of disbelief. In fact, the whole audience appeared riveted, and was staring at him with nothing but keen interest.

A few seconds of silence passed until it was McWhicker who spoke first. 'If someone in our audience had asked that same question a few years ago, I'd have assumed he was some religious nutcase but, given the current climate, I'd now say it's a fair question. We've all heard the rumours surrounding events at the Vatican last December... the shooting of Cardinal Rocca and these revelations by the Pope regarding the second coming. So, were you involved?'

Harker immediately smelt a rat. One of the provisos agreed to before staging this interview was that there was to be no mention of the speculation that had filled the world's press several months earlier. It was a proviso that obviously McWhicker had been keen to get around by placing a mole in the audience.

Ever since the dramatic events at the Vatican, the media had been awash with conspiracy theories surrounding the now missing Pope's disclosure. Every newspaper in the world had been trying to crack the mystery of what had actually occurred. Most of the world leaders had remained silent, though, no doubt not wanting to associate themselves in any way with the story for fear of destroying their own political credibility. No politician was foolish enough to have given an interview regarding the ex-Pope's declaration that the Christ child was now back on earth and that, in his eyes, this signified a genuine second coming. But still rumours abounded. The majority of the globe had moved on from that event in disbelief, but there were many others who had sunk their teeth into the story and refused, understandably, to let go. The papers had, and still did, consider it newsworthy enough to follow these rumours from a distance and they were still reporting Christ sightings with the same passion which Elvis once received. Furthermore, there had been many serious discussions on legitimate news programmes regarding the dramatic events, and the debate on whether we were really seeing a prophecy come to fruition had become prevalent. Most had scoffed at such an idea but the coverage had nevertheless left an air of uncertainty and curiosity concerning the whole affair, creating very real whispers amongst ordinary people and Christian churches throughout the world. Without proof though it was only gossip, although tinged with a general *wish* to believe, and that power of belief had proved to be a strong one.

'I've heard the gossip, yes, but from my understanding, that's all it is. The shooting at the Vatican shocked us all, as did the disappearance of Pope Adrian, but the one thing I can be certain of is that I myself wasn't involved in any way. Besides which, if I thought the second coming was a reality, then I can assure you I would be the first to voice it.' Harker paused for a moment, eyeing the same audience member intently. 'So, I think you may be taking the slogan on your T-shirt a bit too seriously.'

'Really,' the conspiracy theorist, whilst pulling a photograph out from under his seat and holding it up in the air for everyone to see. 'Then how do you explain this photograph taken on the very same night showing you leaving St Peter's Basilica just before the shooting, in company with a young girl wrapped in a cardinal's cloak?'

The cameras immediately zoomed in on the photograph in question, displaying it on all the studio's monitors, including the one directly behind Harker. The image was in colour and, although somewhat blurred, it clearly showed Harker glancing over his shoulder at the expanse of media covering that night's event and guiding a woman with long black hair away from the Basilica.

'Well Professor?' the same man continued with an accusing stare.

The whole studio had fallen silent, with seconds seeming to evolve into minutes, and Harker felt a nervous flush run through him. It was only slight, though, because thankfully he had prepared an answer to this question months earlier, under the guidance of Brulet, but had never had to voice it. Until now.

'That's me all right, but I'm afraid the reason for my being there is going to disappoint you. As some of you may know, I was, at one time, a Catholic priest and I still have many close friends at the Vatican. I asked to attend the event in support of my friend Salvatore Vincenzo who was organising the evening and, as many will know, has since become the new Pope. I brought with me my then girlfriend, but she was sick as a dog after the long flight over and managed to throw up all over her dress, so I took her outside for some fresh air. One of the cardinals was good enough to offer his robe to save her the embarrassment of being photographed by the world's media with vomit down her front.' Harker let out an awkward laugh. 'The good news is that I wasn't asked to pay for the cleaning bill.'

No sooner had he finished speaking then almost the entire audience raised their arms in unison, and the conspiracy theorist disappeared behind a wall of bodies all wanting to ask the next question. As Harker struggled to hold in the gasp of relief threatening to emerge, it was McWhicker who quelled the tumult by waving his hands in the air. Maybe he was not expecting his ploy of a planted conspiracist to be so completely overshadowed by the rest of the audience.

'We can't hope to answer everyone's questions so allow me to pose a few myself.' He turned to face his guest with a glint of unshakable resolve in his eyes that to Harker seemed almost comical. 'Professor. I wasn't going to bring this up but I must be fair to my audience.' McWhicker managed to sound almost magnanimous. 'You can't honestly expect us to believe that obviously well-rehearsed story of yours? I mean the shooting of a cardinal inside St Peter's and the subsequent absconding of the Pope himself has been one of the biggest stories of the decade. Then the rumours, from credible sources, that the same Pope had been right in the middle of revealing to world leaders his belief that the second coming has already happened,' McWhicker began shaking his head wildly, 'and you're really saying that you know nothing about it, even though you just happened to slip out of the Basilica within minutes of the shooting taking place?'

Harker allowed the studio to fall silent as the talk show host stared at him with eyes full of accusation before finally, after a few uncomfortable moments, replying in the most relaxed tone he could muster. 'Yes, Vinnie, that is exactly what I am saying. Because it's the truth. I'm sorry but I don't know what else to tell you except that if there was some alternative agenda, as the man in the audience seems to think, then I am just as uninformed as he is.'

Murmurs of discontent now broke out around the studio as McWhicker clicked his head to the side, no doubt getting word through his earpiece to drop the subject and move on. Begrudgingly he nodded his head. 'Well, that's good enough for me,' he declared and ignoring disbelieving moans from the audience. 'Professor Alex Harker, thank you for being my guest here tonight.'

Harker offered a courteous nod, then he reached over and shook McWhicker's bandaged hand squeezing it deliberately tightly until the host winced and pulled back from that tight grasp. Despite gritted teeth he maintained his smile as he turned to address the audience. 'Ladies and gentlemen, give him a hand.'

The audience managed to respond with a polite patter of applause, though many of the guests were eyeing Harker with a look of distinct mistrust.

'The Vatican, shootings and throwing up... what a story. But I'm afraid that's all we have time for in this session of The Midnight Hour. My thanks to all tonight's guests, and also remember that you can see the new Caesar exhibit for yourself as of next month, so just log on to our website for all the details. Have a good night and I'll catch you next time.'

The programme's theme tune had barely begun playing before Harker was out of his seat and off the stage, shooting Doggie an unhappy glare as he began heading straight for the exit. He wanted to get out of there before someone else tried to corner him, and was already reaching for the door handle when a voice sounded from behind.

'Professor Harker, I need a word.'

Harker snapped his head round to see a man wearing jeans and a leather jacket, who was waving his hand vigorously. He was about to ignore the fellow's pleas when he then noticed the white dog collar poking out from under his jacket, stopping him in his tracks more through an instilled reaction than a deliberate choice. The man seized this opportunity and hurriedly made his way over.

'Thank you for waiting.' The casually dressed priest began. 'My name is Father John Strasser... and I'm here on behalf of an old friend of yours.'

'An old friend? Who?' Harker replied curtly, trying to subdue the anger he still felt at having been ambushed on stage.

'A friend who needs your help. May we talk somewhere private?' The priest continued. 'There's a coffee shop just around the corner, if that's suitable?'

Harker glanced back at the ruckus now being created by a small section of the audience, led by the T-shirted guy, who were trying to force their way past the security guards, as Doggie stood waving his arms agitatedly in the air.

'Of course.' Harker replied and continued heading out of the exit. 'Anywhere else but here.'

Chapter 3

Harker raised to his lips the grimy white coffee cup, with the words 'Meridian Cafe' printed across it, and took a sip before placing it back down onto the chipped matching saucer with a clink. 'That's nasty... tastes like sewage water.' He gagged visibly before wiping the last traces of the offending liquid from his lips with a paper napkin. 'Not that I've tasted raw sewage mind you but I'm fairly sure that's how it tastes.' Harker dropped the napkin down on to the table top and, with a final wince of disgust, he turned his full attention to the man who had guided him to this cafe not five minutes' walk from the ITV studios. 'So are you going to reveal who this old friend of mine is, or should we continue with the small talk?'

Harker waited as Father Strasser eyed him with the all the nervousness of a man in the dock. At only five feet two inches in height, the softly spoken priest's oversized front teeth and hunched posture endowed him with the look of a rodent. The way he clutched his miserable cup of coffee protectively with both gloved hands helped contribute to his remarkably rodent-like appearance, although admittedly, one that was rather old and declawed. But it was the man's eyes that distinguished him and Harker couldn't ignore the sparkling intelligence that clearly lay behind those light-blue irises.

'I am working with a group that was specially formed in the wake of your recent exploits,' Strasser took a moment to anxiously clear his throat, 'or perhaps the word discoveries is more appropriate. I of course refer to the supposed birth of the Christ child and the subsequent disappearance of his holiness Pope Adrian VII.'

This mention of the pontiff's title drew a contemptuous scowl from Harker. 'I think you mean John Wilcox and, believe me, there's nothing saintly about him.'

'That may be the case and, for the record, I agree with you,' Strasser replied with a conciliatory nod. 'But nonetheless he was elected to the papacy under that name, and it has been deemed appropriate that the title remain.'

'Appropriate so as to keep things quiet?' Harker mused sarcastically.

'No Professor Harker – I mean appropriate for the protection of our faith. What would you have us do? Tell the whole world this charlatan conned his way into the highest position in Christendom, before attempting to deceive the entire globe by faking the second coming with a clone of Jesus Christ! And, while we're at it, why not also disclose to the world that this same pretender then disappeared – along with the child.'

Even though Strasser's voice remained calm and discreet, his eyes burnt with genuine distress, and it was clear that this priest was still wrestling in his own mind with the consequences of those events.

'OK, well, maybe I wouldn't tell them everything.' Harker offered, not wanting to contribute to the man's increasing agitation.

'Some secrets should stay hidden, Professor. Besides which, the decision was not mine to make.' Father Strasser paused and sucked in a deep breath. 'But nevertheless it is ours to rectify.'

'*Ours?*' Harker almost spat out the word. 'I'm not sure I follow you?'

Strasser glanced around the otherwise empty cafe, briefly pausing to study the overweight male member of staff stood at the counter who strangely had his head buried in a copy of *Woman's Own*. Satisfied that the man was more concerned with the magazine than with his two remaining customers, Strasser turned back to face their table, rested his elbows on its surface and leant inwards. 'When it was discovered what John Wilcox had been planning,' the priest continued offering a courteous nod to Harker at this mention of Adrian VII's real name, 'a special council was set up to deal with the implications of Jesus Christ himself once again walking the earth... or perhaps *crawling* is a more accurate statement.'

The attempt at a joke forced a lame smile out of Harker. 'Amusing, Father, but what implications exactly? The child was merely a clone copy. This whole second-coming 'business' was a charade. It was no more genuine than...' he pointed to the cup in front of him, '... than this cup of coffee!'

Strasser sat still, his eyes fixed on Harker. 'If I fill a cup with water and that cup has a crack in it then soon the cup will drain away and become empty. But what if I picked up that same cup and tipped the water out myself… the same conclusion would be reached since the cup would still end up empty. So the question is: would the very act of my tipping out the water have had any real bearing on the outcome?'

'How very Zen of you, Father Strasser,' Harker joked. 'You're wearing the wrong outfit; you should have been a Buddhist.'

Strasser gave a slight shake of the head, his expression resolute and unyielding. 'I am serious, Professor. Would it have made any difference?'

'OK, I'll play along.' Harker replied, discerning instantly the point that was being made, but not wanting to seem discourteous before this man had reached the conclusion of his analogy. 'It would at least make a difference to anyone watching the spectacle. That I know.'

'Maybe so, but it wouldn't make any difference to the cup itself now, would it.'

'And the second coming is the cup, right?' Harker replied, just wanting to make sure they were both on the same page.

Strasser sat further back into his seat and gave a nod, his eyes full of concern. 'The fact that this event has been brought about by the hands of man is unimportant. The fact is it has happened, however, and that truth cannot be reversed… which means repercussions.'

'Repercussions!' Harker said it so loudly that even the *Woman's Own* enthusiast briefly looked their way, before quickly losing interest in them and returning to his magazine for more tips on the female mind.

Harker massaged his brow in frustration, seeking a way of not completely insulting the peculiar little man sitting opposite him. 'Father Strasser, I think it's important, before we go any further, that I be totally honest with you concerning my feelings on the subject.' He took a moment to steal another sip of his rank-tasting coffee, then rolled his shoulders as if limbering up for a fight. 'Yes, it is true that the plot to fake the second coming of Christ through cloning techniques is without a doubt the most amazing, most crooked, boldest and frankly terrifying idea to gain control of the Catholic church I could ever have dreamt of. It is without doubt the stuff of movies and that it was perpetrated by the very person that sought and succeeded in becoming the Pope, and head of the Catholic world, is nothing short of a dark miracle. But…' Harker laid both his palms on the table and leant across it. 'If you really think that tragic scam has anything to do with the reality of Christian doctrine, then I would put it to you, Father, that you are as crazy as the man who started all this.' Harker pulled away and settled back in his seat, his eyes ablaze with contempt. 'I myself do not believe that for a second and, if I can be blunt with you Father, were you really to believe that then I would say you're as loony as Pope Adrian himself!'

Across the table, Strasser maintained his expressionless stare, responding with a voice still calm and confident. 'Your belief is not a requirement one way or the other and, if it helps, I myself was filled with a similar sentiment.' The priest replied. 'That is until the recent incident.'

'What incident?' Harker spat out, now wishing he had remained silent until the end of Strasser's story.

'Two weeks ago, we received word of an attack on a priest... one Father Danilo Baziak.'

'An attack?'

'Yes, an animal attack.' Strasser replied, already loosening the straps secured by a shiny brass buckle on the black leather satchel next to him. He pulled out three colour photos and passed them over to Harker. 'The poor soul was found simply dumped somewhere near Kiev, barely alive and bleeding to death from bite marks that couldn't be identified.'

The first photo offered showed a man lying on a hospital gurney in the emergency room. The patient was wearing only jeans and the left trouser leg had been cut away to reveal an horrific pear-shaped bite mark that had shredded most of the man's thigh down to the bone. A second bite mark visible on his shoulder was of the same shape, but there was no tearing this time, only puncture marks similar to those made by a dog, but far too big for any canine Harker knew of.

'There was saliva still in the wounds, which we had tested,' Strasser continued, 'but the results failed to identify the animal responsible. Stranger still, when the DNA was mapped further, it was determined to come from an animal of unknown origin. The scientists had never encountered the genetic make-up before... not from anywhere within the animal kingdom.'

Harker said nothing but resumed his examination of the second and third photos, showing each of the wounds in close up. He felt the onset of nausea as he passed them back to Strasser, who carefully slipped them back into his satchel. 'Those are nasty wounds, and no doubt a mystery worthy of Bigfoot but, without sounding heartless, so what?'

Strasser secured the satchel's buckle and leaned closer once more. 'So what, Professor, is that the priest was still rambling in and out of consciousness while asserting that he had been attacked by *demons* and, what's more, that they gave him a message to relay to his masters, as they put it.' Strasser licked his lips nervously. 'The message consisted of only a few words: *The three Secrets are upon you. Prepare for the end.*' The rodent-faced little priest clasped his hands together and squeezed them. 'Are you aware of the three Secrets of Fatima?'

To Harker the remark appeared more of an insult than a question. 'Father, it was my faith in the church I lost, not my memory.'

The priest raised his eyebrows apologetically but said nothing, allowing Harker a chance to demonstrate his knowledge of the subject.

'The three Secrets are a prophecy from the early 1900's,' he began. 'The story goes that three Portuguese shepherds, merely children, were visited by an angel who related to them three truths concerning the future of the world. The first two disclosures were related to a vision of hell predicting the two world wars that would follow...'

'And the third?' Strasser interrupted.

'The third was supposed to be released in 1960, but instead it remained in its sealed envelope until a few years ago, when Pope John Paul II finally approved its release. It apparently referred to the attempted assassination of Pope John Paul himself, back in the eighties.'

'Why do you say apparently?' Strasser questioned, his gaze unblinking.

'Because, beside the Pope and a select few, no one else has actually laid eyes on these three Secrets. Not the originals, at any rate.'

'Exactly.' An uneasy smile crossed Strasser's lips. 'You are correct in saying that only a select few have ever viewed the Secrets, but it is the contents of them that is the troubling part. Despite what the Catholic world has been led to believe the third was actually opened in 1960 by Pope John XXIII, and he was so troubled by the text that he had it and the other two locked away in the depths of the Vatican archive, under the papal mandate that only a reigning pope should have access to them. It was here that the Secrets of Fatima remained under close protection for another fifteen years, until Pope Paul XI saw fit to break the papal mandate by forming a council of three church scholars to revise and fully interpret these Secrets once and for all. After almost a year, the council of three reported their finding to the pontiff, and within days he determined that the Secrets were too dangerous to be kept in one place, and it was just as dangerous to reveal them to the public. Pope Paul entrusted a close confidant to distribute just two of them throughout the Catholic world so that no one would ever have access to all three at the same time.'

'That seems a bit drastic.' Harker remarked, his response sounding a tad more sarcastic than he had intended to. 'If they were considered that dangerous, why not simply destroy them?'

'We don't know,' Strasser replied. 'But what we do know is that a note was written by Pope Paul which was placed along with the first secret in a safe in his holiness's private quarters, for all future pope's eyes only. On the death of a reigning pope, the safe key is retrieved from around the pontiff's neck and held secure by a designated member of the pontifical guard before being passed on to his successor. So when John Wilcox did his vanishing act, along with the key, the safe had to be broken into and both the note and the first secret were retrieved.' Strasser stopped and took another sip of his coffee, taking his time about it as if to heighten the anticipation for his coming revelation.

'Well?' Harker grunted as he became increasingly annoyed at what seemed like the older man's deliberate stalling for effect. 'What did they say?'

'Well, the note said the three Secrets would lead to a change so massive, so all-consuming, that the world would cease to be as we know it – and that this 'process' would begin with a single happening.'

'A happening?'

'Yes, a happening such as was described in the first Secret – the one discovered along with the note.'

'OK then,' Harker dropped his gaze, and was now looking highly curious, 'what did the first secret say would start this whole thing off?'

'It said the *happening* would be the second coming of Jesus Christ,' Strasser shuffled uncomfortably in his seat, 'reborn and returned to us in the twenty-first century.'

Harker shook his head in astonishment as the statement sank in. 'Then, in that case, I'm not surprised Pope John Paul and his prede-cessors kept it quiet... Not surprised at all.'

Strasser nodded agreeably. 'Yes, can you imagine the chaos it would cause if the pontiff announced to the world a specific timetable for the second coming?'

Harker let out an ironic laugh. 'More to the point, can you imagine if he announced it and it never occurred? Talk about a loss of credibility to the Church at large.'

'Exactly,' Strasser agreed. 'That's why details of the happenings predicted in the other two Secrets were never made public. The damage would be potentially appalling, since the Church is meant to be the authentic voice of truth and authority. But that's not all, for the note also declared that the only way to impede this oncoming cataclysm is to know all three secrets.'

'Know all *three*? What does that mean?' Harker was genuinely puzzled.

'That we don't know.' Strasser murmured through gritted teeth, his frustration showing through. 'With a foreknowledge of the Christ child's rebirth, the content of the other two Secrets would become extremely important to millions of the faithful. Now more than ever.'

Harker took a moment to eye Strasser carefully. The priest was the picture of sincerity, but still he shook his head dismissively. 'Father, I want to know where the child is more than anything but for the record, and as I already said, that child is a clone: it was a man-made event. It has, therefore, no relevance to whatever these Secrets are referring to.'

The older man let out a deep sigh. 'Maybe… maybe not. But many of the cardinals now believe that the child, along with those two other secrets, are the key to stopping this cataclysmic event. And whether this happening is man-made or not, it has forced them to take the Secrets of Fatima all the more seriously. Some are even saying that the discovery of all three will prove to be mankind's salvation, and so they must be retrieved at all costs.'

Harker slumped in his chair and took a few seconds to absorb this information. Human history was saturated with prophecies and spiritual messages of impending doom which never amounted to anything, yet the very existence of a Christ child gave an unsettling and real dimension to what he was now hearing. 'Didn't the note indicate where the *other* two Secrets had been hidden?'

Strasser was already shaking his head. 'The note they found had been torn in half, and the best guess is that missing portion was taken by the previous pope.'

'Wilcox?' Harker moaned.

'Yes, since he was the only one with access to the safe. And with his whereabouts unknown, it seems unlikely we will find out any time soon.'

'Does anyone in the Church have a clue where these Secrets are hidden – even a rough idea?' Harker pressed, and becoming ever more aggressive in his tone.

'No.' Strasser replied, pausing to chew thoughtfully on his bottom lip. 'With the exception of perhaps one man. Does the name Marcus Eckard mean anything to you?'

Harker mulled it over for a few seconds before replying, 'No. Who is he?'

'You know that council of three I mentioned earlier, to whom were charged the task of reviewing the three Secrets in full.'

'Yes,' Harker replied.

'The three men selected were highly respected scholars and deemed trustworthy by the then pope. The first, Father Yohansen, who was vice-head at the Vatican's archives, sadly passed away some years ago due to natural causes. The second was Cardinal Winchowser, who worked for the Vatican's Governorate dealing with security issues, but unfortunately he has also since passed on, leaving just one man left.'

'Marcus Eckard?'

'Yes. Eckard was never a man of the cloth, although he was the president of the Vatican's Academy of sciences for some years. He's a mathematical genius and physicist with an extremely trustworthy character, and also a cunning linguist. When I say 'genius' I'm not exaggerating; he was the youngest person ever to graduate MIT and has enough accolades and awards to fill a warehouse – and he gained them all before he was eighteen!'

The man's résumé was indeed impressive and Harker let out a gasp of respect. 'I get it, he's a very smart man.'

Strasser nodded unemotionally. 'It was he that Pope John asked to hide the Secrets, and it is for that same reason that those worried cardinals I spoke of would like you to talk with him and discover what he knows… as a personal favour to the Church.'

The request was an odd one and Harker's expression said it all. 'So why don't one of those same cardinals pay him a visit? Why are you asking me?'

Strasser cleared his throat and lent closer even though the coffee shop was otherwise empty of customers. 'Because firstly you already have knowledge of the Christ child's existence but, just as importantly, the council feels it prudent to keep the Church at a distance from this one. You see, he's at Blackwater.'

The name meant nothing to Harker and he raised his shoulders in defeat. 'Blackwater. I've never heard of it. What is it? A government research facility? A private university for the gifted?'

This answer drew a solemn look from Strasser, who gave a slow shake of his head. 'A university? No, nothing of the sort. It's an asylum.' He licked his lips distastefully. 'For the criminally insane.'

Chapter 4

'Marcus Eckard – or Doctor Dread as he's known amongst the staff – has been here since '76, therefore well before my time. They say he was a child prodigy and genius but you would be hard pushed to tell as much these days. As a member of the nursing staff here, I have not been apprised of all the gory details, but what I do know is that one day he left his place of work and just vanished. He was gone for over two weeks, then out of the blue he arrived back home with no recollection of where he had been. The following day a police officer went round to his house to put the missing-persons report to bed, where he encountered Eckard who very pleasantly offered him breakfast. The policeman was halfway through the meal when he noticed part of a cooked human eyeball concealed under a piece of bacon, and the Doctor was arrested on the spot. The other remains of his wife and child were never found, but by then it didn't matter. There was enough evidence to convict him and he ended up here by reason of his insanity. I must confess we rarely get visitors to Blackwater, as this facility, I am sorry to say, is the end of the line for these patients. It's true that we do receive release orders from time to time, but for the majority this institution means never again seeing the light of day. As for Eckard, I can't remember the last time he had a visitor.'

Ward Nurse David Decker halted in front of an imposing-looking green metal door, before pressing a buzzer to the side of it and glancing briefly up at the security camera scrutinising them both overhead. 'You didn't mention the nature of your visit... Professor Harker is it?'

Harker offered a thin yet polite smile. 'No... No I didn't, did I?'

It had taken him over an hour of driving around the neighbourhood to locate the obscure Blackwater facility, tucked away amid the York-shire hills. Concealed behind a high security wall, it was as foreboding as it was strangely reassuring. Add to that a thunderstorm, which had been hurling down rain mercilessly, and the trip here had been something of a nightmare. Strasser had given him the asylum's address and some directions, and had then made an abrupt and annoyingly swift exit. Harker's gripes were exacerbated further when he was next collared by Dean Lercher, who had managed to track him down, as always, and had caught up to Harker just as he was leaving the Meridian Cafe. Doggie had been most inquisitive to see where Harker had disappeared to in such a rush, but his curiosity evaporated in a flash on the mention of a trip north to an asylum for the criminally insane.

'A nuthouse!' Doggie had stammered, in his usual politically incorrect way. 'Well, be careful and if you do get into any trouble, don't call me, just call the police.' Harker was already pulling away in his dark blue BMW 325i before his old friend even had a chance to ask exactly why he was taking this trip. After all, what business did he have visiting an asylum for the criminally insane?

On arriving over four and a half hours later at the facility's secure-entrance checkpoint Harker had been relieved to find his name on the visitor's list, just as Strasser had assured him, and after parking he had swiftly made his way into an elegant building which looked like a country retreat, with intricate stonework and a long lush green lawn at the front. Harker had quickly headed through the main double doors and into the waiting-room. Sadly, that was where the elegance ended and the interior soon revealed the building's true purpose. The rear of the asylum was divided into separate modern wings connected by long corridors and secured by a series of hefty steel doors, each equipped with security cameras and access buzzers giving it the disconcerting feel of a prison. At the reception area, which was protected by a Perspex safety barrier adding to his continuing feeling of unease, Harker had been met by the night nurse David Decker, who had promptly led him on the tour he now found himself on. At six feet tall and with cropped ginger hair over an abnormally high forehead, the nurse resembled Lurch from the Addams family, and upon meeting him Harker had observed him with the same curious stare that now graced the orderly's own face.

'Very well, Professor, I won't pry further,' The nurse replied, and then waited for the next door to buzz open before leading Harker further into the hidden depths of the asylum. 'We have three categories of patients here at Blackwater: types A, B and C. Type A are what we consider to be low risk, with minimal security needed. Type B are considered medium risk; these patients are mainly here for GBH and various degrees of assault although, with regular medication, we have few problems from them.' Nurse Decker paused at another large, yellow steel security door containing a thick Perspex viewing panel in the middle. He pulled out a key from his pocket and slid it into the hole. 'And then there's type C.'

He pushed open the door and ushered Harker into a long grey corridor, with suspension lights cocooned in a steel mesh hanging from the ceiling and running the entire length of the corridor, before closing and locking the door behind them with a clink. Lining either side of the walkway was a series of solid cell doors with sliding observation hatches kept open with nothing but pitch darkness visible behind them. It was clear that bedtime was still in effect, but the scratching noises fused with a few light groans suggested that not all the guests were taking full advantage of their opportunity to sleep.

'Patients assigned to C category are our most challenging residents,' Decker explained quietly, as he led Harker further down the long corridor. 'Most are here for the worst criminal acts imaginable: rape, murder, necrophilia and everything in between. Such colourful characters make up the most violent and deranged criminals Great Britain has to offer.' Decker paused briefly at a door labelled C8 then tapped his finger on it lightly. 'You ever heard of John Dervish – or, as the papers dubbed him, 'Mr Sweetbread.'

The very name caused a feeling of cold panic to rise in Harker's chest. 'The child killer?'

Decker gave a slow, ominous nod, obviously taking great relish in Harker's visibly edgy demeanour. 'Mr Sweetbread, the one and only. He cooked and ate most of his victims… Although I'm glad to say that these days he gets to dine mainly on vegetables and pasta.'

This response was voiced with such eeriness that Harker could feel a thin bead of nervous sweat beginning to develop across his forehead, and he glared at Decker with annoyance. 'Look, I get it, OK' he growled in a low tone, more annoyed at his own instinctive reaction than anything his tour guide had actually said, 'you obviously don't like me because of I wouldn't tell you why I'm here. But that really has to remain a private issue.'

'Not at all,' Decker looked offended. 'It's none of my business why you're here. Now let's get you properly introduced to Eckard, shall we.'

With that, the Addams family *doppelgänger* continued along the corridor with Harker following close on his heels.

'There's a lot of grey.' Harker remarked, as he surveyed the bland corridor in front of him, anxious to prevent Nurse Decker from continuing to divulge any further details of what lay behind these walls. 'Don't the inmates here find it depressing?'

His comment drew a restrained laugh from the orderly. 'I doubt half of them even know where they are, and as for the other half... bright colours only stimulate them, and not in a good way.'

'How do you manage to control such dangerous patients?' Harker persisted.

'Regrettably there is only a minor chance of rehabilitation when dealing with warped minds such as these, so regular drug therapy is key and, of course, the whole of Blackwater is automated in its security.'

'Automated, how?'

'The system is still controlled by supervisors but it means we can secure a prisoner inside his cell in temporary restraints, and exit before the system releases him, which cuts down on potentially violent contact between the most dangerous and the staff.'

Decker's answer fuelled Harker's growing realization of how dangerous these patients actually were. 'You must have some tales to tell during your time at Blackwater. How long have you worked here... you never said?'

Reaching the last door on the left, Decker stopped, eyeing Harker sarcastically. 'No. I didn't, did I?'

Harker let out a defeated sigh, much to Decker's amusement. 'Touché, Mr Decker. Touché.'

Satisfied he was now back on a par with his guest, Decker gave a courteous nod and lightly tapped on the door in front of them. 'I've had him specially secured for your visit but not sedated, so no sudden moves.' Decker shook a finger warningly. 'That makes him extremely edgy as does bright light, so only one of the main lights has been left on.' The troubled expression appearing on Harker's face was not lost on Decker. 'There's really no need for you to be concerned. Like I said, he's fully restrained.' The orderly slipped his key into the door and then paused to remove a silver metal clipboard, with pen attached, from a hook on the wall before placing it in Harker's hands. 'I almost forgot, you'll need to sign this before entering.'

Harker scanned the printout, catching words like 'physical endangerment' and 'liability'.

'It means you can't sue us for any injuries received whilst you're at the asylum.'

'You're not filling me with much confidence.' Harker replied before signing the form.

'I know,' Decker said apologetically, and promptly whisking the clipboard from Harker's hands, 'but during his last assessment hearing, the good Doctor here managed to gnaw off his solicitor's finger when the poor fellow got too close, so now we prefer to cover ourselves against any future such incidents.'

The tall orderly leaned towards the observation hatch and peered inside. 'If you need me press the red panic button next to the door and I will be with you in seconds.'

As Nurse Decker continued to scan the inside of the cell, Harker began to reason what factor was making him feel more on edge: that he was about to enter the cell of a maniac or the fact that the patient was considered so dangerous there was a red panic button next to the door.

Obviously satisfied that everything was in order, Decker popped the lock, swung open the door and waved his guest inside. 'Enjoy.'

Harker edged his way tentatively into the darkened fifteen-by-ten-foot cell, with all the caution of a mouse surveying a mousetrap. A solitary uncomfortable-looking metal-encased toilet sat directly below a small Perspex box window as the rain outside lashed against it in waves. To Harker's left had been placed a grey plastic chair, no doubt in an effort to match the overall decor, and a thick, painted black line ran down the middle of the room across the brown vinyl flooring tiles with the words 'DO NOT CROSS' just beside it. These words alone were enough to induce from Harker an involuntary gulp but the door clanking firmly shut behind him caused him to skittishly jump a step towards the chair.

As Nurse Decker had mentioned, the narrow strip light, protected by the same grey metal mesh enclosing the lighting in the corridor outside, illuminated only half the room, resulting in the chair facing a wall of murky darkness that the cell's occupant was surely inhabiting. As Harker strained to see beyond the gloom, he could just begin to make out the outline of a man perched on what must be a bed, with only the end of one foot peeking out into the light, its sole covered in hard calluses.

Harker gently slid into the visitor's seat provided, which creaked ever so slightly under his weight, and squinted into the shadows ahead.

'Doctor Eckard, may I speak with you?' A few uncomfortable seconds passed as that wall of darkness seemed to merely absorb his words before a reply was forthcoming.

'That depends entirely on who you are,' came the response. The voice was calm, controlled and well-spoken, with an inherent air of confidence that one might expect from a child prodigy or perhaps a narcissist.

'I'm a professor at Cambridge University.'

'A professor, indeed? Come to observe me, have you?' There was real curiosity evident in the man's tone. 'Well I haven't got any time for you. I'm far too busy.'

The pronouncement was deadly serious, and Harker treated it so. 'Might I ask doing what?' he replied, briefly surveying the static surroundings of the cell.

'No, you might not,' came the speedy response, 'but nonetheless it's nice of you to ask. So what brings you're here, Mr Professor at Cambridge University, if that is your real name?'

'Of course, my apologies. My name's Harker – Alex Harker.'

The reply caused the shadowy figure to sit up more attentively. 'Harker, Harker, Harker? That name sounds familiar. Have we met? I pride myself on never forgetting a face, or a name.'

'No, we've not met before, Doctor Eckard... Not face to face, anyway.'

In an instant, the cell's occupant lurched towards him, and into the light, as far as the man's arm restraints would allow, thrusting his face forward and prompting Harker to jolt backwards into his seat.

Such an instinctive retreat could have been interpreted as due to the Doctor's face coming within a foot of his own, or maybe just the shock of having someone suddenly thrusting their face forwards without warning but that wasn't the reason. That wasn't the reason at all. Eckard's features were a roadmap of self-harm and physical abuse, the likes of which Harker had never seen. Scores of healed cuts and tears scoured the man's skin, some fresher than others but all truly horrific in their own right. On both cheeks there were deep indentations where fingernails had ripped through flesh and then healed into thick bluish rake marks not just once but repeatedly, and across Eckard's forehead ran a zigzag of lesions inflicted with such ferocity that the scars had buckled the skin like a plough tearing through hard soil. More disturbing still was the black triangular eye patch that concealed his right eye, held securely in place by a narrow strip of dark-coloured nylon that ran around the Doctor's bald head, which was equally disfigured. Eckard's arms were splayed outwards due to his wrists being secured by metal restraints, each attached to thick plastic rings on either side of the bed frame which had individual electronic locks that could be opened and closed remotely. This was no doubt part of the safety mechanism that Decker had spoken of earlier.

'Are you sure we've not met before?'

'No,' Harker said calmly, while trying to overlook the Doctor's dreadful facial injuries, 'I'm pretty sure that I would remember.'

His remark elicited a wide smile from Eckard. 'Of course you would,' he replied before rhythmically grinding his teeth together a few times, 'I've got one of those faces that people tend not to forget.'

Seeing as Doctor Eckard was responding well to the honesty of the questions raised so far, Harker decided to gesture towards the scars adorning the patients face. 'That's quite a collection of scars you have, Doctor.'

'Thank you,' Eckard smiled. 'It's a work in progress.' He paused briefly to roll his head in a clockwise motion, allowing Harker to get a full view of every facial scar, before resuming his penetrating stare. 'Of course some are family mementos... mementos from a long time ago.'

This remark was potentially distracting to Harker and he immediately pushed the conversation forward, not wanting to get caught up in reminiscing about Eckard's previous crimes. 'Well, thank you for seeing me at such short notice. I appreciate it.'

'Anything for a professor.' With one eyebrow now raised, the grisly-looking Doctor leaned in closer to examine his visitor's face, 'especially one with such lovely eyes.'

This last comment sent a shiver down Harker's spine, as he now recalled the orderly's account of how Eckard had served up a boiled eyeball for the policeman shortly before his arrest. 'Thank you. I inherited them from my mother.'

The remark drew a further smile from the restrained patient. 'Really... well, I hope she doesn't miss them.'

Harker forced a brief laugh which received a stony glance from Doctor Eckard. 'I don't know why you laughed there. It wasn't funny.'

'Then why say it?' Harker replied calmly.

'Just to see if you would laugh. You're not a professor of psychology, are you?'

Doctor Eckard gave a look of mistrust, then slowly swivelled his neck until it emitted a loud satisfying crack, before turning to face Harker once again. 'Ah, that feels good. I get so stiff in these restraints – you know it's tantamount to torture. I don't suppose you could loosen them, could you?'

Harker almost laughed out loud at the idea, but it was raised with such sincerity that he resisted. 'I'm afraid that's not possible Doctor.'

'Very well… It's probably for the best.' Eckard nodded empathetically. 'So… what brings you to the nuthouse, then?'

'The nuthouse!' Harker gawped, genuinely surprised by this casual use of such a disparaging remark.

'Professor Harker, in the cell to my left is a convicted murderer who spends every waking hour masturbating furiously, so much so that they now have to restrain him most days for fear that – and I kid you not – he will tear his own penis off. On my right, is a serial rapist who when free, was not solely content with sexually abusing young college boys and so engaged in 'making love', as he puts it, to as many farm animals as he could get his wandering hands upon, much to the distress of many a farmer… and undoubtedly the animals in question.' Doctor Eckard craned forward and flicked his head towards the cell next door. 'He went by the name of The Night Jockey?'

'That's him?' Harker spluttered, remembering the unpleasant bestiality story from some years earlier, which had filled the tabloids.

'That's him all right,' the Doctor replied dryly. 'So when I refer to this place as a nuthouse, believe me when I tell you that it is the nuttiest.'

Eckard took a moment to slouch back into his restraints, but still keeping his head in the lit portion of the cell. 'So, now we've done away with the embarrassments of my current residence, how about explaining to me what you, Professor Alex Harker at Cambridge University, are doing in it?'

The tone of Eckard's voice had changed during these last few words, sounding more impatient and Harker sought immediately to get to the point. 'Doctor Eckard I'm here concerning your research on the three Secrets of Fatima.' This mention of the Secrets brought about not an ounce of change in the Doctor's demeanour. 'I'm not sure how up-to-date you are on current events, but recently the Secrets have become of great concern to many within the church. In fact, it was a friend within that fold that asked me to speak with you. I've been led to believe that you are the only one to have viewed all three, and I was hoping you would be willing to discuss them.'

Eckard's eye rippled with excitement or recognition or maybe even realisation. It was difficult to tell which but, regardless, one thing was certain. The Doctor was interested.

'Harker,' he murmured, his lips barely moving, 'Alex Harker.' Eckard's eyes closed for a moment, as if lost in thought, and then he was back, his eyes now full of scathing mistrust. 'Who sent you?'

'As I already said, a friend within in the church.'

The Doctor slowly shook his head, his single eye trained squarely on his guest. 'No… who *really* sent you?'

He growled the question with such menace that Harker felt his cheeks begin to heat up in the beginnings of a flush. Did this lunatic know something about the Templars or the Magi? That had to be near impossible unless Nurse Decker had lied about the Doctor never receiving visitors.

'I'm not sure what it is you're getting at, Doctor Eckard, but I can assure you that I'm here as a favour to a friend… A Vatican friend, if that helps.'

Doctor Eckard held his accusing stare for a few moments longer before finally slumping against the edge of his bed, though with his face still visible and displaying a sly grin. 'Now, now, Professor, you're not being entirely honest with me are you. This visit of yours may be on behalf of a friend, but there's only one reason you yourself would be enquiring about the three Secrets.' Eckard ran his tongue across cracked lips, allowing its tip to investigate each individual crevice as a roguish smile took form. 'He's back isn't he? For a second visit?'

Over the next few seconds Harker sat still, his expression emotionless as he debated how much to disclose to this shackled patient whose widening manic grin would have given the Cheshire cat a run for its money. He wasn't sure if telling Eckard of the Christ child's existence would make any difference in the grand scheme of things, but he was certain of one thing: if the Doctor did know anything relevant, then there would have to be some give and take. Besides, the man was locked away in an insane asylum, so who in the world would ever take this lunatic seriously. 'Yes, he is.'

The reply had Eckard immediately bouncing up and down on his bed, as best as his restraints would allow, his excitement palpable. 'I knew it,' the Doctor almost screamed, staring into the empty corner of the room. 'You thought I was crazy, didn't you? You thought I dreamt it, but I *knew*. I knew it was real… so stick that in your pipe and smoke it. Actually you can stick it up your arse, for all I care.' Eckard snapped back to attention and then laughed out loud. 'He never believed me, never had faith. And faith is the key you know.'

Harker was just about to ask who he was talking to, when Eckard noticed the confusion in his guest's eyes and he shook his head from side to side dismissively. 'Oh, don't worry about him. He's been on my case for years, but this vindication is its own reward.' The Doctor released a deep, triumphant sigh and stared at Harker keenly. 'You don't have any idea why you're really here, do you, Mr Alex Harker, professor at Cambridge University' – the madman paused and raised and lowered his eyebrows comically – 'and the owner of such a lovely pair of eyes?'

Somewhat taken back by the man's outburst, Harker simply offered a shake of the head. 'No… but I'm hoping you could help me with that, Doctor.'

This courteous mention of Eckard's erstwhile title appeared to soothe the patient and he sat up somewhat proudly, if not regally. 'Then allow me to reward your honesty,' he began, before expelling a cough to clear his throat, thereby adding to his now professional manner. 'The three Secrets provided a map of events to come. Some things are set in stone and some things are not… The three Secrets, they are both.'

'I'm sorry Doctor,' Harker replied, clearly confused, 'I'm not sure I understand what you mean?'

'The three Secrets tell of a prophecy – a prophecy deemed so powerful by the church that it was carefully hidden away. But they are also a road map to that prophecy… a series of events that will take place, culminating in the fulfilment of the prophecy itself. Yet the prediction is not set in stone, it has no destiny – it can be avoided.

'How?'

'By discovering the nature of the *fourth* Secret.'

'There's a fourth Secret?' Harker blurted out.

'Yes. Few people know that but…'

'But what?' Harker blurted out and struggling not to spoil Eckard's enthusiasm on the subject.

'The three Secrets tell that the Christ child reborn will once again save us all, and so must be protected at all costs from those who wish to bring about the great change predicted...' Eckard had barely finished speaking before a deep frown appeared across his ravaged forehead. 'The child is safe, isn't he?'

'I'm afraid not,' Harker's reply was immediate since he had already made a conscious decision not to hold anything back because the man in front of him might be crazy but he was not an idiot. 'He was abducted some months ago but there's a search in progress even as we speak.'

At the news Doctor Eckard began to shrivel in his seat. 'Listen to me carefully, Professor. The people that have taken him have no wish to stop this prophecy from becoming reality. They wish only for it to be fulfilled, and the death of that child can ensure it. The fate of the child can either cause or prevent these events. You must act quickly, as time is of the utmost importance.'

The suggestion was beguiling to Harker, and he jumped in without hesitation. 'Doctor, does the word Magi mean anything to you?'

'Magi!' Eckard spat. 'Never heard of them, and whoever they are, those are not the ones seeking to kill the child.'

The man's reply only compounded Harker's confusion. 'Can you tell me how you know who the real perpetrators are, considering you've been held in this asylum for over thirty years?'

'How do I know?' Eckard glared as if insulted by the question. 'Because those bastards put me here.' The Doctor shook his head in frustration. 'But you don't have time for this, now just follow the Secrets and you will find the child, thus avert the prophecy and save us all...' Eckard trailed off and sat looking upwards, muttering to himself as if weighing up an argument in his head, going back and forth between its pros and cons.

'Prophecy!' Harker sputtered, his own frustration now boiling over. 'What is this *prophecy* people keep talking about?' His question stopped the Doctor's muttering instantly, and the man's head swivelled around to face Harker again.

'The prophecy is *change*.'

'Change to what?'

'To everything... To belief, To the planet, To life itself... Simply put, Professor, the end of the world.'

'End of the world! Oh, for God's sake.' Harker literally howled his disbelief. And even if Eckard had not been restrained, he still would have reacted exactly the same way. 'Is that what this is all about? Some Armageddon prophecy? That's ridiculous.' Harker's outburst seemed only to calm Eckard, who raised a single eyebrow in surprise as Harker continued. 'I'm trying to save the life of a child... I'm sorry Doctor but this meeting has been a waste of your time and mine.' Harker had begun to stand up, with his eyes already on the door, when Eckard called out.

'Please Alex, allow me to finish.'

The Doctor's request was voiced with such feeling that Harker paused and then sat back down with a gentle sigh. 'I apologise, Doctor, of course, please go on.'

Eckard nodded thankfully. 'You're not a believer, are you, Alex?'

'In prophecies? No, I am not.'

Eckard gave an empathetic nod of the head. 'That's fine, but understand this: the ones who have this child *do* believe and they will kill him despite what you may judge to be the truth.'

The calm logic of this remark had a strangely soothing effect on Harker, and for a fleeting moment he wondered why, aside from the obvious, this man was still kept locked up. 'So how do I find him?'

Eckard's single eyelid began to flutter and his expression becoming more distant as his gaze honed in on Harker's face. 'You really do have the most exquisite eyes, Professor,' he said hungrily, once more licking his lips. 'I would so like to partake of them.'

It was clear the Doctor's attention was now beginning to fade. 'I'll make you a promise,' Harker offered. 'Finish what you were going to say and you have my word: if I ever decide to get rid of them, you'll be the first person I think of. Deal?'

The strange proposal lit up Eckard's face and his blemished and discoloured fingers twitched in anticipation at the thought. 'I would like that very much. Very much indeed... You have a deal, Professor, but be warned that the Secrets, and especially the fourth, will challenge everything you think you know. It will dissolve everything around you and then put it all back together before your very eyes and, in doing so, change your perception of the world around you until your last dying breath. Remember that it does not matter if you believe in the power of prophecy or not, because *it* believes in you and that is all that is required. The very reading of these Secrets is enough to bring about the stepping stones that will lead to either destruction or salvation, but never forget the same path must be travelled to reach either conclusion.' Eckard paused momentarily and his stare became glassy-eyed. 'Be extremely wary, Professor, because the simple fact that you're sitting here in front of me right now signifies that the ball is already rolling, and with it comes dark storm clouds.'

The Doctor's seemingly irrational and nonsensical answer induced a sickly feeling deep in the pit of Harker's stomach, and he shuffled uncomfortably in his chair. Were these words just the ramblings of a madman or was there something more to it? *Something real.* 'Dark clouds?' he queried.

Doctor Eckard gazed up to the cell's small window as a flash of lightning crackled outside in the distance, illuminating the forbidding moors that lay just beyond the asylum's white security walls. 'The darkest.'

Harker was still trying to decipher the meaning of Eckard's cryptic response when the Blackwater patient decided to return his full attention back to his guest, his eyes now glinting with energy and zest. 'Go see the Dame and ask for Eizel. He'll set you on your way. Tell him... tell him... I forget now,' the Doctor shook his head violently from side to side, dispersing saliva from his torn lips to the floor. '... Yes, I remember now. Tell him the darkest part off the night always comes before the dawn but... but... Damn, it's been so long since...'

Harker watched in bemusement as the Doctor continued shaking his head back and forth in an attempt to remember the instruction he deemed so important, until he stopped suddenly and began to click his tongue against the roof of his mouth.

'Of course, I'm being an idiot. Eckard, you fool.' The Doctor cursed and leant over to his right arm and began to slowly nudge back his sleeve with the butt of his chin, revealing a series of deep cuts and a scrawl of lettering scarred upon his forearm. It took a minute or so for him to edge the arm sleeve back as much as needed, and with no attempt to help by Harker, who was more than content to stay on his side of the black line and wait patiently.

'Here it is.' Eckard rejoiced. 'I wrote it down so I would never forget. The drug therapy they keep me on has never been conducive to a clarity of memory. Yes, I remember now. The darkest part of the night always comes before the dawn, but in...'

Eckard was only halfway through his sentence when overhead the light began to flicker, and a series of clinks echoed along the corridor outside.

'Oh, my God, they're coming,' Eckard suddenly gasped and he began to struggle violently against his restraints, the veins in his hands bulging as he attempted to break free. 'I shouldn't have said anything, I'm sorry.' The Doctor stared up at the ceiling, tears now streaming from the corner of his functioning eye. 'Do you hear me…? Can you hear me…? I'm sorry.'

Harker shrunk back into his chair as Eckard thrust a tear-stained face towards him, spittle dribbling down his chin and frothy bubbles emerging at each side of his mouth. 'You must leave now. They're coming… They're coming.'

The light overhead suddenly cut out, plunging the cell into darkness. Harker instinctively froze, clasping the arms of his chair as he fought against the feeling of sheer dread now creeping into his chest. Apart from the furious sound of heavy rainfall outside, the only noise he could hear was the shallow but rapid breathing of Doctor Eckard from somewhere on the other side of the room.

In desperation, Harker tried to assess this situation logically and thus keep his fear from winning outright. It had to be just a power cut, so he just had to stay calm and not let his emotions get the better of him, which can be a sufficient challenge during a power cut at night in the safety of one's own home. But whilst locked in a room with a criminally insane patient who has a thing about your eyeballs? Well that's another thing entirely.

Before Harker could make any decision on his next course of action, a deep metallic clink sounded in the direction of the cell's entrance, followed by the familiar creak of a metal door opening. There was now a total silence, before eventually the rasping voice of Eckard sounded out of the darkness directly in front of him.

'Too late… They're here.'

Chapter 5

In the distance a deep and sorrowful moan echoed down the corridor as Harker fought to loosen his frozen muscles, his whole body still firmly rooted to the plastic chair he clung to with tensed palms. To his left he could hear Eckard whimpering uncontrollably and was about to call out to him when a lightning bolt flashed outside the window, offering Harker a brief peek of the room's interior. The Doctor was out of sight and evidently cowering on his bed which was still in the shadows but Harker managed to steal a glimpse of the cell door, which was now wide open. He experienced his first sliver of relief since the overhead lighting first cut out. It had to be a simple power cut and the staff would unquestionably be attempting to rectify the problem, so he expected to see torch beams approaching at any moment. That's what he was telling himself anyway, but in truth the eerie comments that Eckard had voiced, just moments before the blackout occurred, only served to engender an enveloping sense of paranoia which was seeding his mind with numerous unpleasant possibilities – *Who were they?*

Feeling a cold sweat forming across his brow, Harker wiped it away anxiously with his sleeve and now realised that his muscles were not quite as frozen as he had first thought. He stood up cautiously and was already feeling his way along the wall towards the cell's entrance, when a faint torchlight flickered into life and slowly slid along the murky corridor outside, then settled on the open doorway just as he reached it.

'Decker!' Harker uttered quietly, relieved that the orderly had been true to his word in coming to his aid so quickly. Without needing further encouragement, he stepped out of Eckard's cell and diligently made his way along the empty corridor towards the inviting beam of light glimmering through the Perspex viewing window of C wing's main security door. Thankfully all the other residents were still securely locked in their rooms, and that knowledge helped to calm his nerves. An encounter now with some of the UK's most dangerous patients was something he could do without, and just the very thought encouraged him to pick up his pace. He had reached the viewing window within seconds and the torchlight shining through it was, to Harker's mind, like a beacon of sanctuary. Squinting against the glare, Harker raised his face to the observation window and tapped his hand against the Perspex. 'Decker, is that you?' He hissed before glancing back down the gloomy corridor just to reassure himself that he was still alone. 'I'm ready to leave.'

The torch remained motionless but continued to shine directly into Harker's face.

'Decker, can you hear me?' Harker was now raising his voice.

The torch slowly jerked up and down.

'Then, can you let me out… please.'

The torch began to move again, but this time swaying slowly from left to right.

A dark sense of dread began to fill Harker's body and he pulled back slightly from the viewing window. 'You're not Decker, are you?'

The torch once more moved from left to right but firmer and faster this time.

This disturbing response chilled Harker to the core and he anxiously watched as the torch turned round on itself and illuminated its owner's face and, for the first time since arriving at Blackwater, he was actually glad to be on the patient's side of the security door. There in front of him, and gazing back with an emotionally hollow stare, was one of the most sinister-looking men he had ever seen. Under the hood of his black robe, the man's face looked almost childlike and the skin had a plastic texture to it. His lips were shiny and taut and above them glared a pair of unblinking pale-blue eyes.

It took a few more seconds for Harker's own eyes to adjust, and he gradually realised that the figure was wearing a mask. But it was a creepy, unnatural-looking mask that would take pride of place in the collection of any horror enthusiast.

'Who are you?' Harker croaked, struggling to vocalise his thoughts as an adrenalin spike shot through him, tensing his jaw muscles.

The other said nothing, instead simply raising his free hand and pressing a piece of paper to the window. The note was written with red marker in a childish scribble.

You should not be here. A penance must be paid.

As Harker digested these words, he found himself so preoccupied with studying the note that the muffled clinking sounds behind him barely registered. The hooded figure then raised an arm and extended a thick finger towards him, pointing over Harker's shoulder towards the darkness of the corridor behind. Harker spun around and peered into the gloom, as a number of unnerving sounds began emanating from the pitch blackness. It included the grinding of teeth, some heavy panting and the scuffing of socks on a tiled floor.

Instinctively Harker pushed his back flat against the security door, just as the lights overhead flicked back on, flooding the entire corridor with a brightness that Harker would have welcomed just a few minutes earlier, but now seemed nothing more than a torturous punishment. The sight that greeted him came straight out of his worst nightmares. For all of the cell doors were lying open and the occupants were already shuffling out into the corridor, with palms upheld to shield their eyes from the brightness of the lights overhead. All, that is, except one whose focus was firmly locked upon Harker himself. The man was only around five foot five inches high but his broad shoulders and thick forearms were tensing menacingly, and his dark black eyes, although penetrating, seemed dull and void of any intelligence, as if their possessor's mind worked on instinct alone. The sight was daunting enough, but it was the familiarity of this figure that really made an impact. Harker recognised that face from the news reports of some years earlier. The papers had dubbed him 'the Night Caller' and, if his memory served him correctly, the man had killed close to twenty people by bludgeoning them to death in their own beds, after committing a horrendous sexual attack on each victim, whether male or female. Harker particularly remembered one chilling report that described how the murderer enjoyed watching his victim's life slip away with those very same eyes that were now fixed upon him so resolutely.

Harker immediately broke eye contact, not wanting to invite any more interest, but at the same time he kept the killer constantly within his peripheral vision. He quickly scanned the corridor for any way out and within seconds had arrived back at his initial impression: there was none.

With his panicked heartbeat thumping in his ears, Harker glanced feverishly at the patients in their white fabric two-piece pyjamas, as the majority of them began honing in on the only person not dressed in similar attire… *himself.*

Up ahead, the Night Caller was taking his first steps forward, and Harker was already considering dashing into the nearest empty cell, with a mind to holding the door shut… when a loud knocking sound echoed along the corridor. At the far end of the wing he could see a woman's face pressed against the viewing window of the security doors, her eyes wide in alarm, and gesturing her hands backwards, motioning Harker towards to her. Seeing that she had finally gained his attention, the woman then continued banging the door, attracting interest from the patients.

The distraction worked and within moments the attention of all those in the corridor was now fixed on the source of the racket with the single exception of one patient who seemed far more interested in pulling his pants down to his ankles and waggling his genitals from side to side.

Harker was now running, the plastic soles of his shoes providing excellent grip on the tiled floor and he thanked God he wasn't wearing his usual leather-soled brogues. He took off with such a ferocity that the Night Caller was only just turning back to face him when Harker shoulder-barged the man with the full weight of his body, sending the multiple killer flying back into his cell with a harsh thud.

The next few minutes were a blur of grabbing hands and rough shoving as Harker made a furious dash for the far door. At one point he was close to being herded into a nearby cell by two of the larger patients, but he managed to keep up his momentum and slid between them, ducking the grasp of one and accidently tripping the other, so as to send him face-first to the floor with a bone-cracking thump. By the time he reached the security door, he was throwing wild punches and kicking anything that got in his way but, as ever more pairs of hands grasped roughly for his neck and shoulders, he began to slow. There comes a moment when a person is so physically overwhelmed by others that a drastic change can occur within them. At this moment one of two things will happen. The first response is to give in to the onslaught, allowing their own fear to devour them, and they weaken to become limp and accepting of what they now perceive as the inevitable. With the second, though, something clicks, a survival mechanism perhaps, when fear and terror transform into blind rage and every ounce of power and force the victim possesses gushes to the surface and is unleashed into every fibre of one's being, regardless of how futile that endeavour might be, as if acting on auto-pilot. As Harker slowed to a near halt, with more hands grappling, pinching and clawing at his body, and the sheer weight of it all becoming unbearable, it was the latter reaction which now consumed him as he yelled in anger at the top of his voice. He slammed his head backwards again and again, feeling noses crumple under each blow and he slammed his elbow into the nearest attacker. The loosening of strangleholds around his neck, coupled with the yelps of pain from those on the receiving end, only boosted his resolve and, with elbows thrusting back and forth, he began kicking out at any unguarded shins he could reach. The hand grips began to loosen even more but the weight pressing on his back, as other new patients piled in from behind, was becoming too much and his knees had begun to crumple just as the security door was flung open. A hand lunged out to grab him firmly by his hair, then tugged him sharply forward and, with his knees acting as a fulcrum, he lurched straight ahead and scrambled through the opening, leaving the crowd behind him to topple to the floor. Harker was still clambering to his feet as the security door was slammed shut, catching a number of unwary fingers clawing at the door frame, which were quickly retracted amid cries of pain from the other side.

'Jesus Christ.' Harker spluttered before turning to see a young woman with long silky black hair, and wearing a white lab coat, still ensuring that the security door was properly secured.

'Doctor Stanton actually.' The woman corrected him while she blew a loose strand of hair from her face. 'Are you OK?'

Harker offered her a thankful nod and then sucked in a much needed breath of air. 'What the hell is going on around here, Doctor?'

'I'm still trying to figure that out.' She replied grimly and then flinched as numerous fists began pounding on the observation window, leaving blurry smudges of spit and grease. 'More importantly who the hell are *you*, and what are you doing here?'

'My name is Alex Harker,' Harker answered staunchly, and tried to regain some composure before offering his hand, 'and I had an appointment here with Marcus Eckard.'

'An appointment with Marcus?' Stanton blurted. 'I wasn't informed about any appointments.'

'It was a very short notice thing.' Harker guessed and drawing her attention to his still out-stretched hand.

Doctor Stanton gave him the once-over before finally shaking his waiting hand. 'Nice to meet, you Mr Harker, and I doubt that explanation, because Marcus is one of my patients. So I would have been the first to be notified.'

Another round of fists now began banging at the door, whereupon Stanton beckoned Harker to follow her as she made her way up the steps to the exit. 'Enough with the pleasantries. I need to get this place under control, and half of the facility is already in lockdown. Follow me.'

Harker followed dutifully, rubbing at the part of his head where a clump of hair had been used to pull him to safety. Stanton noticed this and briefly raised her hands.

'Sorry about your hair.'

'No need to apologise.' Harker replied sincerely. 'For all I care, you could have grabbed me by the ears. I'm just glad you got me out of there when you did. Thank you.'

The Doctor said nothing, merely smiled, and then continued up the stairs with Harker in tow.

'If half the facility is in lockdown, how did you reach me so quickly?' he asked.

'I didn't even realise you were here in the first place.' Stanton reminded him. 'I was up on the first floor when the lights went out, so I headed down to check on the patients and...' Stanton reached into her coat pocket and produced a silver-coloured multi-key. 'It helps if you carry one of these. Without it I never could have reached C-Wing, so that was lucky for you.'

'I'll say.' Harker replied, with a deep sigh. 'Well, Doctor Stanton, as you've seen for yourself all the doors down there have been opened... How is that even possible?'

'It shouldn't be.' The physician replied and shook her head. 'All the cell doors are automated, but they still require a manual override.'

'So how do you get the inmates back into their rooms?' Harker persisted.

'*Patients*,' Stanton corrected, 'and that will depend on whether any of the other wings have been compromised. If the breach in security is confined to C wing, then the five staff on duty with me tonight should be able to handle it, but if not, then we have a far more serious problem.'

'The police?'

41

'Yes.' Stanton replied. 'But if it is that bad, we will need every other member of staff brought in. We have one hundred and twenty patients here at Blackwater.'

'Well, you should know that it's now one hundred and twenty-one.'

Stanton stopped as she finally reached the stairwell's upper doorway and she stared at Harker, clearly puzzled by his reckoning. 'One hundred and twenty-one?'

'Yes.' Harker nodded. 'There was someone else in C wing with me, and I would wager a guess that he's the one responsible for all this mayhem.'

'What! Are you sure it wasn't just a member of staff?'

'Not unless your orderlies have taken to wearing Halloween masks.'

'Halloween masks!' Stanton gasped, clearly unaware of that extra presence roaming loose in the facility.

'Yes.' Harker emphasised gravely. 'I think you need to make calling the police your number-one priority.'

Stanton looked baffled. 'Then we need to get to the front desk,' she decided opening the stairwell door and heading through. 'We can use the phones there and check the security cameras at the same time.'

The walk back to the main entrance took just a few minutes, the multi-key proving its worth by allowing easy access to three security doors along their way. Both Harker and Stanton were silent meanwhile and it was not until they had emerged into the fully illuminated hallway leading to the main reception area that either of them said a word.

'That's strange,' Stanton murmured. 'The blackout hasn't affected this part of the building.'

Harker glanced over towards the reception area where he had originally met Nurse Decker. 'Where's the nearest phone?'

'At the front desk,' she replied, and they both hurried over to it with Harker reaching for the phone itself while Stanton began examining a series of security monitors ranged behind the counter.

'Oh good God.' Stanton cried in dismay, taken aback by the footage now being displayed. 'Most of the cells inside the facility are open.'

Harker had already picked up the phone's receiver but finding there was no dial tone, he dropped it back down into the cradle. 'Phones are dead,' he announced in frustration and then moved around to Stanton's side of the counter to view the screens. What he saw was bedlam, literally. There were scenes of near anarchy as patients roamed the hallways, some fighting with each other whilst others seemed hell-bent on destroying anything they could get their hands on. Despite all this, the one screen which stood out revealed three men in orderly suits waving frantically up at the camera. 'Where are they?' he asked, pointing to the screen in question.

'That's the night shift,' Stanton explained, taking a moment to scrutinise a board on the wall that was flashing with red and white lights – mainly red. 'The red lights signify areas in lockdown, and they,' she said tapping at the screen, 'are members of staff trapped right in the middle of it.'

This revelation was disheartening and Harker was already contemplating the options when he heard voices approaching down the same hallway they had just come from. He grabbed Stanton by both shoulders and thrust her to the ground, then pushed her under the reception counter even as she fought against him.

'What the hell do you think you're doing?' she yelled, and Harker immediately slapped his hand across her mouth.

'Quiet, there's someone coming,' he whispered, before he removed the hand and raised a finger to his lips.

Stanton remained silent, despite looking furious, and with a clenched fist she walloped Harker in the biceps. The punch was unintentionally weak and she glared at him through wide eyes. He raised one finger in warning and gestured to the source of the voices that were getting louder – one of which in particular was familiar to both of them.

'You have to understand it's almost a miracle that I was able to trap most of the staff on the ground floor at all.' The voice protested.

Harker peered up through a gap in the desk to see Nurse Decker, who was following another man wearing a dark leather overcoat, black boots and a plain navy baseball cap. The unknown man's chiselled face was rugged and weathered and had it not been for the emotionally dead green eyes and a deep scar running from just below the left eye halfway down his cheek, he could have been the magazine favourite of many a bored housewife.

'The problem with that statement of yours is the word *most*,' the man responded lightly yet sternly.

Behind him, Decker continued to plead his case. 'You hardly gave me any notice, so what did you expect?'

The lack of respect in the orderly's tone stopped the other man in his tracks only metres from where Harker sat watching them. He then swivelled on his heel and directly faced Decker, who lowered his eyes to the floor uneasily.

'Now is not the time for you to grow a pair of balls '*Nurse*' Decker, and instead what I expect from you,' the man growled, 'is competence... something you lack in volumes. You are paid a great deal of money to be ever at our beck and call – and don't forget it.'

Decker looked genuinely nervous but his next words created a different impression altogether. 'With respect Captain McCray, you don't pay me that much.'

Without hesitation, the man named as McCray reached into his inside jacket pocket, pulled out a handgun with a silencer and then promptly shot a bullet into each of Decker's shins, dropping the man to his knees. The gun's three-inch-long barrel was then brutally jammed deep into the orderly's mouth, thereby and suppressing the man's impending scream of pain before it even had time flourish. 'Then, with respect, consider your contract now rescinded.'

A flash from the gun's muzzle lit up the hallway as a bullet ripped through the back of Decker's skull, sending a red splattering of blood out on to the white plastic tiled floor behind him, followed closely by the twitching body of Decker himself.

Harker watched as, without so much as a pause, McCray continued past the reception desk and along the corridor, when a metallic banging sound brought him to a standstill.

Harker ducked his head back around to see Stanton steadying the metal waste-paper bin she had just knocked over, her eyes wide and panic-filled at further sounds that could only be attributable to a muffled gunshot and then a body hitting the floor. Harker raised a single finger to his lips before returning to scan the corridor, and what he saw there sent shiver down his spine. McCray was now slowly making his way back towards the reception desk, gun drawn and his neck craned alertly as he attempted to pinpoint the location of the unexpected noise.

Harker pulled back from the crack and promptly searched about for a convenient weapon, but the only instrument he could see was a spent Parker biro with a metal nib lying in the same waste-bin that the Doctor had disturbed moments earlier. Perturbed by his only choice of defence, he carefully picked it up, taking care not to rustle the crumpled bits of paper it sat upon, and clasped it with both hands like a knife.

Harker readied himself, as McCray made his way around the opposite side of the reception counter. As the man's footsteps got closer, there was only one thought at the forefront of Harker's mind. One solitary thought blotting out the fear that he surely should have felt.

How the hell do you disable an armed man with just a pen?

Harker was still debating whether to leap out and go straight for McCray's neck or else stab him in the shin and then wrestle him for the gun, when he overheard the sound of a radio crackling.

'Captain, the entrance doors have been secured and we have movement on the first floor. It could be Harker and the missing Doctor.'

Harker could hear McCray breathing heavily through his nose less than a metre above him, with only the thin wooden counter between them offering safe haven from a bullet to the head. There was no reply for what seemed like a couple of minutes before eventually a response was forthcoming.

'This is McCray. Get back here to the main reception area and have the security doors unlocked. I'm on my way'

'Does that go for all security doors, including the rest of the patient wings?'

'Affirmative, let them loose. This situation needs to look like it was caused internally,' McCray paused and stared down at the lifeless body of Nurse Decker. 'And you'll need a clean-up crew when you get here… There was an issue that needed to be resolved.'

'Understood,' came the reply, and with that the captain, as he had been addressed, casually made his way back along the corridor in the carefree manner of a man just out for a stroll.

Harker remained motionless until the footsteps had faded away, before slipping out from underneath the reception counter and then helping Stanton to her feet.

'Who the hell was that?' Stanton gasped as Harker dropped his token weapon back into the metal waste-bin.

'I've no idea… and honestly right now I don't care,' Harker replied while cautiously peering out into the empty corridor beyond. 'We need to get ourselves out of here now. Will your multi-key open up the entrance door?'

Stanton was already shaking her head. 'No, the key is for internal doors only.'

This was not the response Harker had hoped for and now it was his turn to shake his head. 'OK, fine,' he said with a sigh. 'If we can't get out through the main entrance, then how about a fire exit?'

A glimmer of hope appeared in Stanton's eyes. 'We can get up to the roof through there.' She was pointing to a green fire door on the opposite side of the lobby, 'and there is also a set of fire stairs leading down to the car park.'

'Good, then that's where we're going,' Harker replied, encouraged by the news. 'My car's parked nearby.'

With a wince of revulsion at the bloody spectacle of Decker's sprawled-out body, Doctor Stanton took the lead and headed across the lobby towards the green door on the other side. Suddenly a scuffling noise caught their attentions as down at the far end of the corridor, Captain McCray peeked out from round a corner with a pleased grin on his face.

'Well, hello there,' he exclaimed gleefully.

'Run!' Harker yelled in warning but McCray was already raising his weapon and they had to duck as bullets zipped over their heads and embedded themselves into the wall, launching puffs of plaster into the air all around them. Harker kept expecting to feel the sharp stab of a bullet thudding into his back but suddenly the zipping noises stopped and, just as they both darted through the green-painted fire exit, he glanced back to see why. At the far end of the corridor McCray was engaged in fighting off two of the asylum's patients who had emerged through a nearby security door, which was now swinging shut. The taller one kept attempting to claw the gun from McCray's hand whilst the second, stockier one – who Harker recognised as the Night Caller – was busy pounding at the Captain's chest. The bizarre thing was that McCray showed no sign of flinching at all even as the Night Caller administered yet another powerful blow.

Harker tore himself away from the sight, now actually feeling glad that those maniacs were on the loose, and he took pleasure in knowing that the Captain was receiving a well-deserved beating. '*Enjoy yourselves boys*' was his immediate thought as he followed Stanton up the stairs and through the fire exit door leading on to the roof.

The heavy downpour hit them like a wave as they scrambled across the rain-sodden rooftop and down a green metal set of external stairs. Most of the outside lights were still off and it was only the flashing of lightning overhead that enabled them to maintain their footing on the slippery metal steps. Harker had retrieved his car keys by the time the stairs reached the car park and was already pointing the clicker towards his BMW waiting in the corner. The car's lights flickered in acknowledgment and he pulled open the driver's door and slid inside as Stanton jumped into the passenger seat.

'Where to?' she coughed, brushing away the droplets of rain that were dripping off her forehead and into her mouth.

Harker jammed his finger down onto the oval start button and the car engine hummed into life. 'Anywhere but here.' He growled over the sound of rain lashing against the windscreen. He jammed the gearstick into reverse and then stopped and took a deep breath. 'Bloody hell that was close.' He had hardly said it before something crashed down upon the bonnet with such a force that the back of the vehicle lifted off the ground, then slammed down again with a heavy thump. Harker raised his head to peer through the cracked windscreen and came face to face with the lifeless expression of the Night Caller. The serial killer's body was splayed out across the bonnet, but with one of his arms dislocated and bent grotesquely across the back of his neck.

Harker looked upwards to the top of the building above them but could not see a thing, the darkness of the night sky and the relentless pounding of the rain on his windscreen making it near impossible. He released the clutch and, in a flurry of spray and spinning tyres, began to reverse as a flash of lightning lit up the cloudy sky to illuminate the silhouette of a lone figure standing high up on the rooftop.

McCray glared down with his finger pointing towards them and, as the car came to a momentary stop, Harker locked eyes with the Captain just as the light faded into darkness before taking off at high speed down the length of the driveway, towards the main road and the Yorkshire hills beyond.

-

Back inside the asylum, Cliff Johnson was discovering for himself that the phone lines were all dead. The young orderly replaced the handset and exhaled a deep sigh of frustration. 'Great,' he murmured to himself, 'what next?' He was still considering what to do next and staring out through the wire-meshed window, across the unlit grounds of Blackwater beyond, when two arms clamped vice-like around his body and a cold face pressed closely into the back of his neck.

'I'm sure we can think of something,' a voice whispered loudly in his ear. 'Have I ever told you what wonderful eyes you have, Mr Johnson?'

Chapter 6

John Wilcox stared down at his cup of coffee and tapped its rim impatiently with his fingertip. He then sipped the last few drops and dumped it heavily back on the desk with a solid thud.

This was taking far too long?

He had left his third message over two hours ago and his patience was disintegrating fast. This was no way to be treated by one's underlings, and especially now. He slammed his fist down hard on the desktop and let out a frustrated growl.

Heads would roll for this impertinence.

Wilcox next pulled a pack of Marlboro Lights from his shirt breast pocket, flipped open the lid and reluctantly pulled a cigarette from the packet and glared at it. He had never been much of a smoker but, after spending the past few months in this place and rarely seeing the light of day, he had needed a distraction and so had thought *what the hell*. He knew he had strong lungs and decided that a few months of smoking would do him no long term damage. Unfortunately, he had underestimated just how alluring the nicotine craving would become and his indulgence was now turning into a full-blown obsession. He tutted loudly at the offensive white stick of tobacco and was about to slip it between his lips when the iPhone next to him started to vibrate.

About time!

Wilcox tapped on the incoming call button and pressed the device to his ear. 'Speak.'

'John, it's been a while. Where are you?'

The casually demanding tone of the man's voice served only to fuel Wilcox's already growing irritation.

'Where am I? Where the hell are *you*? Not only have I been waiting hours for you to call but then you dare address me by my first name! You will henceforth refer to me by my title and show me the respect I deserve.' Wilcox felt highly insulted by the caller's informal manner.

'I apologise. Do you wish to be known as Pope Adrian or just His Holiness?'

The remark was so brazenly disrespectful that the total lack of deference sent a sobering chill coursing through Wilcox. 'No, but *Sir* will do.'

'Of course sir,' came the reply, and this time the tone seemed totally void of any disrespect. 'May I ask if your plastic surgery was a success?'

'I am pleased to say that the scars have almost healed,' Wilcox replied, gently rubbing at the fading lines around his nose and across his forehead. 'From a distance I should be unrecognisable, but I'm not sure how it will stand up under any closer inspection. Still, I am sure you can give me an opinion of your own when we meet.' Wilcox croaked to clear the annoying phlegm from his throat, and silently cursed the new habit that had caused it. 'So, back to the point, has it been organised yet?'

There was silence at the other end of the line.

'Well?' Wilcox demanded.

'Sir, the general consensus is that to arrange a meeting of the entire Magi council would not be prudent at this time.'

'Not prudent?' Wilcox yelled, gripping the phone tighter. 'And why is that, exactly?'

The voice now hesitated to reply and when it did it sounded far more tactful. 'It is concerning that very matter that the Council expressed its wish that I speak to you in person.'

Wilcox deliberately held back an answer and waited a few moments in the hope that this would add an air of authority to a conversation he felt he was struggling to maintain control of. 'Very well,' he replied, 'then you will come to me?'

'Agreed,' the voice continued. 'I will join you in person as soon as I can.' The line then abruptly went dead... and along with it vanished Wilcox's restraint.

'Those scheming bastards,' he raged, reflecting on the flippant tone of the call itself and sensing the beginnings of a potential coup for leadership of the Magi. The peasants were clearly becoming restless, and his being out of sight was only making them bolder. 'If the Council think they can usurp my authority, then they are about to have a nasty awakening,' he ranted inwardly. 'I *am* the Magi.'

Within seconds, the ex-pontiff began punching another number into his phone, his breathing starting to calm as the line connected.

'How can I serve you, my lord?'

'We have a guest on the way and I will need one of your men on hand when he arrives. Someone persuasive.'

'Of course, sir. I have just the man for you and I will make sure he is ready for your summons.'

'Good, because dissension is in the air,' Wilcox licked his lips, 'and we might therefore have to do a spot of house cleaning.'

Chapter 7

'I have never encountered the name McCray therefore I certainly don't know him, and for the record, even though my circle of friends is a bit small at the moment, I can assure you it does not and never has contained any psychopaths. Anyway, seeing as he turned up the same time as you did, I would suggest you might know more about him than I do.' Doctor Chloe Stanton stole a sip from her glass of orange juice, and sat back in her chair with arms folded. 'But I will tell you what is suspect, Professor Harker. What is suspect, is that this maniac turns up on the very same night that you decided to visit us.' Chloe was now glaring across the table accusingly. 'So how about it, Mr Professor? Are you ready to share?'

Harker rubbed at his tightened lips angrily, then turned away only to come directly face to face with an old man wearing a thick cream jumper, corduroy trousers and a pair of blue wellingtons, who was seated at the adjacent table. The man's ruddy cheeks bore tribute to a lifetime of overindulgence in alcohol.

'I'd dare say you're in a lot of trouble here, boy,' the old man quipped, obviously fascinated by the conversation going on at the table next to him.

'Thank you for that,' Harker replied drily, scanning the room for any other inquisitive faces. Fortunately, the pub's other patrons were all far too preoccupied by their own beverages in the warm and cosy surroundings of a small country tavern.

It had taken almost a full five minutes before Harker had felt willing to ease up on the BMW's accelerator, after tearing out of Blackwater's front entrance gate. Luckily the car's engine had not been overly damaged by the Night Caller's 'high dive' from the asylum's roof, even if the bonnet itself was a complete write-off. Doctor Stanton – or Chloe as she told him she preferred to be called – had immediately contacted the asylum's director to inform him of the break-out, or to be more accurate the break-in. Initially her superior had been livid that Chloe had chosen to leave the facility, but his attitude had soon mellowed at the mention of a killer with a gun and of her hazardous escape. It was only after she revealed the senseless murder of Nurse Decker that the aggressive tone from the earpiece subsided and she was sternly given two orders:

1. not to notify anyone of the incident but allow him to contact the authorities; and
2. find a place to sit tight and wait for his call.

After that, Chloe had directed them both to the nearby Fox and Hound pub, the only place open at this time of night. After finding a secluded place to park Harker's damaged BMW down a back road and out of sight, the two of them had made their way inside for a restorative drink. The not calling the police part had jarred on Harker initially but he had soon agreed because getting himself dragged back to the asylum by the authorities would have potentially put him right back into McCray's line of sight.

'Well Professor?' Chloe continued, with a glare 'It's interesting how this all began with your arrival.'

'My arrival!' Harker gasped irritably, the implication angering him. Of course she was right, partially at least, but that wasn't the point. 'I'll tell you what's interesting; what's interesting is that you just happened to turn up at exactly the right time.'

The vague accusation drew a deep look of disbelief from her. 'The right time! You mean the right time to *save your life.*'

'Or the right time to ingratiate yourself into my good books.' he responded boldly, then ticked himself off for not articulating the allegation more precisely. Still, when making a mistake while directing an accusing remark of that type, there's not really a lot you can do. You just have to move on and hope your opponent does likewise. Unfortunately, Chloe did not.

'Trying to get into your good books?' Chloe seethed.

'Look, I just don't know if I fully trust you, all right.' Harker replied.

'Well, that's fine by me because I'm not sure I can trust you either, you arrogant sod. I save your life and you then think I'm just trying to endear myself to you. You complete and utter connard.'

'Connard?' Harker echoed with a look of surprise.

'Yes, it means asshole in French.'

'I know what it means,' Harker replied with a smirk. 'Why not say it in English?'

'Because I have manners, that's why.' Chloe shuffled in her seat. 'But you are, without a doubt, one of the biggest connards I have ever met.'

'OK, I was wrong and I apologise.' Harker held his hands up in surrender.

Chloe assessed the sincerity on Harker's face, before her shoulders sagged and she offered him an accepting nod. 'Apology accepted.'

'Thank you.' Harker replied, letting out a sigh. 'It's just been a long time since I was insulted in a foreign language.'

'Not any more.' Chloe informed him cheerfully, now enjoying the air of defeat that Harker was deliberately exuding.

'Thanks again, and I am genuinely grateful that you turned up when you did.'

Chloe offered him an appreciative nod. 'And thank you for helping me get out of there without being shot.'

'We good now?' Harker raised his pint of bitter towards her.

Chloe clinked her glass with his. 'We're good.' '

To their right the old man sitting at the next table raised his glass as well. 'We're all good.' he remarked with a lonely smile.

Harker grimaced back at him. 'Again thank you, but this really is a private conversation.'

The smile on the lone drinker's face evaporated. 'Damn, boy, you really *are* a connard.' The old man then cursed quietly before turning his back on them both.

'Told you,' Chloe said with a sarcastic smile, and was taking a self-congratulatory sip of her drink when the mobile in her pocket began to vibrate, the surprise of it causing her to spill some on to the lacquered-wooden table top.

'Serves you right.' Harker grinned mockingly as Chloe put down her drink and pulled out the offending item to answer it.

'Hello?'

Harker continued to nurse the pint in front of him while he watched Chloe's expression shift from curious to complete disbelief as she digested the caller's news.

'Doctor Wenson, I can assure you it was not a dereliction of my duties. And given the circumstances... that's impossible, I saw the body... wait just a minute you can't do that. Hello... Hello!'

Chloe snapped shut the flip-top phone and placed it back in her pocket, her eyes glazing over. Harker already pretty much guessed what had just happened, because the Magi – if that's who these psychos were – had a habit of making bodies and evidence disappear. It formed the cornerstone of their ability to evade the authorities so well. After all, if there's no body there's no crime. 'Who was that?' he asked, nevertheless.

'Doctor Wenson, my department head,' Chloe muttered, the incredulity in her voice blatantly obvious, 'I'm now being held responsible for negligence in the deaths of two inmates.'

'*Two?* Since when was Nurse Decker an inmate?' Harker already had an idea but decided to play dumb, not wanting to become the unwitting focus of Chloe's mounting anger.

'He wasn't,' she managed, expelling a controlled sigh. 'His body wasn't even found, so he's simply being considered missing. As for the dead, they found one of the inmates exactly where we left him in the car park.'

'And the other?'

'The other was Marcus Eckard. He attacked one of the orderlies but was fought off. When the security team finally got things back under control, he was found hanging by a bed sheet in his own cell. In both cases they're being labelled suicides.'

Even though Harker had been expecting the worst for Eckard, just hearing it confirmed somehow made things worse, but what really got his attention was how disheartened Chloe looked. 'Chloe, it's not your fault. Wasn't Decker supposed to be in charge?'

Chloe eyed him vacantly. 'They checked the security records… and it was my security pass that was used to release all the security doors. They think I did it deliberately.'

'Jesus, I'm sorry, Chloe. If you want us to head back to Blackwater, I would be happy to back you up and explain everything.'

Chloe's blank stare quickly dissolved. 'And explain what exactly? That an insane gunman with a penchant for Halloween masks decided to let loose the majority of the UK's most dangerous prisoners before killing the man in charge – who, by the way, has miraculously disappeared – and then chasing us two within an inch of our lives, and finally attempting to use one of the patients as a makeshift kite.' She paused and massaged both sides of her forehead, then took a particularly deep swig of her drink. 'Oh, yes, and don't forget this maniac has the technical skills to change the records and make it look like I released all the inmates, before disappearing as quickly as he arrived.' She was close to shouting and the occupants of a table in the corner were now staring at her with intrigue.

'Do you mind?' she said, glaring at them ferociously.

'No, I don't,' came the response from one of the other tables, followed by a few laughs. 'I don't mind at all.'

Chloe allowed her anger to pass and, with a strained smile, she returned her attention to Harker who had meanwhile shrunk into his seat, trying to look as inconspicuous as possible, as the surrounding patrons gradually resumed their conversations.

'I think it's time you told me what the hell is going on?' she demanded.

Feeling backed into a corner, and not wanting to draw any more undue attention, Harker offered her a conciliatory nod and then continued. 'Look, I'm as surprised as you are, and before tonight I had never even heard of Marcus Eckard, let alone who or what that psycho was! All I know is that I was asked by a friend to meet with Doctor Eckard.' Harker paused for another gulp from his pint as the grisly image of Eckard's scarred features flashed through his mind.

A Doctor? That was a joke.

'This friend of mine wanted me to ask him about some stupid secret he is supposed to know of and like an idiot I agreed. The next thing I know the lights go out and some crazy wearing a mask unleashes yet more crazies on me. That's before meeting you and finally being chased off the roof by someone whose sole intent was to put a bullet in my brain.'

'Let's not forget the murder,' Chloe corrected and winding Harker up even further.

'Oh, yes,' Harker replied, draining the last drops from his pint glass and dumping it back on to the table. 'How could I forget seeing a man have his head blown off? You see, you're not the only one with problems, Chloe.'

Harker pushed the empty glass to one side and squared up. 'Now… where would you like me to drop you off?'

Chloe allowed the question linger in the air as she inspected Harker's expression, her eyes beginning to glow with interest. 'Who was the friend?'

'The friend?'

'Yes, the friend who asked you to meet with Marcus Eckard.'

'No one in particular.' Harker shrugged his shoulders. 'He's a Catholic priest from my time in the Church.'

His response garnered an appraising look from Chloe. 'Well, that's not at all surprising.'

'What, that he's a priest or that I was in the Church?'

'Both,' she smiled shrewdly, 'but more so that he's a priest – what with Eckard's incessant talk of prophecies.'

It was Harker's turn to smile, and he then laughed sarcastically. 'Don't tell me you buy into all that rubbish?'

Chloe's own smile faded and she let her head loll pensively to one side. 'I'm not sure, but I tell you what I *do* buy, and that is that you know a lot more about this business than you're letting on.' She leaned forward, placing her elbows on the table top and resting her chin on her hands. 'I also know who you are, Professor Harker.'

This unexpected announcement sounded like an accusation, and it caught him off guard. 'And what the hell does that mean?' he asked, shaking his head.

'It means I read the papers and I've read all about your exploits at the Vatican last year.'

Harker's face fell and his puzzled expression was instantly replaced by a look of contempt. 'Oh, you're not one of those, are you?' he uttered with a groan. 'You seem far too intelligent to have been suckered into that ridiculous conspiracy.'

'I may be an atheist, Professor, but it is hardly ridiculous!' Chloe sputtered, now offering her own look of contempt. 'The Pope of the Catholic Church disappears into thin air just after delivering a speech to world leaders that the Second Coming has occurred… and how about that cardinal who was shot the same night inside St Peter's basilica.' She paused briefly to suck in another breath, her face wearing the same look of sarcasm that had adorned Harker's only moments earlier. 'And you now turn up at the asylum and begin discussing with Marcus Eckard about the Second Coming and some prophecies to come…'

'Wait a second,' Harker jumped in, shocked at this revelation, 'how do you know what we were talking about?'

'Because I was watching you on the security camera.' Harker was looking more and more alarmed with every word as she leant closer towards him so as not to attract any inquisitive ears. 'You don't honestly think I would let anyone speak to my patient in the middle of the night without ensuring it wasn't anything detrimental to his mental health, do you? How do you think I got down to the ward so quickly? It's because I was watching you.'

'You told me earlier that you didn't even know I was there. Why?' snarled Harker, riled by the deception.

'Because I did not want it to become an issue – like it is right now – whilst we were in the middle of a lockdown, that's why,' Chloe replied reasonably and sat back in her chair. 'I recognised you the moment you entered the building and I also know what you both talked about and that he directed you to a location. But he didn't have a chance to reveal everything before that maniac turned up and started trying to kill everyone... And, seeing as Marcus Eckard is dead, I would say you're unlikely to ever get that information.'

She anxiously picked up her drink and took two deep sips before continuing, her gaze never leaving Harker's stunned expression. 'That is unless you accept my help – and, believe me I can help. Do you know how?'

Harker raised his eyes mockingly as if wanting to make her forced intrusion into his affairs as difficult as possible. 'Well, you apparently know everything so why don't you illuminate me.'

Chloe ignored the condescending tone and continued. 'Because I know what Marcus was trying to tell you. He had the words cut into his skin and I saw them daily. As I already told you, he was my patient for several years.'

Harker began to assess his newest friend's offer. He searched her face for any signs of deception but found none. In fact, the only thing he could detect was a slight twinge of nervousness from her and the longer he stared the more that twinge grew. But, considering she had almost been murdered tonight, he thought she was holding up pretty well. Such thoughts rapidly began to fade, leaving Harker with a single important question. The most generic and important question there ever is: 'Why?'

'Why! Why would I help, you mean?'

Harker offered her a simple nod.

'Because I want to come with you, that's why.' Chloe exhaled a deep breath as if to steady her voice, which was shaking slightly. 'I'm not a particularly religious person Professor but I find the thought that something remarkable could be happening here extremely intriguing.

Ever since I read about you and those events at the Vatican, I have found myself tantalised by a single thought: *What if?* What if everything I have read is true, and if it is I want to be a part of it. Besides.' Chloe raised her hands in the air. 'Thanks to you I'll now have lots of spare time on my hands.'

Behind them the high-pitched rumble of a dozen or so pint glasses crashing to the floor broke the intense stare that was developing between them, and they both turned around to see a young boy wearing an apron being berated by the chef over the pile of broken shards on the floor in front of him. The cook's tall white hat nodded back and forth as he clapped sarcastically, before disappearing back into the kitchen and leaving the embarrassed-looking teenager apologising to the customers around him, before starting to clean up the mess.

Harker turned back to find Chloe still staring at him and waiting for a reply.

'If it's an adventure you are looking for, Chloe, then all I can say to you is that adventures always sound better in the brochure.'

'Everything sounds better in the brochures, Alex,' Chloe replied. 'That's the point of them.'

'True,' Harker offered flatly. 'But if this does lead anywhere, and I'm not sure it will, then you can expect your attempted murder by that maniac – as you so aptly put it – to be just a taster of things to come.'

Chloe delicately cleared her throat before locking eyes with him. 'My mother died of cancer when I was young, so I never really got a chance to know her. Her passing was one of the main reasons I got into medicine, from a wish to help people. And, if I had not discovered I had a particular talent for psychology, I can promise you that I would be a practising GP.' Chloe gently rubbed her hands as she attempted to sum up her feelings. 'The thing is that I always believed... no, I always hoped that my mother went on to a better place, but of course we don't know that and how could we? However, if there is evidence or some tangible truth to religion and therefore of an afterlife, I want to know about it.' She paused for a moment and Harker watched as any fragility she had displayed earlier now vanished and was replaced with a look of sheer determination. 'You, Professor Alex Harker, are the closest I have ever been to finding out, so how about it?' She reached over and offered him her hand. 'Do we have a deal?'

Harker sat for a while in silence and mulled over this proposition, staring at her outstretched hand. He hardly knew anything about this woman and even though she seemed genuine, he had been conned before and at the very worst he could always head back to the asylum and try to gain access to Eckard's body and the lettering he had carved into his own skin. This idea was soon quashed by the thought of running into the homicidal lunatic McCray again and, as he looked at Chloe, he suddenly felt an overwhelming sense of trust and he realised his mind was already made up. Besides, this whole thing was more than likely going to be a wild-goose chase. His faith in such outcomes was zero and he considered it far more likely for him to come across Lord Lucan riding Shergar than ever witnessing a prophecy come to pass.

'Fine,' Harker announced and gave Chloe's hand a firm shake, 'You have yourself a deal... and from now on call me Alex... no more Professor, OK?'

'And you must continue to call me Chloe.'

'Good. Nice to meet you again, Chloe. And let me take this opportunity to say that you exert blackmail more pleasantly than anyone else I know.'

'Thank you, Alex,' she replied with a laugh.

'Right, so what is the complete line of text that Eckard wanted me to know?'

'The darkest part of the night always comes before the dawn, but in a windowless room the night is never-ending.' As Chloe let the words roll off her tongue, Harker suddenly felt a deep attraction to her.

'Well?' she asked, shaking Harker out of such thoughts of how appealing the Doctor really was without her lab coat and not being surrounded by mental patients which had been of course a major distraction. 'What exactly do you think it means?'

'I don't know,' Harker replied, 'but we're going to find out. First we need to check out train times.'

'Why? Where exactly are we going?' Chloe asked, unsure of their next destination. 'I heard Marcus say to you something like 'Go see the Dane!'

Harker was already shaking his head. 'Not dane but *dame*. Go see the Dame.'

'And who is the Dame?'

'It's not a 'who' but a what. Come on, let's go. I'll tell you in the car.'

'Lead the way.'

They both stood up and began slipping on their coats. 'You know what?' Harker said with a smile. 'You are going to make a terrific assistant.'

Chloe snorted a brief laugh. Heading towards the door, she turned to face him. 'Forget the assistant, Alex Harker. You have yourself a damn partner!'

Chapter 8

High above Notre Dame Cathedral, a gargoyle watched intently as a black taxi pulled up outside the main entrance and dropped off its two passengers, a man and a woman, before turning around and heading back into the bustle of the Paris streets. The man took a few moments to inspect the impressive stained-glass windows looming above him, and then turned his attention to the pair of stone eyes silently observing them from above.

'Welcome to the Dame of Paris,' Harker announced enthusiastically, gazing up towards the roofline of the building. 'You have to love those gargoyles. They must be the most beautifully ugly things of all time.'

Chloe squinted up at the winged figure in stone perched firmly upon its ledge. 'Well, you're right about them being ugly but I'm not sure I could call them beautiful.'

'They are an acquired taste, for sure, but can you imagine what they've seen over the years,' Harker replied, turning his attention back to the cathedral's entrance and the piazza in front of it. 'The French Revolution, the coronation of Napoleon, and *The Wolves of Paris* which has to be one of the greatest films never made.'

'What's *The Wolves of Paris?*'

'The year is 1450,' Harker stated eerily, obviously excited at being able to tell it, 'and the people of Paris are being hunted by a vicious group of wolves who continue to venture into the city at night and terrorise the locals... Led by a huge wolf with reddish fur this villainous pack kills, mutilates and eats over forty Parisians...'

'Mutilates?' Chloe questioned with an unimpressed giggle.

'Oh, yes.' Harker offered while narrowing his eyes comically. 'Finally the citizens decided enough was enough and lured the beasts with bait into the square right here in front of the cathedral, where they were then stoned or speared to death.' Harker motioned up to the gargoyles above them. 'And they saw it all.'

Chloe folded her arms and took a step closer to Harker, an enigmatic smile upon her face. 'Some might say it was just desserts for the almost total decimation of the wolf population here in Europe.'

Harker gave a diplomatic nod of his head. 'And some might say *you* know how to kill a good story. I bet you're a lot of fun at a party?'

'Are you asking me out on a date, Professor?'

The question was a deliberate attempt to make Harker feel uncomfortable, but he batted it away with a smirk. 'In front of the house of God? Never!' he gasped sarcastically. 'Now let's see if we can find this Eizel character.' With that he began navigating his way through the seething mass of tourists and on across the forecourt and up the stone steps and through the central portal entrance and into the cathedral itself, followed closely by Chloe.

The interior of the cathedral was every bit as impressive as Harker remembered. The long nave, lined with rows of pews on either side, stretched for over a hundred metres to the main choir and the enormous altar rising high into the air which was backlit with blue lights and surrounded by angelic figures of cardinals long past sculptured in brilliant-white cracked marble. The three famed stained-glass rose windows positioned along either side of the main hall, with another above the entrance behind them, filtered an intoxicating plenitude of gold and purple rays of light which shone down onto the glossy floor tiles providing a vision that would have brought a smile to the lips of even the most passionate atheist. Thick and weathered stone pillars all around rose high into the canopy of the roof and Harker took a further moment to enjoy the sight. He pressed his palm against the closest pillar and proceeded to brush his fingers over its smooth stonework, this very act of touch adding another ingredient to the captivating visual experience. The hordes of tourists taking photos amidst the chatter of excited voices all melted away, and for a moment Harker found himself alone in enjoying this magnificent building that owed its very existence to a few simple ideas. To *belief* ... and the control of it. The awe of seeing such a monument in past ages must have proved absolute in the confirmation of one's faith, Harker reflected, because for many this building surely had not been created by the hand of man but by God himself.

'Wow, now that is impressive,' Chloe exclaimed having made her way to Harker's side. 'Shame about all the tourists.'

Her comments brought Harker back to reality – and to the mass of visitors most of whom were searching for a perfect photo angle.

'This is nothing,' he replied, motioning to the swelling crowd. 'When it's really busy there can be as many as fifty thousand of them passing through here in a single day!'

'That's a lot of people.' Chloe concurred, sounding genuinely surprised. 'Hey, wait a minute, is that ex-President Sarkozy?' Chloe discreetly pointed out a brown-haired man with a strong nose and wearing an expensive suit standing a few metres in front of them, inspecting one of the cathedral's many statues.

Harker stole a quick glance before shaking his head. 'No, but it looks a bit like him.'

'How do you know for sure?'

'Because this guy's well over six-foot-tall and Sarkozy is pushing only five and a half.'

'Ahh.' Chloe gasped. 'That explains a lot.'

Harker let slip a chuckle at her obvious reference to the short-man complex, before turning his gaze to the far side of the church. 'Right, now let's find the one person we're actually looking for, shall we.'

Harker made his way down the nave towards the main altar followed closely by Chloe who seemed far more interested in the people hovering around them than the cathedral itself. He was about to make a crack about psychology being the right profession for her when the sight of two uniformed security guards in navy blazers caught his attention. The two men were standing either side of an impressive-looking statue of St Angela. It took a few more seconds of manoeuvring past a large party of Chinese tourists who had managed to occupy the entire side aisle before reaching the figures of authority posted at the south end of the cathedral. One of the guards was tall and slender whilst the other was short but broad-shouldered and both wore black-tinted sunglasses.

'Excuse me,' Harker enquired in a thick Parisian accent to the taller of the two, 'I'm looking for someone. Can you help?'

'I will certainly try, sir.' The guard offered. 'Who are you looking for?'

'It's Eizel, a Mr Eizel.'

The taller man deliberated over the name for a few seconds before shaking his head slowly. 'I'm sorry, *monsieur*, but I'm not aware of any Mr Eizel.' He turned to his colleague and repeated the name: 'You know of a Mr Eizel?'

The stocky guard turned his attention to Harker and studied him through those dark glasses for a moment. This silent stare was just about to become uncomfortable when he turned back to the taller guard and patted him on the back, the thick muscles of his shoulders stretching the suit's stitching close to breaking point. 'I may be able to help here, so why don't you take a break?' The guard's voice was unusually husky, and his workmate gave a polite nod and then headed off towards the group of Chinese tourists, who were still not only blocking the entire aisle but appeared to be growing in number.

'Are you already acquainted with Mr Eizel, monsieur?'

Harker shook his head glibly. 'No, but I was asked by a friend to speak with him.'

'What about?'

'I'm afraid I don't know that either,' Harker insisted, feeling like more of a berk with each question, 'but I was hoping he might know more than I do.'

The guard raised his eyebrows above the rims of his glasses and then lowered them, following his curiosity with a deep frown. 'And the name of this friend, sir?'

'Eckard. Doctor Marcus Eckard.'

The guard's mouth fell open ever so slightly, then he pulled down his glasses to reveal two bulging eyes, one of them facing in the opposite direction to the other in a classic case of wall-eye. 'Then you had better come with me.'

The man turned his back on them and began making his way toward a solid wooden door off to the side, with Harker and Chloe close behind.

'I can see why he wears sunglasses!' Chloe murmured.

'That doesn't seem a very enlightened comment for psychologist,' Harker remarked while resisting the urge to laugh.

Chloe let out a faint chuckle. 'Not at all. I'm merely saying that if we don't find this Mr Eizel at Notre Dame, then we can at least say we found the hunchback.'

Harker could not suppress a subdued guffaw which attracted the attention of their guide. The man glanced back and, with a snort of impatience, ushered them down a narrow corridor leading to a room beyond which Harker recognised immediately. Like in a small chapel, its walls were lined with wood-panelled alcoves except these ones contained a collection of numerous gold and silver artefacts protected under glass covers. Above them the stained-glass windows set into the stone walls added to the feel of a small village church.

'What is this place?' Chloe asked as she made her way over to the first alcove to inspect the ornaments it contained.

'It's the Notre Dame treasury,' Harker informed her. 'I've never had the pleasure of seeing it before but the photos don't do it justice.' He was about to follow Chloe's lead and view the items for himself when their chaperone stepped in front of him.

'I would be happy to give you the tour, *monsieur*,' he said, taking off his glasses and dropping them into his jacket pocket. 'But first...' In a single move, the guard slammed Harker back against the stone wall and firmly thrust his forearm up against his chest. With his other hand he then produced a short hunters knife from another pocket and slid it under Harker's chin, pressing it securely across his Adams apple. '...you are going to answer some questions.'

Harker raised his hand towards Chloe who was already making her way towards them both and she stopped and offered an uncertain nod in Harkers direction.

'Who are you?' the guard demanded roughly.

'My name is Alex Harker and I am a professor of archaeology,' Harker spluttered, the knife digging deeper into his throat with every word.

'Archaeology?' the brute growled suspiciously.

'Yes... At Cambridge University. And she is my assistant.'

The burly guard glanced over at Chloe before returning his skew-eyed gaze to Harker... as well as the wall opposite. 'And what do you want with Eizel?'

'As I said earlier, I am a friend of Marcus Eckard.'

'Marcus Eckard doesn't have any friends,' the guard snapped fiercely.

Harker managed another gentle nod, not wanting the sharp blade to actually penetrate his skin. 'Well on that we can both agree. He was murdered last night.'

Harker felt the knife begin to ease away but his attacker continued to scrutinise him, his lips moving silently as if contemplating his next question. This staring match continued until a soft voice sounded from behind the three of them.

'Alphonse! What on earth is going on here?'

Harker turned his head enough to see a man dressed in the official white and silver biretta of a bishop, looking totally astonished.

'I apologise, Father, but these people are looking for Eizel,' Alphonse replied respectfully, though not relaxing his grip on the knife still held firmly to Harker's throat.

If that name meant anything to the bishop he didn't show it but the cleric immediately stepped over and pulled Alphonse's hand away, allowing Harker to rub his throat.

'I apologise Mr...?'

'Harker.' Harker coughed, continuing to massage his larynx. 'Professor Alex Harker.' He motioned towards Chloe, who looked remarkably calm given the situation. 'And this is my assistant, Doctor Chloe Stanton.'

Chloe raised a hand in acknowledgment. 'Actually I'm his partner, not an assistant.'

The bishop nodded to her cordially and switched his attention to Alphonse, who had already returned the offending blade back into his pocket. 'Thank you, Alphonse, I will take it from here.'

The bishop's statement was met with a look of concern from the brawny guard, who inspected Harker intently one final time, then graciously nodded to his superior and headed back out into the nave.

'He doesn't look like an Alphonse!' Chloe remarked.

'Neither did Al Capone,' Harker replied sourly.

'It's not like that all. Please forgive Alphonse's rashness.'

'Rashness!' Harker gasped. 'That man was ready to slit my throat.'

'No, no. I can assure you he would never have gone that far, but nonetheless his actions were inexcusable. Please except my apologises and allow me to introduce myself.' The bishop outstretched his hand. 'I am Bishop Canard.'

Harker hesitated momentarily before grasping the man's hand. 'It's a pleasure and, as I said, my name is Professor Alex Harker and this is my partner Chloe Stanton.'

Bishop Canard turned then to Chloe and courteously shook her hand.

'It's Doctor Chloe Stanton,' she replied firmly, glancing at Harker with disapproval. 'And it is also a pleasure to meet you... I think.'

Canard returned his attention to Harker, who was already gearing up for the next question.

'Bishop Canard, with respect, I think you owe us an explanation.'

'Actually I believe it is *you* that owes me an explanation,' Canard rebuked him softly. 'Why are you seeking an audience with Mr Eizel?'

Harker was not about to initiate a stand-off and, besides, the last thing he wanted was for Alphonse the loveable 'hunchback' to be recalled. 'Fair enough. I was asked to meet Doctor Marcus Eckard by the Vatican.'

Canard's face remained emotionless. 'Go on.'

'There are some in the Vatican who believe that he has information that may have recently gained in significance,' Harker explained, deliberately keeping his answer vague. Then he glanced warily back to the doorway, to make a point.

'Please feel safe to continue, Professor. We are free of prying eyes.'

'OK, I met with Doctor Eckard who, as you may or may not know, has been a resident of Blackwater insane asylum for the past thirty years, and it was he who told me that I should visit Notre Dame and contact someone called Eizel in regards to information.'

The bishop continued to stare at him blankly, his expression still giving nothing away. 'Information? Anything else?'

'Yes, he told me to say... "The darkest part of the night always comes before the dawn but in a windowless room the night is never-ending"... whatever that means.'

Finally, the cleric's blank stare began to fade and was replaced with a cautious smile. 'In that case you are both welcome here. How is poor old Marcus? I've had a few reports over the years but none that were very good.'

'He's dead, Bishop,' Harker replied coldly, as a pang of anger now returned at having been held at knife-point earlier. 'He was murdered last night at Blackwater by someone who also had myself in their sights.'

Chloe took her chance at adding to this disclosure. 'They were trying to kill me as well. I'm his... I was his psychologist.'

This addition to Harker's revelation seemed lost on the bishop, who now rubbed at his forehead and was clearly saddened by the news. 'Then these are dangerous times, my friends. Very dangerous.'

As Canard continued to preoccupy himself with the obvious grief or concern that was visibly welling up within him, Harker decided to press the momentum for fear of losing it. 'I am sorry to have to be the one to give you this news but Doctor Eckard seemed adamant that this information would signify a great change – or a darkness enveloping the world, as he put it.' Harker paused and searched for the right words, not wanting to offend their host. 'Seeing as Doctor Eckard was... not exactly of sound mind, I'm unsure how seriously to take all this... whatever *this* is.'

This comment drew a wide-eyed but unyielding stare from the cleric. 'Marcus Eckard was no madman, extremely disturbed mentally, yes, but never insane.'

Harker was tempted to relay the state in which he had encountered the late Doctor Eckard. The self-mutilation and... well, everything. But he resisted and allowed the bishop to continue.

'Are you a believer, Professor Harker? In the spiritual world, I mean.'

'In God, yes, but everything else?' Harker replied with a shake of his head. 'Not really, no.'

His reply did nothing to dampen Canard's steadfastness. 'Then you are in for a serious shock, my friend.

'Why? What is this darkness he was speaking of?'

The bishop stood up straight, his complexion becoming somewhat grey. 'It isn't *darkness* he was speaking of, Professor Harker. It was something far greater. Simply put, he was to referring to the *end*... An end to humanity and the living world as we know it.'

Chapter 9

'Armageddon? Doomsday?' Harker exclaimed with unbridled incredulity in his voice and, now resting against one of the wood-panelled alcoves lining the walls of Notre Dame's treasury, 'with respect, Bishop, that is the something I expected to hear from Marcus Eckard, not you.'

'There is nothing respectful about it, Professor,' Bishop Canard reasoned, 'and you can be as sarcastic as you like, but remember one thing: you sought me out and not the other way around.'

Harker was still shaking his head when he caught a glimpse of Chloe's disapproving stare, and his shoulders slumped. 'Oh, come on, Chloe, you don't really believe this, do you?'

'I don't know, Alex,' she replied calmly, 'but I do think that at the very least we should hear what the bishop has to say... shouldn't we?'

Her response doused some of Harker's irritation, and he gave their host a polite nod. 'Of course, forgive me. It's just that all this talk of gloom and doom is a bit medieval – especially coming from a bishop. Please continue.'

Canard reached over to place his hand reassuringly on Harker's shoulder. 'I do understand. This is the not the kind of talk one would expect from a man of the cloth... not in the modern age anyway.' He offered a troubled smile. 'So why don't I just tell you what I know.'

The clergyman took a step backwards and pressed his hands together diplomatically. 'When I was initially approached by Doctor Eckard, I had only recently taken up my position here at the cathedral and, although I was expecting a challenge, I freely admit that I never expected to have such a task laid at my feet. I had already met Doctor Eckard a few times whilst visiting the Vatican but he wasn't what you would call a friend, which is why I found it so peculiar that he should approach me with such a request. He told me that a discovery had recently been made that would have unthinkable consequences for the faith and for the Catholic Church.' Canard slowly made his way over to a large painting of St Francis of Assisi hanging between two of the alcoves and swung it aside on its brass hinges to reveal a grey-metal wall safe. He then proceeded to swivel the numerical dial back and forth until, with a click, the metal panel swung open allowing the clergyman to retrieve a small wooden box which he placed on the table below. 'Then he entrusted this item to me and asked that I keep it safely hidden until the appropriate time.'

'And you believed him, just like that?' Harker inquired, taking a couple of steps towards the box.

'Not at all,' the cleric replied, looking somewhat offended. 'I informed him that I wasn't in the habit of holding unknown packages for anyone, regardless of how important they were. Besides which, it was the Seventies,' Canard explained, biting his lip gingerly. 'But when he then produced an official letter from the Pope himself, I began to take his request very seriously indeed.'

'What did that letter say?' Chloe interjected, taking a step closer to the shiny lacquered box.

'It was a personal appeal from his Holiness asking that I honour Doctor Eckard's wishes, and confirming that he had the full authority of the Vatican in this matter. It further stated that it was essential that I conceal any knowledge of its existence until I was called upon to do so, for the sake of humanity itself and all of God's creatures.'

'So how did you know it was us that would come calling?' Chloe probed, but she had barely finished the sentence before the bishop reached under his vestment and produced a small brass key attached to a thin metal tag with printing on it, which he now held up for his guests to read.

Harker had already recognised the words and he read them out loud: 'The darkest part of the night always comes before the dawn, but in a locked room the night is never-ending.'

'Yes.' Canard nodded shrewdly. 'And you are the first person in over thirty years to ever approach me with that password, and using the name Eizel.'

Harker reached over and gently plucked the key from Canard's hand, as the older man continued.

'Even with that official letter I was still uncomfortable about taking charge of this item, but Doctor Eckard assured me that as long as the box remained closed, then the mentioned 'consequences' would have no bearing, but that a time would come when its contents would need to be shared with the world at large, and would be the Church's only weapon in defeating the dark events that would follow.'

'And you never told a soul?' Harker asked, still examining the fine craftsmanship of the metal tag.

'Just one: a trustworthy and extremely protective friend.'

'Alphonse?' Chloe almost shouted the answer whilst jerking her thumb backwards to the doorway behind.

'Yes, a friend that has helped me shoulder the burden of this secret for so many years.'

Harker shot the bishop a surprised glance. 'And you never once looked inside?'

Canard reached over and retrieved the brass key from him. 'Never,' he continued, before slipping it into the lock and then taking a step back so as to allow Harker access. 'That was the burden I carried.' He paused a moment to massage his brow. 'Although I will admit that I came close a few times, but would you yourself readily open up Pandora's Box, Professor?'

Harker approached the wooden container and rested his thumb and finger on the key. 'I am ashamed to say that I probably would have. I'd be far too curious.'

'Then perhaps that is why *you* have been asked to retrieve it,' Canard said knowingly, 'just as I was asked to protect it.'

This comment brought a smile to Harker's lips and he acknowledged the logic with a nod before turning his attention back to the box and the key inserted. But, before he could apply pressure to it, Chloe slapped her hand squarely down on to the lid causing both men to jerk backwards.

'Alex, before you open this, do either of you have any idea what "it" is?'

'I think so...' Harker replied, throwing an uncertain glance in Canard's direction. 'Well, not exactly.'

Harker could see a tinge of mistrust appear in the clergyman's eyes and he immediately sought to eliminate the other man's concerns without giving too much away. 'The information Doctor Eckard gave me was that there are these certain texts that would pave the way for a timetable to those dark events you mentioned, and that these must be acquired if we are going to put a stop to it. He then told me to come to you. That's it.'

'What texts was he referring to?' Canard asked, his eyebrows arching inquisitively.

'The three Secrets of Fatima.'

'The Secrets of Fatima!' Canard spluttered. 'But they were revealed years ago.'

Harker shook his head. 'Apparently not Bishop. The original Secrets were kept... well, secret. The ones in the public domain are merely fakes.

'Fakes!'

'Yes, according to Father Strasser, the same man that recruited me to meet with Doctor Eckard, the Secrets referred to an event so cataclysmic that they must be hidden until the right time, and the knowing of them could prevent whatever perceived nightmare is waiting on the horizon,' Harker then pointed to the box in front of them. 'And I am hoping one of them is contained right here in this box.'

Canard was now looking bewildered. 'So how did you decide the time is right?'

Both the Bishop and Chloe were both staring at him questioningly but Harker was not about to disclose the bombshell that the Second Coming had been faked and that the Christ child was already back on earth. 'I have no idea. You would have to ask the Vatican.'

Before Canard could persist with further questions, a voice spoke up from behind them.

'Your excellency?'

All three heads snapped around to see a choirboy dressed in a traditional white vestment with red sleeves waiting anxiously in the treasury doorway.

'The congregation are seated and ready for the service to begin.'

Canard squinted and shook his head. 'I almost forgot. Thank you, Frédéric. I will join them shortly.'

The young boy looked perturbed by this answer and remained motionless in the doorway. 'But, sir, they are getting restless.'

'Then stall them, my boy,' Canard ordered politely. 'Why don't you go and pass out the collection plate amongst the crowd.'

'But we've already done that.'

'Then do it again. They are mostly tourists anyway, so they should have lots of spending money on them.'

Canard's solution was met with a look of shock from the choirboy.

'I am joking, Frédéric. Have the organist play some music to pass the time, and I will be there momentarily.'

This final suggestion was met with a respectful nod, then the boy headed back into the main hall.

'Are you sure you don't need to go right now?' Harker asked.

Bishop Canard shook his head firmly. 'Professor, I have waited over thirty years to see what is in this box, so believe me when I tell you that, at this moment in time, wild horses could not tear me away.'

'Understood,' Harker replied, returning his attention back to the box. 'Let's take a look.'

The box itself was deceivingly heavy and Harker deduced that the grainy wooden casing must house a much sturdier metal container that offered added protection. He lightly gripped the brass key and turned it. Without warning the lid automatically opened, on its spring hinges, into an upright position. This was followed by the sound of pressure releasing, not unlike a somewhat muted fizzy-drink bottle, but Harker immediately realised it was just Chloe releasing a breath of anticipation, her face huddled close to his own in an attempt to get a good look. The box was indeed lined with a shiny metal interior casing and filled with a fibrous-looking white packing filler similar to cotton wool. Just below this wispy material, Harker caught the glint of an object and he carefully pulled away some of the overlying strands to reveal a small tubular glass container with a piece of white paper folded up neatly inside. He picked it up and held it upwards towards the window light, in order to get a better look.

'What is that?' Chloe demanded roughly, attempting to pull the glass vial from Harker's hands.

'Looks like a piece of paper,' Harker replied, jerking the vial back towards him. 'And there's some writing on it. Just hold on.' Harker reached into his jacket pocket and retrieved a white linen handkerchief which he wrapped repeatedly around the two-inch-long sealed glass container. He then placed the wrapped item down onto the tiled floor in front of him and hovered the sole of his foot over it. Harker brought his shoe down on to the handkerchief with a muffled crunch, and then retrieved the flattened handkerchief and placed it squarely on an adjacent side table. He then proceeded to carefully unwrap the white linen, revealing shards of broken glass and a small folded piece of aged paper. Picking up the note, he then unfolded it directly in front of Canard, as Chloe stared over his shoulder with all the intense concentration of an accountant studying a spreadsheet.

74

The scrap of paper was a few inches wide by an inch deep and was blank except for a sentence handwritten in black ink.

> *And when those all around drop like fallen ash to the floor, the harps will begin to play their song and with it the icy and bright music of destruction will sound out for all to hear.*

The confusion in Harker's voice as he read this aloud was echoed by Chloe's as she swiftly reached over and plucked the piece of paper from his fingers. 'Is that all it says?'

'Well, it's obviously not the whole thing and just a snippet, but… yes.' Harker replied, while pointing to the uneven edges of the paper. 'You can tell a portion of it has been cut away at some point.'

Harker allowed Chloe a few more seconds to examine the note before taking it back from her and checking the reverse side. But it was blank and he now turned his attention to the box itself. He rummaged through the packing filler but, on finding nothing else of worth, he gave Chloe a shake of his head. 'That's all there is.'

As Chloe stood there looking unhappily perplexed, Harker found his attention returning to Bishop Canard who was staring at the box glumly.

'Well, that was worth thirty years of waiting,' the bishop stated sarcastically. 'I cannot even begin to tell you how many times I have needlessly worried over the safe-keeping of that box.'

It was obvious Canard was truly depressed about the box's contents – or lack of it – and Harker could only think of one thing to say. 'Don't you at least want to have a look at the note itself?'

'Thank you but no,' Canard replied indifferently, 'I was told the note was not for my eyes.'

His response drew a laugh from Chloe. 'But you now know what it says''

'True, but no one said anything about *hearing* it with my own ears,' Canard offered with a forced smile, before turning back to Harker. 'Well, Professor, I must say that the last twenty minutes of knowing you have been among the most exciting, intriguing and wonderfully disappointing moments of my life.'

The bishop's sour remark was greeted by a laugh from Harker. 'I'm sorry this has turned out not to be as exciting as you hoped, but even so this is apparently one of the real Secrets of Fatima! That has to mean something?'

The bishop let out a disheartened sigh. 'Yes, apparently... but more likely that it is a fugazzi.'

'A fugazzi?' Chloe queried unfamiliar with the term.

'It's Italian,' Harker offered, 'and its slang for anything that's fake. In the past, Vatican couriers were given fake packages to test their reliability, as it were. If they were found to have been opened, then the courier was deemed unreliable and not to be trusted with the more important items.'

'Or in most cases it was a way of making the cleric feel more important in his position,' Canard declared matter-of-factly, 'which I'm guessing is the case here, and that is most embarrassing if not somewhat insulting.' The bishop gave a polite nod of his head and moved over to the open doorway leading back into the main cathedral. 'Now, if you will excuse me, there are a hundred or so people all waiting for the service to begin,' he announced. 'You are of course both welcome to stay for the service, then afterwards I would be happy to discuss further this,' the Bishop raised both hands and flicked his fingers sarcastically, 'mini adventure of ours.'

'Thank you, Bishop, we might just do that.' Harker replied.

'Very well, I will see you after the service.' Canard gave a friendly wave of his hand as he headed back towards the main nave leaving Harker and Chloe starting at each other in disappointment.

'Well, that was a let-down.' Chloe scowled. 'I honestly thought the box was going to unravel a mystery or something.'

Harker glanced down at the note still sitting in the palm of his hand. 'I did too. I really did,' he replied, before slipping the note into his jacket pocket. 'Apparently Marcus Eckard was plain crazy after all, but it still doesn't explain why that psychopath McCray turned up.'

'Maybe he was conned into believing there was something more to this, just like we were.'

'Maybe,' Harker agreed, 'but it still doesn't make any sense.'

'Nope, and it probably never will. God, I can't believe I allowed myself to get dragged into all this through heeding the imaginative ramblings of one of my patients.' Chloe looked humiliated and down-cast by the whole escapade.

Harker rested his hand on her shoulder reassuringly. 'Don't forget the murderer who almost killed both of us.'

She pulled away with a genuine look of shame now. 'That may be true, but to allow myself to be so influenced by a patient's flights of fancy is unforgivable. I should have just gone back to Blackwater in the first place and explained what happened, instead of jumping on a train to Paris with a complete stranger, with grandiose and idiotic hopes of unravelling some spiritual mystery.' Chloe clapped her hands over her face and let out a lengthy frustrated sigh. 'Jesus, when I say it out loud, it sounds even crazier.' She slumped back against the thick stone wall of the treasury and stared down at the floor miserably. 'What the hell was I thinking?'

The sorrowful figure in front of him elicited a tinge of sympathy from Harker but, considering the good doctor had pretty much black-mailed him into coming along, he was also finding it hard to feel any real empathy. Still there was something about her he genuinely liked, but whether that was down to pure physical attraction he wasn't sure. 'You did exactly the right thing. Remember your supervisor told you to go home and wait for his call, right?' The remark drew a slow nod. 'And he still hasn't called you yet, has he?'

Chloe's eyes remained fixed on the weathered tiles below her feet. 'I suppose that's true.'

'And you survived an attack on your life, which I consider a success in itself. So what if this little trip of ours came to nothing – big deal. I don't care and neither should you.'

Harker's upbeat words made her glance towards him with an encouraging glint in her eyes.

'Look, Chloe, whatever this Secrets' malarkey was about it was a long shot at best. And besides,' he glanced up at the impressive stained-glass windows and the sunlight pouring through them, 'how often do you get to visit Notre Dame Cathedral and, more importantly, Paris.' Finally, a smile began to emerge on Chloe's lips and she stood up straighter with renewed composure. Harker continued, 'We have the rest of the day to spend in one of the most exciting cities in the world, and we can be back in the UK by this evening and then you can call your boss and get an update.' Even as he said it, the idea of McCray and any unfinished business was still resonating in the back of Harker's mind like a foghorn, but there was little he could do about it at this point in time. He also had to consider that this dead-end at the cathedral may have been just what the psychopath was hoping for, and perhaps their paths would never cross again. 'So what do you say, Doctor Stanton, shall we take a taxi and see the sights?'

The words had barely passed his lips when somewhere in the distance a high-pitched shriek shattered the surrounding stillness, only to be followed by another even louder scream.

'What the hell was that?' Chloe exclaimed and she quickly followed Harker who was already making his way through the treasury entrance and down the corridor. He had only just reached the access door to the cathedral when another scream erupted and he went bolting through the entrance with such speed that he failed to see the woman standing just beyond it, so the two collided. This caused Harker to stumble but sent the woman flying face first onto the marble floor. Within moments Harker was at her side. 'I'm so sorry, I didn't see you,' he offered apologetically, then he gently clasped both hands around the woman's shoulders and carefully turned her over to face him. She had hit the floor hard and in those few frenetic seconds Harker expected to see maybe a badly blooded nose, but the sight that greeted him was far more shocking and he shuddered in astonishment at the distressing image that confronted him.

The woman's skin was a sickly ashen grey with, just below the surface, a dark network of black veins and capillaries weaving through her flesh, adding to the woman's rapidly darkening skin colour. A tight grimace pulled back her lips to reveal bleeding gums that seemed to recede further with each passing second, and her tongue was so purple and swollen she was clearly struggling to breathe. The woman's eyes peered blankly upwards, the whites replaced with a deep crimson red where the capillaries had completely burst. The life fluid ruptured through small tears in her eyeballs, squirting globules of frothy blood over the eyelids and rolling down the woman's cheeks.

Harker heard Chloe gasp in shock behind him, then felt her hand grasp his shoulder for support. That gasp clearly caught the attention of the deathly-looking woman and those two blood-red eyes slowly rolled towards Harker and her body began to tremble, then shake violently, until her whole frame went rigid. This climaxed in the expulsion of a high-pitched shriek, before her body went limp and those staring eyes became glazed and lifeless.

Harker was already shouting out loud. 'I need help here. Please, I need hel...' His words tailed off the moment he looked up and towards the rows of pews up ahead. There must have been over a hundred visitors to the cathedral that day – men, women, and children of all ages – and, as far as Harker could see, every one of them was now writhing in pain while displaying the same ghoulish features as the dead woman before him. Some simply stood shaking uncontrollably, whilst others where punching at their own faces or tearing at their clothes as if the fabric itself was burning into their skin. Nearby an elderly man started banging his head repeatedly against a pillar which such force that the front of his skull finally crumpled inwards and he collapsed to the floor leaving a long bloody smear down the stonework.

One by one, visitors began to replicate such macabre acts, with some fighting against their pain more violently than others, but all eventually were left trembling uncontrollably until finally, with high-pitched screams, they fell to the floor and lay still.

Harker could not tear his gaze away from the gruesome sight and it was only the feeling of Chloe slipping her hand into his own that finally snapped him out of it.

'Alex, we have to go,' she yelled loudly over the ear-piercing wails of the dying and Harker felt a surge of focus returning until every cell in his body demanded one single response. '*Run!*'

Chloe pulled him to his feet and took the lead but within a few steps Harker had outpaced her, their hands still gripping each other's tightly. They began making a path around the outer perimeter of the cathedral. The inner sanctum containing the altar was hidden by internal screening walls but as it came into view, they could see that the same madness was gripping the priests and choirboys, who were all tearing at their robes and screaming for a release from the pain that was clearly overwhelming their bodies.

The screams grew louder as Harker guided them both towards the twitching mass of people, each trapped in their own bloody death throes. At first he attempted to avoid direct contact but it soon became clear that these poor souls were not out to harm anyone, but merely struggling to endure their own hellish torment. Harker ploughed straight into the thinning crowd, stepping over scores of fallen and convulsing bodies, and headed on towards the cathedral's main entrance, with Chloe clamped close to his side. The hefty wooden doors lay wide open, with cleansing sunlight pouring through, and they reached them just as a high-pitched scream, far louder than the rest, caused both of them to turn round. Halfway down the main aisle, Bishop Canard stared after them with burning red eyes, his face a sticky grey and his mouth wide open. Slowly raising his arm, he pointed a long grey finger towards Harker, then stood thus poised for a few moments before unleashing one final ear-piercing shriek and dropping to the floor in a heap.

As Harker felt Chloe tug insistently at his arm, he observed an odd calm descend all around the cathedral and the thrashing of bodies began to ease. Some continued swaying from side to side but most of them became still as statues, with dark red eyes fixed upon nothing but space, until the pain that had consumed them moments earlier was replaced by an unnatural peacefulness. Harker watched in astonishment as one by one each individual then dropped silently to the floor, just as Canard had done. There was no pattern here but all of it totally random. One by the altar, a group in the pews to the left, followed by a woman and her young child over to Harker's right... until finally the last victim sank slowly to the floor, leaving both himself and Chloe the only ones standing. Harker remained transfixed by the sight until Chloe finally dragged him away and out into the fresh air outside.

'Oh, my God,' she choked as Harker turned his gaze from one nightmarish spectacle to another. Scattered across the plaza beyond and up the cathedral steps were yet more corpses with the same distorted features. The sound of sirens drew near and he looked across to see two police cars each containing a number of officers just arriving at the scene. The proximity of a police station had allowed for such a quick arrival and some were already attempting to hold back the shocked onlookers, who were staring in Harker and Chloe's direction and then at the bodies at their feet.

Harker struggled to control his nausea and the hazy numbness in his head, and he turned to see Chloe was now beginning to shiver with undoubtedly the onset of shock. Harker pulled the woman close and rubbed at her shoulders and arms instinctively, trying to keep her warm even though it was a sunny day. 'Are you OK?' he murmured.

'I think so,' she replied, her breath coming rapid and shallow. 'What the hell just happened?'

Harker still held her close as a small group of police began to advance cautiously in their direction with guns drawn. 'I honestly don't know, but there's something else that needs answering.' Harker voiced the question he had no answer for but which was making him doubly anxious. 'Why are we the only ones still alive?'

Chapter 10

A grey Mercedes Benz made its way down the muddy dirt track with ease, its tinted black windows glinting as it passed the numerous path lights leading into a forest clearing and on up to a solitary run-down barn. The car stopped with a skid, its wheels struggling for grip on the damp earth. The headlights cut out and the deep growl of the engine dwindled to silence, as overhead the full moon glowed brightly.

With a click the rear passenger door swung open, revealing a wine-red lit-up interior and a solitary figure in an overcoat stepped out onto the muddy path and made his way over to the entrance to the barn. The man took a moment to glance around before then he rapped firmly on the wooden door. Within seconds it opened to reveal an old man dressed in a set of dirty work clothes. The beige flat cap on his head was just as filthy as the muddy pair of green wellington boots on his feet, and he would have looked altogether the typical farmer had it not been for the silenced Luger pistol held tightly in one hand.

'I'm here to see the owner,' the new arrival stated.

'Do you have the necessary paperwork?'

'No, I find documentation causes unnecessary scrutiny,' came the reply.

Satisfied that the password was correct, the gatekeeper stood back and allowed the visitor inside.

The barn's interior looked as dilapidated as the outside, with all the appearance of a working building. Various pieces of farming equipment hung from the walls and several bored-looking Romanian Simmental cows occupied a number of stalls.

'This way.' The old man instructed and led his guest across the hay-strewn cobbled floor to a small room opening off to the left. It was lined top to bottom with what had once been gleaming white tiles but years of use had left the majority yellow and cracked, and a row of toilet stalls along the back wall had fared no better.

The farmer made his way to the end and stopped in front of one filthy and disgusting, ill-used looking toilet. The pan itself was cracked, but not seeping, and the thick brown crust covering it hinted at the abuse it had suffered over time.

'Just for show,' the farmer explained with a grim smile before he reached over to the flusher and gave it a firm tug. The floor immediately emitted a deep grinding sound, followed by a series of vibrations directly underneath the men's feet and then the entire toilet sunk into the ground, revealing a set of stone steps leading down to a passageway below.

'Follow the corridor,' the old man urged, gesturing into the dark void.

The passage itself was no more than twenty metres long, and the visitor made his way between unpainted cement walls leading eventually to a metal security desk. The guard occupying it wore a black balaclava, bullet-proof Kevlar vest and had a M4 machine-gun hanging by a leather strap from his shoulder. The guard said nothing, he simply offered a nod and stood up before leading his guest into a larger room beyond which, although painted a pleasant magnolia colour, was lacking any décor and was currently occupied by five neatly dressed individuals labouring intently at secured grey work desks. There were several doors leading out of this room but all were closed and the guard ignored them and continued to make his way towards an impressive-looking wood-panelled door upon which he administered a single firm knock.

'Come,' hailed a muffled voice from inside and the guard swung the door open, allowing the visitor access, before gently closing it behind him with a click.

At a large oak desk slumped John Wilcox like a wearied monarch, sitting in an expensive-looking blue leather armchair his hands drooping limply over the arms. 'You took your time.'

'I apologise, sir,' the other man replied, 'but there were some important issues the Council needed me to attend to before I left.'

Wilcox slowly pulled himself to his feet and made his way around to the other side of the desk, coming to a halt within a foot of the new arrival. He then leaned in closer, his face within inches of the visitor and his lips were twitching in annoyance. 'Well, David, you should have informed me, then, shouldn't you?'

The man he called David gave a regretful nod, keeping his eyes directed front and forward throughout. 'Yes sir, but I think I may have picked up a shadow and I didn't want to risk having your location compromised.'

'A shadow?' Wilcox questioned. 'You mean the Templars?'

The Magi Council's go-between gave a brief nod. 'It's hard to say, but maybe. They have been driving pretty hard recently. Many of our station houses have been raided over the past few months.'

'Of course, they have,' Wilcox replied with a smirk. 'They're looking for the child, no doubt.'

The response drew an uneasy glance from his visitor. 'Actually that is one of the reasons I am here.'

The go-between's vague admission made Wilcox's face sag apprehensively, and he eyed the younger man with disdain. 'There's not a problem, is there? Come on, speak up,' he snapped, 'I've been hidden away in this underground tomb for months, so if I've been kept out of the loop...'

David offered a solemn nod. 'I understand, sir, but having one of the most famous faces on the planet has its drawbacks when making travel plans; even with the surgery, which I must say looks far better than I had expected.'

'Yes, not a bad job, if I do say so myself,' Wilcox replied and rubbing at his transformed cheeks. 'But what about the child?'

'The child has disappeared.'

'Disappeared?' Wilcox spat, as his face began to redden and his eyes rolled angrily as a distracting thought came to mind. 'And what about Claire Dwyer?'

'She has also disappeared,' David replied sternly. 'We waited at the meeting point, as planned, but she never turned up. And as of this moment, we have no idea where either she or the child are.'

Wilcox exhaled a deep gasp before slumping against the side of his desk. 'When did this happen?'

David opened his mouth but hesitated for a moment, his lips wavering. 'Just over a month ago.'

'A month!' the other man hissed, his whole body becoming tense. 'And why am I only now hearing about this?'

'The Council thought it best that they deal with the matter themselves, considering your current notoriety,' the younger man replied, seemingly unmoved by Wilcox's increasingly agitated demeanour.

'Oh, they did, did they,' Wilcox fumed, with the last vestments of his restraint evaporating. 'And what have the Council done, in their infinite wisdom, to rectify the situation?'

'I am afraid they have so far drawn a blank,' David conceded, now looking embarrassed by such an outcome.

Wilcox took a step back and shook his head disappointedly. 'Do you have any idea of the importance of that child?' he yelled loudly. 'He is the very embodiment of the reason *we* exist.'

'Maybe so, sir,' the younger man agreed. 'But there are many who believe that the child is of little relevance to the Magi at this time.'

'No relevance?' Wilcox continued to shout. 'Now, why would he not be relevant to us, as protectors of the Catholic church? Oh, I don't know,' Wilcox's jaw muscles were tensing furiously and his eyes beginning to bulge. 'Maybe it's because he is the fucking son of God!'

'Yes, sir,' David replied, resisting the urge to argue the semantics regarding the clone. 'You are right, of course, but the Council are quite adamant in their views.' The younger man was now looking nervous and he gulped as Wilcox slammed his clenched fist down hard on the thick oak table beside him.

'The Magi Council,' he hissed menacingly, 'are *my* counsellors, *my* base, and *my* administrators. They are not my equals, nor are they this organisation's leader.' Wilcox raised one finger to his cheek and tapped it pensively. 'It appears the members of the board think that my being out of sight means also being out of mind and thus allowing them free reign. I therefore think it's time I paid them a visit in person,' he concluded with a wide, threatening smile. 'Just to put their minds at ease, don't you think?'

'Actually, that is the main reason I am here,' David replied confidently, despite his own increasing nervousness. 'Due to the controversy that your leaving the Vatican in such a way has caused, and the worldwide attention you still attract on a daily basis, the Council have decided that your position has, for the time being, become untenable. They have therefore decided to hold a vote for an interim leader, until things have settled down.'

Wilcox remained silent and his eyes began to grow calmer as he gently put his arm around the other man's shoulders. 'You seem to be under the illusion that this is a democracy, David.' Wilcox said patiently as a father would do in explaining to a child about the naivety of his understanding. 'The Magi has endured for over a thousand years as a hierarchy... and it will remain a hierarchy for the next one thousand, you silly boy.'

Wilcox then slid his arm away and leisurely made his way back to other side of the desk with a renewed spring in his step. 'You do know the punishment for treason?'

David watched in silence as his master took his seat and picked up the phone.

'Michael, could you join us please,' he requested, and replaced the handset before turning his attention back to his guest as the same balaclava-wearing guard entered the room and stood off to one side, with both arms crossed.

'Don't worry, my boy, I am not one to shoot the messenger but I would like you to let the Council know that I will be attending their meeting, and I will take it as a personal slight if all of them do not show.'

Wilcox's measured response brought a wave of relief to the younger man and he snapped to attention with any air of defiance now gone. 'Yes, sir, I will notify them immediately.'

With a gracious nod from Wilcox, the go-between was already making his way towards the door when the Magi leader called out after him.

'One last thing before you go,' Wilcox said and then turned his attention to the waiting guard. 'Michael… break his fingers would you.'

'Which ones, sir,' the henchman replied, as David's face began to turn pale.

'All of them,' Wilcox rasped.

In one speedy movement the guard grasped the younger man around the shoulder and forcefully stretched his arm out straight. He then clamped both hands around the guest's fingers, curled them inwards and began snapping them one by one, with a crack inducing a cry of intense pain from David. Once all four fingers had been snapped, the henchman released his grip, allowing the younger man to retrieve his hand and hold it to his chest protectively, sweat now pouring from his forehead.

'Good, that will do,' Wilcox announced. 'Someone will contact you soon with a place and time of my choosing.'

David managed a shaky nod, his eyes welling up with tears at the agonising pain in his fingers, which now hung bent and twisted. 'Is there anything else you would like me to notify them of, sir?' the young man stammered, his eyes fluttering as he fought the urge to pass out.

'No, I don't think so,' Wilcox replied nonchalantly, and then gestured towards the other man's crippled hand. 'I think they'll get the message, don't you?'

Chapter 11

'Do I look like a member of al-Qaeda?'

'With respect, Professor Harker, looks have nothing to do with it these days. There are more Caucasians being radicalised every day. It's a common misconception to assume otherwise.'

'OK, well, don't all of them still end up committing suicide during their atrocities because, if you hadn't noticed, I am still very much alive?'

'You certainly are and, who knows, maybe something went wrong, or maybe you were supposed to survive but never got away in time, or maybe you are just a useless and inept terrorist. Either way, you two were the only people to walk out of the cathedral alive and I want to know why?'

Harker sank back into his grey leather seat and shot Chloe a reassuring glance. His alleged partner in crime was holding up well and the shock which had gripped her some hours earlier had all but vanished. That vacant expression and her taut lip muscles had faded within the first hour and she now appeared to be back in control of her faculties, despite her look of disbelief at the ridiculous accusations currently being heaped upon them.

They had been arrested after exiting the cathedral by a group of police officers who had seemed just as stunned at seeing the piles of bloody corpses littering the forecourt as they were. With jackets pressed to their mouths, two of the law men had then ventured inside, only to make a hasty retreat upon seeing the human devastation within. The younger of the two had retched his guts up on to the stone steps outside, adding to the sheer unpleasantness of the whole scene. Amid the nauseous groans and paling faces, Harker and Chloe had been hustled into the back of a black police transit van to wait until a Haz Mat squad for infection control had arrived. This unit had immediately gone to work by setting up a series of unfolding plastic containment tents, whereupon Harker and Chloe had been escorted into one by two men wearing pale-blue biohazard suits, while others cordoned off all the cathedral's entrances. After four hours of testing and examinations, whereby he and Chloe had been deemed free of any biological threat, the pair had next been released into the custody of Interpol Detective Xavier Rodriguez who had promptly cuffed them and bundled them both into the back of a grey Audi A4 with blacked-out windows. They had been on the road ever since, during which time Detective Rodriguez had continued bombarding them with every question under the sun and then re-asked them again and again and again. Although emphatic about both his own and Chloe's innocence, Harker had remained calm and respectful since, after all, over a hundred people had died back at Notre Dame. No, now was not the time to be forgetful of that fact and it was clear to see from Chloe's submissive demeanour that she was of the same mind-set.

'Detective, I am just as horrified as you are,' she declared softly, 'but our only link to this awful catastrophe is that we both happened to be there at the time.'

'Yet you were the only ones to come out of it without so much as a scratch,' Detective Rodriguez was glaring uncompromisingly into his rear-view mirror, 'and you both know each other. If it had been two strangers that survived, then the odds would be on your side. But the fact that out of a hundred people only two survived, and those two knew each other... that's a coincidence too far!'

Harker released a tired sigh. The Detective's logic was undeniable and he was right in that there was a connection, but revealing the discovery and interpretation of a prophecy was not going to do either of them any good. They would simply think he was crazy and, besides which, Bishop Canard had been with them during the opening of the Secret, and it certainly had not stopped *him* from dropping dead.

Neither Chloe nor he had mentioned their real reason for being at Notre Dame and he refused to believe that this disaster had anything to do with simply reading out a few words. This disastrous event had to be something more, something tangible. Something real.

'What's going on, Detective, is that somehow we were both incredibly lucky. I can't explain it, and we certainly don't know what caused it, but I can assure you that neither of us were involved,' Harker shook his head from side to side. 'And, anyway, since when are official interrogations carried out in the back seat of a car?'

Rodriguez continued to frown with mistrust, then returned his attention to the road ahead. 'When a hundred innocent bystanders drop dead without explanation, that's when.'

Just then the car pulled up to a red-and-white striped pole barrier with a woman in a navy-blue security uniform manning it. Rodriguez pulled out his Interpol ID badge and pressed it flatly against the windscreen, getting a nod from the guard. She reached inside the small monitoring cubicle next to her, and within moments the barrier was raised and they were on the move again. The access road continued between two large tar-covered dome-shaped buildings, one on either side, which Harker recognised immediately.

'Why are we at an airport?' he demanded.

Chloe followed quickly: 'Shouldn't we be going to a police station?'

Rodriguez remained silent for a few uneasy seconds before answering, and Harker got the impression the Interpol agent wanted his two passengers to sweat it out as for as long as possible. 'You're both being flown to Interpol Headquarters in Lyon, for interrogation.'

He barely finished speaking before the car had reached a large tarmacked area upon which was parked a white Gulf-Stream 450 twin jet, with two stocky men wearing black suits and sunglasses standing either side of a short flight of stairs leading up into the open hatch. The entire area was a network of taxiing roads leading from various hangars to the single runway, but it was the boundaries of the airport that betrayed its true identity. The entire perimeter was surrounded by a high chain-link fence which in turn was hugged by a row of tall conifers offering protection from unwanted attention.

'This is a private airfield,' Harker grunted, a feeling of trepidation beginning to rise from the pit of his stomach, as the car came to a stop next to the fuselage of the aircraft. 'And why fly us all the way to Lyon?'

'What's wrong with Lyon?' Chloe snapped, the tension in her voice evident as the two suited men outside made their way over to the car.

'Because Interpol doesn't have an interrogation section there – or anywhere else,' Harker explained. 'Its primary role is to act as intermediator between separate law agencies around the world.'

'Very good, Professor Harker,' Rodriguez remarked sarcastically as both the Audi's passenger doors were suddenly flung open. 'Now get inside the damn plane.'

'Motherfu...' Harker's abusive reply was cut short as one of the men in suits hauled him firmly out of the back seat and, with one hand planted around the chain of the handcuffs, began marching him towards the Gulf-Stream and then up the steps leading to the open hatchway. A few feet from the opening, Harker jammed his foot against the plane's fuselage and thrust backwards trying to catch his burly chaperone off balance. But it was like pushing against a brick wall and the only thing he succeeded in achieving was pulling his own hamstring. Without a weapon he was going nowhere and, even if he did manage to get the handcuffs off, the single strip of spearmint gum in his jacket pocket did not constitute anything he could use in a viable plan of attack. Besides which, he was not the MacGyver type.

Harker therefore ceased resisting and allowed himself to be pushed through the entrance accepting that for the time being they were not going anywhere, even if Chloe – who was yelling and demanding to be released – had yet to reach the same conclusion.

The interior of the aircraft was deceptively spacious and Harker's nostrils were greeted by the smell of leather and fresh fabric, evoking in him a curious feeling of contentment given the circumstances. The cabin windows were covered with drop-down blinds denying admission to even the slightest sliver of sunlight, thus adding to the false sense of security he felt. Up-lighters lining the cabin's floor emanated a cosy orange glow, reflecting off the lacquered walnut strip-panelled edges of a shiny round conference table bolted securely to the floor. Comfy-looking padded-leather business chairs encircled it, with each leg nestling in a deep divot set within the thick cream carpet, thus ensuring they remained in position during any moments of unforeseen turbulence. At the far end, a wall partitioned off the room, with an open doorway on either side leading deeper into unobservable areas of the aircraft's interior beyond. The partition itself had a large LCD plasma screen fixed into its surface which provided much of the ambient light with a plain blue hue. The room was finished off perfectly with an impressive corner bar, its well-secured crystal tumblers sparkling with evidence of their extravagance and cost.

'Please have a seat,' the suit-clad man stated firmly, sounding more of an instruction than an invitation and he pushed Harker down on to the nearest conference chair. Chloe was led past him, through one of the open doorways and out of sight, still protesting as she went.

'Where are you taking her?' Harker demanded loudly, rising to his feet before being thrust back down again.

'She will be fine, sir. You have my word on that,' the suited man replied, now standing back a few paces with arms crossed and allowing Harker some personal space.

'Oh, I have your word, do I,' Harker snapped sarcastically. 'Well that doesn't exactly inspire me with any confidence considering you're obviously about to kidnap us.'

The man in the suit shrugged his shoulders indifferently, then made his way back to the aircraft's entrance where he pulled the door closed and secured it with the large metal locking handle, thus blocking out the last vestiges of the daylight outside. 'Someone will be with you shortly, sir,' the guard informed him and then headed for one of the internal doorways. 'Please take a moment to relax in the meantime.'

'Relax?' Harker gasped, raising his still handcuffed wrists into the air. 'Really?'

A genuine smile of amusement crossed the man's lips before he disappeared deeper into the aircraft, leaving Harker alone with nothing but his thoughts, his surging temper, and a pair of steel handcuffs restricting the flow of blood to his hands.

After a few moments, something stirred up ahead, near one of the cabin's darkened internal doorways. Harker's attention honed in on it immediately.

'I would say you look remarkably relaxed,' a voice declared. 'All things considered.'

Harker watched as the shadowy figure appeared through one of the two doorways and began to make his way into the light cast by the LCD screen. He moved with a familiar gliding motion but the voice alone was unmistakable – as was his sense of relief that Harker felt upon hearing it.

Dressed in a charcoal-grey pinstriped suit, dazzling white shirt and a matt-black tie, Sebastian Brulet, Grand Master of the Knights Templar, continued towards the table with all the graceful poise Harker had come to expect. Neither man said a word as Brulet reached over and slid a slim metal key into the handcuffs, released them with a click and then dropped the uncomfortable restraints into the spare seat next to Harker.

'Sorry about those,' Brulet apologised, 'but you know… appearances and all that.'

Harker was immediately on his feet and warmly shaking the hand of his friend. 'Is there any time you *don't* make a dramatic entrance?'

'Not if I can help it, since it adds to the mystique,' Brulet joked, and for a moment Harker was again transfixed by the unique shape of the Grand Master's truly distinctive if not bizarre eyes, which seemed to exude mystery like no others Harker had ever known. The eyes themselves were normal, of course, but it was the yellow irises and pupils each formed in the shape of a cross that commanded attention, since it looked as if Brulet was wearing special contact lenses. Of course Harker knew this was only the result of a genetic disease, Coloboma, which deformed the pupils in such a way. But, when combined with Brulet's second rare condition called Waardenburg's Syndrome, which affected the body's pigments and gave the Templar's skin a light almost silver tinge, it made the man's overall appearance exquisite. Harker found it just as mesmerising now as on the first occasion he had met the Grand Master.

'Still bewitched by my appearance, Alex?' Brulet remarked casually and without any hint of offence. 'If you keep staring at me people will talk.'

The jest broke any awkwardness that could have entailed, and Harker quickly responded. 'Well we certainly wouldn't want that, would we?'

Brulet gave a friendly nod and then motioned for Harker to resume his seat as he himself took the chair opposite.

'Well, then,' the Templar continued, folding his arms and settling back in his seat, with an expression now all business, 'perhaps you would be kind enough to tell me what on earth is going on?'

A number of questions were already forming an orderly queue in Harker's mind, and first in line was how Brulet's men had managed to get to him so quickly. But by now Harker knew the drill and that the Grand Master would eventually reveal all, and probably already knew more about what was going on than he did. 'I'm not sure where to start, Sebastian.' Harker replied, fumbling for the beginning of his explanation. 'The last 24 hours have been crazy.'

'Of that I have no doubt.' Brulet replied with a wistful smile. 'Hold on one second.'

The Templar stood up and made his way over to the corner bar, where he quickly mixed a drink in one of the crystal glasses. He then returned to his seat and placed it in front of Harker. 'Vodka and Red Bull right?'

'Perfect, thank you.' Harker gave a grateful smile and took his time over a long, deep swig, allowing the potent liquid to soothe his throat and refuel his dipping energy reserves that were waning after the day's events.

'You're welcome,' said Brulet, settling back in his seat. 'Now, why don't you start from the beginning?'

'OK, from the beginning,' Harker agreed and took another satisfying gulp, 'but bear with me because it's... complicated.'

'Isn't it always?' Brulet answered, crossed his legs and listened as Harker began to recount the events that had led him to the chair he now sat in. He detailed the attack on the priest by the *demons*, and the message they had delivered. He told Brulet about the faking of the three Secrets of Fatima, and how the real ones detailed the Second Coming of Christ and that this would signal the beginnings of the prophecy. He went on to explain how many in the church hailed the cloned Christ child's arrival as the genuine Second Coming, and how that very fact meant acquiring the other two Secrets was now imperative. Harker went on to divulge what he had learnt during his meeting with Doctor Eckard and then of his escape aided by Chloe from the psychopath McCray. He told how Eckard's revelation had led them to Notre Dame and the discovery of the second secret, and how, after reading it, everything had descended into chaos and death.

Throughout the telling, Harker had been stealing sips of his drink to combat the unease he was feeling, but this had nothing to do with the events themselves. It was the supernatural overtones contained within his account that irritated him, because the very mention of such outlandish things made him feel like a fool.

Brulet remained expressionless, looking neither surprised nor knowing throughout, and it was only as Harker's account drew to a close that Templar Grand Master began to shift in his seat.

'... and that's it.' Harker concluded before finishing off his drink. 'Right up until Detective Rodriguez dropped us off here.'

Brulet remained still, staring directly into Harker's eyes with those cross-shaped pupils of his. 'That's quite a story, Alex,' he said finally and interlaced his fingers pensively. 'So do you believe it?'

Harker was slightly taken back by the ease with which Brulet asked this question. 'Which part?' he stammered, because he had covered a lot of ground.

'About the three Secrets and this apparent fourth one,' Brulet replied. 'Do you think they actually foretell the timetable for an approaching cataclysm?'

Harker held back for a moment to consider his answer, but that didn't help him much and he instead ran with his gut feeling. 'Sebastian, I may still believe in God, even if my faith in the Church itself is somewhat diminished but...' He shook his head vigorously. '... a prophecy! I don't believe in them for a second, but... if you had seen those people's faces at Notre Dame and the way they just dropped dead; it was so unnatural. It was almost... *supernatural.*' Harker zoned out for a moment as those expressions of pain and despair briefly came to life in his mind, and he dropped his head into his hands and massaged his temples before returning once again to face Brulet's steady gaze. 'Truth is I don't know what to think, but I do know the Vatican believes it, and they also believe that the Christ child is the only one that can stop it from happening. Either way, that little boy appears to be at the heart of it all. Have you had any luck tracking down Claire Dwyer?''

Harker felt his heart sink as Brulet shook his head solemnly. 'I am embarrassed and saddened to say no. Claire Dwyer has literally vanished off the face of the earth, and with her the Christ child that she kidnapped. We have people looking but every lead so far has resulted in a dead end.'

Harker collapsed back into his chair, his energy now deserting him. 'Then my only option is to keep tracking the Secrets and pray something comes of it. I just hope that the hundred people that died today will have been the last.'

'Actually it was one thousand,' Brulet corrected.

'What?' Harker coughed.

'I am afraid so.' Brulet continued, his finger gliding across his lips thoughtfully. 'Apparently Notre Dame was just the start. Over a thousand people died today, Alex... and they all died the same way.'

Chapter 12

'Hello? Is anyone there? Can anyone hear me? Please… anyone please.' Claire Dwyer screamed the last few words in nervous frustration as the sound of her voice was once more consumed by the pitch blackness smothering and besieging every one of her five senses. Her head swirled with the same unanswered questions that had been haunting her since regaining consciousness some minutes earlier. Where was she and how long had she been here? Her mind felt disconnected, her thoughts scattered, with all the unnerving peculiarities experienced during those first few seconds after having just woken from a deep sleep, and not knowing where one is. Except those seconds had become minutes and the fog clouding her mind was still refusing to clear.

Claire closed her eyes and clumsily stumbled through her memories, attempting to recall any reassuring truths that would allow themselves to surface. 'My name is Claire Dwyer,' she whispered to herself gently, the warmth of her own breath tickling her chin and that sensation offering a small measure of comfort in these otherwise cold and damp surroundings. 'I am thirty-six and I was born in… in… Manchester.' The simple recollection brought her a shred of relief, but it was quickly replaced by that same feeling of dread she had awoken with. 'And how did I get here?' Wherever *here* was. The question caused her whole body to slump in self-defeat as she allowed herself the indulgence of self-pity. She shook her head back and forth violently as if the very act itself would shake loose the doubt and fear that were continuing to strengthen their grip. What was the last thing she remembered? There was a car… she had been in a car, with something in her possession. Something important. Something very important. She had a vague recollection of staring out of the window and watching buildings and other vehicles pass by. She was a passenger in a car, and the car was travelling fast; she was sure of that because she could remember the whine of an engine in her ears.

The images in her mind began to fade and she immediately pressed one hand to her forehead and began to massage it stiffly, concentrating on those thoughts with every ounce of mental strength she possessed. After a few seconds, the memory began to fall back into focus and she expelled a sigh of relief at this minor triumph. The car she sat in was chasing another... or were they being chased? She couldn't be sure but what was certain was that she had in her arms something valuable. Something of great importance. Something priceless. No, something irreplaceable. And then a dark shadow had fallen across her. The shadow of another vehicle just before it hit.

Claire shuddered as she relived that moment of impact. There was the deafening sound of crunching and twisting metal. The grinding of glass as it shattered all around her. And the intense force of the collision that sent shockwaves rippling throughout her body... And then nothing. The images captured in her mind were but a few single snapshots of the turmoil unfolding around her. It had all happened within a fraction of a second, but the sensation of it was far more lasting than the single hazy image of the impact – as is commonly the case during the most intense moments of trauma experienced during a car crash.

Claire instinctively rubbed at her right arm, where her first aware-ness of the impact had occurred, searching for signs of injury. But there were none. She slid her open palm down the length of her right side, all the way to the ankle, but there was nothing. No pain. No breaks. Not even any bruising, so far as she could tell in the darkness. Not even a tightness in her muscles. Quite simply *nothing*.

Claire pulled back instinctively and clasped both her hands together as if protecting them from any unseen force that may be maliciously lingering in the darkness. It was impossible! A crash like that should have been punishing to her body, pulverising even, and yet she couldn't find any trace of it on her body. Impossible unless... A dark thought implanted itself into the depths of her cortex. At first she pushed it to the periphery of her mind but within seconds it began to grow, overpowering the rational and logical thought processes that had so far been guiding her. As, the idea became more vivid, so did the fear it induced and the consequences that came with it. Claire Dwyer felt a cold shiver tingling throughout her body as the idea flourished further. The grip she exerted on her hands began to stiffen and her mouth became dry, as an unpleasant constriction took hold in her throat.

Was she dead?

In a person's life there is a moment when the potentially inevitable suddenly becomes inescapable. A moment such as an accident at the crucial moment of impact, when the point of no return has been reached, and your life is literally in the hands of the gods or of fate. When these moments occur and the importance of your own world fades around you and time slows, as it always does, one thought will consume your mind… *Is this it? Is this the moment of my death?* Of course it all happens so quickly that you won't have a chance to worry about it, let alone have time to evaluate it. It just *is*, and in that instance comes a moment of peace. Not because you are OK with it in any way, shape or form, but rather because there simply isn't time to think further. As Claire Dwyer sat motionless in the pitch black, clutching her hands together for comfort, this time-induced luxury was one she would not be afforded. There was only one emotion she could feel and it wasn't one of peace… It was sheer panic.

Claire's mind frazzled with the notion and as a single tear of despair rolled down her cheek, she once again clung to any truth her mind would allow.

'My name is Claire Dwyer,' she stated forcefully, her voice now shaking uncontrollably, 'I'm thirty-six years old and I am alive.'

She dipped her head to her chest and was about to repeat this comforting mantra when, high up above, a tiny glow appeared and from it a thin ray of light shone down onto her head. She looked up and raised a hand in front of her eyes, as the dazzling light sent a shooting pain through her retinas. The discomfort increased, as the thin ray of light from above began to expand until it surrounded her whole body in a circle of light, revealing the moss covered, stone-cobbled flooring of what looked like a medieval prison cell of old. Through blurred vision she could now make out a circular opening overhead, where a rusty metal cover had been lifted back on a pair of dirty and well-oiled hinges. As her eyes struggled to focus, a shadowy figure loomed into the opening, the bright light from behind making it impossible to distinguish any of its features.

'You are not dead, Miss Dwyer.' The voice was unmistakably a man's: deep, gruff and with a strong European accent. 'But your fate has yet to be determined.'

Claire pulled herself to her feet, both hands still shielding her eyes, and she squinted up at the opening in the ceiling which she could now see was about ten feet above her. 'Who are you?' she demanded cautiously. 'Why am I here?'

The mysterious shadow craned its head to one side as if trying to get a better view of the prisoner. 'You are here because you are a sacrilegious heretic and a witch.' The voice sounded extremely composed, considering the insults it was hurling. 'You are here because you kidnapped the son of God for your own political grotesqueries.'

Claire's knees almost buckled under her as her memory came flooding back. The cloned child! The Christ child and her part in his abduction! Where was he? Was he safe? She remained silent while trying to hide the shock she was feeling and, as her eyes grew more acclimatised to the light, she could now see the figure was wearing a hood made of a dark-coloured fabric, covering his face. In fact, she could only make out one feature and that was a pair of glinting white teeth and the lips surrounding them, which appeared to be snarling at her.

'As for who I am, you need to know only that I am your judgment. I will be either your saviour or your executioner.' The shadow's lips now began to smile ominously, the sight sending a chill racing down Claire's spine. 'Tell me, Miss Dwyer,' the voice continued, 'are you ready to be born again?'

Chapter 13

'...one hundred at the basilica in Rhône, one hundred and thirty at a synagogue in Porta Bella, Italy, and lastly one hundred and forty at the central mosque in Madrid. That's just over one thousand people in seven religious institutions around the world, and they all died the same way within minutes of the tragedy at Notre Dame.' Brulet nestled back into his chair. 'So once again, Alex, I am compelled to ask: what is going on?'

Brulet's question was not uttered accusingly but rather more like a probing of the facts. Regardless, though, Harker couldn't help but feel this back-and-forth was more of an interrogation than a debrief, and he struggled to hold back an instinctive feeling of defensiveness that was now rising in his chest and attempting to push its way to the surface. 'You have my word, Sebastian: that's all I know.'

Brulet remained silent and motionless, those eyes of his not blinking or moving but just staring uncompromisingly.

'You don't really think I had a hand in this, do you?' Harker's stunned tone prompted an immediate shake of Brulet's head.

'Not for a moment, Alex – or we would not be having this conversation.' The response was typical of what Harker had come to expect from the Grand Master, affable yet unnerving, demanding a silent respect from any it was directed towards. Brulet rose gracefully, picked up Harker's now empty glass and glided over to the corner bar, where he began to mix a fresh drink for his guest. 'Have you spoken to Father Strasser since he initially set you off on this Vatican-sponsored mission?'

'No. I tried his number after we got arrested outside Notre Dame. It was the only phone call I was allowed but his line had been disconnected.'

'It doesn't sound like he wants to speak to you any more,' Brulet deduced. 'So what do you know about him anyway?'

'Just that he was acting as an emissary for the Pope,' Harker replied, now feeling somewhat naïve for not having checked out Strasser's credentials for himself.

'Very well.' Brulet continued back to the table and placed the drink in front of his guest. 'Then let us at least try and find out who he really is.' The Grand Master leaned over to a small wood-encased speakerphone set in the middle of the conference table and tapped a round grey button on one side. 'Jason, I need a background check, please, for one Father John Strasser – two 'S's I think.' Brulet glanced enquiringly in Harker's direction but was met with an uncertain shrug of the shoulders. 'Better try it with one S as well,' Brulet continued, 'and he's claiming to have direct contact with the Pope, so begin with the Vatican's database. Oh and, Jason, do the same for a Captain McCray. Did the man have an accent, Alex?' Brulet asked, looking back at Harker.

'It was English,' Harker replied earnestly, 'and definitely southern.'

'Did you get that, Jason? I'm not sure if the title refers to some military affiliation but best start there.'

'Right away, sir,' came the response, and the Grand Master released the speaker button and slid back into his seat, with his attention again focused on Harker. 'Now, may I see this so-called Secret that seems to have caused these terrible events?'

The hint of sarcasm in Brulet's tone was not lost on Harker but he didn't take any offence to it, considering he himself thought that the idea of mere words instigating such a tragedy was absolutely crazy. But, still, the cynicism evident in Brulet's voice was unusual from the man he had come to know. Harker pulled the offending piece of paper from his coat pocket and silently placed it in Brulet's waiting palm.

Brulet began to examine it and within seconds was shaking his head, his eyebrows raised in bewilderment. 'Well, its cryptic, and I can see the connection with ashes – or people – dropping to the floor but, Alex,' he waved the piece of paper in front of him like a white surrender flag, ' "sticks and stones may break my bones but words will never hurt me." Whatever this is it cannot be responsible for the deaths of all those people.' Brulet handed the note back to Harker. 'You don't really believe that, do you?'

The question was voiced with such conviction that Harker couldn't help but feel somewhat idiotic, and he slipped the note back into his pocket with a gulp. 'The whole idea of it sounds crazy, I know, yet

I saw it happen with my own eyes. One second everyone's fine and then I read this, and within seconds people are dropping to the floor like flies.'

Harker let out a deep pained sigh before continuing, as Brulet eyed him in silence. 'If you had seen those people... their faces, the colour of their skin, their eyes.' Harker paused to catch his breath as the memory of Bishop Canard pointing a finger towards him with those glaring inflamed red eyes loomed in his mind. 'It just seemed so manufactured, as if it was meant to happen exactly as it did... if that makes any sense.' Harker took a deep swig of his fresh drink and pushed the awful images from his thoughts before returning to face Brulet who was now looking a tad more sympathetic.

'Do you believe in prophecy at all, Alex?'

Harker instinctively shook his head. 'No, never have.'

'And why is that?' Brulet continued.

'Because I believe that those who prophesise usually want to feel they have a special place in this world. That they are here for a reason, regardless of what the truth might be, and prophecy can give them just that. Furthermore, some especially spiritually inclined people, can convince themselves that they even have a direct link to God Almighty.'

Brulet offered a mere nod of his head, those dazzling pupils of his refusing to blink. 'Well, I do believe in prophecy, Alex. I believe in God Almighty and I believe that the Church and those that govern it, although far from perfect, do so at His wishes and in His name. Now, if I believe that, then I must also believe that God must communicate with some of us, and even hand down His knowledge to a few when that is deemed important or necessary.' Brulet raised his finger upwards towards the ceiling, with the conviction of a preacher. 'The real truth, though, lies in separating those with an authentic link from those for whom it is totally imagined.'

'Oh yes? And how do you decide that?' Harker questioned and unable to conceal the scepticism which he had instinctively wrapped around the question.

'With common sense, my friend.' Brulet reached over and lightly tapped him on the shoulder. 'You have just found yourself at the centre of a horrific and truly bizarre event and are left considering the prophetic warning this Strasser fellow heaped upon you, not to mention this psychopath McCray? Well, then I'm not surprised your good judgement has taken a knock,' Harker offered a nod but remained silent, allowing Brulet to present his rationale further. 'But ask yourself this: what makes more sense? That you are somehow responsible for the death of a thousand people around the globe by the mere reading out of a note, or that some terrorist is using you as a pawn in his own twisted plans.'

Terrorist? With everything else going on, Harker had not even entertained the idea, and he sat there somewhat stunned as Brulet pulled a remote from his jacket pocket and pointed it towards the LCD screen behind them.

The monitor instantly lit up to display a split screen of seven news channels, each reporting from one of the places of worship that had recently been targeted.

'They are claiming this is the worst terrorist attack since 9/11, and the world's first global terrorist attack aimed at religion as a whole.' Brulet concluded. 'These events are every bit as shocking as they are wicked.'

With each rolling headline that Harker viewed, his stomach tightened a notch further. Words such as 'chemical attack', 'nightmarish', 'first global terrorist attack' littered the various channels in the general outcry at such a large-scale assault. Everything Brulet was showing him made sense, but there was still one question that nagged him over all others. 'So how is it that Chloe and I were the only ones present to survive?'

Brulet swung his chair back around to face Harker, leaving the rolling news to continue displaying on the screen behind him. 'I will admit it is extremely odd but this attack is still fresh and we still don't know the full extent of what has happened. For all we know, there may be other survivors not yet accounted for. We will have to stay the course and watch the news channels like everyone else.' Brulet gestured back to the screen. 'And meanwhile I am not about to get the Templar organisation involved. The authorities will do a much better job of investigating this than we can and, besides, we have operatives like Detective Rodriguez willing to keep us updated.' Brulet retrieved the remote and began to play with it, rocking it gently from one hand to the other. 'Now, as to the question why you, I think I might have more of an idea.'

Harker watched as the large screen went black for a moment and then flashed back into life to display a variety of magazine covers and articles, all with one constant theme... Alex Harker himself. They were largely interviews Harker had given regarding the archaeological findings he had made during recent months, including the biggest one: that of Caesar's death mask.

'Over the last four months you have had more exposure than the Templars have received in the last millennium – the real Templars anyway.' Brulet remarked with a wink. 'And then there's this.' Brulet clicked the remote once again and the display became flushed with yet more front-page headlines but from mostly tabloids this time. 'Are you aware that you have become something of a poster child for so many of the conspiracy buffs out there?'

Vatican suppresses the Second Coming... Christ walks the earth once more... Alex Harker prophet or deceiver? With every new headline he read, the more uncomfortable he felt. Harker was aware of the various accusations the tabloids had been throwing at him recently but, considering they usually appeared alongside UFO and Elvis sighting exposés, he had never paid them much attention. His boss Dean Lercher, on the other hand, had wanted to use them in a publicity stunt when advertising Harker's latest archaeological discovery. 'Remember, Alex, there is no such thing as bad publicity so long as it gets bums on seats,' the Cambridge dean had argued when wanting to send out a press release reading: 'He discovered the son of God. Come see his latest discovery.' Harker had immediately quashed the idea but it gave proof of the gossip connecting Harker with the Vatican crisis four months earlier. 'It's not something I've deliberately courted, Sebastian,' he stated firmly.

'No, I can see that.' Brulet replied dryly, now using the control to zoom in on a magazine cover showing a smiling Harker shaking hands with the Mayor of London over the top of Caesar's gold death mask and under the banner headline: 'The man with the Midas touch.'

'Now that's out of context,' Harker growled defensively as the embarrassment over his media attention seeped into his cheeks.

Brulet was already waving his hand dismissively before Harker could defend himself further. 'I'm only joshing you, Alex. You've not mentioned a word regarding the child, just as you promised, and I have no problem with the publicity you have sought for your various finds – but I was simply making a point. Regardless of what you have or have not said, you have become the very real focus of attention for many of the general public in regards to the Vatican and also any and all rumours concerning the Christ child. Isn't it possible that these terrorists could have included you in their plans for today's attacks?'

Brulet had barely finished his sentence when the speakerphone crackled into life. 'Sir, I have completed the check on Father John Strasser.'

'Good,' Brulet replied, as both he and Harker automatically leant towards the speaker. 'What did you find?'

'Father John Strasser, aged fifty-five,' the voice blurted out military-style, 'was born in the Ukraine 1959 and joined the clergy in 1979. His parish lay in Warsaw, Poland until last year, when he just fell off the grid. I did find a Polish forwarding address tacked on to his voting registration form, but that was from over six months ago. I also found no record of him working at or even visiting the Vatican, let alone having access to the Pope.'

'Thank you, Jason,' Brulet replied. 'And what about McCray?'

'Nothing yet, sir, but I'll let you know when I do.' Brulet glanced over at Harker, who was already opening his mouth to ask the man a question, but Brulet held up a hand stopping him before he could utter a sound. 'Oh and, Jason, could you text Professor Harker with that address please.'

'Doing it right now, sir,' the metallic voice crackled, before the line went dead.

'It will almost certainly be a dead end, Alex,' Brulet declared force-fully, but it was lost on Harker who was already responding to the ping of the text message on his iPhone.

'Maybe,' Harker replied after taking a moment to view the address and, once satisfied, dropping the phone back into his jacket pocket, 'but if there is a chance of finding Strasser, then I need to take it. That rat-faced little turd knows a lot more than he's been telling.'

For the first time since his appearance Brulet was looking uneasy, and now Harker noticed the Templar tensely tapping the arm of his chair with one finger. 'Is everything all right Sebastian?'

Brulet sat there staring for a further few moments, just silently eyeing his guest through those weirdly misshapen pupils of his. Their odd shape meant it could be difficult to get a read on the Grand Master but, even with this unusual layer of expression protection, Harker had a rough idea what was on the man's mind.

'I'll be careful. You have my word on it.'

'I've no doubt you will,' Brulet offered, 'but I sometimes wonder if you are truly aware of the reality you're now living in?'

The statement wasn't intended to sound threatening, and Harker didn't take it as such, but he was uncertain nonetheless of what Brulet meant exactly. 'I'm not sure I follow you.'

Brulet lent forward, his fingers interlaced together, and rested his chin on his linked hands. 'When you were inducted into the Knights Templar, I said you could be as involved or uninvolved as you wished, do you remember?'

'I remember.' Harker replied with a nod. 'And I was and am thankful for that concession.'

'Of course, and I was happy to offer it, but you do realise that by searching for the child on your own you are delving ever deeper into the murkiness of our world... and the deeper you go, the more dangerous it becomes.' Brulet dropped his hands into his lap and raised his eyebrows. 'Alex, you have already pissed off some very powerful people within the Magi by aiding us, and if you continue to go forward, it will only get worse.'

To anyone else, Brulet's warning may have sounded like a threat, but Harker took it for what it was: concern. 'I understand that, Sebastian, but I've been aware of the dangers from the get-go and I'm still willing.'

'Maybe I'm not being clear enough,' Brulet interrupted loudly. 'You know the Magi as a single organisation, but that is not strictly true. The Magi are actually made up of four individual families, all of whom claim they belong to the original bloodlines of the three wise kings who followed the star leading to the stable where Jesus Christ was born. Even though they are ostensibly on the same side, these families have battled each other for centuries while all clawing for the right to be considered the Magi's prime faction. Each family deals exclusively in a particular area of the Magi: John Wilcox's branch of them dealt within the political arena, where others deal in such areas of expertise as intelligence, assassinations and finance. Each family strives to bring up their own kin with the education and ability to render them top of their game within that family's sphere of influence. These roles are instilled in them from the earliest age, and the moulding continues throughout their education.'

'Surely not everyone is born to suit a particular role?' Harker stated, intrigued by such a concept of destiny.

'Very true,' Brulet replied, rubbing his hands together, 'but certain abilities are passed on genetically. It is no coincidence that children tend to follow in their parent's footsteps in certain areas of expertise such as in sport or the sciences.'

'That's true but it would also be fair to say that many are prone to going in another direction altogether,' Harker ventured, as he found himself being distracted more by the debate than by the actual point Brulet was attempting to make.

The Templar let slip a thin smile at Harker's rather defensive posturing. 'That is true as well but in many such cases children have the ability to follow in their parent's footsteps but lack the wish to do so, for whatever reason. Finally, there are the rest whose abilities do indeed lie in unrelated areas. That is why each of the Magi families are encouraged to have as many children as possible, so as to increase the likelihood of producing a child with the requisite traits and characteristics.'

Harker was already shaking his head in agitation. 'That's a pretty cold way of looking at family life.'

'Indeed it is,' Brulet continued, 'and if you are not a fan of that parental model, then you'll love this. If a child fails to live up to their designated role, they are removed from the bloodline.'

'Removed?'

'Yes, undesirables end up as victims of various accidents and tragedies, many of which are blamed on the Templars.' Brulet licked his lips, wincing ever so slightly. 'It's a reliable mechanism for ensuring that hatred of the Templars will be passed on from one generation to the next.' Brulet paused briefly in reflection. 'I myself was blamed for the death of John Wilcox's father, so am now hated above all else by that family, even though I am pretty sure it was Wilcox himself that took the old man's life in order to usurp his position.'

Brulet expelled a gruff sigh before getting to his feet and placing one arm behind his back as if preparing to deliver a speech. 'Now, even though John Wilcox's branch of the Magi have reached the top position, it does not mean their rule is absolute per se. There is a council comprising the heads of each family and decisions are made according to a vote, but' – Brulet took a deep breath as if the mere explaining of the Magi's inner workings pained him – 'the most powerful of the families has the deciding vote, and Wilcox was therefore in charge because his family had attained the Magi's most important ambition of all time which, as you know, was to steal the papacy. Now that plan has gone to hell, thanks in part to you, and we have no idea who is in charge, and therein lies the problem. Up until now we have only had to worry about Wilcox's decimated family seeking to exact revenge but if you continue to pursue the child yourself, there is a very real possibility that the other three families will descend upon you, Alex. And, unless you are under the protection of the Templars, I can only see them succeeding.'

Brulet snatched another deep breath and settled back into his seat, suddenly looking weary. 'There is something more you should know. Since the Magi kidnapped the Christ child, the entire Templar organisation has rallied around one single objective: the retrieval of that child at all costs. Many within our ranks believe that to allow him to remain in the hands of the Magi is quite literally an affront to God. And although I do not believe there is any spiritual connection to the child, since he was made by man, I cannot in good conscience allow the poor innocent to be destroyed by the Magi's own twisted belief system. What is also significant is that to not take any action could – and I believe would – result in a fracturing of the Knights Templar Order itself and that can never be allowed to happen. So, when the child was kidnapped, it was decided that the Templars would begin an offensive against the Magi and for the past month it been nothing short of a total war between us. We have tracked down and raided one Magi stronghold after another, and the casualties have been high on both sides. But still, after all this, we have not produced a single lead to the child's whereabouts. Then, about two weeks ago, they just disappeared. Every known member of the Magi, every network we had discovered, every listening post and even every legitimately placed member in their various businesses has just vanished.'

Brulet licked his lips apprehensively. 'Right now I have every Templar under my command scouring all the corners of the globe in search of some piece or even a fragment of information that will lead us to the child but, as I said, so far we have come up with nothing. The point is, Alex, that if you choose to follow these leads which, for the record, I believe will take you nowhere, I cannot guarantee your protection... I simply cannot spare a single soul for that at the moment, not with the losses we have taken, I'm sorry.'

Harker shifted in his leather chair with a creak and began to digest the information the Grand Master had just heaped upon him. He had realised that he could become the target of a revenge attack but with Wilcox's brothers all dead and the ex-Pope in hiding, he had assumed the risk was low. However, throwing these other Magi families into the mix was something else altogether. What concerned him most was Brulet's disclosure that so many Templars had been cut down and in such a short time period. The loss of life must have been appalling and realistically it would take years for the Order to replenish its ranks. Templars were born into the Order and seldom invited, himself being a rare exception to that rule. 'I am so sorry, Sebastian, but I had no idea so many members had been lost.'

'Thank you, Alex,' Brulet nodded appreciatively.

'How many?'

'Almost a third worldwide… including two masters of the Templar Council, some of whom attended your own initiation.'

An image of the nameless faces of the men and women holding out their swords in an arc, as he made his way down the ceremonial aisle to be inducted, recurred sharply in Harker's mind. He was never given their names but at this moment he wished more than anything that he could have known them better. To grieve a stranger's death can be an emotional even if detached experience, and his Templar colleagues deserved more. 'Bloody hell!'

'A bloody hell it is indeed, my friend,' Brulet voiced despondently in nothing more than a whisper. 'A truly bloody hell.'

Since his first meeting with Brulet, he had never seen the Grand Master look so disheartened, and Harker suddenly felt an almost euphoric surge of protectiveness towards him. This was possibly in part due to his second drink which Brulet had ensured was a double. 'Then I need to find Father Strasser a.s.a.p. If there is even a chance that Strasser is a member of the Magi, and connected to the child's disappearance in any way, then I can't afford to wait even for a moment. Finding the child has to be my first priority.'

Harker was already on his feet and using his iPhone to take another look at the last known address provided for him, when Brulet's voice growled loudly from behind.

'Did you even listen to anything I just said?' he boomed.

Harker turned to see the Grand Master struggling hard to maintain his composure, the pale skin of his cheeks flushing red with either anger, frustration or a mixture of the two.

'If you chase after the child on your own, the Magi will come after you. And did I mention one branch of that family is known as the house of assassins!' Brulet bellowed as he jumped to his feet. 'So far you have only had dealings with their political branch, and you know how dangerous even they were. The people who will pursue you next have trained since birth to do nothing else but liquidate their enemies. These murderers have been taught to engage in every type of covert espionage in order to eliminate their targets.' Brulet continued to growl as he pushed back a lock of long white hair that had slipped across his face in his rush to stand up. 'And now they will be after you, specifically, Alex Harker.'

A few moments of silence passed as Harker stood there stunned by this outburst. Brulet was not the kind of man to allow his temper to erupt; in fact he seemed the essence of calm and always fully in control. 'I thought you said the Magi didn't have anything to do with this 'terrorist' attack – or with Strasser, for that matter.'

'I don't think they did but, who knows, maybe there is a connection. And anyway putting you back on the street, as it were, gives them all the opportunity they need to take a shot, should they wish to.' Brulet began forcefully tapping a finger on the conference table. 'Just stay here with us until we figure out what these attacks are about.'

Without hesitation Harker was already shaking his head, his own anger now flaring. 'I appreciate the concern, Sebastian, but if Strasser has any connection to the child, I need to know. Actually, forget *needing* to know; with everything that's happened, it's my duty to know.' He spun around and was already making his way to the exit, which proved an ill-conceived idea because he found it was locked tight.

'Thank you, Alex. That is what I wanted to hear,' Brulet called out after him, in his more familiar restrained voice.

Realising he wasn't getting out of the plane without some help, Harker turned to see Brulet calmly resume his seat and motion him to do the same.

'I apologise but I had to be sure that you know what you're getting yourself into.'

'You were testing me?' Harker fumed.

Brulet offered a gracious nod. 'I would never send a man into any potentially life-threatening situation without ensuring he was wholly committed. That would be heartless and irresponsible, not forgetting just plain mean.' Brulet smiled widely and once again motioned for Harker to sit back down. 'Please.'

Harker held back for a few moments, then with a shrug he was back in his seat. No matter how annoying Brulet had been, Harker could see the logic in the Grand Master's words. In truth he had instinctively decided to pay Father Strasser a visit without really considering the consequences or implications, but he still hated being played. 'Fair enough, I get it, but seriously, Sebastian, please don't do that again.'

'You have my word, but I needed to be sure… simply for my own conscience.'

Then Brulet went straight back to business, in typical fashion.

'Now, I can't offer you any manpower, as I have already said, but logistically we are at your disposal. Travel arrangements, personal jets, vehicles, contacts and any information checks you might need are but a phone call away.'

To the uninitiated this change to a more accommodating pace would have seemed bizarre, but it was something Harker was getting used to and he nodded his thanks.

'So there's really only one question left… how to handle your new friend, Doctor Chloe Stanton. I think it would be best to not involve her any further than she already has been,' Brulet advised. 'Do you think could convince her to put all this business behind her and head back to the UK?'

Harker was already smiling confidently before the Grand Master could even finish the sentence. 'Sebastian, I deal with unruly students every hour of the working day, each trying to undermine my authority and pressuring me to accept their own personal ideology. Believe me when I tell you that convincing Chloe this adventure is now at an end will be easy.' He waved his hand casually in the air. 'Trust me.'

Chapter 14

'Of all the crummy excuses… If you're trying to palm me off like one of your first-year students, then think again, mister.' Chloe declared loudly, slamming her open palm down on the British Airways check-in desk with a loud thump. 'You must think I'm an idiot, Professor Harker.'

'Professor Harker? What happened to Alex?'

'I reserve first names for people who are actually my friends, not those simply feigning to be so.'

'I see. Well in that case thank you for letting me know, Doctor!'

'Excuse me, sir, but are you looking to buy a ticket or not.'

The desk attendant's question momentarily distracted Harker's tunnel vision and he glanced over towards the clearly irritated member of staff. 'Just give us a second, will you?' he huffed.

'Sir, if you're not yet ready to buy a ticket, then please step aside and allow other customers to do so.'

Harker glanced back to see the ticket line totally empty, and no one else to be seen except for one lone luggage-handler leaning against the rear wall chewing at his nails lethargically. 'What customers!' He barked loudly, turning back to face the disaffected attendant. 'We're the only damn customers here.'

'That's not the point, sir, and if you continue to swear, I'm afraid I am going to have to ask you to leave.'

'Swearing!' Harker shouted in disbelief. 'That's not swearing. This is swear…' Harker let the words tail off when he noticed a blue-shirted gendarme further along the concourse was beginning to take an interest in their increasingly heated conversation.

'Well, sir?' the attendant continued facetiously, also fully aware of the policeman's gaze.

Harker raised one finger towards to the ceiling. 'We'll be right back,' he replied and gently took Chloe by the arm and guided her out of hearing range of the now smug-looking attendant. 'Chloe, I am not trying to palm you off. I just thought that, seeing as I'm already out of the country, I might as well take the time to visit some friends as well.'

'In Warsaw?' Chloe replied disbelievingly.

'Yes, in Warsaw. I'm already halfway there, so why not kill two birds with one stone? Besides, after everything we witnessed, I could do with a break. So why don't you head back to the UK, and in a few days we can have dinner and try and put these terrible events into context.'

'Context!' Chloe exclaimed. 'Well, that's not a bad idea,' she hissed sarcastically. 'Let's examine it, shall we. We find ourselves at the centre of a terrorist attack, after which we're arrested by Interpol, before being manhandled on to a plane, which doesn't actually go anywhere, at which time I spend almost an hour locked in a flight cabin whilst you apparently are interrogated by Interpol agents who, strangely enough, don't even bother to interview me before hurling us back into a car and dumping us here at Charles de Gaulle Airport, totally free to head home. Oh, yes,' she continued and sucking in a much needed breath, 'and without even having to disclose as much as our names to the authorities.' She continued to stare at Harker incredulously as she took a moment to catch another breath before continuing with the onslaught. 'Can I tell you how all these events could be wrapped up with a big bow?'

'Please do,' Harker declared indifferently, while retaining his poker face.

'Conspiracy,' Chloe leant closer, her lips tightening, 'and unfinished business. Now I want the truth. What the hell is going on, Alex, and what the hell is waiting for you in Warsaw?'

An awkward silence followed as Harker searched Chloe's hazel-green eyes for any sign of weakness that might actually allow him to palm her off for real, but regrettably all he could find was a look of unyielding determination. He would have to give her something, but only enough to mollify her understandable curiosity. Anything else would be a bridge too far and besides, Doctor Stanton was still an unknown quantity in his eyes. 'OK, fair enough. After Notre Dame you do deserve to know what's going on.'

His response drew a relieved sigh from Chloe, and she moved back a few inches so as not to seem so confrontational, even if her stare did continue to remain uncompromising.

'Back in England you were right about what you said,' he began, pausing for a moment to look out for anyone who might be in earshot. Satisfied that the only person in range was the lone baggage-handler, who seemed still only interested in the state of his own nails, he continued. 'Jesus Christ is back. He was reborn four months ago.' Harker couldn't help but feel a total pillock in just uttering those words aloud. He felt like some conspiracy nut or one of those weirdos that parades down the street with a sign reading: *Repent. The End Is Nigh.*

Chloe on the other hand was looking stunned, her mouth hanging open and her eyes wide with excitement. 'I knew it,' she announced in an almost high-pitched squeak of exhilaration. 'I just knew there was something going on there... I mean I didn't know exactly what happened but I knew something big had happened. I mean there were too many strange stories coming out in the papers, so some of it had to be true.'

'Now hold on,' Harker said, placing his hand on Chloe's shoulder in an attempt to quell her almost giddiness at the news. 'It's not quite what you think. The child is in fact a clone.'

'What!' Chloe gasped.

'A clone, constructed from Christ's DNA that was found on a number of relics the Catholic Church had in its possession.'

She didn't utter a word as Harker now revealed more of the truth he had kept so painfully quiet about since its discovery.

'There is a group of people – fanatics – that infiltrated the Church and wanted to use the child to bring about a Catholic revolution. But I and a few like-minded people, managed to stop it before it could get out of hand.' Harker paused there but not to give Chloe a chance to absorb this outlandish tale, but rather to give himself time to figure out how to explain the situation further without giving away too much about the main players. He was not about to reveal the existence of the Knights Templar and its ongoing war to stop the Magi controlling the Catholic Church. 'Unfortunately some of these fanatics managed to kidnap the child about a month ago and then they vanished.'

'The last Pope, Adrian VII,' Chloe stumbled as she began to put the pieces together, 'he's one of these infiltrators, one of the fanatics, right?'

'I'm afraid so,' Harker offered a solemn nod, 'and my friends have been searching for them both ever since.'

'Who are these friends? MI6, CIA?'

'Sorry, Chloe, I can't and won't tell you that, but suffice to say they're the good guys.'

Considering what she had just been told, Chloe was looking remarkably accepting, and Harker wondered if she was simply shell-shocked by the admission but the expression of curiosity spreading across her face made him think again.

'So what has any of that got to do with my patient Marcus Eckard or with McCray at the asylum, not to forget those hundreds of people that dropped dead in front of our eyes.'

'That I honestly don't know.' Harker replied, and it was the truth. He genuinely had no idea what was going on.

Chloe was already opening her mouth to demand more information when Harker waved a hand in the air.

'All I know is that the same man, Father Strasser, who asked me to speak with Marcus Eckard also told me that it would lead me to finding the child safe and sound, but so far it's only led to the death of over one thousand innocent people.'

'One thousand?' Chloe asked, genuinely surprised at the figure.

'Notre Dame wasn't the only place of worship to get hit by a terrorist attack.' Harker revealed as her eyes widened once more. 'There were seven identical attacks – including mosques and synagogues – around the world, and all happening at the same time.'

'Oh, my God.' She raised a hand to her mouth. 'And your friends believe everything's connected to these fanatics?'

Harker shook his head. 'No, actually they don't think it is.'

'But *you* do.' Chloe surmised astutely.

'I'm not sure but I think Father Strasser does, and my friends have managed to locate his address.'

'Warsaw?'

'Yes. And that's where I'm heading next. If there's any chance that he knows where the child is then I have to try.'

'It's one hell of a chance.' Chloe remarked as she leant back against the wall.

'True, but it's one hell of a story.' Harker replied.

'What does that mean?'

'It means that nothing surprises me any more. And if you have a chance, no matter how slim, then you need to take it.'

They both waited patiently as a family of holidaymakers bustled past, the father struggling with the bags as the mother directed two children onwards along the concourse. In all their hurry they completely missed the nearby baggage-handler, who simply watched indifferently as the struggling parents disappeared down one of the terminal lanes, before resuming his spot of self-grooming.

'These friends of yours, Alex, they must be extremely influential considering we just disappeared from an active investigation into a terrorist attack.'

'They have their moments,' Harker admitted, not wanting to reveal anything further. 'But their intervention means you are now free to go home.'

'Now, just you wait a minute. You can't expect me to walk away after everything you've told me.'

'That's exactly what I expect you to do,' he replied firmly. 'You deserved an explanation, and I've been more forthcoming than I needed to be, but there is not a chance you're coming with me.'

Chloe was suddenly looking crushed like a teenager who has been told she cannot go to a friend's party. 'That's not fair,' she stammered. 'I can be of help.'

'Of help!' Harker almost laughed at the comment. 'How?'

'Firstly I saved your life so you owe me, and secondly we work well together. I can act as your support.'

He was already shaking his head stubbornly. 'Thank you, Chloe, but I already have all the support I need. And regarding you saving my life, I'm going to return the favour and save yours by not letting you get involved in this any deeper than you already are.' He brought his hand up between them in an effort to silence her as she was already revving up to make her next argument for being allowed to come along. 'Chloe, these people, these fanatics, are trained killers whose ideology is as vicious as their methodology. They won't take no for an answer and they don't care who they destroy in the process, so long as they get what they want.'

Harker took a moment to look around the empty concourse and satisfy his paranoia that no one was listening to him, before continuing. 'You've been great, Chloe, you really have but I'm not going to be responsible for something bad happening to you. This is as far as you go.' Harker held out his hand, but it was met with an icy stare as if he were offering her a lump of manure instead of a polite handshake.

'It's not your decision to make,' she replied resolutely. 'It's mine.'

'The hell it is,' he blurted out louder than intended.

'Very well, then.' Chloe pointed to the blue-shirted gendarme still hovering in the near distance. 'Then it is my decision to go over to that officer right now and tell him that both you and I were witnesses to the terrorist attack today, and explain that so far no one has even bothered to take a statement from either of us.'

'Oh, please, you're not really going to do that,' Harker replied confidently.

'Why not? We haven't done anything wrong, but I think it might slow down your chances of getting to Warsaw in a hurry, don't you?'

'I don't respond well to threats, Chloe,' Harker hissed intimidatingly through gritted teeth.

'Well, you better respond well to this one, Professor, or you're not going anywhere.'

For the next few seconds Harker stared silently into Chloe's trouble-making eyes before he allowed the feeling of rage that was pounding in his chest to subside and his jaw muscles to loosen. He then ignored her and quietly made his way over to the ticket attendant, sporting the most jovial smile he could muster, and sucked up the fact that he had just got screwed. 'Two tickets to Warsaw, please,' he said politely. 'And may I ask you for a favour?'

The attendant stood po-faced for a moment before resuming that annoyingly smug demeanour. 'You may ask, sir. How can I help?'

Harker pointed back towards Chloe, who still stood on the other side of the concourse, looking mightily pleased with herself. 'I want you to seat me as far away from that woman as humanly possible.'

Chapter 15

The faint rumblings of an argument in full flow grew increasingly louder as Cardinal David Mythias approached the small wooden doorway of the Vatican's Holy See press office. He paused at the imposing entrance and rubbed his forehead vigorously in an attempt to diffuse the worsening headache that had gripped him since learning of the terrorist attacks earlier that morning. The devastating assault on a number of religious institutions was the lead story of every newspaper, TV channel and radio programme throughout the world and, with over one thousand dead from every culture and creed, it was hardly surprising. Within minutes of the attack, the world's social-media networks had erupted in an explosion of furious chatter. Hundreds of millions of people all venting their disgust and outrage at such an atrocious attack upon the citizens of the world. Many of those same voices were now slamming their verbal fists against the Vatican's front door, with hundreds of thousands of emails crying out for the Pope to respond.

Cardinal Mythias rested his hand on the brass door handle and took a moment to clear his head. As one of the new Pope's closest advisors, his recommendation on the day's tragic events held much weight, but unfortunately his was not a viewpoint held by all, and the altercation now playing out on the other side of the door was no doubt as a direct result of that.

Mythias turned the knob and allowed the wooden door to swing back slowly under its own weight, revealing the two men inside making all the commotion.

'I'm not saying it's an ill-thought-out idea, Michael. I'm saying it's a *stupid* idea.'

Michael McKinnon dropped both hands to his sides and angrily glared at the man throwing insults. 'Stupid idea!' he growled indignantly. 'What's stupid is your belief in the misguided notion that you know what you're talking about. Don't forget who's the professional here. I'm the director of this press office, not you.' McKinnon raised his pudgy finger towards the underling and poked the air firmly. 'You're my secretary, so why don't you just fulfil that role and go make me a cup of coffee.' The press director then lifted two fingers up in the air and wagged them condescendingly. 'That's two sugars, remember.'

'I resent that, Michael, I'm the press secretary, not your private lackey!' the man shouted back before doing an about-turn and marching off through one of the side doors.

'That's two sugars,' McKinnon called after him sarcastically, 'not one. Even you should be able to…'

'Well, then,' Cardinal Mythias interrupted the director's mockery, 'I see you got my message.'

McKinnon spun around to face Mythias, having been completely unaware of the cardinal's presence. 'How long have you been standing there?' he puffed, unhappy at being caught off guard.

'Just arrived.' Mythias replied.

'Well,' McKinnon strode his way across the room towards his new visitor, 'they don't call you the mole for nothing.'

'The mole? How so?'

'Because you're always popping up in places unexpectedly.'

'Very good, Michael,' Mythias mused. 'I had not heard that one before.'

The cardinal gracefully closed the door behind him and proceeded to scan the interior of the press room. Ever since Michael McKinnon had been appointed as the Vatican's press director a few months earlier, he had set about placing his own personal stamp on everything under his control including the press office itself which now glittered with numerous photos of the director and a variety of well-known faces. At forty-three, Michael McKinnon was one of Sky News's brightest political editors, with a belly that was equal in size to the man's ego. A self-styled media guru, the ex-journalist had won award after award for his keen and shrewd ability to navigate the political and media land-scape in order to get his story. This was of course not the only reason for his success in attaining the Vatican's press directorship, as Mythias was well aware. The fact that he was a genuinely religious man, with connections to Opus Dei, had helped immensely in securing the position, but it was hard to deny the man's talent for the job, even if

Cardinal Mythias – as well as others – found his demeanour somewhat brash.

'So was cancelling the trip your doing, David, or have I been hammering that little gopher press secretary of yours for no reason?' McKinnon demanded uncompromisingly.

'It certainly was, but haven't you heard of the expression: Don't shoot the messenger?'

'I've heard the expression indeed, but personally I *like* shooting the messenger… It keeps people on their toes.'

'And off your own no doubt,' Mythias replied dryly.

'Very amusing, Cardinal, but what I really want to know is why you have cancelled his holiness's trip to Notre Dame Cathedral tomorrow?'

Cardinal Mythias allowed a few moments to pass as he eyed the director sternly, with all the compassion of a traffic warden. 'For two simple reasons, Michael. Firstly, because this attack appears to be against religion itself, full stop, and his holiness should be seen to act accordingly, in speaking for humanity as a whole and not just for Catholics.' Mythias raised his hand to silence the press director's opinion, seeing the man's mouth was already open and ready to respond. 'And secondly, because I just got off the phone with the chief of police in Paris and as of yet they have no idea what caused the deaths of those people – and so far it is the same for all the other locations where such attacks have taken place.'

'Hold on…'

Cardinal Mythias was already shaking warningly his hand that was still raised between them. 'And nor am I about to allow his Holiness to visit an area that, for all we know, could still be contaminated… I'm afraid his safety must come first and, until we have confirmation from the authorities that there is no danger, it would be incredibly irresponsible for us to put his holiness in harm's way, wouldn't you agree?'

If McKinnon was in any way swayed by the cardinal's reasoning, it didn't show, and that was confirmed seconds later.

'The humanity part I can get on board with,' he reasoned, 'but no one has died at any of those locations since this morning, and to not visit one of the sites today would mean losing out on an amazing opportunity for publicity.' The director was already chewing his lips as if he could actually taste the prospect. 'We have him visit Notre Dame and one of the mosques or synagogues affected, and we then push the idea that he is the… the People's Pope. Or, even better, we promote the notion that he came as a Catholic but left as the leader of humanity.' A deep smile crossed McKinnon's face as he began to visualise it. 'I've not got it quite right yet but if we play this thing correctly, the PR rewards will be huge.'

As the director's eyes continued to widen at his own brilliant idea, they were met by the cold stony gaze of Cardinal Mythias. 'Of course, Michael, we wouldn't want a multitude of innocent deaths to get in the way of a good news story?' Mythias offered sarcastically. 'That would just be short-sighted, wouldn't it?'

'Cardinal,' Director McKinnon replied bluntly, dropping his notepad back on the table, 'the fact that so many people died this morning isn't lost on me, and that loss of life is terrible but don't forget I was brought in by this administration to counterbalance the truly disturbing series of events that have taken place on Vatican soil recently,' McKinnon stated flatly. 'And what would be truly short-sighted is for Pope Gregory not to be seen spearheading that sense of world solidarity that people are already demanding, and will continue to demand in the days to come.'

Cardinal Mythias was already nodding. 'On that point, Michael, we are in total agreement and that is why this evening his holiness will address the people of the world directly from the balcony of St Peters. But,' the cardinal continued with a firm gesture of his hand, 'the coverage will be handled in a respectful and sombre tone, and not as an excuse to incur the throwaway tabloid headlines that you seem to be suggesting. Furthermore, he will visit the affected houses of worship you mentioned, but not until they have been deemed free of any potential dangers to his holiness.'

Mythias had already opened the press office's door and was on his way out, as the director called after him. 'OK, that will work, but you can't blame me for looking at all the angles. And don't forget that I was brought into protect his image, and I won't allow you or anyone else to compromise that.'

'Then don't *you* forget that I am here, amongst my other duties, to protect his holiness's life,' Mythias replied, lingering in the doorway, 'and I will not allow you to compromise that either.'

McKinnon waited for the door to shut then allowed his shoulders to slump. 'Dick,' he uttered under his breath, before noticing from the corner of his eye, a figure standing at one of the side doors. He glanced over to see his young press secretary staring at him with the hint of a satisfied grin beginning to form across his lips. 'Back to work, smiley,' McKinnon barked impatiently. 'Those toilets aren't going to clean themselves, are they?'

Chapter 16

'Look, I won't say it again; you either pay monthly or by the hour,' the sweaty-faced reception manager advised. 'You can be a resident or a visitor but, whichever way, you're not getting in here without paying, so either you show me the cash or get lost!'

Harker took a step backwards and watched disconcertingly as the overweight doorman slammed down the reception desk's metal security grate and folded his arms, that simple motion causing another fold of sweaty fat to form under his more than ample neckline. When Harker had first noted down Father Strasser's work address as '31 Rue Decord, Praga district, Warsaw', he had imagined somewhere far more impressive than the filthy-laden rat shack he now found himself standing in. He had always prided himself on not being too fastidious but the speed with which the taxi driver deposited them here and then drove off coupled with the numerous used condoms they had passed on the pavements outside, was straining this tolerance to breaking point. Chloe clearly wasn't coping much better, and had kept rigidly to the centre of the narrow entrance way as if trying not to brush against the walls for fear of picking up something moist and unsavoury.

'OK, fine,' Harker replied, pulling out his wallet. 'How much for the hour?'

The obese receptionist scratched at the neckline of his stained white T-shirt, which only managed to cover half of his impressive belly, before rolling the security grate upwards again. 'Two hundred euros.'

'Two hundred!' Harker choked. 'You've got to be kidding!'

'Look, Englishman, if you want in, you pay the price,' the fat man replied with a snort. 'And decide today because I'm far too busy for your bullshit.'

A rolling tumbleweed was all that was missing from the otherwise empty reception area, and Harker pointedly took a moment to glance around the empty void. 'Yes, I can see that,' he replied sarcastically.

The fat man just shrugged and once again began reaching for the roller shutter.

'Fine,' Harker growled, pulling the notes from his wallet and dropping them on to counter where they were keenly scooped up, then placed quickly out of sight.

'Fifth floor,' the receptionist announced with a false smile as he handed over a single key clipped to a grubby yellow disk with the number 53 scratched on to it. 'And you two have fun now.'

This last comment drew an offended look from Chloe, who hadn't said a word since entering. 'Oh, please, I've only known him for a couple of days,' she objected, referring to Harker.

'And I'm an ex-priest.' Harker followed up hastily.

The receptionist eyed his latest customers from head to toe. 'Kinky,' he observed, grinning sleazily.

Harker was already guiding Chloe up the first flight of stairs before she could say more.

'What a lovely man,' she remarked facetiously. 'Remind me to leave a star review on Trip Advisor, would you?'

'Will do,' Harker replied with a smile, as they continued on up to the second floor and then towards the third. 'Good manners and pleasantries obviously aren't requirements for working in a place like this.' He directed Chloe's attention to an unpleasant-looking foamy puddle she was about to step in. 'What possessed Strasser to live in a place like this?'

'I thought it was listed as his working address?' Chloe replied, proceeding more cautiously.

'It was but unless Father Strasser swaps his dog collar each night for a red velvet suit and pimp's cane, then I'm guessing that info was wrong.'

'Then what the hell would he be doing here?'

'I don't know but the sooner we find him, the sooner we can get out of the place,' Harker said just as they reached the fifth floor. 'And for two hundred euros it had better be worth it.'

He grabbed the fire-exit door handle and paused. 'You know that could be a world record.'

'Record?'

'Yes. The most a person has ever paid *not* to have sex!'

The fifth floor was just as grimy and unimpressive as the reception area. The only sunlight came from a small arched window at the end of a long and gloomy corridor and the only working light seemed to be a green fire-exit sign above a door next to it. Harker couldn't help but admire how, even in this dive of a hotel, EU health and safety regulations had prevailed. Game set and match to the bureaucrats. He steadily proceeded along the fifty-metre corridor, with Chloe in tow, the sticky carpet fibres producing an unhealthy crunching sound with every footstep until they reached number 53.

'Let me do all the talking,' Harker whispered, 'if something happens and it starts to get out of hand I want you to just leave here and meet me at that coffee shop we saw a few streets along.'

'What are you expecting?' Chloe asked, clearly a touch nervous.

'I don't know but, whatever Strasser's part is in all this, he was the one that got me involved in the first place, and considering what happened at Notre Dame I don't want to take any chances.'

'Understood, Alex.' Chloe agreed dutifully, taking a step behind him as he moved to within knocking distance of the grubby doorway.

Harker rapped his fist heavily against the scratched wood and then let his arm drop to his side, tensing in apprehension at the greeting he might receive. Ten seconds passed before he thumped on the door again and then resumed his cautious pose. They waited like this for what seemed like an age but no flicker of movement disturbed the strip of dull light escaping under the bottom of the door. No shadow fell across the peephole in front of him either. Nothing.

Harker glanced back at Chloe, who not only stood completely motionless but was breathing as quietly as she could. 'Looks like we're going to have to wait,' he whispered and was about to step away but instead grasped the door handle and gave it a twist just in case. To his surprise, the door clicked open and slowly swung back with a creak, revealing a short hallway beyond lit by a single bare light bulb dangling from the ceiling. There was a closed door on either side of the short passage, which itself opened into what looked like a living room, with a brown polyester sofa protruding from one side.

'Hello? Is anyone in here?' Harker waited for a reply but was met only with silence. 'I've got a message from the manager,' Harker continued in his best Polish. After a short wait, and a gentle nudge from Chloe, he ventured onwards towards the main room.

The living room was devoid of anything except for its peeling yellow wallpaper and the muddy brown sofa he had seen from the entrance. A small open kitchen adjoined the main room, accommodating a pathetic-looking single cooking hob and an ancient refrigerator which would have looked more at home at a landfill site than in a contemporary apartment.

'He's not much of a homemaker, is he?' Chloe commented softly as she pushed her way further into the main room. 'And what is that stink?'

Harker pointed over to something in the far corner as he wrinkled his nose. 'That would be the pile of shit over there, I assume.'

Chloe craned her head to get a closer look at the offending object. 'Oh, that's vile,' she said with disgust. 'He could at least take the dog outside.'

'I don't think that's from a dog, Chloe.' Harker winced before making his way back into the hallway, leaving Chloe to take one last look at the nauseating mound of human excrement.

'And this man's a priest you say?' she grimaced and made her way back to join him just as he was preparing to investigate one of the side doors.

'I'm not sure exactly what this man is, but I intend to find out.'

Harker pushed open the door and poked his head inside but retracted it just as quickly as a fresh stench assaulted his nose. 'Well, at least there's a bathroom,' Harker gasped closing the door firmly shut again, 'but he seems to have used everywhere but the toilet!'

Chloe began shaking her head in distaste as Harker lurched towards the opposite door. 'That's just nasty,' she remarked. 'I wonder if he has some type of clinical bowel issue.'

Her comment drew a light smile from Harker who was about to open the second door. 'Bowel problem I doubt, but a clinical problem most definitely.' He glanced back at her challengingly. 'You're the psychologist, you tell me?'

Chloe opened her mouth as if about to deliver her professional opinion, when Harker cut her short by raising his finger to his lips and then gesturing to the closed door. He slowly turned the handle before cautiously taking a step inside.

A haze of red light immediately engulfed him and in that instant a wave of panic flooded into his chest as he attempted to make out the darkly crimson-lit interior. The room was the biggest of the three and the small mattress on the floor suggested the room's true purpose, even though the red lighting exuded the ambience of a chill-out room in some sleazy nightclub. A series of white bed sheets, bathed red by the light bulbs, hung from the ceiling by clothes pins, splitting the room into different sections and the window set in the far wall was covered by a blanket which only added to the claustrophobic atmosphere. *Home sweet home.*

Harker warily made his way deeper into the room and his attention was immediately drawn to a series of framed black-and-white photos firmly secured to the wall. The people depicted were all random; men, women and children dressed in a variety of old-style suits, bowler hats and long, ill-fitting dresses complete with full-length undergarments. The style was unmistakeably late nineteenth century, but it wasn't this attire that commanded Harker's attention. As he struggled to make out the various faces under the crimson light, he became aware of an odd-looking slant to their eyes and the peculiar way in which the bodies seemed to be propped up. He finally realised what he was looking at: these people were all dead. Corpses re-dressed and specially posed for the camera? Harker felt an unpleasant feeling of nausea seep into his stomach. He had seen these types of photos before; they were known as post-mortem photographs and had been all the rage during the Victorian era. Photos were taken as family mementos – or memento mori to be accurate – and it had even been common to place living members of their kin in the picture. Harker had seen more than one picture of an extremely uncomfortable-looking child having to pose with a dead family member, a practice that would undoubtedly leave the subjects with a few choice mental scars for the rest of their lives. Seeing such images had always unsettled Harker, but having them as part of historical record was one thing. Whereas hanging them in your bedroom was just grotesque. He was already pulling himself away from this morbid little exhibition when a loud screech erupting from behind caused him to lurch forward in shock and smack his forehead on the wall display he was examining. Rubbing his brow, Harker spun round to find the doorway behind him was empty.

'Chloe?'

'Over here,' came the answer from further back in the room.

Harker pushed aside the nearest hanging sheets to find Chloe standing in front of what looked like a small wooden altar only a few feet in diameter, with her hand raised to her mouth. He immediately stepped over to her side, until over her shoulder he could see what had caused this outburst. A metal-cast cross, complete with Jesus Christ, hung above the altar, while three glass jars with metal screw-top lids filled with liquid were distributed evenly across its surface. Each of them bore the unfamiliar symbol of a half circle containing a triangle in the middle.

Initially Harker's stomach began to tighten up with the expectation of seeing further examples of Father Strasser's bodily excretions but, as he leaned closer, he began to wish that was all they were. In the left jar a small toe hung suspended in what must have been a preserving solution, and the middle jar contained two fingers in much the same state. But it was the final jar that really gave him a chill, and he instinctively cupped his groin. The small shrivelled penis floating aimlessly in the jar's solution had all the sorrowful appeal and charm of a dog suffering chronic mange.

'What the hell!' Harker gasped as, outside the room, the click of the apartment's front door unlocking could be heard, quickly followed by the sound of footsteps making their way down the hallway and stopping at the bedroom entrance.

Harker and Chloe both froze and stared at each other in alarm. The only thing keeping them out of sight was the single red-tinged sheet hanging in front of them and concealing them from the unknown intruder. As both continued to remain absolutely still, the blurry shadow of a figure slowly began to creep across the surface of the sheet, until it paused halfway across and its head slowly began to rotate in their direction. Harker watched anxiously as the shadow raised its hand and the image became increasingly clearer as the person on the other side moved closer.

Harker glanced again at Chloe, whose face was full of uncertainty, and she was clearly waiting to follow his lead. He gave a slow nod of the head, then waited until the silhouette of the probing hand had come within inches of them, before he made his move. He hurled himself at the shadow, crashing into the sheet with both arms spread wide, ripping it free from the ceiling and wrapping it around the newcomer with such impact that he knocked the unknown person off its feet before landing on top of it with a heavy thud. Harker then leapt back up, and forcefully dragged the now shrouded mass struggling into the hallway, and then into the living room, before slamming the heavy linen bundle against the far wall as hard as he could.

A loud groan emerged from the heap as the intruder fell still, that sharp collision with the wall having done its job. Harker meanwhile bounded into the kitchen and began pulling out drawers until he came across a large carving knife.

Knife firmly in hand, Harker leapt back to confront his captive and, with his free hand, reached down and tore the twisted sheet away in one wrench before tossing it across the room, the steel blade still aimed at the figure on the floor.

Father John Strasser stared up at him blearily, his glasses cracked and dangling off one ear, with a bright red mark already developing across the cheek where it had connected with the wall. The priest's eyes widened as he recognised Harker and he shrank back into himself. 'Are you going to kill me?' he croaked, and straightening his glasses with a shaking hand.

'Kill you?' Harker yelled unnecessarily loudly, a surge of adrenalin affecting his ability to stay calm.

'Well, you're holding a knife.' Strasser gestured towards the sharp metal tip only inches from his face.

Harker glanced down at the weapon still held tightly in his hand, then instinctively loosened his grip as he began to regain control of himself. 'Who the hell are you, Strasser, and why did you stick me in the middle of a terrorist attack?'

'Terrorist attack?' Strasser laughed. 'What terrorist attack?'

Chloe rushed over to Harker's side, and stared down at the odd little man. 'The attack at Notre Dame – and the other thousand innocent people that were murdered.'

Strasser's derisive smile was now replaced with a meaningful scowl. 'There never was any terrorist attack.'

'Try telling that to all the people who died.' Harker seethed, his grip again tightening on the knife.

Strasser stared at them blankly for a few moments, then he shook his head from side to side. 'You really have no idea what's going on, do you – and for that matter, why would you?'

The response sounded genuine and served only to fuel Harker's temper. 'Then how about you tell us, Strasser... *everything*. Why get me involved in all this?'

Strasser sighed contemptuously and rested his head back against the wall. 'You have your part to play in these events, as do I. And, as much as you may hate hearing this, I have no idea why *you* are involved,' the priest continued, gesturing towards Chloe. 'But I swear to you that it was no terrorist attack.'

'Then what was it?' Harker was becoming increasingly frustrated by the priest's vague answers.

'This is what you English would refer to as the real McCoy.' Strasser slowly picked himself up off the floor and brushed himself down, all the while still facing the tip of the knife Harker was aiming at him. 'This is merely just the prelude to the beginning of the end.' The priest's face began to turn an ashen colour and his lips widened in a smile. 'Rejoice, Professor Harker, for the end of days is upon us, and your own day of judgement will come soon enough.'

Chapter 17

Michael McKinnon peered out from behind the curtain of the famed St Peter's balcony and looked down onto the shifting tide of onlookers that had gathered in St Peter's Square for the Pope's address that evening. 'There must be over one hundred thousand people down there,' he decided enthusiastically, pulling away from the curtain. 'That's impressive for only a few hours' heads-up.'

Cardinal David Mythias watched the Vatican's press director rub his hands together with all the zeal of a super-villain. 'Indeed, Michael, your office has done a superb job of organising it all at such short notice, but you should never underestimate how such a terrible tragedy will draw the masses together,' the Cardinal remarked. 'People quite rightly need to feel that we are all united as one against such depravities.'

The excited smile on McKinnon's face melted away at this comment and he folded his arms defensively. 'I take, by that analysis, that you think people would have turned up anyway, regardless?'

The cardinal shook his head. 'On the contrary, Michael, the press department has done a wonderful job. It was simply an observation.' Cardinal Mythias continued woefully, 'I do wish you wouldn't take every word I say so personally.'

'And I wish you weren't so passive-aggressive. But such is life, hey, David.'

Mythias was about to refute this insult when a voice spoke softly behind them.

'Please, gentlemen.'

Both men turned around to find Pope Gregory VII observing them with an attentive smile.

'There are far more concerning events to deal with than our individual qualms, wouldn't you agree?'

'Of course, your holiness,' Cardinal Mythias replied for both of them. 'Forgive us.'

The pontiff raised his hand courteously. 'Forgiveness is not necessary. I only ask for your continuing strength in standing united during these awful events.'

As the two men offered him a respectful bow, Pope Gregory took a few steps towards the red curtain of the balcony and began to peruse the prepared speech he would deliver. 'The speech is perfect, gentlemen,' he declared at last, 'and exactly how I wish to address the world.'

'I'm happy you approve, your holiness,' McKinnon offered respectfully, the Pope's words mollifying any anger that had begun to fester only moments earlier, 'and I'm sure people will respond positively.'

The Pope dropped his arms to his sides and raised his head towards the red curtain directly in front of him. 'Then let us find out, shall we?'

'Yes, sir.' Mythias then turned his attention to the two young attendants standing on either side of the pontiff. 'And three, two, one...'

The red curtains parted and Pope Gregory VII made his way out on to the famed balcony of St Peter's basilica, as down below him two hundred thousand pairs of eyes all locked on to him. Rapturous cheers erupted throughout the square and thousands of welcoming hands were raised skywards, showing their support.

The Pontiff made his way to the waiting microphone and lifted a hand into the air, whereupon thousands of camera flashes from waiting photographers sparkled amongst the crowd below, bathing the balcony in a cascade of flickering light.

Pope Gregory waved to the crowd for a few moments more, then lowered his hand and gently picked up the microphone. In years past, the practice had always been for an altar boy to hold this instrument for the pontiff but, since taking office, Pope Gregory had elected to throw much of the established protocol to the wind. Many of the Vatican's cardinals had disagreed with a lot of these changes, but the new Pope had expressed his wish to be seen by the people exactly as he felt himself to be... *one of them*, even if it meant some within the Vatican had likened his clutching of the microphone to a Vegas lounge bar singer.

As the euphoric and ear-blistering welcome from the crowd finally subsided, the pontiff raised the microphone to his lips and smiled. 'Brothers and sisters, good evening.'

Once more the roar of the crowd exploded, and once again the pontiff allowed a moment for the square to calm, before continuing.

'I come to you tonight not as Pope Gregory VII, the pontiff in Rome, but simply as the man I am: Salvatore Vincenzo. And I speak to you all now, not just as head of the Catholic Church but as a citizen of mankind. My reason for this is because these terrible and unjustifiable terror attacks have affected people of every race and creed, in that it has been an attack on the very moral fabric that binds us all.'

The crowd once more began to cheer, and Vincenzo raised his hand once more in support.

'If this tragedy is truly the world's first global terrorist attack, as has been reported, then its repercussions will only be resolved by all the people of the world working in solidarity, together. It is for this purpose that I intend to host a summit during the coming weeks, for all the heads of all world religions to convene in an attempt to find common ground that will better unite the population of the earth in a common goal. It is a goal we all wish for... a goal we have all prayed for... and that goal is peace. For I believe that our separate religions define who we are, not what we are – and that simple yet crucial distinction allows all of us hope for lasting global peace.'

The crowd's eruption into cheers signified their obvious approval of the pontiff's olive branch to all diverse people, and once again the balcony was illuminated by a blinding series of camera flashes, even as Pope Gregory VII continued his address, obviously encouraged by the reaction.

'And so I say to my brothers and sisters of the Catholic Church, your Church stands united with all the rest of humanity against such despicable atrocities that have no place in this twenty-first century. And to the peoples of the world, whatever your faiths may be, I say that if we stand together in this darkest of hours there is nothing that we cannot endure... nothing that we cannot protect... and nothing we cannot aspire to.'

Vincenzo placed the microphone back into its holder and raised both his hands into the air as the crowd began to sway with hands joined together in a show of solidarity, and as roars of support boomed across the square. Vincenzo continued to hold his hands aloft as he waited for the cheering to subside, but after sixty seconds and realising the outburst was unlikely to cease he lowered them and reached for the microphone again in preparation for the rest of his speech. It was then that he felt a mild tremor beneath his feet. The curious sensation caused him to look down as that gentle trembling began to intensify, rapidly spreading up his legs and then expanding throughout his entire upper body. Vincenzo instinctively reached out for the balcony ledge in a bid to steady himself, only to find it vibrating to the same rhythm.

Down below, the sounds of elated cheers suddenly tailed of into an eerie silence, as the entire assembled crowd began to notice the tremors for themselves. Many of them began exchanging nervous glances as a succession of powerful quakes started to spread throughout the entire square.

Above them Salvatore Vincenzo, both hands now clinging to the balcony ledge, glanced back to see Mythias clutching onto one red curtain with such strength that its fittings broke away from the rail, sending the cardinal hurtling backwards on to the tiled floor with a painful-sounding thud. Next to him, McKinnon also lost his balance as an intensified wave rippled across the floor tiles which were in turn thrust upwards, flipping the press director head first into the nearest wall with a sharp crack, whereupon he dropped to the floor with a trickle of blood oozing from one ear.

Still with a firm grip on the quivering balcony ledge, Vincenzo returned his attention to the chaos of St Peter's Square just as high above them a tremendous flash of light lit up the sky to reveal swirling dark clouds gathering overhead, followed by a clap of thunder so deafening that it sent most of the panicking crowd underneath down onto their knees in shock. Thick bolts of blue lightning began to erupt in the skies above, revealing more of these looming clouds unlike any Vincenzo had ever witnessed before. They swirled in a clockwise direction, like some gigantic vortex threatening to suck up anything below it and, stranger still, they appeared to hang directly above Vatican City, and nowhere else.

The tremors now began to peak in ferocity and Vincenzo watched in horror as the entire square below him started undulating up and down in waves, causing the ground itself to tear apart and creating deep gaping chasms into which thousands of people instantly plunged to their deaths. Wailing and screams of pain and fear could be heard all over as the ground continued to shake ever more violently. Then the pillars of surrounding colonnades began to twist and crumble under their own weight. Massive blocks of stone fell to the ground, crushing anyone underneath and leaving large spatterings of red, before disappearing into the darkening abyss below.

A hand grabbed Vincenzo by the shoulder and he turned to see one of the pontifical guard attempting to pull him away from the weakening balcony. But the man was stopped cold as a large piece of white masonry struck him from above, crushing the unfortunate would-be protector in a twitching mass of scarlet pulp. Overhead, the basilica's east façade also began to ripple and sway, the bone-shattering tremors now intensifying in ferocity. As jagged lumps of stone crashed all around him and the entire front of St Peter's gave way underneath him, a single question entered the mind of Pope Gregory VII. It was a question that would go unanswered: 'Oh, my lord, why have you forsaken us?'

Chapter 18

'The end of the world! Here we go again and how original of you,' Harker muttered sceptically as he stared at John Strasser with a weary shake of his head. 'That's the third time I've heard that rubbish in the past couple of days.'

'Then perhaps it is time you stopped taking it for rubbish,' Strasser replied resolutely, his face exuding new confidence.

The comment received a disbelieving smile from Harker. 'Considering the first time was from a patient in an insane asylum, you'll forgive me for not taking all your gloom and doom too seriously.'

'Ahh,' Strasser considered. 'So Marcus Eckard had a similar viewpoint, I take it?'

Harker said nothing, simply offering an apathetic nod of his head.

'One man's delusion is another man's vision.'

'Oh, he's deluded all right.'

'I was talking about you, Professor.'

'*I'm* deluded?' Harker gasped, the response catching him by surprise. 'I'm not the one with a taste for eyeballs but, that aside, what the hell has any of this got to do with the Secrets of Fatima?'

Strasser's eyes widened at the mention of the three Secrets. 'That is not for me to say, but I wasn't lying to you when I said that finding all three will determine the world's destiny.'

'Well, that's good, because I have no idea where the third Secret is,' Harker fumed. 'And what about the fourth?'

'A fourth? I haven't ever heard of a fourth but I do know where the third is.' Strasser was now smiling like a maniac. 'It's to be found at the Temple Mount in Jerusalem to the north under the protection of the old man of the rock.'

Harker was stunned at the ease of Strasser's admission. 'If you already knew the locations of the Secrets, why the hell didn't you tell me in the first place?'

'As I already told you, Professor, we all have our parts to play.'

'Enough, both of you!'

Harker turned to find Chloe glaring furiously, her cheeks flushed red with impatience.

'At this very moment there are only three questions I want answered,' Chloe demanded and she raised a finger and began to reel off each one. 'Firstly, what have you got to do with the Notre Dame terrorist attack? Secondly, where did you obtain those human appendages in the other room? And thirdly,' she pointed to the far corner of the room and wrinkled her nose, 'what on earth made you take a poo in your living room?'

Chloe's determined outburst shook Harker out of his own stupidity. The stupidity of allowing himself to be drawn into an argument with a man who was clearly not of sound mind.

'Thank you, Chloe. That needed to be said.' Harker turned his attention back to Strasser, whose gaze had lost none of its intensity. 'So tell me then, Strasser, what's with the poo in the corner and the penis in the pot?' The words came out sounding far more comical than Harker intended, and he swiftly moved on to his next query as an attempt to suppress his own feeling of morbid amusement. 'More importantly, I want to know how you're involved in all this.'

Strasser stared at his interrogators condescendingly, his eyes filled with self-importance. 'There is one word that offers truth for the world and which blinds the eyes of every heretic on God's earth. It is the beginning of the new, and will stand at the end, when all others fall and are incinerated in hell's fiery depths.'

'Very poetic,' Harker declared, already tired of the bravado, 'and that word is?'

'Skoptsy,' Strasser said, his body bristling with self-belief and pride. 'The word is Skoptsy.'

The ever-widening stare from the priest seemed to create an invisible force pushing at Harker's chest, and he felt an unpleasant surge of queasiness that quickly spread through his stomach.

'Skoptsy?' Chloe looked confused by the answer. 'Is that Polish?'

Harker ignored her question and instead glanced back towards the bedroom containing the collection of unpleasant jars, as suddenly everything began to make a disturbing kind of sense. 'You're lying, Strasser. The Skoptsy died out over half a century ago.'

'Did they, now?' Strasser hissed. 'Then I am just a crazy man and you have nothing to worry about, do you, Professor?'

Seconds ticked by as Harker silently considered this latest revelation, his eyes never leaving the darkly robed figure who returned his stare stubbornly. Could he be telling the truth? Was this really possible, or just the latest lie that Harker had come to expect from the shadowy and deceptive world of the Magi – if indeed Strasser was even affiliated to that organisation. Theirs was a world where subterfuge and deception were more of a science than a tool, and common sense and logic were utilised to ensnare the mind rather than set it free. Harker was still pondering this question when he felt a light prod in the ribs and turned to find Chloe at his side, with her face still full of questions.

'Well, is anyone going tell me what the Skoptsy is? Are they some kind of murderers who take bodily trophies, or something?'

Harker lightly shook his head. 'They're not trophies, Chloe, and the people they belong to haven't been murdered.' He turned his attention back to Strasser and motioned towards the priest's hands. 'Take off your gloves.'

Strasser remained silent, his smug smile still proudly on show, as he peeled off his left glove to reveal the two purple-scarred stumps where his little and ring finger used to be.

'You're not really a priest, are you?' Chloe declared, her eyes focused intently on Strasser's hand or lack of it.

'Oh, he's a priest, all right but not the type you're familiar with,' Harker explained to her, before glancing back in Strasser's direction. 'That is if you are telling us the truth about the Skoptsy.'

Strasser continued smiling in silence.

'The Skoptsy are… were a Russian sect, a kind of twisted offshoot of Christianity, or Christ believers, back in the early eighteenth century. Its members dedicated themselves to a life of abstinence whose remit included no alcohol, sex, marriage or even bad language.'

'They don't sound too bad.' Claire said, glancing over to see that Strasser was following Harker's history lesson intently.

'True, but what I haven't mentioned is that they rejected the holy bible and placed their entire faith in the Holy Spirit. You see, the Skoptsy believed that all the evil in the world was as a result of sexuality and that the beauty of the human form was a sin, which is why the holy spirit became their sole focus and the cornerstone of their belief.'

'I'm not sure I understand. Why?'

'Think about it,' Harker continued, 'the Holy Spirit was able to impregnate the Virgin Mary without resorting to sex and so in the eyes of the Skoptsy, it stood as the ultimate example of a world without sin. And it was an example they expected all their members to live up to.'

'How?'

'We dispose of the sin,' Strasser interrupted, 'in order to purify our bodies.'

Harker focused on Chloe, who was still looking bewildered. 'Or, to put it more accurately, they would castrate every clan-member and I am not just talking about the men. The women would have their breasts and labia removed in a process known as the fiery baptism, which was an enigmatic way of saying they used razors and a red-hot branding iron.'

The vile thought drew a minor frown from Chloe, who was now staring at Father Strasser in revulsion. 'Most Skoptsy were castrated before puberty, so their bodies missed out on the adolescent phase signified by testosterone production which, simply put, means—'

'They never developed properly,' Chloe interjected, her eyes still firmly planted on Father Strasser.

'Exactly,' Harker concurred as a small chill rippled through his body at the thought. 'The men would develop unusually long arms and legs, and their faces would eventually appear almost triangular in shape,' Harker reached over and gently lifted Father Strasser's chin upwards with one finger, 'much like his.'

Strasser's smile widened further, obviously pleased at Harker's knowledge and the recognition that came with it.

'So what happened to them?'

'They swelled in numbers if you can believe it, until there were tens of thousands of them. But when the Russian empire discovered this twisted religion it was deemed a threat to the state and outlawed. Some of the Skoptsy did survive… at least until the Soviet era, whereupon the authorities hunted them down and the sect soon disappeared into the dark annals of political history. But…' Harker tailed off as he paused to gaze in curiosity at the robed man standing in front of him.

'But *what*?' Chloe demanded loudly, her curiosity getting the better of her.

'There were stories… folk law really, that the group merely went underground to hide from Soviet persecution, in preparation for the day when they would return as God's chosen few, and then reclaim humanity under the banner of the Skoptsy.'

'That's pretty creepy.' Chloe said, in nothing more than a whisper.

'Yes, it is,' Harker replied and intrigued by the idea, 'but if we're to believe the Father here, then parts of it are based on fact.'

'Not parts of it, Professor… all of it,' Strasser insisted, as he now rejoined the conversation. 'And I'm impressed by your knowledge of the subject.'

'Well, I do enjoy a mystery, Father, especially one involving bizarre religious sects that apparently vanish into thin air.'

'Christianity, please.' Strasser protested, clearly irritated by the notion of the Skoptsy being labelled a bizarre sect.

Before Harker could begin to argue, Chloe stepped between them, raising both hands.

'Before we go any further there is something that, although it might seem irrelevant, I want answered before I listen to anything else.' Chloe lowered her hands and pointed once more to the corner of the room and the unsightly mess that had been dumped there. 'Why the poo? Are the Skoptsy some kind of faeces loving sect or is it just that they have an appaling grasp of interior decorating?'

Harker sighed loudly and was met with a cold look of disdain from her.

'It isn't a joke,' she protested furiously. 'That is disgusting.'

The question had been directed at Strasser but it was Harker who provided the answer.

'You know how priests used to prostrate – or whip themselves – as atonement for any sin? Well, the Skoptsy believed it an act of faith to surround oneself with evil and yet still maintain one's… purity.'

'I would hardly call that pile of crap over there *evil*.' Chloe replied. 'It's just disgusting and unpleasant.'

'As is the world all around us.' Strasser interjected. 'To remain pure of mind and thought when everything surrounding you is corrupted and damned, that is the truest show of faith possible.'

'Hence you living in this charming hotel,' Harker added bluntly.

Chloe stood back and shook her head slowly. 'You need help, Mr Strasser – and that is my professional opinion.'

John Strasser eyed his two visitors with the same contempt that was being levelled at him, and he took a few long breaths in preparation for his answer, the room's stench seemingly having no effect upon his senses. 'Despite what you both may think, I can assure you I am of sound mind.'

'Oh, yes,' Harker remarked sarcastically, glancing around the oddity that constituted Strasser's home. 'Without a doubt. You're a picture of sanity.'

'And the same goes for Marcus Eckard,' Strasser continued, ignoring the quip.

'Mr Strasser, I was Marcus Eckard's doctor for over five years,' Chloe announced, 'and I can assure you that his problems were very real indeed.'

The Skoptsy priest nodded his head as if in total agreement. 'You're right about that but those problems were never neurological in cause, but rather an inner-manifestation. They were a direct result of the truth he had discovered…' Strasser took a moment to ponder his words '…not unlike a kind of post-traumatic stress disorder.'

Harker glanced at Chloe questioningly, seeking any type of validation for what the priest alluded to.

'It is true that Marcus's scans never showed any abnormalities of the brain, and he did exhibit certain symptoms associated with stress disorder, but I doubt…'

'Doubt nothing, Doctor Stanton,' Strasser interrupted impatiently. 'When the mind opens itself up to certain facts – unsettling facts – about the nature of one's own reality, it can have devastating consequences upon the unprepared psyche. In fact, consequences that have no cure.' Strasser's bottom lip trembled ever so slightly and an involuntary gulp slid visibly down his neck, as if the words were being pulled back into his chest. 'If a person finds himself taking a journey of knowledge into the abyss, you cannot expect him to return without paying a price. And the fee required is different for everyone… for Marcus Eckard that cost was his sanity.'

'So what was the knowledge?' Harker demanded.

'Simply put, Professor Harker, it's the fact that God, angels, Satan, demons, heaven, hell… they're all very real.' Strasser leant back against the wall and watched his two guests stare at him in disbelief, before continuing. 'The only untruth is how religion has depicted them, but believe me when I tell you that the basic concepts are absolutely sound… a force for good and a force for evil and that one day it will all end. Then the world will be judged by these two opposing forces,' Strasser smiled wildly, 'and that day has now arrived. The knowledge that became so mentally devastating to Marcus Eckard will soon be experienced by every single person living on this planet. The knowledge that, after billions of years, the earth is coming to an end and the dark forces of Satan are readying themselves to implement it. But some knowledge is so great that it must be actually seen to be believed, and you – along with the rest of humanity – will soon have the chance to see it with your own eyes. I tell this to you because firstly, you are to become a participant in the coming events, whether you like it or not, and secondly,' a grim smile spread across the priest's face, 'because there is absolutely nothing you can do about it.'

Harker stood silent for a moment, stunned by such delusional beliefs, until one single question came to the forefront of his mind. 'And the child? Do the Skoptsy have him?'

Strasser's uncompromising smile now gave way to a look of surprising seriousness and clarity, before he glanced down at his watch. 'Not yet but we will and, when we do, the Christ our saviour will once again surrender his life to ensure salvation for his people… Those that make it, of course.'

Harker almost choked on hearing Strasser's admission. 'The Skoptsy are going to kill him!'

Strasser nodded calmly. 'He will be sacrificed so that the Judgement may begin.'

'But that doesn't make any sense,' Harker winced in disbelief, 'if you believe the child is your salvation, then what good does it do to murder him?'

Strasser remained motionless and merely displayed a sly toothy grin. 'You'll find out soon enough.'

Harker immediately motioned to Chloe. 'Have you got your phone on you?'

She nodded and pulled out her iPhone from a pocket and held it up.

'Then call us a taxi.'

She nodded once more and began tapping away, as Harker turned back to Strasser. 'You're going to take us to him right now.' He pulled out his own phone while Strasser simply smiled away as if he didn't have a care in the world. 'And I'm now going to call a friend of mine at the Vatican and see if we can't get some more information on your Skoptsy story.' Harker was already dialling, when Chloe reached over and brushed his hand away from the keypad.

'That's going to be difficult, Alex.' She raised her phone in front of his face and Harker felt his heart sink as he took in the BBC news flash displayed on its screen: 'Thousands dead as earthquake destroys St Peter's. Pope Gregory VII missing and feared dead.'

'Oh, my God,' Harker uttered under his breath, much to the evident delight of Strasser who had craned his head around so he could also read the headline.

'And that is just the beginning,' the priest declared, placing his hands together in a praying gesture. 'And now that my part in all this is finished, I have only one thing left to say.'

Harker gazed at the still smiling priest, his eyes wide open with shock at what he had just learned.

'Find the third Secret and you will find your answers, and with it the destiny of the entire world.'

With that, Strasser launched himself backwards, crashing through the window glass covered with newspaper directly behind him, and disappearing out of sight as the fresh evening air poured into the room.

Harker leapt to the window just in time to see the priest conclude the last few feet of his fall, thudding on to the cement pavement with a loud crack. The fall completely demolished the back of the priest's head, releasing a dark pool of blood right in front of a mother pushing a pram. The aghast woman automatically looked up toward to the smashed window and Harker jerked back inside and out of sight to find Chloe looking as shocked as he felt.

For a few moments they both stood staring at each other in silent disbelief until finally Chloe managed to mouth a few words, 'what do we do?' Harker's mind raced through the options until he came upon an answer. He reached over and gently grasped her arm as reassuringly as he could.

A look of determination now took hold, as he replied, 'Jerusalem… We go to Jerusalem.'

Chapter 19

Dusk was settling over the rolling Tuscan hills and casting a warming red hue across the terracotta roof tiles of the modest four-bedroom villa that nestled between the folds of a rocky outcrop and was surrounded by a dense clump of Cypresses. Inside the house, three men sat impatiently around a large round cherrywood dining table, each eyeing one another warily. They had been waiting here for over two hours and the initially comfortable black leather chairs were now becoming increasingly hard and painful to sit upon.

'He has ten more minutes and then I am leaving,' announced the podgy grey-haired man with a mild German accent.

'*You* are not going anywhere,' declared the slender man opposite pointing at him with a gloved finger. 'Don't start getting delusions of importance now, Dietrich.'

'What the hell does that mean?' Dietrich's face beginning to flush in anger.

'It means you'll sit there and like it, you fat little twerp.'

Dietrich glared at his insulter with scorn. 'You may frighten the others, Davidson, but I am not susceptible to your brutish ways.'

John Davidson placed his elbows on the table top, before resting his chin on his hands. 'We'll see how susceptible you become after I nail your hands to that chair.'

'Gentlemen, please,' the third man intervened calmingly, not wanting this childish wrangling to escalate. 'Are we not all of us part of the same greater whole?'

'Oh, please,' Davidson hissed as he turned his attention to the same man who was dressed in a light-brown corduroy suit and wore a white patch over his left eye. 'Stop trying to play the diplomat, Alonzo. We all know how you want nothing more than to usurp a position that is not yours by right.'

'And neither is it yours,' Alonzo replied icily. 'Let none of us forget why we are gathered here today. This meeting will determine whether

John Wilcox can continue as First Prime of the Magi. And it is then, and only then, that we will consider looking for his successor.'

Alonzo's conclusion received acquiescent nods from both Davidson and Dietrich, and the three men then relapsed into silence again with the crackling of logs from the open-hearth fire set in one wall providing the only sound in the room.

A few more minutes of silence passed before the double doors at the far end of the room were flung open, and John Wilcox strode through them and up to the table with all the self-importance of a dictator about to address his minions.

'Gentlemen, what a pleasure it is to see you.' Wilcox greeted them. He then slipped off his black leather gloves and slapped them down hard on the table top. 'It has been quite a while since we all met face to face... how long? Six months? A year?'

'Just under three, actually,' Alonzo replied for the group and with an air of mild scorn.

'Really?' Wilcox continued cynically, having of course known that all along. 'Doesn't time fly when one's having fun... or being a symbol for a billion Christians around the world?'

'Not any more,' Davidson reminded him coldly, clearly unimpressed by Wilcox's upbeat manner.

Wilcox's confident expression remained steady, and he sat down elegantly on the one vacant chair, with his back to the fire so that all the other faces were lit up except his. 'The unfortunate events surrounding my self-imposed papal exile have been tragic, and I do not have to remind you that I have lost three of my brothers along the way.'

'That was, as you say... tragic,' Alonzo proffered as the other two nodded their heads in solidarity, 'but it does not change the facts.'

'And what facts are those?'

'The facts are that even with your facial surgery, which I have to admit isn't bad,' Alonzo concluded, gesturing towards Wilcox's face, 'I can still tell it is you, John, and there is a feeling amongst those of us seated here that your position has therefore become untenable.' The group spokesman sat back in his chair. 'You are just too high-profile to be sitting at the top of the pyramid.'

'That sounds to me like treason,' Wilcox replied in a low gravelly tone.

The accusation had Alonzo immediately shaking his head. 'Not treason, John, just common sense. And we, the Council, feel that regrettably it is time for you to stand down and make way for a new First Prime of the Magi. We ask therefore, that you renounce your authority officially to all your associates and instruct them to await news of a new hierarchy. We further ask that you make available to this board all details pertaining to Magi funds that you have held in your possession since assuming the position of First Prime, as the Magi codex demands.'

Wilcox's shoulders slumped ever so slightly and he rested both elbows on the table with his arms stretched out in front of him. 'Is that so?' He glanced over at Dietrich and then Davidson, both of whom were now looking uncomfortable. 'Just like that?'

'Yes, just like that,' Alonzo replied firmly. 'It is time to relinquish your authority. And might I remind you that, when you took over the position as First Prime from your father, it was only agreed upon because of the long-term plan of infiltrating and taking control of the Catholic Church. A plan that I am extremely unhappy to admit has failed, and along with it thirty years of careful planning.' Alonzo suddenly sat forward and slammed his fist down on the table. 'For thirty years now the other families represented here have been commanded by your father, then by you and your brothers. During that time our resources and manpower have been guided by your hands towards this common goal, and now, after nearly two generations, it has amounted to absolutely nothing. We others have sat on the side lines,' Alonzo continued furiously, including his two partners with a flick of his hand, 'and watched as you have drained away billions of dollars from our coffers in your misguided and narcissistic grab for papal power. And all the while we have been ignoring the Templars, who are, and always have been, our one true obstacle in gaining power over the masses as is our divine right.'

Alonzo fell back into his chair in exasperation, and it was Davidson who now seized his chance to reprimand Wilcox.

'And now this debacle at Notre Dame Cathedral involving none other than that Harker idiot who you should have eliminated well before he even became an issue.'

Wilcox still looked calm, even though underneath he was fuming, and he remained in control at this mention of Harker. 'I don't know what has happened there at Notre Dame, or if the professor had anything to do with it, but after this meeting I intend to have my people look into it.'

'Don't bother,' Alonzo replied firmly. 'We already have one of our own operatives following Harker even as we speak, and I have no doubt he will resolve any remaining questions for us.' Alonzo had been shaking his head and tutting loudly. 'Your stewardship of our holy organisation has proved nothing short of sacrilegious and at complete odds with the Magi's holy codex, which many of us still believe was dictated by the Lord God himself.'

Even Dietrich was nodding his head in support of the accusations being hurled at Wilcox, as Davidson continued with his attack. 'Did it ever occur to you that the reason for your failure lies not in this fly in the ointment – this Harker person you have seemed so ready to place the blame upon in the past – but instead serves as a penance from God Almighty after growing tired of your continued attempt to desecrate his one and only son's flesh with this cloned child?' Davidson seethed. 'The only person responsible for the deaths of your brothers, and the total mess you have contrived for us, is you yourself and your own baffling incompetence. You and the legacy of your father have betrayed us with your ungodly acts and far-fetched plans for too long now and there is only one punishment for a betrayal of the Magi. *Death.*'

'Yes,' Dietrich said, finally joining the inquisition and now looking encouraged by Davidson's mention of treachery. He folded his arms across his swollen belly and eyed the accused through small beady eyes. 'The codex demands it.'

John Wilcox didn't look troubled in the slightest by the charges that were being levelled at him. He calmly assessed each one of their condemning stares before getting to his feet and placing his hands lightly on the back of the chair. 'You all speak of the codex and of betrayal,' he said, pursing his lips, 'and you would be right to do so.'

His words drew a look of surprise from the others.

'So you admit it!' Alonzo stammered, obviously not expecting such a blatant omission.

'Yes, I do,' Wilcox maintained. 'But it is not a betrayal perpetrated by me but rather by someone else in this very room. And furthermore it is a betrayal that has penetrated to the Magi's very core.'

The other three men sat there in astonishment as Wilcox continued with this defiant revelation.

'I have reason to believe that one of us has been working from the very start against our attempts to secure control of the Catholic

Church, in a selfish and unforgiving act of deception. It is a deception that was intended to doom us all to failure, and to elevate this person high above us. A deception that I have managed to uncover and will reveal to you, my brothers.'

All three other men were now glancing at each other suspiciously, but it was only Alonzo that spoke up. 'I think you need to explain yourself, John.'

'With pleasure,' Wilcox replied. 'But first...' The Magi Prime clicked his fingers and a group of six men wearing identical dark suits entered the room, each of them armed with a holstered handgun, hanging from his waists. Four of these men took up position on either side of the room's two entrances whilst the other two stood on either side of Wilcox, who now sat back down and eyed the Council grimly. 'None of us is leaving until this lone and traitorous fiend has been revealed. Then the only difference is that two of you will leave the same way you came in.'

'And the third?' Dietrich asked, looking particularly edgy.

'The third will leave rolled up in that rug.' Wilcox replied and indicated an expensive hand-woven tapestry hanging on the far wall. 'As the codex requires, of course.'

Chapter 20

'So, is this your first trip to Israel?' the taxi driver inquired with a glance back at his latest fare. 'Because to truly appreciate the city you need about a week, and even then you'll only begin to scratch the surface.'

'No, I've visited many times before,' Harker replied politely, 'but never during the rainy season.'

This reply drew a vociferous chuckle from the driver, who ran his free hand over his short black hair and he nodded enthusiastically.

'We don't get that much,' the driver said, pointing out a group of children on the opposite pavement, all throwing their hands in the air and squealing with delight at the few meagre drops of rain that were falling. 'It won't last long, so you should enjoy it while its here.'

Their flight to Tel Aviv had been uneventful considering what preceded it, and Harker was thankful for that. After watching Father Strasser plunge to his death from that grimy fifth-floor apartment window, he had hustled Chloe briskly out of the building through the fire exit and into the adjoining street. The fire alarm had immediately gone off but the area was void of any witnesses, and a few streets along he had managed to flag down a taxi to whisk them away. Harker had used the journey to leave a brief message for Brulet, so as inform him of their next destination. But he decided to withhold any mention of the Skoptsy's involvement for fear of who else might hear it first. If the Templars were divided regarding the child, as Brulet had stated, then he didn't want to make things any worse. Therefore, a face-to-face conversation with the Grand Master himself seemed the best move.

Chloe had remained silent throughout the short taxi ride and, although still visibly shaken, the drive had helped calm her frayed nerves. But upon arriving at Warsaw airport the sight of armed guards patrolling the concourse had soon made her jumpy again.

'Are they here for us?' she had muttered, her paranoia starting to get the better of her. 'Because getting arrested at gunpoint again is not how I saw my day ending.'

Harker managed to reassure her that this heightened security was doubtless due to the global terrorist attacks and, as far as anyone here was concerned, they were just two holidaymakers making their way home. Unfortunately, and due to the heightened terror risk, many of the flights had been cancelled and they ended up spending the next twelve hours hanging around the main concourse for an available flight. The long wait had been long, tedious and full of dread that they were going to be arrested at any moment. Chloe had managed to get some sleep while Harker had used the time to reflect and try to make sense of events, with little success, and had also tried numerous calls to Brulet and the Vatican, but bizarrely neither his mobile or the airport's landlines seemed to be working properly.

Finally they had managed to board a flight to Jerusalem at about midday and once in the air and feeling secure Harker was able to pour over, methodically, the bizarre nature of their journey so far. Strangely, the unexpected death of Father Strasser had not primarily occupied his thoughts, but instead the terrible events at the Vatican. The story had been running constantly on all the airport monitors, then continued to feature solidly on the inflight TV. Seeing the images taken from numerous helicopters had been shocking: the entire front half of the basilica had literally disappeared into a dark chasm in the ground where St Peter's Square had once been. The white rubble scattered at the bottom of the pit was barely visible through the thick clouds of dust that hung above it, spilling out across the famous via Della Conciliazione like an unnatural fog tainting everything it touched with filthy black residue.

Harker had used the inflight telephone to call the Vatican numerous times, but unsurprisingly it had never connected, so he had reluctantly resumed his seat to watch the unfolding devastation along with everyone else travelling on the flight. As those same images of destruction looped over again and again, all he could think about was his friend Salvatore Vincenzo, better known to the masses as Pope Gregory VII. There was no way anyone could have survived such catastrophic devastation, let alone an old man in his seventies, and even though the death toll was now reported as over the eighty thousand mark, his friend's life was the only loss he could think about. In truth,

Vincenzo would have been wholly disappointed that Harker's feelings were for him alone and not the many thousands of other dead, and oddly this had made Harker smile as he continued to brood quietly cocooned in his own little bubble of thoughts.

Chloe, on the other hand, couldn't stop commenting and exclaiming, even if the conversation had been totally one-sided. Harker had eventually turned off his own TV screen and opted to sleep for the rest of the flight, a choice he was inclined to resume under the bombardment of questions their taxi-driver was now throwing at them.

'So what's your profession, sir?' the taxi driver continued, blissfully unaware of the lack of enthusiasm his questions were being met with.

'I'm a lecturer in archaeology at a university,' Harker muttered despondently.

'A lecturer! Does it pay well?'

'Pays the bills.'

The man was already opening his mouth for another question when a motorway sign caught Harker's attention.

'Why are you taking us by route 6? Surely it's route 1 that leads right into Jerusalem.'

'Not today, I fear. There was a bad crash earlier,' the man replied, following a turning for the nearest off-ramp. 'A fuel tanker jack-knifed across both lanes, so we have to go round.'

This answer elicited a double-take from Harker, as the vehicle continued down the curving exit lane that lead underneath the highway itself.

'Go around what? The whole of Israel!'

Before he could finish his complaint, the taxi came to an abrupt halt at a fenced-off area directly below route 6 and in between the highway's support arches. Harker was already pulling at the door handle when the barrel of a gun, thrust over the top of the driver's seat, stopped his escape attempt cold.

'Stay where you are,' the man ordered. He then exited the car and made his way hurriedly around to the passenger side, with the gun still aimed in front of him. He pulled open the passenger door and with a jerk of his gun ordered them both out. 'Don't say a word, and don't try anything foolish,' the driver growled, cocking the compact .22 calibre, semi-automatic model 71 Beretta as a reminder of the consequences if his order went unheeded. As the armed man now guided them through a metal gate into the fenced-off area, Harker was already considering trying to grapple the gun out of the man's hands, but then thought better of it and dutifully did as he was asked. He was no commando and, even though the driver was small with a wiry frame, getting shot during a struggle was not going to do him or Chloe any good.

Inside the fence, the area looked like a mini junkyard with a couple of cars stripped down to their chassis, and the remains of a number of old refrigerator units had been piled up at the far end. The only thing Harker could see of any significance was the large rusty shipping container in one corner that they were now being herded towards. The taxi-driver kept his gun trained on them both, even as he moved towards the container and pulled open the metal door with a creak. It was very dark inside and the only things visible were a couple of plastic chairs positioned by the opening.

'Take a seat,' the man instructed and, once they were both inside and had taken their seats, he swung the door shut behind them with a hefty clank.

The interior of the container was chilly, so the beads of sweat across Harker's forehead from the heat outside made the droplets feel like frost stinging his skin. In the gloom he could just make out Chloe seated to his left, her hair swaying from side to side as she surveyed their surroundings.

'Are you all right?'

'That depends on what comes next,' Chloe answered and with a remarkably calm tone given the circumstances. 'Where are we?'

'In a storage container.'

'Yes, I know that, you fool,' Chloe gasped. 'I mean what are we doing here? Are we about to get shipped somewhere.'

Up ahead, there was a scuffing sound and the metal floor creaked as someone or something shifted its weight.

'I don't think this is used for shipping, Chloe,' Harker replied, straining his eyes to catch any flicker of movement. He was about to call out when a gruff voice with a thick Israeli accent sounded out from the blackness.

'That assumption would be correct, Professor Harker.'

Overhead a single strip light flickered into life, bathing the interior in yellowish light that forced them both to look downwards. It took a few moments for Harker's eyes to adjust as, in front of him, a blurry figure gradually took form. At a guess the man was in his late forties, totally bald but with a thick bushy moustache that covered a good expanse of his extremely pudgy face. A white linen, short-sleeved shirt complete with darkening sweat marks underneath the arms, was tucked in at the waist, revealing an ample barrel of a stomach which protruded flabbily over dark khaki trousers.

'So, then, Professor,' the fat man said coldly, 'and you too, Doctor Stanton... What brings you to my country?'

Harker was already considering jumping up and rushing to attack the newcomer but the sight of a black 9mm Glock holstered at the man's belt made him to reconsider. 'We're here on business,' he replied calmly. 'Official university business.'

The answer drew an amused sneer from their host, who raised a finger to his lips and tapped them. 'Official university business? Well, that kind of authority might transcend UK borders but it has little weight in this part of the world. I am afraid I'll need something a little more precise.'

'I'm here to negotiate an exchange of exhibits with the University of Jerusalem,' Harker continued, unflustered, the smooth delivery of this lie serving to increase his confidence. 'I was recently behind the discovery of Caesar's death mask in Italy and, amongst other items, we are looking to promote an exhibit exchange programme sometime in the near future.'

His response was received with a look of disbelief from the fat man, who raised his eyebrows. 'I read an article about your discovery of the mask in Time magazine. It was intriguing but I find it hard to believe that our university would have any interest in such an artefact.'

'As I said, Mr...?'

'Mr will do just fine.'

'Very well,' Harker continued grimly unfazed by the man's wish for anonymity. 'As I said, that was just one of many items that The University of Cambridge, alongside the British Museum in London, wishes to offer as an exchange. If you want, you can call your own university and check with Professor Malik Phipps. He'll be able to confirm my visit.'

This was, of course, a lie. Harker knew the professor by name, though he had never met the man let alone organised a meeting with him, but it was certainly worth a shot. 'So perhaps it is *you* that should be doing the explaining, and why *you* are interrogating us?'

The fat man looked wholly unconvinced and ignored the question, then he turned his attention to Chloe who was also managing to look sincere. 'And you can confirm this story as well, Doctor Stanton?'

'Yes, I can,' she managed, offering a polite nod in the fat man's direction. 'I am his assistant, after all.'

The use of the word 'assistant' drew a surprised look from Harker, who automatically threw her a brief glance that was immediately seized upon by their interrogator.

'Now, you were doing well up until that point,' the fat man stated unsympathetically. 'But, for future reference, when you are being questioned you never take your eyes off the interrogator, and you should never look at one another except in mutual surprise.' A smile began to emerge from underneath his bushy moustache. 'That only induces curiosity in an interrogator and makes him think you are hiding something. OK, my name is Mendel Rabin and we have a mutual friend, Professor,' the man continued. 'A friend who has the ability to see things others do not.' Rabin motioned towards his face with two chubby fingers. 'It is all in the eyes, you know.'

Harker let out an unguarded sigh of relief, for it had to be Brulet their new acquaintance was referring to. 'He's a good friend.'

'Yes, he is. But before we go any further I need you to understand that although you will be allowed all the co-operation that his friendship deserves, you must be aware that I am not happy to have you in my country.'

The last few words were said with such a ferocity that Harker tensed up again for a moment. 'And why is that, Mr Rabin?' he asked cautiously.

'Because death seems to follow you, Professor, wherever you go.'

Rabin reached down and pulled a single A5 photograph from a leather satchel lying on the floor next to him, which he then placed it in Harker's waiting hands. The black-and-white image exhibited all the tell-tale signs of having been taken by a security camera. It showed the front entrance of Notre Dame Cathedral littered with dead bodies and there right in the middle, looking shocked, stood Harker with his arm around Chloe and surrounded by armed police.

'That image and others like it are being pasted all over the internet. They've not appeared in the mainstream news yet, but they inevitably will.' Rabin retrieved the photograph and placed it back in his satchel.

'And then there is the death of John Strasser in Warsaw, whose apartment building you were both seen entering shortly before his death.'

'That was a suicide, plain and simple,' Chloe protested.

'That may be the case, Doctor Stanton, but there is nothing plain or simple about any of the events that have occurred during the past few days. It might be worth reminding you that Notre Dame was not the only house of worship to suffer a terrorist attack. The main synagogue in Tel Aviv was also hit, with over one hundred deaths.'

An uncomfortable silence hung in the air. 'Who exactly are you, Mr Rabin?' Harker asked, all of a sudden feeling enormously vulnerable.

'All you need know is that I work for the Israeli security services, and the clue is in the name itself. I keep Israel *secure*, regardless of whether it is from an internal...' – Rabin dipped his face closer to Harker's – '... or an external threat.'

The reply was all Harker needed. 'You're Mossad, aren't you?'

Rabin continued to stare at Harker intimidatingly, his silence an answer in itself.

'Fine,' Harker replied drily, 'that's good enough for me.'

'As so it should be.' Rabin replied, disconcerted at almost having to say it out loud. He took a step backwards and folded his arms. 'Now, our friend explained the reason for your trip, so I had the Temple Mount checked from top to bottom, but they found nothing out of the ordinary. I also have a team watching the place, so if any undesirables do turn up then they are in for a rude awakening.'

'It's not the terrorists I'm concerned about,' Harker replied seriously.

'Oh, yes, I know about your secret pieces of paper,' Rabin scoffed sarcastically. 'Personally I think it's a load of bullshit but, like I said, you have quite a knack of surrounding yourself with death and tragedy, so I'm not about to take any chances. You are free therefore to travel to the Temple Mount, and our friend has arranged for a private jet at Atarot airport should you need it, but... one of my men will be at your side during every moment that your feet are on Israeli soil.'

Rabin reached over and thumped at the wall, and the door of the storage container swung open to reveal their taxi-driving kidnapper standing outside, minus his gun.

'This is Avi, and he will be your chaperone.'

'You know you could have just introduced yourself at the airport,' Harker remarked to Avi, getting out of his seat.

'I could have, yes, but we don't take chances on unknowns – and you are exactly that,' Avi replied, gesturing with one hand for them to follow him.

Harker was already doing so when Chloe grasped him by the arm. 'Aren't you going to tell me who our mystery friend is, then?' she asked, obviously referring to Brulet.

Before Harker could reply, Rabin's voice boomed out from behind. 'No, he is not, and furthermore you should just be glad to have such a friend.' He aimed a large forefinger at her and wagged it from side to side. 'No more questions now.'

Avi was hurrying them both towards the taxi when Rabin called out one final time. 'Oh and, Professor Harker,' the Mossad agent offered a wide grin and raised both his arms upwards as if offering an embrace, 'Welcome to Israel.'

Chapter 21

'No, no, no,' the Waqf guard shouted. 'No one is allowed inside the mosque at this time of day – especially an Israeli!'

Avi glanced back at Harker and Chloe, who were doing their level best to look as non-threatening as possible whilst surrounded by a group of Israeli policemen all equipped with scoped Galil assault rifles.

'They are not Israelis,' Avi replied to the increasingly irate guard. 'They are UN inspectors and they have permits.'

The Mossad agent once again brandished the documentation in front of the guard's nose, who in turn waved his hand and shook his head, his other hand never leaving his holster. 'I have received no word regarding a UN visit, and without that you go no further. No word... No access.'

Harker looked on as the two men continued to argue. He was surprised they had even made it onto the Temple Mount, considering the troop of Israeli police they had gradually picked up upon entering the Temple's west entrance.

'Alex, one question.' Chloe's soft voice was in stark contrast to the deep-throated barking of the two men up ahead. 'How did you expect us both to get inside the Dome if we hadn't been given an escort in the first place?'

'I have a few good friends in this city,' Harker replied quietly, not wanting the policemen surrounding them to take any interest in their conversation. 'One of them is even on the Waqf committee that oversee this whole area.'

'Would he have been prepared to help?' Chloe whispered back, following Harker's lead in avoiding attention.

'Not sure, but he's a good man and he knows me. So I was hoping I could convince him.'

Chloe nodded politely. 'Bit of a long shot.'

'Chloe,' Harker finally pulled his attention away from the still arguing men ahead onto her, 'this whole trip has been a long shot. Why should this moment be any different?'

His answer drew a smile from her and, content that she was satisfied by his answer, he turned his gaze to the darkening Jerusalem skyline in the distance. Despite all his travels, both professional and personal, he had never yet visited the famous Temple Mount. The gold-domed Temple or Temple of the Rock as it was known – was one of the holiest places in Islam. For the Temple housed the actual piece of ground, known as the Foundation Rock, where the Muslim prophet Mohammed was said to have ascended to heaven with the Angel Gabriel to meet with God and all the prophets that had preceded him, in what became known as 'the Night Journey'. He was said to have witnessed God sitting on his throne surrounded by angels – a pretty impressive trip by anyone's standard. The historical truth was a little less jaw dropping though, as this story had not appeared in any of the Islamic texts until a few decades after the Dome was built, and so was widely believed by Western scholars to have been contrived simply to celebrate the Islamic victory over the Christians at Jerusalem. If or when Mohammed had 'ascended', it was unlikely to have taken place at this spot but, regardless, to millions it remained a place of worship, considered the third most holy in all of Islam, and therefore must be protected at all costs. In fact, the location was still a major flashpoint in the ongoing Arab–Israeli conflict. Situated on top of a thirty-five-acre artificial plateau known as the Haram al-Sharif, the Temple Mount was surrounded by four walls – including the famous Wailing Wall on the Israeli side, where devout Jews came daily to pray. The Dome of the Rock was also said to have been built directly above Solomon's temple, which had once housed the Ark of the Covenant. All in all, the site was an immensely sacred place for Islam, Judaism and Christianity alike, regardless of who now laid claim to it.

'Impressive, isn't it?' Harker remarked noting the wide-eyed enthusiasm with which Chloe was surveying the structure.

'I've always wanted to visit this place,' she confessed, flexing her back against the cool evening breeze. 'My mother came here shortly after discovering she had cancer... she also visited the Vatican.' She glanced at Harker glumly. 'When it was still there.'

'I suppose she was looking for answers?' Harker quickly suggested, not wanting to revisit the still painful subject of the Vatican.

157

'Something like that,' Chloe replied lethargically.

'Did she find any?' Harker continued softly.

'I'm not sure. She was a tight-lipped individual even towards the end, but I think it probably helped her find some peace.'

In the short time Harker had known Chloe, she had proved herself extremely resilient. Firstly after the disturbing event they had witnessed back at Notre Dame and then regarding Strasser's suicide, but this was the first time she had looked frail, with cracks beginning to appear in that tough mental attitude of hers. 'This isn't just an adventure to you, is it?'

'No,' she replied with a shake of her head, turning to face him. 'I meant what I said back in England, about wanting to know if my mother has gone on to another place.' She expelled a curious laugh. 'I didn't really expect to get any answers but...'

'But now?' Harker resisted the feeling of excitement rising up in his throat.

'Now? Well, I'm still not sure but, given everything we've seen...' She paused and gave a sigh. 'Let's just say my mind is open to the possibilities. Although, for the record, I still think it's terrorists.'

The response induced a deep gulp from Harker. 'God, I hope you're right because if not...'

His reply was met with a smile from Chloe, who gently nudged her shoulder into his arm. 'Why, Professor Harker, are you maybe regaining your faith?'

'I wouldn't exactly say that,' he was not prepared to go that far, 'but since the earthquake at the Vatican, let us say I too am keeping an open mind.'

'OK, Professor, we're in.' Avi announced on re-joining them. 'They will allow us ten minutes inside, but that's all.' The Mossad agent then turned his attention to the four policemen waiting patiently. 'Thank you, I'll take it from here.'

With an acknowledging gesture the law officers made their way back down the steps towards the entrance into the west wall, leaving them alone with the displeased-looking Waqf guard, who now headed back to his post.

'They're not happy with it,' Avi explained, guiding them across the spacious enclosure towards the Dome's entrance, 'but I managed to convince them that an international incident would not be in the best interest of either my government or theirs at this time. Even so, we should keep this visit as short as possible.'

The Dome itself was about twenty-metres wide by twenty-five high, consisting of a wooden shell gilded in pure gold which shone like a beacon over the city of Jerusalem. The support building beneath it amounted to an octagonal drum, the outer eight walls of which were equally stunning, the lower half of each being panelled in rich white marble and the upper parts covered by a mosaic of fine Turkish tiles coloured in a stunning myriad of cobalt-blue, white and gold.

Harker paused at the entrance and marvelled at the wondrous building. Non-Muslims were usually forbidden from entering and to gain access had always been on his own personal wish list. Sadly, this special moment was sullied by the Waqf guard jabbing his finger aggressively towards them.

'Ten minutes and then you leave,' the man barked, before pulling open the main doorway.

'Thank you, and As-salaam alaikum,' Harker replied politely, using the traditional Muslim greeting.

'As-salaam alaikum,' the guard responded begrudgingly before gesturing them inside and then carefully closing the door behind him, leaving the three of them alone.

The sight that met them was awe-inspiring and Harker felt his whole body tingle at the stunning display of craftsmanship. He had seen dozens of pictures over the years but none of them did this place credit and he felt a flood of excitement wash over him. Right in the centre, and directly under the Dome, stood the Foundation Rock itself and the reason this entire building existed. The large central slab was encircled by a number of arches supported by majestic marble pillars, and a chest-high wooden partition bordered the edges to protect the humble rock lying within from any over-enthusiastic visitors eager to touch this piece of religious history for themselves. The flooring was composed of royal-gold and red tiles spreading out from the room's centre, and they served to complement the intricate green and gold artistry of the wall tiles.

Harker took another moment to enjoy this sight, and it was Chloe who finally broke the silence.

'Wow. Now, that's impressive,' she gasped. 'So this is where Abraham offered up his son Isaac as a sacrifice to God in the Book of Genesis? Amongst other things.'

Chloe's statement received a look of surprise from Harker. 'You seem pretty knowledgeable.'

'I said I was an atheist,' she replied contemptuously, 'not an ignoramus.'

'Ignoramus! I haven't heard that word in a while.' Harker grinned.

'Then you should get out of your classroom more often. Besides,' she waved her mobile phone in front of him, 'who needs an education these days when we have Google.'

'God help us,' he sighed and shook his head.

'You have nine minutes left, Professor.' Avi warned, tapping at his watch, 'so I suggest you get on with whatever it is you're here to do.'

Harker acknowledged the reminder with a casual salute before he made his way over to the large slab in the centre of the room, while giving Avi a curious glance. Up until that moment he had assumed the Mossad agent must be aware why he had so badly wanted access to this place, but it seemed that Rabin had kept it quiet from his own underlings. Yet Harker could have revealed it to Avi at any moment, so evidently Rabin had complete faith in his agent's ability to keep any curiosity he possessed to himself. Either that or the Mossad chief believed this whole exercise to be a complete waste of time and not even worth discussing with his juniors. Harker dismissed the thought as he reached the waist-high white, wooden barrier, and stared down at the slab of rock contained within it.

The Foundation Stone did not have any particular shape. If one imagined a rectangle with a half circle attached to one side, that would not be far from describing it. Like Chloe, Harker had also Googled on the plane trip over from Warsaw, just to refresh his memory, and had managed to download a few images.

The edges on all sides were relatively straight, but the upper surface of the stone was a mismatch of uneven indentations. Some were the result of natural weathering whereas others were clearly man-made – such as the large cavity in the upper left corner.

Harker thought back to the words uttered by Strasser shortly before his nose-dive out of the top floor window to his death. '*It's at the Temple Mount in Jerusalem, to the north under the protection of the old man of the rock.*' Harker had hoped that seeing the stone itself would enlighten him further as to exactly what Strasser was referring to, but so far that wasn't happening.

He turned to their chaperone: 'Is there a curator for the Dome?'

'No,' Avi replied gruffly. 'The site is administered by members of the Waqf committee, and some archaeologists are allowed in, but nothing permanent. So it's the guards outside or nothing.'

Harker was already continuing on around the rock, his frustration beginning to show as his pace became faster. Ever since Strasser had told him where to find the third Secret, he had spent little or no time actually thinking about it, with instead the death of Salvatore Vincenzo looming at the forefront of his mind. In truth it was only after his meeting with Rabin that he had begun to contemplate what the 'old man of the rock' part could refer to.

'The old man of the rock,' Harker repeated as he began to make his way around the stone's perimeter a second time. If it did not refer to a curator or a site administrator, then who was it referring to? A mosque stood on the Mount's plateau, no more than thirty metres away, and it would have an imam present, and he was most likely pretty ancient, but nothing to do with the Foundation Rock – or any other rock Harker was aware of.

Harker rested his forearms on the encircling wooden parapet and gazed down at the large stone block below, exhaling a deeply discouraged breath. *Where the hell was he going to find an ancient old rock man in this...*? Suddenly it dawned on him that he had just answered his own question. 'Rock man? Wait a minute!' he exclaimed, then made his way around to the other side of the slab. 'Strasser said the third Secret was to the north, under the protection of the old man of the rock.' Harker raised an arm and pointed directly in front of him. 'Over there is north.' He continued staring down at the rock below and then pointed it out. 'If you don't look at it from the right angle, you could so easily miss it.'

Chloe and Avi were already beside him at the partition, trying to see what he was referring to.

'What is it?' Chloe asked.

'That's what we're looking for,' Harker replied triumphantly, a wide smile forming on his lips. 'Ladies and gentlemen, allow me to introduce you to the Old Man of the Rock.'

It took a moment for Chloe to make out what he was pointing at, then suddenly she too saw it and, like an auto stereogram picture from a Magic Eye book, once you could see it you couldn't imagine how you ever missed it in the first place. There, etched on to the rock's surface, was the image of a man with his arms pointing in either direction. You had to look at it from just the right angle and then, when you did, even the smaller details of his hair, eyes and nose became visible.

'Oh, my God, you're right,' Chloe uttered, shocked by spotting the image that seemed to have materialised right out of thin air.

Avi stood on tiptoe to look over Harker's shoulder and get a better view. 'Oh, that,' he remarked indifferently. 'I've seen that before. They say it was done by Roman soldiers a few millennia ago.'

The casual comment made both Harker and Chloe spin around to face him, and with the same look of surprise.

'Then why didn't you say something?' Harker demanded, indignant because they were up against the clock.

'I thought you were looking for someone real, that's why,' Avi explained, though looking ill at ease. 'Besides, Professor it's you who are the archaeologist. Shouldn't you already know about this sort of thing?'

'I have a lot on my mind at the moment,' Harker said defensively, reluctant to explain himself further.

'Clearly you have.'

Harker ignored the man's jibe and turned his attention back to the rock. The man's image had both arms outstretched in opposite directions and Harker traced a line with his finger outwards from the first, but there was nothing of any interest in that direction. He then switched over and followed the other pointing hand, until his finger indicated the only object in his line of sight: one of the inner stone pillars encircling the room.

'There!' Without another word Harker made his way over to the pillar, with the other two close behind. The pillar itself was devoid of any markings but Harker spent a few seconds running both his open palms down its sides, hoping to feel for anything out of the ordinary. Sadly, finding nothing, he turned his attention to the base and the stone block it sat upon. The sides were free of any obvious markings but, as he began to examine the side closest to the pointing hand of the man of the rock, he noticed a thin crack where it joined the adjacent sides. Harker placed one palm squarely upon the middle of the stone and gently pushed. Immediately a clicking sound could be heard, and a square section of the base retreated to reveal an inner cavity.

'What the...' Avi exclaimed loudly, and watched intently as Harker reached into the darkness beyond and retrieved a small box identical to the one they had found at Notre Dame, the only difference being that this one had no keyhole. Harker gently pulled out the box and placed it on his lap. Then with a nervous glance in Chloe's direction, he carefully opened the lid.

The interior was lined with the same packing material as its sister, and lying snuggly in the middle was another glass vial containing a familiar-looking slip of parchment. Harker stood up again and both he and Chloe eyed the glass tube with distrust.

'Are we really going to open this?' Chloe asked cautiously, 'considering what happened the last time.'

Harker was already shaking his head. 'No, not here,' he said. 'I think it's time we contacted Rabin before we do anything else.' He then turned to face Avi. 'Can you get in contact with...?' His voice tailed off as he found himself staring down the barrel of Avi's gun.

'Thank you, Professor, but this is not your burden to bear any more.'

Chloe took a step back at the sight of the weapon, then froze as Avi flicked the barrel slightly in her direction.

'Everyone stay calm,' Avi said, 'and slowly pass that box over to me.'

Harker remained silent for a moment as a sense of confusion swept through him. 'That's the second time you've aimed a gun at me today.'

'Yes, it is,' the Mossad agent replied flatly. 'And if you do not want this gun to be the last thing you see, I suggest you pass the box over to me now... slowly.'

'Who are you?' Harker questioned, as Chloe shifted closer to his side.

'I am the one holding the gun, Professor. That should be explanation enough, don't you think?'

'No, it's not.' Harker replied, his hands tightening around the wooden box in his grasp.

'That is the same inquisitiveness that has already caused us so much trouble,' Avi replied with an unamused grimace. 'You truly are a meddlesome son of a bitch, aren't you?'

This reply removed any other doubts in Harker's mind. 'You're Magi, aren't you?'

Avi said nothing, but a thin smile appeared on his lips alerting Harker to the fact that, despite the man's silence, deep down he really wanted them to know who he was. The agent could have smacked him over the head with the gun and simply snatched hold of the box but the man's ego would not allow for that. He was Magi all right.

Harker broke off from Avi's ever-hardening stare and looked down at the box held tightly in his grip. Inside was another signpost to finding the child. That is, at least, if he believed what Marcus Eckard had told him: *Follow the Secrets and you will find the child*. Harker shook his head at the thought because, so far, the only thing that had been revealed was death and destruction. It didn't even make any sense that something as trivial as reading aloud a piece of text could produce such tragic outcomes... unless you believed in the power of prophecy. But if one did believe, then it stood to reason that they would also believe that whoever possessed the Christ child had the power to either prevent or cause the whole cataclysm. What had Eckard said? – *the child's fate would either cause or prevent these events* – So, if that was the case, then why would the Magi care less if Harker found any of the Secrets? That is if one *believed*.

'Wait a second,' Harker returned Avi's increasingly impatient stare, 'the Magi don't have the child, do they?'

Avi remained silent, his smile suddenly evaporating and his nostrils flaring slightly with anger, no doubt at having his own organisation's competence questioned.

'In fact,' Harker continued and gaining in confidence at his own summation, 'you're just as confused at these events as we are, aren't you?'

Although Avi's eyes remained firmly fixed on Harker, his lips began to twitch and the barrel of the gun quivered as the man's fingers tightened around the grip. 'Very good Professor, very good. But you should be far less concerned over that and more so with the weapon I have pointing at your head,' he replied with a waiting hand now extended, 'and I intend to shoot you both dead if you do not pass over that box right here, right now.'

As Avi thrust the gun barrel menacingly towards them both, Harker felt Chloe move even closer to his side, and his grip on the box began to loosen. 'Fine, it's yours,' he said before slowly reaching over and placing it in the agent's waiting palms.

'Good. Now over there, both of you.' Avi flicked his gun towards the white stone column directly behind them, 'and I want you to place both hands up against the pillar.'

Harker stepped backwards and did as he was told, followed closely by Chloe who placed her palms flat against the opposite side.

'Good.' Avi repeated, retreating a few paces and placing his gun back into its holster. 'Now if either one of you lift your hands away from that pillar I will execute both of you.' He now began to turn his attention to the wooden box in his possession.

Harker and Chloe watched closely as their captor lifted open the box's lid and retrieved the glass vial from within. He then dropped the empty box to the floor sending a clattering sound echoing around the Dome, and raised the glass tube itself up towards the central light overhead. 'It is remarkable, is it not, that something so small and seemingly insignificant has the ability to incur such devastating consequences,' observed Avi. As he inspected the object, the refracted light glinting off the glass projected bright specks of light across his face. 'It is often said that the Secrets offer hope and salvation to those brave enough to unearth them.'

This benign remark was voiced with such conviction that it sent an unnerving sensation through Harker's chest. 'That depends on what your notion of salvation is,' he replied, his hands still planted firmly on the pillar.

This comment produced a devious smile from Avi, who shifted his attention from the vial and towards Harker, one hand still held towards the light. 'Power, Professor Harker, plain and simple.' And with that he let the vial fall from his fingers, dropping to the tiled floor where it shattered and sent glass splinters shooting in all directions. This was so unexpected that Harker managed only to yell in protest by the time some of the fragments had reached his shoes.

'No!' Harker shouted again, as Avi reached down to pick up the single piece of paper. 'You don't understand...'

'I'll tell you what I understand.' The man stared lovingly at the folded piece of white parchment. 'I understand how the Secrets hold great power. You only have to see evidence of what happened at Notre Dame to know that.'

'Then you know that it killed everyone who was inside there,' Harker yelled, allowing his frustration to get the better of him.

'Not everyone,' Avi replied calmly, studying both Chloe and Harker with a subtle raising of his eyebrows. 'You and Doctor Stanton seem perfectly healthy to me.'

Harker was suddenly lost for words. What could he say? Avi was right. Out of over one hundred people only he and Chloe had walked out alive, even if Harker was not yet prepared to put that all down to simply reading out lines from a piece of paper.

After a few moments of silence, it was Avi who clarified the matter. 'It was because you yourselves read the Secret or are you still reluctant to accept that truth?'

The agent waited again for a response but, seeing that Harker was unwilling or unable to give one he continued with his analysis, all the while holding the slip of parchment between the fingertips of both hands in a ceremonial like manner. 'These Secrets were meant for the eyes of the Magi, and the Magi alone. They were meant for persons of true religious conviction. They were not meant for either of you, but worry not,' Avi unfolded the scrap of paper and scanned its contents, 'that is a mistake that I shall now correct.' The agent pursed his lips, drew in a shallow breath and began to read aloud.

'And when burning lakes of fire lap at your feet and the gnashing of teeth and tearing of flesh fills your ears, then you will know you have failed and that hell on earth is now upon you, and with it hope shall become nothing more than a word, and he will reign evermore.' The man's voice reverberated around the Dome and he turned his attention back to Harker. 'I can feel it working. It is remarkable,' the agent said with a look of delight. 'The power... in my blood, in my veins...' He emitted a euphoric roar of laughter, his eyes wide with glee. 'Goodbye, Professor,' he continued, enjoying the moment, 'May you now watch events unfold from the depths of hell.'

Harker glanced towards Chloe, who was staring back at him fearfully, and he felt the same. He couldn't tell if it was hearing Avi's shrill sentiments or his own uncertainty about what might happen next, but these new feelings of terror surprised him. He surely didn't believe in all this prophecy crap... did he?

The unnatural grunting noise now coming from the other side of the room pulled him away from such thoughts, and he turned to see Avi beginning to tremble all over, and with that the man's confident smile began to melt away. With his mouth open wide, a piercing scream burst from his lungs. His jaw muscles started to tighten and a thick vein, protruding from his forehead now throbbed to the point of bursting.

Harker pulled away from the pillar in astonishment as Avi began scratching at his forearms with such force that his fingernails tore away small chunks of flesh sending drops of crimson blood down onto the white tiled floor around him.

'Jesus,' Chloe gasped as Avi now started on his face, digging his fingernails into both cheeks and dragging them downwards leaving three deep red cuts on either side. With each new mutilation the agent bellowed in pain, enduring the torture of a man not in control of his own actions but having to suffer its consequences nonetheless.

'Chloe.' Harker turned away from this gory sight and reached over to pull her to his side. 'Get yourself over there.' He pointed to the other side of the security barriers surrounding the Foundation Stones, which offered some protection at least from whatever might happen next. He ended up having to shove her as she struggled to break her gaze away from the gruesome spectacle of Avi, who had now dropped to his knees as he was consumed by a series of violent spasms. Finally, his hands fell to his sides and his head drooped downwards. He spewed a mouthful of blood, splattering onto the floor directly in front of him like some kind of vile offering. The convulsions then quickly decreased and finally the Mossad agent's shoulders slumped and he remained motionless, but with his body still upright where he had fallen on to his knees.

Harker remained still for a few seconds, then he began to check his own hands for any sign of the convulsions that had plagued Avi. Satisfied that everything appeared normal, he turned and called to Chloe. 'Are you OK?'

'I think so,' she replied, deathly pale, before returning her attention to the motionless, bloody mess that was Avi. 'Is he dead?'

Harker didn't reply but instead began to make his way slowly towards the bent-over body of the Mossad agent, whose wispy black hair was now hanging over of his face, making it impossible to see if there was any spark of life in his eyes. Harker paused a few steps away and studied the body for movement, but detected no sign of breathing. The grisly image took his thoughts back to Notre Dame: whatever had just happened to Avi was similar, yet this time the symptoms seemed far more violent.

Satisfied it was safe to approach, Harker moved to within a foot of the body and dropped down on one knee in an effort to get a glimpse of the man's face. Avi's eyes were still open, yet lifeless, and the numerous self-inflicted wounds on his cheeks were still actively oozing blood that dripped on to the floor with a nauseating pitter-patter. At first Harker thought that same blood must have trickled into the agent's eyes, but on closer inspection, he could tell that the blood vessels must have ruptured with such force that even the irises had turned a vivid red. This was another similarity with the victims at Notre Dame, but also reminded Harker of someone else. The torn skin and horrific self-mutilation of Marcus Eckard's strange self-harm back at the asylum. *Could there be a connection?* Avi's arms bore similar gouges yet many of the veins underneath his skin had ruptured separately, causing blue patches giving the appearance of rot having set into the flesh. In short it was disgusting. What a horrible death.

He was about to stand up and head over to check on Chloe when something moved in his peripheral vision. Harker immediately returned his gaze to the source of the movement, to find himself staring directly into Avi's lifeless red eyes. He continued to do so for a few more seconds until something dawned on him. The man's eyes were most definitely staring back.

In one startled movement Harker jerked backwards, losing balance and landing squarely on his rear, as the blood-red eyes continued to remain locked with his. Harker jumped back onto his feet, struggling to keep his composure. 'Avi?'

Without out a hint of warning, the young Israeli burst into life with both arms thrust towards Harker, and shrieking loudly at the top of his voice. Harker stepped back just in time to avoid Avi's clawing fingers and he made a run for the cover of the closest pillar as the Mossad agent, now hissing through clenched teeth, launched off his haunches and propelled himself towards Harker. The impact caught Harker square on the shoulder, sending both of them tumbling across the floor in a heap and Harker immediately flipped onto his back and scrambled to get back up but was met by the sight of Avi's hand already clawing its way up his trouser leg. The agent's grip was powerful and he pulled himself closer until he was able to throw his hands around Harker's neck, spitting globules of foamy blood in a frenzy. Harker thrust his knee hard into his attacker's groin, which stunned the man for a moment giving Harker a chance to push him off to one side, revealing the gun still securely holstered to the agent's belt. Harker immediately reached for it and he managed to unbutton the holster but, before he could retrieve the weapon, Avi was back on him and trying to gnaw at his hand. The blood-soaked madman was just inches from sinking his teeth into the side of Harker's palm when a large leather-bound book was slammed down hard against his head with a load thud. Harker glanced up in time to see Chloe lower the hand that had hurled it. The impact sent Avi reeling, whereupon Harker seized the moment to lunge again for the gun and pull it from its holster.

He then hauled himself to his feet and aimed the barrel at the Israeli agent, who was already struggling to get up again.

'Don't move,' Harker yelled, thrusting the gun out in front of him, but the warning made no difference: Avi was now fully on his feet again and already preparing to lunge.

Harker cocked the Beretta. 'I said stop!'

This second warning was as useless as the first. The man hurtled towards him with eyes glaring frenziedly, bloody spittle foaming on his mouth like a rabid animal.

The explosive sound of a gunshot thundered around the Dome as the bullet ripped through Avi's chest and dropped him to the floor with an undignified thud. Standing above him, Harker continued to hold the smoking barrel of the beretta out in front of him, his breathing fast and shallow with the shock of what had just taken place. He had never fired a gun in his life let alone shot anyone before... never *killed* anyone. Nausea began to well in his throat at the thought, and his mind began to cloud as he lowered the gun to his side. He felt numb and his flushed cheeks began to tingle with a stinging feeling. He was still gazing down at Avi's lifeless body when Chloe uttered something from behind him. He turned around to find her looking shocked and her eyes seemed somewhat glazed over.

'Are you OK?' Harker asked, his own voice sounding muffled due to the ringing in his ears, caused by letting off a gun in an enclosed space.

'I think so.' She replied shakily, rubbing at her ears. 'But I'm struggling to hear you.'

'Don't worry, it will pass.' Harker offered as his naturally protective instincts began to focus his mind. 'We have to go now.'

The remark was met with a look of total disbelief from Chloe. 'What! We need to wait for the authorities, Alex.'

Harker suddenly felt a deep sense of concern. It wasn't the thought of the authorities that caused this feeling, but rather the lack of them. Surely the sound of a gunshot would have brought the guards racing inside, but they were still on their own. An uncomfortable thought came to the forefront of his mind, and he hurried over to where Avi had dropped the second Secret, retrieving the piece of parchment and placing it in his inside jacket pocket. He then made his way over to Avi's corpse and cautiously rummaged in the man's trouser pockets, thankfully retrieving the car keys on the first try. The bloodstains on his cheek left by his struggle with Avi, caused him to pause momentarily as he became aware of the stains, and he instinctively wiped them with his sleeve before returning to Chloe, grabbing her hand and heading for the door.

She didn't offer any resistance and if she was having any moral dilemma about leaving the scene of a crime, she certainly wasn't showing it. 'Where are we going?'

'Outside,' he replied, and speedily made for the exit. 'I need to see something.' Harker swung open the door and stepped out into the courtyard and the cool evening air outside. What he saw there was something right out of his nightmares, as his worst fears were realised.

All across the city, numerous fires could be seen burning, their flames rising high and licking at the skyline. And the air was filled with screams and shouting, even from far off in the distance: hundreds if not thousands of voices all overlapping in a dreadful harmony of pain and anguish. Just across the way, the famous garden of olives was engulfed in an inferno of swirling gases, illuminating dark clouds above, and the sight of this made Harker's heart sink in despair.

It looked like hell... Hell on earth.

Chapter 22

'Look out!' Chloe shrieked as Harker careered the white taxi cab past a small group of pedestrians who were fighting off a frenzied-looking man stripped to the waist and displaying the same manic expression worn by Avi back at the Temple Mount. Navigating the narrow Jerusalem streets was difficult enough during the day but in near darkness, with clusters of people all fleeing for their lives, it was close to impossible.

The short dash to the parked taxi from the Temple Mount court-yard had offered little challenge but upon reaching it the entire electrical grid of Jerusalem had cut out, plunging the whole city into pitch darkness. If it had not been for the flickering orange glow of fires burning everywhere, Harker doubted he could have made his way through them without ploughing down scores of people.

Whatever had happened following Avi's reading of the third Secret was quickly spreading throughout the entire city and, even though Harker had felt like a bastard for leaving innocent people to be violently assaulted by crazed assailants out on the streets, it would have been lunacy for him to stop the car and attempt to help. Those affected were now completely void of reasoning, and mercilessly attacked anyone they could catch with the brutality of wild animals in the throes of bloodlust. A mile back they had witnessed a pack of five crazed individuals literally tearing apart an old man, as another victim had her face ground into the pavement until it was a bloody mess of flesh and sinew. Just as the third Secret had alluded, it was a vision of hell – although that word alone did not do the reality of it justice.

'Have you got any idea where you're going?' Chloe demanded, gripping the dashboard tightly.

'Atarot airport.' Harker yelled to be heard over the wails and screams of people fleeing all around them. 'Rabin said there would be a jet waiting for us.'

His response drew a look of wide-eyed disbelief from Chloe even as a bump in the road threw her back in her seat. 'And you believed him?'

It was a fair question considering the way his colleague Avi had turned on them, but in Harker's mind the Magi operative had been the only rogue element in their midst, and besides their options were now limited. After all, who knew how fast and far this thing was spreading. 'We'll find out soon enough,' he replied hesitantly, just missing a police car hurtling past them with its lights blazing red and blue. 'But anywhere is better than here.'

After a few more minutes of dangerous driving, the roads began to free up as they left the claustrophobic and chaotic streets of the old city. As they turned on to the main 417 Highway leading out of the city, the air began to grow thick with a smoke like a heavy fog.

'Look at that.' Harker called out and directing Chloe's attention to a nearby hillside which was on fire, its trees and bushes consumed by intense flames that sent sparks and bright red embers spiralling high up into dark sky above.

'What is it?' Chloe leant over towards Harker's window, peering out at the inferno.

'It's the Mount of Olives we saw earlier from the Temple Mount,' Harker replied softly, with a genuine sadness in his voice. 'It's where Jesus Christ was meant to have ascended to heaven, and where the Jews believe the messiah will first appear on his return.'

Chloe shook her head, her eyes still focused on the fire ravaged hilltop. 'Not today, he won't.'

The comment brought a defeated smile to Harker's lips. 'No,' he replied, 'not today.'

Harker was returning his gaze to that same burning glow of destruction when something struck the passenger-side window with such force that a jagged crack appeared down its length. He slammed down the brake, bringing the car to screeching halt, and they both swivelled around to see a man pick himself up off the road and stare back at them through a pair of blood-red eyes, with a deep gash on his forehead where it had struck the glass. The apparition snarled at them, revealing a set of abnormally long teeth. In fact, the teeth themselves were normal but the gums had receded massively making them appear longer than they were. As this freak began racing towards the taxi, his distorted fangs gnashing at the empty air, Harker threw his weight on to the accelerator and left the pursuer to disappear in the rear-view mirror, within a swirl of thick white smoke.

'What the hell was that?' Chloe yelled, 'did you see his teeth?'

'I saw them,' Harker managed, his sole focus now on the smoggy road ahead.

'What the hell is going on?' she yelled again, but louder this time.

'I don't know,' – he bit his lip reflectively – 'and now is not the time to find out.'

'Could all this be real, Alex? The Secrets and the prophecies, I mean?'

'I don't know that either,' Harker replied. 'Let's just focus now on getting to the airport in one piece shall we?'

He said it with such firmness that Chloe did not persist. Instead she turned her attention to the nearby hills and the gloom cast by the power outage over the surrounding countryside. Events were becoming too strange to apply any reasonable logic to them, and they both knew it. After Notre Dame, Harker had actually found solace in Brulet's belief that such terrible events were part of a global terrorist attack but, ever since the earthquake at Vatican City and now seeing Jerusalem burst into this unearthly wave of violence and chaos... well frankly he was struggling not to be convinced that some higher power was at work. He found himself pondering upon the same thought that Chloe had voiced moments earlier. *Was this for real?*

The rest of the twenty-minute journey to Atarot airport passed in silence. Even as they continued to drive by further scenes of chaos – abandoned police cars and people scurrying to find refuge from the ever-growing numbers of red-eyed abominations – neither of them spoke a word. They just watched and took it all in and by the time they had reached Atarot, they were both feeling pretty numb.

The main entrance to the airport consisted of nothing more than a steel-gated wire fence, and the shrubbery leading up to it was just as unimpressive, giving it less a deserted and more a dilapidated feel. Harker came to stop within metres of the gate and, after a few moments spent scanning the area for any signs of anything that might want to rip them to shreds, he climbed out of the taxi and headed over to the fence. He had passed this way a few times over the years, and recalled that it always had at least one Israeli security jeep parked outside, but as far as he could see there was not a vehicle in sight. He pushed against the gate, gave it a nudge and to his surprise it slowly swung open. Once again, he cautiously surveyed the surroundings to see if their arrival had drawn any undue attention but everything remained eerily still, and exactly what one would expect from any deserted facility.

The airport here had been closed to the public since 2001, after the second intifada which was an escalation of the Arab-Israeli conflict when Palestinian forces had once again challenged Israeli occupation. It had initially been designated as the Palestinian international airport some years earlier, but after continuing outbreaks of violence, which mainly consisted of rocks being hurled onto the runway, it was closed and placed under the direct authority of the Israeli defence force. This had seemed to many as an overreaction on behalf of the Israelis but when the other side won't even acknowledge your right to exist, then molehills can very quickly become mountains – and this was one such instance.

He headed back to the taxi and made one last scan of the immediate area for any sign of an Israeli jeep hidden somewhere, but there was still nothing. It was odd to see the place unguarded but, given the chaos that was unfolding in Jerusalem itself, it was becoming difficult to define anything as odd. He jumped back in the vehicle and drove through the open entrance in the direction of the main runway.

'I thought you said this place had round-the-clock security?' Chloe chided, plainly unsettled by the lack of a police presence.

'It usually does.'

'Maybe they were recalled because of what's going on?' she reasoned.

'Maybe,' Harker replied, half expecting the intruding taxi to be bathed in a dazzling bright security spotlight the moment they entered. 'It does seem empty, though.'

They continued on past a series of small reception buildings and down a side road leading to a security area, whose gates lay unlocked and wide open. Then out on to the main tarmac, arriving just short of the actual runway. The whole place looked totally abandoned and he was about to turn around and head back towards the main buildings, in hope of finding their contact, when the shadowy silhouette of a jet parked up at the far end of the runway caught his attention.

'That must be it,' he whispered. 'Let's go.'

It took less than a minute to pull up beside the aircraft which, without any lights, blended in well to its deserted surroundings.

'Stay here while I take a look,' he said and, with a confirming nod from Chloe, he stepped out of the taxi and made his way cautiously towards the aircraft's side door.

This white Gulfstream G450 was capable of holding up to sixteen passengers, which to Harker's mind seemed a bit excessive considering it was here to pick up only two. He reached up and knocked twice on the foot of the door, and almost immediately heard the familiar click of an unlocking mechanism. He then stood back as the door slowly lowered to reveal a series of steps leading up into the pitch black interior.

'Hello,' he called out, but the only answer he got was having the barrel of a snub-nosed Glock handgun poked towards him from the shadowy interior.

'Professor Harker?' The voice had a thick Texan accent.

'That's me,' Harker replied with scarcely a shred of nervousness evident in his tone. He was now getting used to guns being pointed at him.

'I wasn't sure you'd make it,' came the reply, whereupon the interior cabin lights were switched on to reveal a bald man in his forties, wearing a white pilot's uniform adorned with navy and gold lapels. 'Glad you did, but I was told there would be only one of you.' The man gestured towards Chloe, who was still sat in taxi.

'Change of plan, I'm afraid,' Harker replied 'And you are?'

The pilot immediately lowered his gun and emerged with hand stretched out. 'Captain Harry Jones and I'm your ticket outta here.' He raised a hand in greeting to Chloe who had already slid out of the passenger side and was making her way over to join them. 'And, judging by the radio chatter, you most definitely need it. You got any idea what's going on out there?'

'I'll explain once we're on board,' Harker replied, already nudging Chloe towards the jet's doorway, 'but suffice to say your help is extremely welcome.'

'Mr Brulet gave me strict instructions to take you wherever you need to go. So just give me the destination.'

The simple mentioning of Brulet's name caused Harker to freeze because it was rare for the Grand Master of the Knights Templar not go by an alias, and Captain Jones immediately picked up on this.

'Don't worry, Professor Harker,' he assured him, 'we're all friends here. Now, are you ready to leave?'

The response was good enough for Harker, and he couldn't nod his head quick enough. 'The sooner the better.'

Jones gave another smile and then waited for Chloe to make her way up and into the cabin, before signalling for Harker to do likewise.

'Captain,' Harker paused, 'do you know what happened to airport security here? Usually there's a military unit posted at the front gate.'

'There was one up until twenty minutes ago, when they just up and left in a blistering hurry. Can't say I blame them, considering the news reports I've been picking up on the airwaves. I asked them to leave the gates open for you.'

'It pays to have friends,' Harker murmured thankfully.

'Ain't that the truth?' Jones replied, urgently beckoning him inside.

Harker was already halfway up the steps when the sound of foot-steps on the tarmac nearby made him look back, and the familiar sounds of growling quickly turned into a series of wailing shrieks. At first the light shining from inside the cabin obscured his vision, but within seconds he could make out a number of silhouettes no more than thirty feet away, and moving fast in their direction.

'Time to go.' Jones shouted, hauling Harker through the entrance before pulling the door closed and locking it securely. Jones then rushed past them to the cockpit and began starting up the engines, as the pounding of fists against the jet's metal frame began to vibrate throughout the cabin.

Harker slid into a seat and stared out of the oval window just as the aircraft's landing lights flickered into life and lit up the surrounding tarmac, to reveal a crowd of attackers clawing at the fuselage. They were screaming intensely, mouths contorted in furious anger, and each one had those red blood-soaked eyes that looked black when not directly facing the light.

'Strap yourselves in,' Jones yelled over the deep rumbling of the engines as he throttled up. 'It's gonna be a bumpy take-off.'

To Harker this warning suggested that there might be a problem with the runway but, as the aircraft lurched forward, he felt a series of thumps against the floor beneath them and he realised Captain Jones had been referring to the poor souls being run over and not the state of the tarmac.

Harker turned back to the window in time to see one of the crazed maniacs get blasted directly in the face by the blue plume of flame coming from the jet's engine, as Jones throttled up to full power. The force of it sent the unlucky recipient hurtling back into the darkness, consumed in a ball of fire and smoke as the Gulf Stream began to gather speed until, with an almighty roar, it lifted up into the air. As the aircraft began turning, Chloe let out a loud thankful sigh and slumped back into her seat but her sense of relief evaded Harker who was still glued to the window. The sight of glimmering fires infecting the landscape down below was captivating, and reminded him of images he had seen during the bombing of Baghdad prior to the invasion of Iraq: unsettling yet riveting, but it was the shape they created that was even more intriguing. The fires ran in a straight line, running southwards all the way to Jerusalem, and then joining up with the scattering of larger fires throughout the city.

Harker remained glued to this sight until they veered off and turned northwards, when his view was impeded. He rested back in his seat and gazed down at his lap lethargically, the images still vivid in his mind.

My God, he thought to himself. *It was like something straight out of the Bible.*

Chapter 23

'I would like to make a one-time offer of amnesty to anyone who wishes to come clean right now,' Wilcox announced, as he stared over at the three members of the Magi council. 'You then have my solemn promise that, even though there will be consequences, your life will be spared.'

The three men took a moment to scrutinise one another and, satisfied that none of them was about to make any startling admission, they all turned back to face Wilcox with a collective defiance.

'I think it would be appropriate for you to explain exactly what these allegations are,' Davidson said sternly, with a remarkable air of authority considering the armed guards watching over them.

'Someone has been working with McCray,' Wilcox snapped.

'McCray!' Alonzo blurted out. 'That's impossible. That mad dog was disposed of years ago.'

Wilcox clicked his fingers and another guard appeared in the doorway, holding a Sony laptop. The man strode over to the table and placed it in front of Wilcox, then flipped open the lid before disappearing back the way he came. Wilcox tapped at the screen and it flashed into life, then slowly turned the laptop around to reveal an image of McCray. 'Apparently not,' Wilcox replied with a sneer. 'This photograph was taken late last night at Blackwater Asylum in the UK and, as you can see, he is very much alive.'

The other men studied the image for a few moments and then began to glance at one another, each looking mystified, as Wilcox continued to reveal what he knew: 'And I have also unearthed information that the child that was meant to be 'in your possession' is in fact in his.'

It was the first time since the meeting began that the subject of the child had been brought up, and the mere mention of the Magi's failure to acquire him drew a look of unease from all three, but especially from Alonzo. 'Yes, as you know, that operation did not go as planned but it will be rectified,' Alonzo declared, still endeavouring to appear in charge. 'But to say that McCray is back from the dead, and in possession of the child, is simply ludicrous.'

'Is it? Then perhaps we should ask the one person here who was responsible for his demise...' Wilcox now turned his attention to Dietrich, whose beady little eyes appeared to shrink even further into their sockets. 'So then, Dietrich, why don't you regale us with that story you were once so proud to share with us and which, I might add, propelled you to the headship of your family.'

Dietrich licked his lips apprehensively, then he straightened up in his chair with an air of defiance. 'My men had him removed, in accordance with the Council's decision, and I have no reason to believe otherwise.'

'Do you, now?' Wilcox replied challengingly and tapped at the computer screen with his finger. 'Then let me tell you what I think. I believe that you have been in collusion with McCray ever since he was banished from the Magi, and together both of you have the child somewhere in your custody.'

Both Alonzo and Davidson were now both eyeing Dietrich suspiciously.

'Is this true, Dietrich?' Alonzo demanded, as Davidson's fists began to tighten.

'No, of course not,' Dietrich yelled. 'Why would I do such a thing?'

'The *why* is not yet fully clear to me,' Wilcox remarked, 'but I have no doubt it is part of a power-play to take over this Council as sneakily as you did in the case of your own family.'

Dietrich leapt from his seat as quickly as his bulging stomach would allow, and glared down at his accusers. 'That is an absolute lie. I have never challenged this Council and I never would.'

Wilcox stared at the plump little man with his eyebrows raised doubtfully. 'And we can take your word for that, can we?'

Before Dietrich could answer, a loud throaty cough sounded from behind, and all four of the council turned around to look for the source of the noise.

'You can take *my* word, if you like.'

Captain McCray stood in the doorway with his arms folded across his chest, and he looked extremely relaxed given that the armed guards were now pointing their handguns in his direction.

'McCray!' Wilcox gasped in astonishment, then called out to the guards, 'Secure him!' Immediately the six men surrounded McCray as he raised both hands up in the air, as if to ward them off.

'There is no need for that,' McCray said, before folding his arms once again. 'I just wanted to stop by and offer this Council my congratulations on failing the Magi, and having become what I always said it would be... *Useless.*'

Wilcox seemed to ignore the slight while the other members of the Council remained silent, clearly stunned at McCray's sudden and unexpected appearance. 'You're very energetic for a dead man,' Wilcox finally remarked.

'Aren't I,' McCray replied with an amused grin.

'And very cocky for someone with six gun barrels pointed at him.'

'Ah, yes... let's change that situation shall we,' McCray said, and with a click of his fingers all the armed guards did a 180 degree turn and trained their guns on Wilcox and the others instead.

'What!' Wilcox gasped as, behind him, Alonzo got to his feet.

'I demand an explanation,' Alonzo growled.

'You may demand all you want but you deserve nothing,' McCray replied. Then, with a shake of his arm, a slender dagger dropped from his sleeve into the palm of his hand, and in an instant he hurled it directly towards Alonzo. It struck him in the neck, sending the man back into his chair in convulsions and gripping at his throat as blood gushed deep into his lungs. After a few strained gurgles, his expression became blank and his body motionless.

'So sit down and shut up?' McCray ordered, motioning the guards to close in on the rest of the Council, which they did dutifully. 'Now, unless you want to end up like your friend there, I recommend that you all keep your mouths closed and listen to what I have to say.'

McCray made his way over to Alonzo's body and, with a sharp kick, toppled the still bleeding corpse off the chair and sent it to the floor with a thump. He then sat himself down in the empty seat, dropped his feet up on the table top, and shuffled about until he was comfortable. 'Even though you tried to have me killed... which, as you can see, was a wasted effort... I have forgiven you for your betrayal and I am willing to make a trade. You keep your lives and I take control of the Magi.'

Wilcox was already looking totally outraged with his mouth wide open as, with a shake of McCray's other arm, a razor-sharp arm-sword slid down his sleeve and over the top of his hand. The Magi's official weapon of choice then clicked into place with the tip only centimetres from the Magi Prime's neck. 'Now, now... no interruptions,' McCray reminded, as Wilcox struggled but finally succeeded in restraining himself, his cheeks becoming ever redder.

'Since taking over the Magi you have all been guilty of wasting its potential, and in doing so brought all the work of successive generations to a monumental stall. Dietrich, your betrayal is the worst and you are without a doubt the most useless of the lot. Let me offer you a piece of advice.' McCray swivelled his eyes towards the fat little man. 'If you choose to murder your way to the top, brother, then you should first make sure you are actually capable of taking on the role in the first place... As for you,' McCray continued, his gaze moving on to Davidson, 'your continuing corruption of the position you hold, coupled with your devilish preoccupation with lady boys, makes you without doubt the wrong man for the job, wouldn't you agree?'

Davidson now looked highly embarrassed at this revelation of his sexual tastes, and even Wilcox took a moment to mouth the word 'lady boys!' in both surprise and disgust.

McCray continued with his reasoning. 'As for Alonzo,' he said and gesturing to the limp body lying on the floor next to him, 'I don't think that really matters now, does it? And then there is our illustrious leader, Pope Adrian VII, who is quite possibly the most sought-after person on the planet.' McCray shot Wilcox a look of disappointment. 'It's not really a situation that suits a highly secretive organisation such as ours, is it?'

Wilcox remained silent and his eyes drooped slightly at the reality with which he was being forced to confront.

'Under your guidance the Magi has become a bloated and directionless slug, your holiness, and the time has come for new leadership and a return to the values that have guided it successfully for almost two millennia which, I might add, you have fazed out in just a matter of years.'

McCray pulled the arm-attached sword away from Wilcox's neck, then stood up and, with a shake, it retracted back up into his sleeve. He placed his hands behind his back and turned to face his captive audience. 'In light of your recent notoriety and entry into the glare of the world's most wanted, the Magi are expecting a change of leadership. Therefore you, John Wilcox, will contact them and announce that I have been appointed as your successor. I will also need an official endorsement from two Council members and, seeing as Alonzo is no longer with us, that leaves just you two.' McCray gestured to both Davidson and Dietrich.

McCray's demand was met with a look of seething defiance from Wilcox who, incensed by the outrageous suggestion, finally broke his silence.

'You insolent little shit. If you think you can threaten us into giving you the keys to the Magi, you are as stupid as Alonzo is dead,' Wilcox fumed, motioning to Alonzo's still haemorrhaging corpse. 'The position of Magi Prime is not something that can be bartered... it must be earned.'

'Then I will set about earning that right this very instant.' McCray replied, making his way back to the open doorway where, with a flick of his finger, he signalled for the nearest guard to join him. 'I need you to make all of them agreeable in this matter and then have them inform their respective families by video phone, just as we planned, but just make sure you leave their faces unblemished. They can't look like they have been tortured into submission. As for Alonzo's clan, have Wilcox make the announcement.'

The guard gave an understanding bow of his head. 'Yes, my lord. I will notify you when it is done.'

'Good,' McCray replied, glancing back at his captives who looked increasingly twitchy. 'Because when it is done I think I would rather like to kill them myself.'

–

Down below, in the grounds of the chalet, one of the perimeter guards on watch took a moment to enjoy the sight of the night's bright moon bathing the mountainous skyline and the surrounding forest in a cold silver light. The view was stunning and the guard waited for a few more moments before continuing his perimeter sweep of the property, as the rustling of a cool breeze carried itself through the hedges. The sounds and the views on offer were as close to heaven on earth as the guard could imagine and, had it not been for the screams and squeals of agony now coming from the chalet, it would have seemed perfection itself.

Chapter 24

'Professor,' Captain Jones called out from the cockpit, 'I've got an incoming call for you.'

Harker was already looking around for any sign of a phone, when Jones called out, again his voice muffled by the drone of the jet's engines.

'In the arm-rest,' he shouted, turning briefly to point at the side of Harker's chair. 'Flip it open.'

Harker tugged at the grey leather-lined arm rest, which opened up to reveal a tiny storage compartment, and the top of a small plastic-encased monitor comfortably hidden inside. He pulled at it and the device automatically extended upwards on miniature hydraulic pistons, unfolding directly in front of him. The screen then flickered into life revealing a close-up image of Sebastian Brulet.

'Alex can you hear me?' the Templar Grand Master squawked, due to the bad interference.

'Yes, I can hear you,' Harker replied loudly as Chloe, seated behind him, took an interest and poked her head over his shoulder inquisitively.

'Ahh. And hello to you too, Doctor Stanton. It is nice to finally meet you. I had a feeling you would still be with us.' Brulet said it with a hint of sarcasm and briefly glanced towards Harker with raised eyebrows.

'Nice to meet you too,' Chloe replied and having absolutely no idea who this man was.

Brulet offered her a polite nod and returned his attention to Harker. 'I see you've found the third Secret then?'

'Yes,' Harker replied, 'but there was a problem.'

'I know,' came Brulet's blunt response. 'I've been watching the coverage of Jerusalem. It's all over the news.'

'No, not that' Harker said, now fumbling his words. 'I mean, yes, that's a problem but—'

'I would say that is a major problem, Alex,' Brulet interrupted, leaning closer to the screen.

'Sebastian, there was a Magi operative with us back at the Temple Mount,' Harker blurted out, eager to get the conversation immediately back on course. 'It was one of Rabin's men. He pulled a gun on me and he opened the third Secret himself.'

'He pulled a gun on both of us!' Chloe interrupted and was immediately silenced by a dismissive wave of Harker's hand.

'OK, us! But the important thing I found out is that the Magi don't have possession of the child, and they are just as much in the dark as we are regarding the Secrets... That's why they were there,' Harker continued gruffly, allowing his vehemence to get the better of him.

Brulet pulled back from the monitor and raised a finger to his lips pensively. 'It seems I owe you an apology, Alex. I should have given you considerably more attention after Notre Dame.'

The Grand Master turned away and stared off to one side thoughtfully, before refocusing with renewed enthusiasm. 'We need to determine who this Father Strasser was working for.'

Before Harker could say anything, Chloe forcefully pushed Harker to one side and thrust her head closer to the small camera embedded into the top of the monitor. 'They're called the Skoptsy.'

'Do you mind,' Harker exclaimed pushing her back to her previous position, 'this is a private conversation.'

The anger evident on his face did nothing to dissuade her and she squared up to him with a look of equal irritation.

'Not this time, Professor,' Chloe fumed and this use of his formal title received an unamused blank response from Harker, 'I'm just as much involved in all of this as you are, whether you like it or not. So deal with it!'

The uncomfortable silence and unyielding stares exchanged with one another was finally broken by Brulet's calming tone.

'I must say Doctor Stanton, you have a persuasive knack for implanting yourself in other people's business.' The Grand Master paused until both Harker and Chloe had returned their attention back to the screen. 'Not wholly unlike the man sitting next to you, I might add.'

This friendly observation brought a smile to Harker's lips, as he remembered the vigour with which he had forced himself into the

Templar's affairs. Even if initially it had been a matter of circumstance rather than Chloe's less tactful approach.

'Fair enough, Chloe,' Harker said reluctantly, 'but allow me to do the talking until I've brought you up to speed.'

'Thank you, Alex.' Chloe replied graciously, and swiped an imaginary zip across her lips as Harker returned his full attention to Brulet.

'Before Strasser committed suicide, he told us that he was a member of a group known as the Skoptsy. They were... are... a semi-Christian religious sect commonly thought to have died out during Stalin's purge of Russia's religious community back in the nineteen-fifties. Strasser implied that the group was involved or would benefit from the 'end of days' as he put it, brought about by the revealing of the Secrets and the prophecy thereby foretold. He also said he knew nothing about a fourth Secret and, far more importantly, that the Skoptsy would soon have the child in their possession and...' Harker hesitated as he prepared to mention the single and most important fact he had left out during his message to Brulet back in Warsaw. 'And that they planned to sacrifice him, for lack of a better word, which they believe will ensure that their version of the prophecy comes true.'

'What!' Brulet yelled, his eyes widening, offering a clearer view of those cross-shaped pupils of his. The sight produced a soft gasp from Chloe, who had only now noticed the Grand Master's unusual appearance. 'Why didn't you let me know?' he fumed.

'Because you already mentioned how many of your people were divided over what to do about the child, and I thought it was best if I explained the situation to you directly rather than pass it on in a message, having no idea who might read it first.'

The sincerity with which Harker delivered his explanation appeared to ease Brulet's anger and the Grand Master resumed his calm demeanour once more, remaining silent as Harker continued.

'And what with the earthquake at Vatican City and then the chaos in Jerusalem... well, events just took over and I've not had a chance to speak with you until now.'

Brulet took a few moments to consider, then a smile began on his lips, 'I understand,' he replied, 'and we should put aside the notion of a fourth Secret and now simply concentrate on finding the child.'

Harker watched as Brulet exhaled a deep frustrated sigh but not as a result, Harker sensed, of his own omission but rather due to the problems they now faced. 'What happened at Vatican City was a tragedy, and now with the appalling events unfolding in Jerusalem...' Brulet let the sentence taper off, not knowing how to adequately verbalise such a terrible loss of life. 'And you were right not to mention it in your message. In light of recent occurrences, my people are becoming ever more fractured in their attempts to agree on a course of action. But, knowing now that these Skoptsy have the child – or at least soon will – and the implications, I think we can begin to move forward.'

Brulet's positive response was as relieving to Harker as it was confusing. 'How so?'

'After you left the message concerning Strasser's death, I took it upon myself to dig a little deeper into his background,' Brulet declared with a heavy frown. 'I had a contact of mine gain access to his apartment before the police sealed it off as a crime scene, and she came up with some interesting if not peculiar findings. Apart from his morbid collection of bottled remains, which now that I know he is Skoptsy makes a grim kind of sense, she found a data disk containing the names of hundreds of thousands of people. Now, we have not had time to fully sift through it – the list is too vast – but they all seem to have a single connection: they are all devout church-going Christians.'

Before Harker could voice the most obvious question, Chloe asked it for him.

'How did you managed to figure that out?'

'Because, other than a name, address and an identity number of some type, the only other piece of information was which parish they attended. We did some checking and, for the ones we have verified so far, I can tell you they were all dedicated and active members of their local church. Now,' Brulet continued swiftly, 'we've only been able to check a couple of hundred names on that list, but so far that consistently appears to be the case.'

'Could those churches themselves become targets for attacks like at Notre Dame and Jerusalem?' Harker posed and still hoping to put a more down to earth reason on the day's events.

'Unlikely,' Brulet replied flatly. 'So far as we can see none of these churches have been affected in any way. No, whatever the reason for that database, it seems to relate directly to the people listed themselves.'

Harker sat back in his seat and tried to comprehend the reason for making such a data file but nothing immediately came to mind. And before he had time to think about it further, Brulet unloaded another more immediate piece of information garnered from Strasser's stench-ridden apartment.

'My contact also found a notebook containing a log of all Strasser's travels during the past six months. The man was obsessive in the details. Everywhere he's been, flight numbers, restaurants he visited, even the taxi firms he used. Everything neatly logged in this one little notepad and, even though the locations are far and wide and all over the world, he kept returning to one single location again and again.'

Harker was almost salivating at what he hoped Brulet was leading up to. 'Where?' he pressed impatiently.

'In the Ukraine.' Brulet replied. 'About ninety miles from Kiev.'

'Isn't that where they found the priest who was attacked by supposed demons?' Chloe asked.

'Father Baziak, yes. He was found dumped just outside Kiev. It has to be the Skoptsy's headquarters,' Harker assumed, 'and I'll bet there's a very real possibility that the child is being held there.' He continued eagerly, 'So that's where we're going now.'

Harker was already out of his seat and halfway past Chloe towards the cockpit when Brulet's scratchy voice called out after him, the satellite connection beginning to encounter major interference once again.

'Alex, wait.'

Harker stopped immediately and turned back to face the screen.

'I am going to have the exact address sent to Captain Jones, so please take a seat. There's something else you need to know.'

Both Brulet and Chloe's synchronised calm suddenly made Harker feel like a bit of an idiot, and he made his way sheepishly back to the seat. 'Is there a problem,' he enquired in his most professional tone hoping it would absolve him of his embarrassing childlike excitement moments earlier.

Fortunately, Brulet continued without comment. 'I took a look into this Captain McCray fellow you mentioned, and it seems we do have something on him – information we received some years ago from a Magi contact we managed to turn. His full name is Donald McCray and at one time he was being groomed to become the head of one of the Magi families, but something happened and his younger brother was promoted instead.'

'Do you know what it was?' Harker asked, glad to finally be getting some details on the man that had tried to kill him.

'Some internal disagreements between the brothers regarding the direction the Magi was heading. All we know is that the younger brother, Dietrich, had him killed – or at least he thought he had – and then seized the position for himself... Strange though.'

'Why?' Harker asked.

'Because, as I told you once before, the Magi families seek to cut off only the dead wood, as it were, and Dietrich was and is without a doubt the weaker of the two and, considering his family is the Magi's branch associated with assassinations, it makes for an odd choice.' Brulet paused for a moment and then put his curiosity to the back of his mind. 'Anyway, with McCray back, I am working under the assumption that the Magi could well be in the midst of a civil war.'

'That has to be a good thing,' Harker replied happily and encouraged by the idea.

Brulet looked unconvinced and he pursed his lips. 'That all depends on what McCray is seeking to achieve. Given Strasser's own admission that they would soon have the child in their possession and if the Magi are not connected, then it could be McCray himself who is associated with Skoptsy in some way.'

'So the Ukraine it is.' Chloe announced, as if wanting to involve herself in the conversation in any way she could.

'Yes, but we do have another problem though.' Brulet was now looking concerned.

'Why, what is it?'

'The problem,' Brulet replied, 'is that for the time being you are both on your own.'

'How so?'

'The news channels have been awash with stories of the terrorist attacks since Notre Dame but with the Vatican and the unfolding crisis in Jerusalem there has been a near total clampdown across all of the major airlines, and I am embarrassed to say that, even with all my connections, I am well and truly stuck where I am for the moment... as are the majority of my operatives.'

The news that Chloe and he would be acting alone was not as unsettling for Harker as he might have expected. So far they had managed to track down the Secrets without any direct help from the Knights Templar. Still, the idea that they would be going truly solo, without any assistance from Brulet should they need it, was enough to induce a feeling of apprehension.

'I'm sorry to do this to you, Alex, but rest assured I will be doing everything I can to resolve the situation. And, besides which, I do have some friends I can reach out to that may still be of help to you once you reach the Ukraine.'

'I understand, Sebastian. I know you'll do what you can,' Harker offered, 'and until then you count on us to find the child and do what is necessary to ensure his safety.'

Harker's bold statement was meant to reassure the Grand Master but did not appear to have the desired effect.

'I have no doubt of that, Alex, and for the record you have my total confidence but, should you locate the child, I want your word that you will not do anything until you have contacted me.'

In any other circumstance Harker would have agreed to Brulet's request without hesitation but, given the importance Harker had himself placed from the outset upon the child's wellbeing, he was reluctant, and Brulet detected this immediately.

'That is, of course, unless you deem it absolutely necessary, then I will leave it to your own judgement but I urge you to remain cautious,' Brulet said with a stern jab of his finger. 'Remember we have absolutely no idea who or what these Skoptsy are or what they're capable of, so play it safe.'

'I will.' Harker assured him glancing at Chloe who nodded in appreciation and gratitude for the inclusion. 'You have our word.'

A satisfied smile crossed Brulet's face even as his image on the monitor began to fuzz.

'We're starting to lose you, Sebastian.' Harker began tapping at the screen. 'I'll contact you once we learn more.'

'Wait!' Brulet said urgently, moving closer to the screen and realising they were running out of time. 'Two final things. Firstly to you, Doctor Stanton. Even though you are now involved in all this, let me tell you that I am appreciative of your help but I must make it clear that Alex is in charge, and I expect you to defer to his judgement at all times and without exception. Agreed?'

'Agreed.' Chloe replied unwaveringly and without any hint of resistance.

'And secondly, Alex, I need to bring you up to speed regarding...' Brulet paused looking somewhat uncomfortable at what he was about to disclose. 'Claire Dwyer.'

The name hit Harker like a swift punch to the stomach and he stiffened in his seat. 'What is it? Have you found her?'

'No, not yet. Not exactly,' Brulet continued as the monitor's reception became increasingly worse, so only fragments of the Grand Master's voice crackled through the speakers. 'But there… something you need… know. I tried… you see she's…'

The audio abruptly cut out, as did the picture and Harker was left staring at a blank screen. He shook his head in frustration at this lousy timing. 'Damn it,' he muttered angrily. Not a day had passed that Harker's thoughts had not strayed to Claire Dwyer and her supreme betrayal back at the Vatican months earlier.

'Who's Claire Dwyer?' Chloe asked, as Harker folded the monitor back into the armrest.

'Just someone I once knew,' Harker replied, not really wanting to pick at an old wound. He took in a deep breath and began to get comfortable in his seat, when Chloe reached over and lightly placed her hand on his forearm.

'Alex,' she uttered softly, 'isn't it about time you told me what's going on?'

Harker looked up and, seeing the placid inquisitiveness in her eyes, he offered a slow nod. It was indeed about time he gave her all the details and, considering they were going into another potentially life-threatening situation, she at least deserved to know. Not to mention that Brulet's recent blessing on the partnership meant he didn't have to hold back any more. 'Of course. What would you like to know?'

'For starters, who is Sebastian Brulet and why was he wearing those weird contact lenses?'

Her misguided observation made Harker laugh and he took a final deep breath so as to prepare. 'Firstly, those are not contact lenses and, secondly, Sebastian Brulet is the Grand Master of the Knights Templar.'

'What, like the Knights of Malta that Tony Blair belongs to?'

'No. I mean like the original Knights Templars from medieval times.'

His answer caused Chloe to drop her head in disbelief. 'Please,' she replied sarcastically, sinking back into the leather-cushioned seat next to him. 'You must think I'm a moron!'

'I don't think you're a moron, Chloe.' Harker replied smiling at the thought of his own disbelief upon learning of the Templar's survival from the lips of Brulet himself. 'I actually think you are remarkably smart.'

Chloe's eyes brightened at the comment, even though she continued to stare at him suspiciously.

'Sit back and relax, Doctor Stanton,' Harker instructed as he began to enjoy the feeling of being at the enlightened end of things for once, 'and prepare to have your view of the world turned on its head.'

Chapter 25

A hushed silence fell across the waiting onlookers crowding the walls of the twenty-metre-high domed rotunda as the initiate was led in through a side passage carved into the rock and then on towards the three thick wooden posts arranged in a triangle protruding from the floor. Accompanied by two heavily built male escorts garbed in white ceremonial gowns, the initiate – barefoot and clothed in nothing but a black woollen robe – struggled against the yellow rope binding the wrists. The black canvas hood secured tightly around the prisoner's head was held in place by a noose around the neck made from natural fibre, its loose ends hanging down behind like a braid of hair.

The escorts dragged their inductee to the designated position and untied the constraints before each taking a wrist and securing it to the metal rings which were attached to the posts on either side with thick iron screws. With arms splayed out either side, the initiate continued to struggle furiously in an attempt to break free, but after a few feeble attempts the captive's body went limp and seemingly resigned to the fate awaiting it. The escorts now grasped the two pieces of rope dangling down the initiate's back and tied both ends tightly around a third post fixed directly behind, so the noose pulled the victim's head firmly upright until no slack remained.

With a few short tugs, and satisfied that all the ropes were fixed correctly, the two escorts made their way to the edge of the rotunda and took their place silently amongst the other spectators.

Somewhere high above, the low monotone of a blown horn rang out to signal for one of the spectators to make his way towards the captive. Dressed in a dark purple robe secured around the waist with a gold tassel, the man approached the initiate and outlined the sign of the cross with both his index and middle finger before turning to address the audience lining the edges of the room.

'Once again we have in our midst a person plucked from the depths of sin and seeking reconciliation,' the man announced in Russian, his tone gruff and raspy. 'Many times before have we seen one of our own undertake the right of passage: the hard path… the righteous path. The path to enlightenment.'

A soft murmuring of agreement rippled around the arena as the master of ceremonies raised his hands and smiled. 'And now we are blessed with this opportunity to save yet another soul from the clutches of a world that seeks to wallow in the foulness of Lucifer's bile… A world that takes gluttonous pride in the filth and debasement that only false gods can offer… A bleak world that has been raped of its last vestiges of salvation and now stands on the precipice of destruction. A destruction that will finally cast out the sinful and raise up the righteous to bask in the Lord's warmth for all eternity.'

The murmurings now amplified into a louder chorus of appreciation, until their leader raised his hands once again and brought the whole room to silence.

'Here and now we shall allow a lost soul to escape the torment that is to come and grant instead an opportunity to join our ranks. But that path is arduous,' the speaker turned to face the initiate and grasped the tip of the hood firmly, 'and only those possessing the sturdiest of faith may know the wonders that it can provide.'

The speaker swiftly whipped off the black hood and threw it down on to the floor. 'So, outsider,' the man exclaimed, now in English, 'are you prepared to be judged by God almighty and withstand the purging of those demons that you have so readily lain down with – for now is the time to decide.'

Claire Dwyer stared back at the speaker with sweat pouring down her face, and her eyes darted around the rotunda at the many faces all now focused upon her. She tried to speak but only a gurgling could be heard through the thick gag wedged firmly in her mouth.

The speaker listened to the muffled sounds emanating from Claire's throat before deciding for himself what her answer was, and with that he offered an approving nod. 'Good, my child, you have made the right decision.' He reached into his cassock and retrieved a foot-long, curved flaying knife with an intricately carved wooden handle, and raised it in front of him as Claire's eyes widened in panic. 'Rejoice,' he cried out, 'and let the fiery baptism begin.'

Chapter 26

'So they've been around for almost a thousand years, then?'

'Well, the Templar organisation has, but Brulet's family go back much further to a time even before the pyramids at Giza were built,' Harker explained to Chloe, who was still looking highly sceptical.

'Can we put that whole Templar thing to one side for a moment,' Chloe requested with a frown, 'and clarify who the Magi are exactly?'

'You've already met one of their illustrious members back at the Temple Mount.'

'You mean Avi – the man who turned into a drooling psychotic and tried to eat us?'

'Yes, that's the one and, for the record, he tried to eat me not you.' Harker gave a smile in acknowledging the comical nature of Chloe's description of his brush with death. 'Maybe it's best I give you a short history lesson, but let me finish it before you ask any more questions.'

Chloe gave a nod in assent and then, with the teacher in him now taking charge, Harker set about explaining the illustrious chronicle that was the Brulets' family tree and with it the history of the Order of the Templars and its ascension to the position it held today, and the shadowy power and influence it commanded.

'Brulet's ancestors were amongst the first followers of Jesus Christ, and then later on became part of St Peter's devotees following the crucifixion. They actually witnessed Jesus perform the feeding of the five thousand near the Lake of Galilee.'

It was obvious that Chloe was already entertaining doubts from the way she raised her eyebrows, but she remained politely quiet as he resumed the story. It was weird somehow because he had expected to feel like a total idiot on giving this account of Brulet's family background but, after everything he had experienced recently he felt no awkwardness whatsoever, as if the truth itself offered a protective shield against any embarrassment he might have otherwise felt.

'Anyway, the family remained loyal to the newly founded church for hundreds of years, surviving the hostility of the Roman Empire until finally Emperor Constantine declared Catholicism to be the one true faith. 'Now,' Harker instinctively raised his index finger towards the ceiling, 'this is where the Magi come into the picture. A council was established to decide upon how best this new religion should operate; how and where people would worship, and what the edicts and rules would be. It was known as the First Council of Nicaea, and Brulet's family were part of its ruling body. They preached freedom and respect for all men but there was another powerful family on the council who believed that the church should be used as a tool to dominate and enslave the populace... the Magi.'

Harker paused as Chloe politely raised one hand. 'Sorry to inter-rupt but why are they called the Magi?' she asked curiously.

'That's a reasonable question,' Harker assessed, still in teacher mode. 'The Magi believe they are direct descendants of the three kings that paid homage to Jesus at the time of his birth. Those three kings were known as the Magi, so they took this designation for their own'

Satisfied with this explanation, Chloe resumed her role as pupil, even resting her head in her palm like an enthralled schoolgirl.

'After a lot of debate, the Council of Nicaea found a middle ground regarding the mechanics of the Church, but with serious opposition from the Magi who were ultimately ostracised for their extreme views. Nevertheless they continued on the periphery, gathering power and money with the aim of influencing the Church at any opportunity. Brulet's family, on the other hand, grew along with the Church and were eventually instrumental in the formation of the Knights Templars, which has been their role ever since.'

Chloe once again raised a hand. 'But, if my memory of second-year history serves me correctly, aren't I right in saying that the Templars were disbanded centuries ago?'

'That's true, they were, but the reasons for that are far darker than the word 'disbanded' implies. Over the centuries the Templars had become extremely wealthy and the French King Philip IV, who, as luck would have it was a childhood friend of the reigning pope, wanted to acquire their assets for himself. So a plan was hatched to destroy the Templars, under the pretence that they had turned their back on the Church. Many of the Templars were subsequently arrested and tortured but when King Philip raided the Templar's treasure vaults, he found them completely empty. Led by Brulet's family, the remaining Templars had escaped to Scotland on a fleet of ships, with all the Order's wealth on board.'

'Why Scotland?' Chloe now asked, now not even bothering to raise a hand.

'Because back then Scotland was well out of papal reach. The Scots had been considered savages ever since Hadrian built his famous wall cutting off their country from the English mainland. It was the perfect place for wealthy crooks – as the Templars were unfairly labelled – to hide out in. A little bit like Switzerland today,' Harker added with a smile. 'And so, from that day onwards, the Templars used their money and expertise to guide the Church, albeit from a distance, along a different path. A path that was guided by their own agenda.'

'Their own agenda!' Chloe blurted out. 'That's terrible, not to mention completely immoral.'

'It would be,' Harker replied, 'if that was the whole story, but I left out one very important fact.'

'Go on.' Chloe said suspiciously.

'After the battle for Jerusalem AD 1123 towards the end of the Second Crusade, the surviving Templars set about excavating the area believed to have housed the temple of Solomon. The temple was said to hold secrets that could prove devastating to the Church, and to Catholicism at large. Now, the Templars believed it was their sworn duty to prevent these secrets from ever seeing the light of day and, in doing so, protect the Church and the faith. What they discovered, however, would begin the process of the Templar's reformation that changed it into the secret organisation that it has since become.'

'What did they find?' Chloe's keen, demanding look brought a smile to Harker's face as he found himself getting caught up in the story.

'They found numerous Christian relics but the game-changer was a book. A book bound in leather. A book written in Aramaic. A book…'

'I get it, Alex.' Chloe cried out impatiently, increasingly annoyed by Harker's dramatic recital, 'It was a book plain and simple.'

'Do you want to hear this or not,' he replied sharply. 'Do you know how many times I've wanted to tell this to someone, since Brulet first told it to me? Do you have any idea how frustrating it is to know so much and yet be able to impart so little of it to anyone else? I just wanted to have a little fun with it, that's all.'

Chloe already looked slightly guilty and she offered an apologetic smile. 'Sorry, Alex, please continue. There was a book... a leather book...'

'No, forget it.' Harker replied with a wave of his hand. 'You've ruined the moment.'

'Please,' Chloe asked pleadingly, with an exaggerated fluttering of her eyelashes.

'Fine,' Harker continued but this time in a much more serious tone. 'The book they found was a gospel – and not just any gospel. They found *the* gospel.'

'What do you mean? Whose was it?' There was no trace of sarcasm.

'Jesus Christ himself. It was the gospel according to Jesus Christ, in his own words.'

Chloe was now clearly riveted. 'Is that true?'

'Yes, it is,' Harker replied. 'I know because I myself have read it. Initially I only saw a copy but some months back I was given access by the Templars to the original, and it is genuine.'

'What did it say?' she asked in nothing more than a whisper.

'It said a lot but there was one passage that affected the Templars to their core...' Harker prepared himself to recite the excerpt. 'And so I say to all God's children who wish to follow my teachings, do not do so in a place of worship set apart from where it truly matters. If you wish to honour me, then observe my teachings in your daily life and in full view of the world around you. For my message is not something to be regulated, like in a Roman court of justice, but must roam free in the hearts and minds of those who wish to see the Lord's kingdom that lies beyond, and in doing so will change the face of both man and earth forever.'

Chloe remained silent as she chewed over these words and their implications. 'That contradicts the entire way the church is set up, from attending mass to the governing hierarchy!'

'That's what the Templars concluded,' Harker confirmed, 'and even though they decided to remain silent and keep it hidden, that all changed when they were betrayed by the very people whom they were sworn to protect.'

Chloe shuffled to the edge of her seat as if closing the distance between herself and Harker would make his revelation somehow more real. 'So what exactly have the Templars been doing for the last seven hundred years?'

'They've been pushing the Church in a different direction, whilst doing their best to protect the *old* one.'

'How so?'

'It was Templar advisers that encouraged Henry VIII to create the Church of England, by supporting the idea of Protestantism at every turn. If you think about it, they've been remarkably successful at it, too. All Catholics are Christian but no Christian would necessarily consider themselves Catholic, and there are more Christians in today's world than merely Catholics.'

Chloe took a moment to soak up this information, then glanced up with a renewed glint of inquisitiveness in her eyes. 'So what about the Magi? What have they got to do with all this?'

'Whilst the Templars have spent their time trying to create a new path for the church, the Magi have been trying to control it. You'll recall Pope Adrian VII?'

'He's a Magi?!'

'Yes, and they were going to use the cloned Christ child that they created as a tool to bring about a new spiritual revolution, with the Magi standing at the helm.'

'That's cunning,' Chloe replied.

Harker nodded. 'And they would have succeeded, if it hadn't been for the Templars.'

'And you, from the sounds of it,' Chloe remarked frankly.

'I played a part, yes,' Harker replied though not wanting to sound too pretentious.

'So where is the child now?'

'The Templars had him and his mother in protective custody – until Claire Dwyer kidnapped him.'

'That's the name Sebastian mentioned.' Chloe motioned to the armrest and the monitor contained within it.

'She was a friend of mine who turned out to be a Magi spy.'

'Magi? So that's why you thought the Magi had the child?'

'Yes. But, since we confronted Strasser back in Warsaw, I now know that's not true.'

He turned his attention away from Chloe and stared thoughtfully though the window and into the dark skies beyond. 'There are two things that connect the Templars, the Magi and the Skoptsy, and each of them points to a single disturbing conclusion and a question that for the moment is unanswerable, yet must be answered if the conclusion is in fact correct.'

'What are these two connections?' She edged still closer.

'One is that all three now believe that the Secrets, prophecies or whatever you want to call them, hold some kind of power that can affect the real world around us. And secondly they believe the child is the key to determining the outcome.'

'So what's the disturbing conclusion?' Chloe asked, already suspecting the answer but still wanting to hear Harker's take on it.

'With everything we are now seeing, the disturbing conclusion has to be that humanity, after two thousand years of its religious history, is finally approaching the end of the world as we know it... namely Armageddon.'

Chloe's eyes dulled as the logic of her own existence deserted her and she felt like nothing more than a shell, an empty husk with nothing to fill it. 'So, with all that on our shoulders, what's the question?'

Harker turned away from the window and offered her a confused smile. 'Where and what the hell is the fourth Secret?'

'I thought Sebastian said to forget about that.'

'He did,' Harker mused, rubbing at his chin, 'but I just can't shake off the feeling that somehow it's at the centre of all this.'

Minutes passed as they stared at one another in silence, each filled with a sense of hopelessness that seemed to radiate from their bodies like an unnerving vortex of invisible energy tugging at their self-confidence. Eventually it was Chloe who broke this mood of increasing futility with six simple words that pulled Harker instantly back from the depths of depression.

'Do you want to have sex?'

Her question drew a surprised laugh from him as a wide smile crossed his face.

Chloe continued and completely seriously, 'I mean if this is really it, then why not go out with a bang? No pun intended.'

Harker was already opening his mouth in readiness for a reply when Captain Jones's voice crackled over the intercom.

'I've received the exact location in the Ukraine, and am now adjusting our heading, but we're coming up against some severe electrical storms, so I'd ask that you both strap yourself in. This is going to be a rough trip.'

Both Harker and Chloe burst into laughter, their eyes still fixed on one another and, when this finally subsided, Harker was the first to speak.

'Rain-check? If, of course, we survive.'

'If we survive? Maybe,' came Chloe's answer and she was now looking somewhat flushed.

Harker shook his head at the *maybe* part and then turned towards the cockpit. 'Captain, what exactly is our destination?'

'You gonna love this,' Jones replied. 'It's Pripyat.'

'Pripyat!' Harker replied with disbelief in his voice.

'Yep. Should take us a couple of hours but I've got no idea yet where the hell we're gonna land.'

'Pripyat?' Chloe questioned, as Harker turned back to her. 'I've never heard of it.'

'That's because most people know it better by the town it's next to.'

'Why, what's that town called?'

'Chernobyl,' Harker yelled as he struggled to be heard above the thunder now booming outside. 'It's the abandoned and radiated city of Chernobyl.'

Chapter 27

'Welcome to the Ukraine, Professor Harker. I'm Michael Shroder.'

Harker made his way down the Gulfstream's exit steps, followed closely by Chloe, and shook their host's waiting hand. 'Call me Alex and it's a pleasure to meet you, Michael. This is my friend Doctor Chloe Stanton.'

'Nice to meet you, Mr Shroder,' Chloe said before shaking the man's hand.

'I know who you are, Doctor Stanton, and please, call me Michael.'

She nodded courteously and shot Harker a questioning glance, encouraging him to voice what they were both thinking.

'We appreciate the welcome, Michael, but without sounding rude... who are you?'

'Of course, my apologies and, given the circumstances, you have every reason to be wary.' Shroder took a step backwards so as not to appear threatening in any way and he retrieved a small leather wallet from his trouser pocket. 'Sebastian Brulet asked me to offer you every bit of support I could.' Shroder held out the wallet in front of him before flipping it open to reveal an ID card.

'MI6?' Harker seemed impressed by the credentials. 'You're a spook?'

Shroder gave an amused laugh. 'Well, I prefer the term *Government agent*, but essentialy yes, and I am now at your disposal.'

'Then we're very grateful for the assistance.'

'You're welcome. I would have contacted you earlier but, as you may have found out for yourselves, the mobile network has gone down.'

This was news to Harker. He had connection issues back in Warsaw airport but that had rectified itself upon arriving in Jerusalem. He retrieved his iPhone and noted for himself the lack of signal strength. 'When did that happen?'

'Just during the last few hours,' Shroder explained. 'There's no news as to why yet, but it does mean things have become a bit isolated for the moment.'

'Which networks have been affected?' Harker dropped the iPhone back in his pocket.

'So far as I can tell, all of them.'

'That's strange.'

'Yes it is. Very strange.'

Shroder pointed behind him to a white Vogue Range Rover parked at the side of the runway. 'I've arranged for you all the necessary permits to enter Chernobyl's exclusion zone, so if you're now ready to leave...'

'Just one moment, Michael,' Harker said as he gently took Chloe by the arm and guided her to one side. 'I need you to stay here with the plane.'

Her look of indignation caused Harker to immediately raise his hands in front of him defensively. 'Look, I know you want to come, but I have no idea what we're going to find, and I would feel much better knowing that you're safely here.'

But Chloe was already shaking her head firmly from side to side, clearly not prepared to accept his suggestion in the slightest. 'So you're worried about my safety? I can take care of myself, as I think I've proved already.'

'It's not *your* safety I'm worried about, Chloe... It's mine.'

'Yours?'

He moved closer to her so as to be out of earshot of Shroder and Captain Jones, who were now standing at the aircraft's exit hatch making small talk.

'I'm not going to get myself double-crossed again, so if this Shroder character returns without me, I want you to get the hell out of here and make contact with Brulet as soon as possible. You must tell him that he needs to get his own team out to Pripyat as quickly as possible, because if I do disappear, you can guarantee that I uncovered something.'

She remained silent as she scanned his face for any hint of a lie.

'You're the only one I really trust, Chloe.'

She continued to study his expression for a few more moments, then her shoulders slumped reluctantly. 'OK, I'll do it, but how do you know Captain Jones back there isn't a double-crosser as well?'

Although relieved that she was acceding to his wishes, Harker didn't show it and he continued to wear a serious expression. In truth he didn't want to have to be concerned with Chloe's safety, and it would be easier for him to do some snooping alone because it would attract less attention. But if Shroder did turn out to be another Avi, then Chloe would be vital in getting word back to Brulet, assuming the mobile network didn't come back online any time soon.

'I'm pretty sure Captain Jones is on the level, and any way Brulet knows he's with us so that's a good enough indication, but I need you to be our last resort if anything bad happens, OK?'

Chloe finally nodded. 'I understand. I'll stay here. But Alex,' she continued, taking his hand in hers and squeezing it reassuringly, 'You be sure to make it back, you understand?'

'I understand,' Harker replied, then made his way over to the Range Rover before briefly turning back to face her. 'Besides, I've got that potential rain-check to cash in, remember.'

The comment drew a guarded laugh from her, and she offered him a brief wave as he climbed in through the Range Rover's passenger-door and slammed it shut behind him.

'Just us, then?' Shroder asked, while strapping himself in.

'Yes, I don't want her getting further involved if I can help it,' Harker gestured back towards Chloe. 'There's too many unknowns and I've no idea what we're going to find here.'

'Well, that makes two of us, Professor. Sebastian seems convinced that Pripyat is connected with all those global disasters, but he was very sketchy on the why.'

'That's because the details themselves are sketchy, I'm afraid,' Harker offered respectfully.

'But you do reckon that these Secrets,' Shroder probed further as he started up the Range Rover's engine and began navigating his way towards the airstrip's entrance gate, 'are responsible for everything that's been going on?'

'It is a definite possibility,' Harker replied cautiously. 'Even if I am having a difficult time accepting that without feeling like a nut. What do the intelligence services think?'

'Well, of course, none of them has an inkling about these Secrets of yours,' Shroder answered firmly. 'MI6 deals in fact not fantasy, so naturally they're scrutinising the numerous terrorist organisations.'

'And what do you yourself think, Michael?' Harker pressed, feeling slightly idiotic at Shroder's use of the word *fantasy*. 'Are you at all religious?'

'If I wasn't a tad religious I wouldn't be associated with the Templars, but I'll admit my faith has waned somewhat over the years,' Shroder replied. 'However, when I saw half of Vatican City disappear into the ground... I won't lie to you that my belief was stirred a bit.'

They reached the airstrip's entrance, which was no more than a gap in the surrounding hedge, and turned on to the main road leading towards Pripyat. Shroder was still mulling over Harker's question regarding his belief. 'It's an odd sensation, you know.'

'What is?' Harker asked checking that his seat belt was secure as a deep pothole in the road sent the Range Rover and both its passengers bouncing upwards.

'Retaining Christian belief, in the modern world.'

'How so?' Harker asked, rubbing his knee where it had impacted with the dashboard.

'A person can have absolute belief in religion, and the concept of miracles and prophecies is part of that acceptance on some level, but when confronted with these notions head-on, such as with recent events, the same people usually have a great difficulty in taking them seriously and immediately look instead to terrorists.'

Harker managed a nod but remained silent.

'The strange thing is that it's usual before any terrorist attack for the chatter to go quiet.'

'Chatter?' Harker questioned being unfamiliar with the term.

'Communication between terrorist groups and their people,' Shroder explained. 'We term it chatter and it always goes silent right before an attack in case we could pick up any communication that might reveal details of the planned strike. I contacted one of my American friends with the Company and he told me that the chatter being received at the NSA didn't even blink throughout, and even increased during it.'

'What does that imply?' Harker asked, although already understanding its significance but wanting to hear Shroder's professional assessment.

'It implies that the usual terrorist groups were just as surprised as we were.'

Their forty-five minute journey to the exclusion zone proved a welcome respite for Harker, even if he had managed to grab some sleep during the continual electrical storm that Captain Jones had correctly predicted for their flight over. Chloe had not been so fortunate, given her terror of thunderstorms, and she had remained silent and rigid throughout. In stark contrast, Shroder had seemed highly curious about Harker's reason for venturing into this radioactive area that had seen the worst nuclear-reactor disaster of all time, when one of the cooling towers had gone into meltdown back in '86. The poisoned dust cloud thrown into the atmosphere had then circled the globe and was thought to have caused a million cases of thyroid cancer worldwide, even if the Soviet government had recorded only thirty-six deaths, and almost all of them related to accidents occurring during the subsequent clean-up. Typical Soviet propaganda in action. A thousand-square-mile exclusion zone had been set up around Chernobyl within days of the accident, and its thousands of residents evacuated.

'There are still some highly radioactive hotspots hereabouts,' Shroder informed 'however hundreds of people have moved back into the area over the years, and tourists from all over the world make visits to Pripyat every day,' he explained, 'but I personally wouldn't want to spend any length of time there.'

Shroder's assurances that the zone was now safe to visit was reassuring, but Harker was nonetheless relieved when the MI6 agent pointed to the two electronic Geiger counters laying on the back seats.

'These will help us navigate any seriously dangerous areas,' he offered assuredly. 'But it would help if I knew exactly what we were looking for.'

'I only have this address in Pripyat to go on, but it seems connected somehow to the Secrets. I'm afraid we're going to have to play it by ear,' Harker replied not wanting to divulge the existence of the Skoptsy just yet. If Brulet had not mentioned it, then Harker would follow suit until necessity demanded otherwise.

'There it is now.' Shroder was pointing to a grey army checkpoint, with a red and white striped barrier, and the two well-built soldiers in Ukrainian military uniforms patrolling it. 'Should be no trouble but let me do the talking.'

Shroder pulled up to the barrier, exited the car and approached the two guards with his permission papers in hand. A few pleasant exchanges later and the guards were waving them through with polite smiles.

'That was easy.'' Harker remarked, surprised that the soldiers had not wanted to search the car.

'I told you, they get dozens of tour visits every day.' Shroder then lifted aside his grey duffel jacket to reveal a silver Browning semi-automatic holstered securely underneath his armpit. 'Just don't flash a gun at them and you'll be fine.'

The sight of the handgun made Harker tense up ever so slightly, but Shroder noticed and was already shaking his head.

'Just a precaution,' the agent assured him, 'but when I'm asked to go into a place with no questions asked, it pays to be prepared. It seems you're a jumpy one, Alex.'

'Well, I've had an extremely unpredictable time of it recently,' Harker replied ruefully.

'Yes, Sebastian told me about that Magi agent back in Jerusalem. They're nasty little shits.' Shroder added with a distasteful snarl.

It was the first time the MI6 agent had exposed any depth of knowledge regarding Templar business, and it relieved Harker to know that he wasn't the only one in the car with the burdensome secret.

'I'm surprised, though, that Rabin got duped by him,' Shroder continued, referring to the Mossad chief Harker had been detained by upon first arriving in Jerusalem. 'The old man must be losing his touch.'

'You know Rabin, then?' Harker asked.

'The intelligence services form a surprisingly small community and, besides, he's a Templar.'

'So you are also a Templar?' Harker guessed. Apart from Shroder revealing his connection to Brulet, the MI6 agent had not, until now, imparted any further personal details during this trip.

'Not exactly,' Shroder replied, 'but Sebastian and I have a long history. And, besides, finding the child transcends all other loyalties, as far as I'm concerned.'

'So you know?'

'Absolutely.' Shroder declared firmly. 'It's one of the main reasons I am here with you right now. What I don't know is who has him and why Pripyat?'

With this admission Harker now felt comfortable laying out exactly what he knew. 'They're called the Skoptsy.'

'The Skoptsy? I'm not familiar with the name.'

'They're a radical quasi-Christian group with a proclivity for self-inflicted castration as a way to prove their faith.'

'Ouch,' Schroder exclaimed with a wince. 'They sound a fun crowd.'

'I know, right.' Harker agreed. 'I ran into one of them in Warsaw, a fellow called Strasser, and it was he who confirmed they had the child – or would do by now – and how they believed he would be instrumental in ensuring the prophecies are fulfilled in their name.'

'What, like a sacrifice?'

'That's what the man said.'

Shroder patted the side of his duffel jacket with a thankful expression. 'Then I'm glad I brought the gun.'

'So am I,' Harker replied, 'because if I am right then Pripyat may be their centre of operations, or whatever you want to call it.'

This last information earned a deeply concerned glance from Shroder, who began to accelerate. 'Then we should hurry.'

It took a further ten minutes of speedy driving before the tall grey building blocks of Pripyat loomed into view on the horizon. Covering an area only four square miles, the now deserted town resembled a snapshot of old-time Soviet life, albeit a weathered one. The entire population had been evacuated immediately upon news of the meltdown at the Chernobyl nuclear plant, which could be seen just a few miles off in the distance. The inhabitants had all dropped whatever they were doing at the time and just left, abandoning their homes along with all their worldly possessions, and even highly valued Soviet-style Lada vehicles had been left there to rust for fear of having been contaminated from the radiation spill. The approach roads, without regular upkeep, had split and cracked due to the weather, and the majority of them were now overgrown by dense vegetation, as nature continued to reclaim the evacuated area. As the Range Rover turned into one of the many neglected streets, Shroder slowed down in order to navigate around dense bushes and sprouting trees, and it took a few minutes of negotiating similarly decaying streets before they reached their destination.

'That's the place,' Shroder announced, pointing towards a shabby-looking block of grey flats. He then parked the vehicle in the first available clearing and turned off the engine. 'It looks totally abandoned,' the man remarked, as Harker opened the passenger door and stepped out onto a tarmacked street with large cracks created by the encroaching vegetation that had pushed the surface up from beneath. The sound of the Range Rover's doors slamming shut echoed down the empty street to announce their arrival, and Harker was immediately aware of how quiet it was. There was no sound at all, not the chirping of birds or even the wind bristling through the trees. Just total silence.

'Eerie, isn't it?' Shroder observed, now making his way round to join Harker on the other side of the car. 'I'm bringing these with us, just in case,' he said holding up two gas masks before clipping them to his belt. 'And don't forget this.' He handed his companion one of the compact yellow Geiger counters Harker had seen on the trip over. 'I've set it up so as to flash on detecting any dangerous level of radiation.' Shroder pointed to the LED display. 'Then you know it's time to turn back and find another way around. There are pockets of heavy radiation all over this place, so keep an eye on the display at all times.'

'I will,' Harker replied, clipping the counter to his jacket, about halfway down, so he could easily glance down at it.

'And don't pick anything up in case it's absorbed enough radiation to cause sickness. Oh, and, really important, this one.' He pointed towards the clumps of green vegetation lining the edges of the pavement. 'That type of moss is completely irradiated, so don't get too close and, for God's sake, don't pick any of it up.'

Harker watched patiently as Shroder scanned the area for other things to avoid. 'You know, in fact, it's best if you just don't touch anything, not if you value retaining a full head of hair.' He said it with a smirk before he raised his Geiger counter and inspected it. 'The reading is still low, but I've got a pair of hazmat suits in the boot of the car if we need them... OK, let's go take a closer look.'

With Shroder in the lead, they made their way along the road to the corner of the nearest residential block, then stopped at the entrance. Two doors lay in front of it that had rotted off their hinges.

'Before we go in,' Shroder held his hand out in front of Harker, 'you should be warned that some of these buildings are inhabited by the local wildlife.'

'What kind of wildlife?' Harker asked, grasping firmly his Geiger counter as if it were a weapon.

'Well, there are the packs of wild dogs but they mainly keep to the surrounding forests, and apparently there are some black bears that occasionally take up residence in these delightful buildings.' Shroder gestured towards the vast concrete blocks towering above them. 'But I've never myself seen any. Still, its best to keep that in mind.'

'Thanks,' Harker replied uneasily, wishing now that he had a gun of his own, 'I'll do that.'

Shroder was already making his way up the steps leading into the dark murky interior, when something caught Harker's attention. A few metres to the side of the entrance a Russian signpost was poking out of the ground, but it wasn't the notice that caught his attention but something scratched on it. Something familiar.

'Hold on.' He called out and made his way over to the now redundant sign, followed attentively by Shroder. As he got closer to the rusting piece of metal he was able to fully make out the image that had caught his interest. In the top right-hand corner, a symbol had been roughly scratched into the surface.

'What does it mean?' Shroder asked, motioning to the half circle with a triangle in the middle of it.

'I saw it at Strasser's apartment.' Harker replied, thinking back to the label adorning the tasty jars they had found in the man's bedroom. 'It's definitely the same symbol.' He stood back and, with his finger, followed the direction that the signpost was pointing – over to a gap forced through the bushes at one side of the building. 'Let's have a look over there.'

Harker covered the ten metres in seconds and was already preparing to make his was through the opening, when Shroder called out.

'Wait,' he commanded, and hurried past Harker with his Geiger counter extended. He spent a couple of seconds checking the display, before allowing them to continue. 'The readings are low,' he stated confidently, 'but I'll go first, and try not to brush against any leaves.'

Harker nodded in silence and then followed his guide into the leafy breach.

Once inside, they found a neat passage had been hacked through the vegetation, with the surrounding bushes offering cover and thus making it impossible for it to be spotted from the air. They followed this gloomy trail further until through a cluster of twisted branches, they began to see hints of white and gold somewhere off in the distance through gaps in the dense undergrowth. Another thirty metres and the trail opened up into a circular clearing, finally revealing the source of those colours.

The weathered white wood-ribbed chapel sat comfortably wedged inside the clearing, surrounded by towering pine trees. Long green strands of ivy ran up its sides, curling themselves around the black bars covering the plain-glass windows as well as the cracked and punctured gutter that lined the roof. The single spire was topped by the familiar bulbous tulip-shaped cupola that adorned most Russian Orthodox churches, supported by the typical single square room that had once provided the interior place of worship.

'Nicely hidden.'' Harker remarked quietly, so as not to attract attention from any possible occupants.

Shroder offered a nod of agreement and followed Harker as he made his way along the chapel's nearest external wall to its farthest end, where he paused and cautiously poked his head around the corner. Once certain that the coast was clear, he began to carefully make his way through the tight one-metre wide gap between the chapel wall on one side and the thick hedge of bushes on the other. All this while he had to make sure his clothes did not come in direct contact with the thick vegetation, as per Shroder's previous instruction.

The wood-slated arched porch revealed a thick white-painted double door, and Harker placed his ear next to it, listening for any sign of activity inside. There was nothing but silence and, with a wary nod to Shroder, he turned the weathered black handle and slowly pushed one door open with his jacketed forearm.

The charming rustic appearance of the chapel's exterior turned out to be the only positive thing the building had going for it and Harker felt a twinge of disappointment at what he found inside. The single room comprising the building had been mostly gutted except for a few cracked pews lying abandoned on the floor. The remaining floor tiles were broken, and the missing spaces in between revealed a layer of filthy black concrete coated with dust and mildew.

Harker made his way further into the chapel as Shroder closed the door behind them, all the while still checking his Geiger counter.

'It doesn't look as if it's been used in a while.' Schroder concluded, as he placed the implement back in his pocket once satisfied that there was no call for alarm.

'No, it doesn't,' Harker agreed, making his way further inside, 'but that's what they would want you to think.'

Harker cast his eyes around looking for any sign of an interior door, but there was none so far as he could see. Then a dark-red stain on the opposite wall drew his attention. 'Looks like blood,' he said, thinking back to the deep bite marks Father Baziak had displayed. As he continued to scrutinise the ruined interior, Harker suddenly froze with the feeling that someone was watching him. He remained still as his eyes darted back and forth before finally settling on two white dots in the darkest corner of the room. He stared at them... and the dots stared back, as Harker felt a heavy knot begin to tighten in his stomach. They weren't dots, but a pair of tiny eyeballs and as he attempted to get Shroder's attention, the eyeballs began to flicker nervously from side to side.

'Michael!' Harker managed to yell just as the eyeballs leapt forward from the dark corner, revealing a frightened-looking stoat which scurried past them and out through a small hole in the wall, sending Harker stumbling backwards with a jerk.

'Bloody hell,' he gasped before shaking his head in embarrassment.

'They're pretty small these Skoptsy, aren't they?' Schroder chuckled as his companion offered an embarrassed smile, and then returned to his inspection of the room.

'What about that?' Harker said pointing to an outline on the floor. At first he thought he must be looking at the faded sun mark where the base of an altar had once stood, but on moving closer he could see that it was a line of dust in the shape of a rectangle. He kneeled down for a closer look.

'That could be a trapdoor,' Shroder remarked, pointing out the tiny ridge of dust outlining the rectangle, and his observation was met with an agreeing nod from Harker.

Harker pulled a plain white handkerchief from his pocket and, using it as a protector, he ran his finger along the line of dust until it sank into a circular crevice. He then used the piece of linen to delicately wipe away the surface, revealing a small iron ring handle. Harker carefully cleaned away more of the dust until a floor-set doorway was visible, cleverly edged with an overlap so there was no obvious sign of the entrance unless someone was actively looking for it. Harker grasped the ring handle and glanced back at Schroder. 'This is either going to lead us to the salvation of the world or to a stinky old basement.'

'I'm going to go with the basement,' Shroder offered before retrieving the silver Browning from his holster, 'but I'm a cautious fellow nevertheless.'

'Well, I hope you're wrong,' Harker replied, pulling on the ring handle and lifting the trapdoor to reveal a wooden ladder leading downwards into pitch blackness. 'Because, if not, we've hit a dead end... and so has the child.'

Chapter 28

'Are you kidding me? If some idiot had called in with a drunken spiel, do you honestly think I'd waste my time with it?'

Eric Paulson stared blankly at his boss as the CNN news van's front left tyre sank sharply into one of the road's many potholes, which sent his forehead smacking hard against the windshield. 'Ow, Russell you prick, take it easy,' Paulson yelled as he rubbed his head, which was already beginning to swell with a nasty red mark.

Russell Taylor may have been one of the up-and-coming reporters at the news channel, but it hadn't stopped him from being an asshole. What had one of the other cameramen called him? *A legend in his own mind.* Cameraman Eric Paulson had been working with this prima donna for less than a week but that was long enough for him to know their working relationship was, and would remain, non-existent. Of course that was fine by him so long as the stories they were chasing were good enough but, from what Taylor had told him so far, this latest one was far from anything special. 'So we're going after a dog-attack story then?' Paulson asked in a tone that suggested he was struggling to get inspired by the idea of a canine scoop.

'No, you fucking idiot,' Taylor shouted as the van's tyre hit another pothole that sent them both bouncing into the air this time. 'It's like a pack of wolves, only bigger.'

'What, like a group of Saint Bernards?' Paulson replied sarcastically, trying not to laugh out loud at the idea. They were here in Spain to get political coverage of the newly elected Prime Minister, not some pet-related yarn. 'Do you think they'll have the mini barrels of whisky hanging from their dog collars?'

'I swear to God, Eric, if you don't start taking this seriously I'm dropping your bearded ass for another cameraman.'

'OK, OK, I'm being serious now,' Paulson replied firmly and sobered by the threat. 'So what exactly are we looking for?'

Taylor took a moment to narrowly miss another pothole before glancing over at his subordinate with a look of wild-eyed excitement. 'The police radio's been lit up over the last twenty minutes with dozens of reports that the village of Valdemanco is under siege from a horde of wolves, except these animals are apparently twice the size and, if the reports are true, they've already killed twelve people.' Taylor stopped to catch his breath and was clearly thrilled at the prospect of an ongoing body count. 'It's fucking anarchy out there,' he yelled excitedly, 'and we're gonna be the first ones to cover it.'

Within five minutes they were pulling into the village's main street, where Taylor brought the van to a screeching halt just in time to avoid running into a crowd of terrified inhabitants fleeing in the opposite direction. Paulson jumped out of the passenger side and slid open the side door to retrieve his camera equipment, as Taylor hustled past the flow of frightened people and pulled himself up on the vehicle's bumper to see what was happening further down the street.

Anarchy was right, Taylor thought as he watched a surge of freaked-out faces all pushing their way towards him. Further up he could see a teenage boy trip up and disappear underneath them as an elderly woman was barged off the pavement by two petrified-looking men who then trampled right over her. He jumped down off the bumper just as Paulson arrived with the camera perched on his right shoulder, and immediately pointed out the old lady who was now being crushed by yet another group of frantic people trying to escape.

'We have to do something. She's being flattened!' Taylor shouted.

'I'll get her away,' Paulson shouted over the ruckus of the crowd, and he began to pass the camera over to Taylor who immediately shoved it back into the cameraman's arms with a look of astonishment. 'Don't try to help her, you idiot,' he fumed, repeatedly pointing towards the frail old woman whose raised arm was beginning to go limp. 'Film her!'

As Paulson busily burned up tape of the old lady slowly being crushed to death, Taylor leapt back on to the van's bumper and scanned the street for any sign of the wolves he had heard about on the police radio. At first he couldn't see anything other than screaming people but, finally, as the crowd began to thin out, something else caught his eye at the top of the street. Something black. Something big. It was too far away to make out any of the features clearly, but he called out to Paulson and pointed in its direction. Turning back to get a better look he just caught the dark apparition darting away down a side street whereupon Taylor jumped off the bumper, grabbed Paulson and pulled the cameraman in front of him.

'OK,' he said, taking the microphone from Paulson's jacket pocket and holding it up to his mouth. 'Keep the footage fluid and follow me. Be ready because I want to get some close-ups of these creatures.'

Paulson nodded warily. 'Where are they?'

'Along there,' Taylor replied, gesturing towards the end of the street where he had last spotted the dark shadowy form. 'In three, two, one... I'm Russell Taylor reporting to you from Valdemanco where there have been reports of nature reclaiming this once idyllic village in the form of a pack of ravenous wolves that are currently attacking the residents. We have unconfirmed reports of over twelve people already dead and, from what we have gathered since arriving here, something has got the entire populace running scared. We can confirm we are the first outsiders on the scene, and the police have yet to arrive. Presumably they will bring specialised units capable of handling these vicious animals. Come with me now as we attempt to shed some more light on this horrible event that could be taken straight out of a Hitchcock movie...'

From somewhere up ahead a deep growl echoed down the street, silencing Taylor mid-sentence. He dropped the microphone to his side and signalled for Paulson to follow him, even as a dark shadow appeared from one of the side streets. The animal's thick coat was jet-black in colour, making it difficult to clearly determine its features in the gloom, and the only thing Taylor could make out for sure was that it walked on four legs.

The reporter watched as the animal made its way into the centre of the street and then it stopped and stared back at the pair of them. Further high-pitched whines could be heard as yet more of the beasts emerged from the shadows and joined the first one, until there were four of them in all, silently staring in Taylor's direction.

Behind him Paulson continued to film. 'Russell,' he called out nervously, 'Those things are not wolves. We should get back to the van.''

Taylor was still gawping intently, as if mesmerised by the creatures, when one of them did something that caused him to take a step backwards. The leader reared up to stand on its two hind legs with the balance of a human being, and sniffed the air for a moment before dropping back on to all fours. It then took a step forward, and then another and another… with each step becoming quicker until it was running full-pelt towards them.

'Run.' Paulson cried out as he dashed back to the van, leaving Taylor standing frozen to the spot. Paulson flung open the passenger door, jumped in and then aimed his camera back towards Taylor, just in time to catch the creature reaching him.

The force of impact sent the reporter flying backwards on to ground, with the animal clinging to his struggling body. It began to tear into his neck with a set of sharp, jagged, white teeth that sent an eruption of dark blood spraying on to the road around them like a burst water balloon. Further down the street, the rest of the pack were now sprinting with the same ferocity as the first. But when they reached Taylor's lifeless body, instead of joining in, they kept going and headed straight towards the van.

Paulson had already thrown the camera on to the dashboard and he was frantically twisting the ignition key, and the engine burst into life just as the animals reached him. Two of the beasts went to either side as the third jumped up on to the bonnet and head-butted the windscreen with such force that the safety glass, although remaining intact, shattered and thus prevented Paulson's view of the creature as it continued to slam against it.

He threw the engine into reverse and sped backwards before sliding the vehicle round almost one hundred and eighty degrees, sending the one on the bonnet flying off and down on to the road, just as another of the beasts collided with the side door with a weighty thump. Paulson then flipped the van into first gear and sped off like a maniac, clipping two parked vehicles in the process, as deep growls and snarls resonated alongside the van. As he began to gain some distance, he could hear the sounds of howling begin to fade and he allowed himself a small sigh of relief.

'What the fuck,' he muttered, struggling to relax his shaking hands that were clasped so tightly around the steering wheel. Whatever those things were, they weren't wolves. He now took a moment to steady himself, thankful that the only sound he could now hear was from the van's engine as he accelerated faster.

Regrettably for the cameraman, he would only have a few more minutes of such calm before the road beneath him began to tremble.

Chapter 29

The bolted-on ladder creaked beneath him as Harker warily made his way deeper into the murky void, the dim sunlight shining down from the chapel above illuminating only the wooden steps themselves. He could just make out a floor at the bottom before, with one final stride, he stepped off the ladder and onto it, chips of gravel crunching under the soles of his shoes. The air was cool but not at all damp, as Harker had been expecting, and he pulled out his iPhone and switched on its light, holding it out in front of him to reveal his surroundings.

It wasn't any ordinary basement, that much he was certain of, and as he swung the tiny beam of light around him, he realised he was standing in an excavated stone passage about three-metres-high and with roughly hewn side walls. This narrow channel ran for a further twenty or so metres, until it turned a corner that was illuminated by a dim glow of light coming from somewhere further up. At first Harker thought it was from a torch held by someone moving it back and forth, but on second glance he realised it was the flickering of a flame that cast dancing shadows along the intervening walls.

'Are you coming back up?' Shroder hissed from overhead. 'Or am I coming down?'

Harker said nothing but instead gestured for the MI6 agent to join him. He didn't want to risk making any noise until he was sure the light source up ahead wasn't in human hands.

Shroder understood and unclipped the two gasmasks from his belt and dropped them on the floor next to the opening, before silently making his way down the ladder to join Harker who was already taking his first steps into the passageway.

'We won't need gasmasks deep down here,' Shroder whispered on turning his attention to the dark passage. 'It's not just a basement, then?'

Harker shook his head and motioned forwards with his hand before continuing quietly towards the corner up ahead. There he gingerly poked his head round the corner to see what lay further on.

The passage shortly opened up into a larger cavity which was empty bar a solitary oil lamp held in place by a rusty bracket attached to the wall with metal rivets. The hollowed-out space acted as a crossroads for another two passages, leading left and right, with the original alleyway continuing directly ahead of them, lit only by an identical oil lamp placed further along.

'We follow the light,' Harker whispered quietly, after flashing his phone torch down the other two passageways and seeing nothing but gloom.

Shroder nodded silently and, with his automatic clasped firmly in both hands, he followed closely as Harker continued along the lit passageway.

They had covered just a few steps when a shuffling noise forced both men to swiftly retreat and duck into the darkness of the passage leading off to their left. Harker immediately turned off his torch as both men moved deeper into pitch blackness, each hugging the wall. They then waited as the now recognisable sound of footsteps got closer.

A hooded and robed figure emerged into their line of sight, then came to a halt right in the middle of the crossroads. Carrying a small wicker basket containing an assortment of vegetables, the figure placed it on the floor and then slowly pulled back his hood to reveal a sight that made Harker feel sick as he watched from the shadows. The man was missing his left ear which appeared to have been crudely ripped off, leaving tags of flesh, and even though long healed the sight brought one single thought to Harker's mind: *Skoptsy*.

The mutilated man lifted his nose and began to sniff the air around him with interest and then turned and stared in their direction with a pair of piercing, dark-brown eyes.

Harker was sure the man must have seen him but he remained motionless holding his breath and all the time cursing that small bottle of cologne he had found and made use of during the flight over.

The man took a few more sniffs and once satisfied he replaced his hood, picked up the basket, taking a moment to light another one of the wall lamps with a plastic Bic lighter, before continuing around the bend until well out of sight.

Harker expelled a breath of relief even as Shroder tapped him on the shoulder and motioned towards the now better-lit passage, urging him to follow. They made their way cautiously down to the bend and then stopped as, further along, the robed man came to a halt next to a wooden door. He then unlocked it and made his way inside, leaving it open behind him.

Before Harker had time to decide on what to do next, Shroder was already making his way quietly towards the open door. Then, with the butt of his gun raised ready to strike, he waited. A few seconds later the same man reappeared and, as he turned to close the door behind him, Shroder brought the weapon down hard against the back of his neck. The robed man fell to the floor and was promptly dragged back inside by Shroder, even as Harker hurried over to join him.

Inside, Harker found the earlier man splayed out on the stone floor wearing nothing but a pair of filthy longjohns while Shroder, having whipped off his belt and relieved him of the robe, was already hog-tying him.

'Put on that robe.' Shroder urged as he finished securing the unconscious victim but this instruction was met with a look of defiance from his companion, who was wrinkling up his nose at the smell of the filthy and heavily stained garment.

'I've got another idea,' Harker replied resentfully. 'Why don't *you* put it on?'

'Because I've got the gun, remember,' Shroder said, waving the Browning automatic in front of him, 'and you need a disguise.'

Harker once more glanced down at the foul-smelling robe, before turning back to Shroder. 'How about I take the gun and you take the disguise?'

His request was met with an uncompromising stare from Shroder, and Harker exhaled a disheartened sigh.

'Fine,' he said, picking up the robe and begrudgingly slipping it on over his clothes, and then inspecting the garment further. 'Is that a urine stain?'

A light murmur coming from a pile of loose hay in the corner stopped him from answering his own question and they both spun around with Shroder's gun raised defensively.

They watched in silence as a hand reached up above the pile, then flopped limply back down, as another deepening murmur could be heard. Harker instinctively moved towards it whilst Shroder continued to cover him. He reached the hay pile and his eyes followed the hand to a body lying directly behind it, out of sight from where they had been standing. Harker reached over and brushed away wisps of hay to reveal a woman's face. In an instant all thoughts of the noxious robe vanished as he found himself staring into the eyes of someone who had occupied his thoughts frequently over the past four months.

'Claire?'

Claire Dwyer stared back at him, wearing a similar if not vastly cleaner robe than his own. Her eyes were glazed, her lips dry and cracked, and she winced in pain as she struggled to speak. 'Alex? Is that you?'

He had mulled over many times exactly what he would say to this woman that had betrayed him so callously back in Vatican City all those months ago. But, as he looked down upon her in such a weakened state, he couldn't help but feel sympathy for the miserable and wretched-looking creature that lay in front of him. 'Yes, it's me, Claire.' He began pulling her up off the floor and gently laying her on top of the pile of hay, even though she yelped in pain.

'You know her?' Shroder asked, closing the door for fear of the interest another yelp might attract.

'It's a long story,' Harker replied, glancing back at him before returning his attention to Claire and the skin discoloration now visible through a gap in her robe. Harker reached over and carefully tugged at the cloth, and it slipped away to reveal such a horrific and disturbing sight that he raised his wrist to his mouth to stop himself gasping loudly. Both of her breasts had been removed and the open wounds then cauterised by a branding iron, in some kind of medieval mastectomy. The burns looked fresh but there had been no attempt to dress or bandage these wounds and, judging by the amount of pain Claire was in, no drugs or painkillers had been given.

The sight would have made Harker vomit had it not been for her eyes staring up at him as if looking for any sign of reassurance, compassion or *anything* for that matter.

Behind him Shroder lowered his gun and his eyes widened at the gruesome sight, while Harker began to wipe away the thick beads of sweat covering her face.

'Oh, my God, Claire,' he murmured trying to remain strong for her sake. 'What have they done to you?'

Claire's lips quivered as she struggled to talk, the pain clearly so absolute that it clouded her mind and scattered her thoughts. 'The Skoptsy have… the child,' she managed to hiss through clenched teeth. 'You have… to save him.'

'Don't talk, Claire. It doesn't matter right now.' Harker glanced around the cell for anything that might offer her even an ounce of comfort – water or anything – but all he could see was the basket of vegetables in the wicker basket that had been brought here no doubt for sustenance. He turned back to her as she clasped his hand, her sweaty palm slipping against his, but he held on firmly as she continued to force more words from her mouth.

'No, you need to know the truth,' she spluttered while fighting the fresh wave of pain that overcame her. 'I'm… I'm…'

'I know you're sorry, Claire,' he guessed, not wanting her to strain herself any more than she had to.

She shook her head forcefully as she struggled to control the spasms convulsing her. 'I'm not sorry…' she continued, as her eyes begin to flutter. 'I'm a Templar.'

With those last words, Claire's whole body seemed to wilt, her limp hand slipping from Harker's and falling to her chest.

'Claire!' he shouted, pressing his finger to her neck and feeling for any trace of a pulse. But there was nothing. 'I can't feel a pulse,' he yelled back towards Shroder who dropped the gun and pushed Harker to one side before beginning to administer CPR.

Harker watched completely numb as the MI6 agent lifted up her neck into the correct position, then placed his mouth over hers and exhaled fresh air into her lungs. He then placed both hands on her scarred, seared chest and began to push up and down rhythmically. 'Did you know she was a Templar?' he questioned, as he worked on Claire's still lifeless body.

'No,' Harker replied and completely shocked by her admission. 'I had no idea.' His mind was buzzing so hard he was finding it difficult to focus. Claire Dwyer a Templar? Could it be true? And why didn't Brulet know? Harker shook his recognising at the obvious illogical assumption on his part. Of course Brulet knew. He just didn't tell him… but why?

'She's gone, Alex,' Shroder uttered despondently, before wrapping the robe back over her body and resting his back against the wall. 'I'm sorry but there's nothing else I can do.'

All the questions and accusations flying through Harker's mind were suddenly replaced with a furious anger at the sight of Claire's motionless body, and he turned towards the unconscious Skoptsy lying tied up on the floor next to him. 'How the fuck could someone do that to another person, especially a woman?' Harker uttered aggressively, his fists clenching and a feeling of uncontrollable rage fizzing in his veins.

'These people are sick bastards, that's how,' Shroder answered, and he began to say something else but Harker didn't hear it because all he could do now was focus on the Browning handgun discarded on the floor. He lunged over and snatched up the automatic and then leapt on to their hog-tied captive, pushing him over on to his side and pressing its muzzle against the man's temple. He then cocked it and, with a shaking hand, fought a growing impulse to pull the trigger. 'What kind of man does that to a woman?' Harker repeated, searching for a reason not to give in to absolute and complete bloody rage.

But it was Shroder who answered him. 'Alex,' Shroder said, kneeling next to him, 'I wouldn't blame you for pulling the trigger but, before you do, I ask that you just think about it. Firstly, if you pull that trigger those other sick bastards are going to come scurrying quick and fast, and the child which you, I and Claire want so much to protect won't stand a chance. And secondly, killing someone *changes* you... and it's a change that can never be reversed. I heard about that Magi operative you had to shoot at the Temple Mount, but you were clearly defending yourself and any sane person would have done exactly the same thing. But...' Shroder paused for a moment and took deep breath, '... if you do this, it's cold-blooded murder and you're not a murderer, Professor Alex Harker, you are a good man.' Shroder raised his open hand in front of him. 'So how about now we make sure Claire Dwyer didn't die for nothing and let's get this child as far away from these creeps as possible?'

Shroder's final plea had the desired effect, and Harker began to ease his grip on the automatic. With a shake of his head, he expelled a deep breath and dropped the gun into MI6 agent's waiting palm.

'You're right,' Harker said taking off the robe and dropping it to the floor, 'but I'm doing it without this stinking thing.' He turned his attention back to Claire's still corpse as Shroder nodded and ripped a piece of cloth from the discarded garment and used it as a gag on the captive Skoptsy.

'This should keep him quiet for a while.'

Harker knelt down beside Claire and closed her eyes with a brush of his hand. 'I know you weren't sorry, Claire, but I am,' he whispered, 'and I promise you I will find the child and make sure no one can ever get to him again.'

'Are you ready?' Shroder urged quietly after checking that the passage outside was clear.

'As I'll ever be,' Harker replied, stepping into the lead as Shroder closed the door behind him and followed.

They navigated back to the junction of passages and then further on down the one they had previously decided upon. They were less cautious this time and whereas before Harker had been hoping to avoid coming face to face with one of the Skoptsy, he now found himself eager for a confrontation.

Harker's thoughts of violent retribution were interrupted by the sinister sound of chanting coming from the end of the passage where it looked like it opened up into another wider area. Any other time he would have slowed but he now found himself speeding up. However, upon reaching it he was met with a sight that caused him to immediately halt and duck low. The narrow passageway opened up into a large cavern with a short walkway high above it, like a look-out post, and Harker crouched upon it, allowing him a vantage point of the area below. The cavern was split into three sections. The first, and largest part, consisted of what must have been living quarters, if you could call them that. There were no carpets or decorations but only a collection of grimy looking wooden huts, positioned in a circle and surrounding an area that must have been used as a communal kitchen/mess hall. A large soot-stained pot sat over an unlit pile of charcoal, surrounded by a selection of rickety tables and benches that looked as if they had been put together by a first grader.

The second part, on the farthest side of the cave, was enclosed by a low level fence which housed a couple of weary looking cows, complete with hay and water troughs, each animal adding their own aroma to the already stinky and claustrophobic ambience of the habitat. Things got a little cleaner in the third section, on the opposite side of the 'neighbourhood', where an open forum, not unlike a mini Greek amphitheatre, had been constructed, with curved walls. The walls only surrounded half of the stage, so it was possible to see the interior and, as well as being the least filthy structure in the cavern, it was also the source of the chanting. Inside, forty or so people lined the periphery of the room, all dressed in the same shabby brown robes as the earless freak they had left back in the cell.

Because of the robes, it was impossible to tell what other disfiguring acts they might have committed upon their bodies, but if their bared faces were anything to go by, it was likely to be substantial – and suddenly the mutilation of the one-eared man seemed pretty tame by comparison. Harker thought back to the masked individual back at Blackwater Asylum and now realised without a doubt he too had surely been a Skoptsy and, judging by the people down below, the mask he wore had been more of a necessity than a choice. Few of them even had hair and in many cases the scalp had been peeled away, leaving jagged white scars that had healed in uneven ridges of hardened skin. Many had both their ears missing, leaving only small dark holes visible in the sides of their heads, and a few were also missing their noses, with the cartilage beneath ground away and dark scars on top where the incisions had been cauterised with a red-hot instrument of some kind.

One person had, amongst other disfigurations, dozens of cross-shaped symbols gouged into his face and neck but it was a man near the front of the audience that made Harker feel most queasy. He was clapping enthusiastically with a pair of hands that only retained a total of four fingers and one thumb, but it was his lack of ears, nose and lips that really made him stand out. He looked like a ghoul from a horror film, and Harker wondered how anyone could stand the pain of such brutal surgeries and surely even a branding iron could not always have prevented the many potential infections that would result. He thought back to Claire's injuries and realised the answer. Not all of them did make it, but the few that did survive would have proved their faith immeasurably, and become worthy disciples in the eyes of the Skoptsy.

'Damn,' Harker muttered to himself at this display of lunacy and debasement. It was astonishing how warped the human mind could become, given the necessary indoctrination and being confined in such an enclosed and squalid environment.

Beneath him the faithful now held lit candles up in front of them with both hands as they chanted a melancholy and monotone series of notes in unison, all of them staring into the centre of the room where a man in dark purple-coloured vestments stood directly above an empty carved wooden crib and now began addressing the congregation in Russian.

'Can you see the child?' Harker whispered.

'No,' Shroder replied, having taken up a kneeling position next to him, 'I can't.'

'Then maybe we should grab one of them and force him to talk.'

The belligerence in Harker's tone received a deeply concerned glance from Shroder, who shook his head. 'No, we wait,' he insisted sternly, and Harker was immediately aware by the man's tone that the MI6 agent was becoming alarmed by Harker's increasingly hostile manner.

'I'm calm, Michael,' Harker said, turning to face his uneasy companion.

'Are you, really?' Shroder replied bluntly.

'Yes,' he replied with a sigh. 'I know I lost it back there but I'm OK now.' He raised his eyebrows in a show of sincerity and patted his chest lightly. 'I'm OK.'

Shroder eyed him further for a few moments before finally nodding his head. 'So what have you got in mind?'

Shroder's restored faith in him was a great relief to Harker because for a moment, and because of the way his gun had been pointed directly at him, he feared the MI6 agent might even take a shot at him. 'I'll go back and fetch the robe, and then we figure out how to get down there and take a look around.'

Shroder was already shaking his head. 'And what if they catch wind of what you're doing? What do you expect me to do – hold them at bay with harsh language?'

'Use the gun,' Harker suggested, pointing to the Browning in Shroder's hand.

'This gun only holds ten rounds,' Shroder replied and motioning to the crowd below, 'and they seem like a pretty committed lot.'

This answer already had Harker shaking his head in bewilderment. 'I thought you were an MI6 agent?'

'I am, Alex,' Shroder replied angrily, reminding him who the professional was, 'but I deal in counter-intelligence and we only fight battles that are coordinated and therefore the cards are dealt in our favour. I'm not a bloody commando.'

Shroder's incensed response had Harker raising his hands and glancing behind him to check no one else was close by. 'OK, then,' he replied as soothingly as possible, 'what do you suggest?'

By the look in Shroder's eyes, he had undoubtedly formulated his own plan and he was just about to deliver it, when something else drew his attention down below and he pushed Harker's head down out of sight.

'Stay down,' he hissed and pointed towards the only individual in the room beneath who did not look like a hobo. Dressed in a clean-cut black suit, white shirt and black tie, the tall man made his way in past the gathered audience, who all parted in front of him to allow him access to the centre of the room, whereupon he shook hands with the preacher. With the newcomer's back still to the audience, Harker couldn't tell who he was, but one thing he was sure of was this new arrival didn't fit in with crowd.

'Brothers and sisters,' the preacher announced in Russian, 'we are blessed to have with us our brother in arms, a defender of the true faith. He is here today to place in our possession that which will allow the Skoptsy to attain true salvation in these final days before the heavenly apocalypse begins.'

Harker glanced towards Shroder who was following the words closely, and it was obvious he too understood Russian, as the preacher continued with his welcoming of the new guest.

'Our faith and our dedication to God have never waned in over two hundred years, nor our resolute belief that the Day of Judgment will arrive and that the death of Jesus Christ, reborn to this world as a cloned and therefore false prophet, would ensure that the Skoptsy receive the salvation they so much deserve by placing us as rulers of the new world to come. Now, please,' the preacher continued, 'hear what our benefactor, friend and ally has to say.'

The visitor was greeted by a clapping of hands to show their support and only when the applause had died did he raise his hands and turn around slowly in a circle, making eye contact with each of the audience members. It was only then that Harker finally got to see the man standing in front of the empty wooden crib.

Captain Donald McCray offered a wide smile to the people of the Skoptsy as he stretched out his arms in a victorious pose and waited for the clapping to fully subside.

From up above Harker watched as the killer continued to receive a rapturous welcome and his look of surprise must have caught Shroder's attention, because the agent reached over and tapped him on the arm.

'Do you know him?' Shroder asked, scarcely audible over the hand-clapping.

'It's McCray,' Harker replied, but the blank expression on Shroder's face suggested the MI6 agent had never heard that name before. 'He's an assassin with Magi connections.'

Harker glanced back down at McCray, who still had his hands raised high, then leaned over to Shroder anxiously. 'How many shots did you say you had?'

'Ten,' Shroder hissed in a whisper.

'Only ten!' Harker gritted his teeth. 'We're going to need more bullets.'

Chapter 30

'Thank you all for such a warm welcome on this holiest of days that has been foretold since the dawn of mankind,' McCray proclaimed as he addressed the rows of eager eyes all fixed upon him. 'The world outside has long decided that it has no need for the truth that sustains the faith of everyone in this room, choosing instead to submit to the animalistic urges that have polluted their souls for too long. Even now those sinners scurry to find earthly reasons for the events that are now unfolding across the globe but, as with Sodom and Gomorrah, they will realise too late that their lives are forfeit and the end of days is truly upon us. But for us this end of days represents the beginning of divine enlightenment and a new chapter in the Lord's plan.'

His words were met by a murmur of approval and he reached over to rest a hand on the preacher's shoulder. 'Your leader has served you well, as you have served me well during all these years in preparation for the day of reckoning that awaits us, and my promise to deliver the Christ child will now be upheld.'

McCray turned his attention to the rear of the large room, where a group of eight men had appeared, all dressed in similar black suits to his own. He beckoned to the one holding a bundle in his arms wrapped in a blanket and the crowd instantly fell back, allowing the summoned man to make his way over and place the linen parcel in McCray's arms. He then retreated to the rear as Harker and Shroder exchanged glances up above.

'The trumpets of heaven and the harps of angels will soon ring out and deafen the non-believers with their truth, like the roar of the demons that you already saw with your own eyes smite that whore of a priest who dared venture into this place of worship only a few weeks ago.' McCray clasped the bundle more tightly in his arms. 'As the Lord rides his chariot down from the heavens he will embrace his true disciples in a warmth that will last forever.'

McCray now gestured for the congregation to join him, and the crowd of ghouls edged closer. Meanwhile the eight dark-suited men at the back formed a semicircle round them, wanting to gain for themselves a better view, even if it was at a distance from the foul-smelling crowd.

'With the sacrificing of this false prophet,' McCray continued, 'we will prove our worth to God and after he graces us with the true second coming, in the days and weeks that follow he will allow us to rule over his new kingdom and stand by his side in the subsequent banishment of evil that has plagued this world he created for too long.'

The Skoptsy crowd were still applauding him, with what was left of their hands, as McCray began to lift away the top fold concealing the bundle in his arms. 'My only regret is that none of you here will get the chance to witness it.'

He let the bundle drop to the floor, revealing the slim hunter's knife he held in his hand and, before anyone could react, he plunged it deep into the preacher's neck.

It all happened so quickly that it took a moment for even the preacher to realise what had occurred. He gripped at the protruding handle with a look of sheer disbelief, then hunched over as his body reacted to the impact of the wound, before collapsing to the floor in a heap.

The Skoptsy members didn't move, each and every one of them unsure how to respond, as all around them the eight suited men pulled compact Uzi sub-machine-guns from inside their suits and began to fire indiscriminately into the crowd.

Harker and Shroder watched from above as blinding flashes and the thunderous sound of automatic gunfire echoed around the dome. The entire huddle of Skoptsy reacted like domesticated cattle, not knowing what to do except glance around at each other wildly in panic as they dropped, one by one, on to the hard stone floor.

While McCray's men stood over and executed the remaining and wounded Skoptsy, with a double tap to their heads, Harker was overcome by a feeling of numbness and only a solitary thought preoccupied him as the last victim was summarily murdered down below. *Justice.* The complete lack of empathy he was feeling unnerved him, but regardless he couldn't suppress the belief that these vile, pathetic, self-inflicting butchers had got exactly what was coming to them.

He felt a tug on his shoulder and turned to find Shroder looking remarkably calm, given the bloodbath they had both just witnessed.

'This is over,' Shroder whispered as the last gunshot rang out. 'We have to go.'

Harker was already shaking his head. 'But they must know where the child is.'

'We can't take on eight heavily armed gunmen,' Shroder replied forcefully. 'So instead we follow them.'

'Agreed,' Harker concurred and pointed down the passageway they had come through. 'Let's get back to the car and see where they go next.'

Shroder was already heading into the passageway when behind them a voice called out from below.

'Alex Harker... is that really you?'

Harker swivelled around to see McCray staring up at him with a look of astonishment in his eyes.

'It is you!' McCray exclaimed as Harker's face came into full view over the side of the walkway. 'My God,' the killer exclaimed, still stunned by his presence. 'For a mongrel, you seem to have the nose of a pedigree bloodhound.'

'And you're a murderous bloodsucking parasite, McCray,' Harker yelled back with disdain, as Shroder crouched out of sight behind him.

The insult elicited a wide smile from McCray even as his men encircled their boss protectively and prepared for any attack that might be launched from the walkway overhead. 'I assume you're here looking for the child?'

Harker remained silent as McCray stood on tiptoe, trying to get a better look at him.

'He's not here, I am afraid, but there is an old friend of yours somewhere in this dump and I am sure she would love to catch up.'

McCray had to be referring to Claire Dwyer and the very mention of her name had Harker clenching his fists. 'I've seen her,' he seethed.

'Oh, good. How is she?'

Harker said nothing and a smile spread across McCray's lips. 'I'll take it from your silence that she's not doing very well. Shame about that but, after intercepting her intended meeting with the Magi, we had to keep her drugged up for a while. And when the Skoptsy grew impatient for the child, we offered her to them as a way of keeping them preoccupied and giving us the extra time we needed.' McCray glanced down at the corpses strewn all about him. 'They do... I mean they did love a chance to redeem a sinner.'

'Time for what?' Harker yelled back and unwilling to get dragged into the horror of Claire's demise.

McCray ignored him and continued to peer up at the walkway. 'Anyone else up there with you, Alex?'

'Well, the place is surrounded if that's what you mean.' Harker's response had the assassin glancing around the upper levels for a moment, before returning his attention back to the walkway.

'I am sceptical about that,' he remarked slyly. 'I doubt you even knew I was going to be here.'

'Oh yes? And why are you here, then?' Harker probed, ignoring McCray's correct assumption.

'Wrapping up some loose ends, you might say.'

'That's more of a reason than an answer, McCray... I mean what exactly have you got to do with the Skoptsy and their terrorist attacks?'

The question drew a sarcastic laugh from McCray, who shook his head with incredulity. 'Are you trying to enforce your own vain sense of logic upon things you can't possibly understand... or are simply unwilling to believe?' The assassin motioned again to the numerous dead Skoptsy. 'Everything I just said to these wretched troglodytes is true. The end of the world is being played out even as we speak. The divine wheels have been set in motion, and there is nothing that you or I can do about it. You yourself must have noticed the events now occurring throughout the world.'

'I've noticed a lot of things,' Harker replied in a far more knowing way then he felt.

'Good,' came the reply. 'Then you too will know, as I do, that no earthly hand could have been involved.'

'Maybe,' Harker offered, 'but what have the Skoptsy got to do with it?'

'This pathetic sect have had their uses, Alex, but not in the way you might think. They have been surprisingly helpful in our preparations.'

'Preparations?'

'Preparation for the coming war.'

'War?' Harker almost spat the word out.

'Yes, the coming war between the divine forces of our Lord and the dominion of evil led by Lucifer himself, for the control of this world.'

McCray's answer was too out there for Harker to engage with credibly, but he played along nonetheless. 'And you think, after all the bloodshed you've caused, that the lord God is going to anoint you as his right-hand man.'

'Oh, don't be so naïve,' McCray refuted bluntly. 'The bible is full of countless deaths perpetrated by people with God's wrath in their hearts, and I am no different. If I had handed the child over to them instead of killing these creatures, then they would have murdered a helpless infant in the misguided notion that he was a false prophet. I, on the other hand, know better and it is my actions that have saved the child's life. The son of God... for this child is not only our salvation but an invitation to sit at the Lord's table.'

There were so many things wrong with what McCray was saying that Harker struggled not to shake his head and sigh in disbelief. He decided instead to continue playing to the man's obvious psychosis. 'Why the Skoptsy? Why not have your friends the Magi lay down the preparations? You see, I know who you are, Donald.'

McCray's face suddenly turned ashen and he looked for the first time like a worried man. 'Then you will know that I was betrayed by my own brother, and when the Magi turned their back on me, I turned to the Skoptsy and utilised their services accordingly.' McCray's confident demeanour suddenly returned to him and he beamed up at Harker. 'It doesn't matter anymore because the Magi are now back where they should have been in the first place... under my control.'

McCray had hardly managed to finish his words when the ground beneath him began to shake and Harker watched as his men began struggling to maintain their balance while dodging the small fragments of rock that were now crumbling off the dome overhead.

'Well, it looks like you've pissed *somebody* off,' Harker shouted, but McCray was already ordering his team to retreat.

'Go,' McCray barked, and they began to hurry out of the arena before he called out one last time. 'Goodbye, Alex,' the assassin shouted gleefully, 'and enjoy your tomb.'

Before the Magi death squad was even out of sight, Shroder was dragging Harker away from the edge, and then the two of them were running back along the stone passageways that were already beginning to disintegrate all around them, until the grating noise of stone grinding against stone became almost deafening. The vibrations were getting ever more violent and, as they reached the crossroads, a large jagged part of the ceiling dropped loose and crashed to the floor just inches away from Harker, sending Shroder jumping to one side and slamming against the wall.

'Here,' Harker shouted, grabbing Shroder's outstretched hand and pulling him to his feet. 'You go first.' He pushed the agent towards the passageway leading to an exit. As Shroder continued his zig-zagging up to and around the bend, Harker paused and glanced down the side passage to his left, and he thought of Claire Dwyer. He had made a promise to himself earlier that he would get her body out of here, but it was one promise he would be unable to keep.

Above him a thick crack appeared in the stone ceiling and Harker instinctively dived into the passageway up ahead just as the whole corridor behind him collapsed in on itself, propelling a thick plume of dust his way which engulfed him in a foul mist that stung his eyes. He clambered to his feet and headed further on up the passage towards the only source of light he could see. Figuring that Shroder had by now reached the trapdoor, he raised his shirt to his mouth so as not to inhale the choking dust and then hurried towards it as fast as he could, dodging fragments of rock that continued to drop all around him.

On reaching the ladder Harker hurled himself up and onto it with such ferocity that one of the steps snapped underneath him, jamming him painfully, groin first, into the one below it with a hefty whack. Harker was already reaching for the top of the ladder and cursing the pain he felt, when more dust from the disintegrating passage behind made it nearly impossible to see, but Shroder reached down and clutched at his jacket, hauling him upwards and up on to the relative safety of the chapel floor.

Harker was still coughing violently as Shroder helped him to his feet and thrust into his hands one of the gasmasks he had discarded earlier. Without need for any direction, Harker slipped it over his face just as the chapel tower overhead, along with the whole building, began to sway back and forth.

They burst through the doors leading back outside, and it was only Shroder swinging Harker up against the chapel's external wall that stopped him plummeting head first into a clump of potentially radioactive bushes directly opposite. They hugged the outer wall of the chapel all the way to the path, before racing down it all the way to the end where the Range Rover was parked across the street. As Shroder sorted through his keys, Harker turned around to see the grey-concrete apartment block opposite began to fracture and twist.

When he turned back Shroder was already inside the car. The agent flung open the passenger side door with such force that the door smacked into Harker and sent him flying backwards on to the ground. The impact dazed him for a moment and he looked up to see the street ahead begin to undulate, and then to roll towards him in a rippling wave of earth and debris. As this wave passed the apartment block standing at the far end of the street, it disappeared into the ground with a thunderous roar, and a cloud of smoke billowed into the sky high above.

Harker immediately dragged himself back to his feet and jumped into the passenger side.

'Get the suits,' Shroder yelled, pointing to the two yellow haz-mat suits lying on the back seat. Harker reached back and scooped them up passing one to Shroder and then slipped into his own as Shroder did likewise. After a few uncomfortable and fumbling moments they were fully suited and as the sound of the car's engine burst into life Shroder jammed the vehicle into first gear and began speeding down the main road that led out of Pripyat, as the next apartment block totally disintegrated.

Harker looked back and watched in trepidation as the final three apartment blocks also disappeared into the ground, before turning back to face the windscreen just as a stout pine tree was uprooted by the collapsing ground and began to fall across the road in front of them. 'Look out,' he yelled but Shroder was already manoeuvring the vehicle up onto the pavement and past the obstacle as it smacked down on to the cracked tarmac behind them.

'That was too close,' Harker yelled, struggling to be heard above the roar of the Range Rover's engine and through the mask covering his face, even as Shroder accelerated faster. 'Did you see McCray?'

'I didn't see any other cars,' Shroder replied as overhead the flapping of rotor blades had them both craning upwards to get a glimpse of a Russian-made Hind helicopter through the top of the windscreen. The helicopter rose into the air and then peeled off to the west, before disappearing into low-level clouds and out of sight. Both Harker and Shroder stared at each with impressed looks on their faces. The Magi, as always, had been well prepared.

'There must have been another exit to that chapel.' Shroder yelled as they hit the main road with a screech from the tyres and fortunately, after a few hundred metres, the earth tremors began to ease off until after a few miles they were barely registering.

'What the hell was that all about?' Shroder shouted from beneath his mask.

'I don't know but I'm sure about one thing,' Harker replied. 'That spiel about the end of the world… McCray believes it completely.'

Shroder glanced into his rear-view mirror to see the large smoking hole in the ground, with pitch-black storm clouds hanging above it where the town of Pripyat had once stood. 'Yeah, well you know what?' He said continuing to accelerate down the road that would lead them out of the exclusion zone and back to the airstrip. 'He's not the only one.'

Chapter 31

By the time they reached the airport Harker and Shroder were still engaged in the same heated discussion that had been preoccupying them since leaving the exclusion zone.

'I just can't believe that you didn't realise Claire Dwyer was a Templar!' Harker persisted, unwilling to let the topic go. 'You're a close friend of Brulet's... and let's not forget you're MI6. You boys are supposed to know everything.'

'I'm telling you I had no idea. Sebastian doesn't keep me fully apprised of absolutely everything,' Shroder moaned, refuting the allegation that was being levelled at him for the umpteenth time. 'Shit, I'm not even a Templar myself, and as for MI6 they don't even know that organisation exists!'

'No, I'm sure they don't,' Harker replied sarcastically.

'Believe me, if the security services knew about the Templars, they'd have them under a bloody microscope.'

Harker shook his head dismissively as Shroder continued.

'Do you really think the intelligence community would allow an entity like the Templars – and the resources they have at their fingertips – to operate without impunity? Because if you do, then you're crazier than the Skoptsy!'

Harker rolled his eyes at this mention of the Skoptsy. 'Maybe but, until I see Sebastian, I'm reserving judgment on everything. He and I need to have a serious talk.'

'Well, it looks like you're about to get your chance,' Shroder declared calmly as the Range Rover pulled up in front of their Gulf Steam 450 jet, allowing them a view of the second, identical Gulf Stream 450 jet parked directly behind it. 'Because, if I'm not mistaken, that's his aircraft.'

The vehicle had barely stopped before Harker was out of the car and briskly making his way towards the newly arrived plane and its waiting set of steps. He climbed them two at a time and hopped inside, almost colliding with Captain Jones who was looking wholly relieved to see him.

'Glad you made it.' Jones said with a thankful smile. 'We felt the shockwave.'

Harker gave him a complimentary nod, then turned his attention to the cabin beyond.

'Alex!' Chloe she jumped up out of her seat and greeted him with a heartfelt bear-hug. 'I was getting worried.'

Behind her, Sebastian Brulet was also already on his feet and looking just as pleased. 'We were *all* getting worried.' The Grand Master offered and then turned his attention to Shroder who had just appeared through the jet's entrance. 'And likewise you, Michael. Thank you for your assistance at such short notice.'

'You might not want to thank me just yet, Sebastian,' Shroder replied, glancing towards Harker who was eyeing Brulet with deep mistrust.

'I see,' Brulet said gravely. 'Then perhaps you had better tell me what happened?'

'We found the Skoptsy is what happened,' Harker announced drily. 'And we also found Claire Dwyer... what was left of her anyway!'

Harker's brutal disclosure made Brulet scowl in dismay and the Grand Master rubbed at his eyes with a sigh.

'Tell me, Sebastian,' Harker continued scornfully, 'were you ever going to tell me that Claire Dwyer was a Templar?'

Brulet stared back with a sad glint in those cross-shaped pupils of his. 'Please, Alex, allow me to explain.'

'I wish you would,' Harker replied flatly, 'because at this moment in time I'm not sure how much I trust you.'

Brulet nodded compliantly and sat down with a sluggish sagging of his body. 'I tried to tell you during our last conversation, before we were cut off.'

'Yes, I realise that now,' Harker replied, having already figured it out on the drive back, 'but it was still a little late in the day to tell me about her, wouldn't you say?'

'Yes, it was and for that I am sorry, but I had my reasons.'

'You always have your reasons, don't you, Sebastian.' Harker replied scathingly. 'I've spent the last four months cursing that woman and the way she deceived me, the Templars and even her own brother, and now I find out that all the time she was working for you!'

'She was, yes,' Brulet confirmed, as Harker brought his palms together with a loud slap.

'She tried to have me killed!' he shouted angrily. 'On more than one occasion.'

'No, she didn't, Alex,' Brulet said firmly, but with a compassionate tone in his voice. 'She actually saved your life.'

'What!' Harker yelled furiously, and so loudly that it made Chloe flinch. 'How the hell do you figure that?'

Brulet placed his hands together and raised them to his lips as some of his usual and familiar confidence began to return. 'The Templars approached Claire shortly after we learned about her brother Archie's involvement with the relics that eventually led you to the Vatican last year, and to the consequences that followed. We knew Archie would never join an organisation such as ours, but Claire was more than willing and in a unique position, as his sister, to dig deeper. When she was approached by the Magi soon after her brother's death, she realised she was in the perfect position to infiltrate their ranks and discover what the rest of us could not… their creation of the Christ child and the sect's sordid and ambitious plan to take over the Catholic Church.' Brulet paused as he interlaced his fingers and assumed a serious pose as if for fear of appearing flippant in his explanation. 'And then you entered the picture and, as it turned out, played almost as significant role as she did. It is important that you know that at no time did she alert the Magi to your location. I'm afraid that was down to the mole within our own ranks.'

'Lusic Bekhit?' Harker asked, suddenly surprised at himself for having all but forgotten about the Templar double agent. The treacherous snake that had changed sides and had since vanished of the face of the earth.

'Yes.' Brulet gave a confirming nod. 'It was he that passed on your movements to the Magi, allowing them to track you both at all times, and in doing so always managing to stay one step ahead.'

'But she left me to die down in the catacombs at the hands of the Magi. She just abandoned me.'

'No,' Brulet said with a wave of his finger, 'it was a calculated risk on her part. If Claire had revealed herself, she would have been killed on the spot along with you. Her intention had been for us to save you but I am afraid it took us a little longer to reach you than hoped. Thankfully your ingenuity knows no bounds, or it could have been a very different outcome.'

Brulet's answer had Harker's mind swirling but one factor stood out. 'You're saying that she contacted you in order to save me and the child's mother.'

'That's exactly what I am saying,' Brulet replied as he now leaned closer to Harker. 'Didn't you ever ask yourself how it was that we turned up at Vatican City so quickly, and just in the nick of time to stop the Magi from butchering you and the unborn child?'

Harker remained quiet, stunned by what he was hearing because everything he was being told was starting to make a disturbing kind of sense.

'Without Claire we never would have found you in time, albeit a little late.'

Harker took a moment to shake off the daze as Brulet sat back in his chair and waited for the barrage of questions he was now expecting.

'So *why* did she kidnap the child?'

'She didn't,' Brulet replied unemotionally. 'After the deaths of his brothers John Wilcox believed, quite correctly, that he had been betrayed and that Claire was the weak link. She was sure that he would kill her soon enough, so she contacted me with a plan for us to get to him first and finally eliminate his cruel bloodline once and for all.' Brulet lowered his head regretfully and rubbed at the back of his wrist. 'It was a plan that I foolishly went along with.'

'She told Wilcox she could get the child back,' Harker guessed. And knowing now what Claire's true intentions had been, he had no doubt at what she would have done next.

'Yes,' Brulet confirmed, obviously ashamed by having gone along with it. 'Claire and the child and his mother, Ms Genowa, were supposed to meet Wilcox under the guise of a kidnapping. We had teams already waiting at the arranged meeting place that were supposed to take Wilcox and his group down before Claire even arrived, but something happened. They were ambushed when a truck slammed into their car, killing Ms Genowa instantly, and then Claire and the child vanished.'

'The Skoptsy?'

'Apparently so,' Brulet replied, clearly encouraged by Harker's engagement in this conversation, 'but I'm hoping you can provide us with more information regarding that, now you have returned from your visit to Pripyat… one that has ended in the complete destruction of the area, I might add.' But Harker was far from finished with his questions.

'So why wait until now to tell me all this?'

'Because you have been very high-profile in recent months and if the Magi had wanted to, they could have abducted you very easily, and after a few days of torture you would have told them anything they cared to know. I don't mean to that to sound like a slight but under torture everyone cracks… eventually. The Templars have been searching for Claire ever since her disappearance, and we were always hoping for the best but preparing for the worst. If getting the child back had meant Claire being reconfirmed as someone the Magi could trust, then your knowing about it could have got her killed.'

'She *was* killed,' Harker said with renewed sadness in his voice.

'I know that now, but up until you arrived here a few minutes ago, I had hoped she was still alive and safe.'

Harker exhaled a long deep breath before sliding into the seat facing Brulet. He didn't have any guilt about his previous feelings of hatred towards Claire, since she had appeared to betray him back at the Vatican – and how could he have known she was actually working with him – but he did feel a profound sense of sadness at the loss of his erstwhile friend. Part of him was actually relieved to learn that she hadn't become the treacherous and disloyal person he had come to believe she was, but knowing how she died – and that it was in such a terrible way – made his anger boil, the focus of it now solely aimed at Wilcox and at the Magi organisation that wrecked anything it touched.

'I'm not happy about this, Sebastian… but I do understand your reasons.'

Brulet reached over and placed his pale white hand on Harker's forearm with an understanding look on his face. 'I am so sorry it happened like this, Alex,' he offered, 'but I warned you once that we operate in a dark world where we are rarely allowed to act the way we wish to but instead the way we have to.'

This sentiment did little to alleviate any of the despondency Harker was dealing with, but it did spur him on to reveal in full what had transpired back in Pripyat, in the hope that something good might still come out of it. 'The Skoptsy had created a settlement directly underneath the town. Talk about a great hiding place from the world. There must have been thirty or forty of them living there, practising their twisted version of Christianity. We found Claire confined in a cell.' Harker paused as the bruising image of her mutilated body burned once again into his thoughts. 'She had been subjected to one of their rituals... They had performed a double mastectomy on her and cauterised the wounds with what looked like a heated poker.'

'Why would they do that?' Chloe gasped, looking sickened by the thought, as next to her, Brulet shook his head in disgust.

'As I said, it was some kind of ritual to cleanse her body and spirit... or some ridiculous nonsense like that,' Harker declared bitterly. 'She died in my arms. The pain for her must have been unbearable. That's when she told me she was a Templar. And, even though she must have been suffering so much pain, her thoughts were only that we save the child.'

'But the child wasn't there.' Shroder interrupted, realising that Harker was still somewhat traumatised by the whole experience. 'The Skoptsy were expecting him to be hand-delivered to them by Donald McCray, but the only thing he and his cronies gave them was a quick and nasty death. Not a pretty sight.'

'That's right,' Harker continued. 'McCray gave them this speech about how they had helped him and that they were all preparing for the end of the world and that the child would be their salvation, etc. They were all pretty excited about it until the Magi gunned the lot of them down in cold blood.'

'And the child?' Brulet asked and expecting the worst.

'Nowhere to be seen, but then McCray spotted me and he gave this big song-and-dance about how the end of days really is upon us, and that he thinks the child will basically put him in God's good books when he returns to earth, and therefore name him as his right-hand man.' Harker was already shaking his head. 'He sounded totally crazy but he also suggested that he now is in control of the Magi. And then the entire place started to fall apart so we got the hell out of there and headed back here. One thing I feel for sure is that he really does believe that this stuff is happening and, judging by the confidence he was displaying, he definitely has possession of the child.'

'McCray's taken over the Magi?' Brulet gasped.

'I know, it sounds implausible doesn't it but that's exactly what he said,' Harker replied.

'Actually it doesn't sound as far-fetched as you might think. There was a recent news report that the body of John Wilcox, the ex-Pope, was found along with three others in a burnt-out villa in Tuscany, but that has not been confirmed by the authorities.' Brulet now fell into deep thought. 'Perhaps there has been a coup d'état within their ranks.'

'Did McCray escape?' Chloe asked and still shocked by the idea of so many people being gunned down in such a cavalier fashion, even if the Skoptsy had deserved it.

'I think so,' Shroder interjected. 'We saw a helicopter flying past us before the entire area disappeared into the earth.' The MI6 agent turned his attention to Brulet, who was now silent as if just absorbing it all. 'I've never seen anything like it, Sebastian. The whole town just sank into the ground leaving behind nothing more than a gaping hole. Now you know I'm not overly religious but, after what I saw well… it's enough to make a rational man think twice.'

The agent's reaction to the situation received a wide-eyed expression from Brulet. 'You're not the only one,' he replied before picking up a small remote sitting on the table next to him. 'There's something you need to see.'

Brulet pressed a button and a section of panelling on the far side of the cabin raised itself upwards to reveal a flat-screen TV, which promptly flashed into life. A Sky News report began to play, showing an aerial view over Jerusalem and the fires which Harker and Chloe had witnessed first-hand. The banner headline at the bottom read: *Anarchy in Jerusalem*.

'They are saying that the death toll could amount to hundreds or even thousands,' Brulet declared, as more pictures of burnt-out shops and cars rolled across the screen, interspersed with images of members of the Israeli defence forces in their olive-green uniforms, firing tear gas into crowds of people.

'We were there, Sebastian,' Harker remarked, gesturing towards Chloe who was standing next to him. 'We saw this with our own eyes.'

'I know but it's what happened afterwards that you are probably not aware of,' Brulet said and pointing at the images of Israeli soldiers, each of them wearing a protective face-mask, throwing bodies on to a burning pyre. 'About an hour after the initial outbreak, everyone affected simply dropped dead.'

'All at the same time?' Chloe inquired with a tone of disbelief.

'No one is sure of that,' Brulet answered, 'but not one of those raving lunatics has been found alive since... only corpses. The Israelis are treating this as a viral outbreak and there are so many bodies they have begun burning them on mass pyres.'

'Weird,' Shroder commented, straining to get a closer view of the screen as behind him Captain Jones looked equally concerned.

'Weird indeed,' Brulet agreed. 'I managed to get a recording of this coverage before the story dropped off the networks.'

'Dropped off the networks, how?' Harker was astonished by Brulet's comment. 'What happened in Jerusalem must surely be the lead story on every news channel in the world.'

'It was,' Brulet replied, 'but it has since had competition.'

Harker and Shroder both looked confused. 'What's happened?'

'A lot,' Brulet offered solemnly, turning the channel to a live CNN broadcast. 'Take a look at this.'

On the screen a news reporter was frantically attempting to hold his ground against crowds of screaming people surging past him. The journalist was saying something unintelligible into the microphone while pointing off camera in the opposite direction of the fleeing crowds.

'What's he saying?' Harker asked, but Brulet was already shaking his head.

'Doesn't matter... just watch.'

The reporter lowered his hands as the crowd began to thin out, then something enormous and black leapt into view and landed right on top of him. Then the camera began zipping from side to side as evidently the cameraman attempted to steady himself and regain the focus of his shot. Harker watched the blurred image come into clear view and a series of screeching howls could be heard over the screams of the reporter until finally the picture refocused and then paused on a still frame of something that caused everyone in the cabin to recoil with gasps of shock. That is except for Brulet, who didn't even flinch.

The grainy image showed a creature with thick dark black fur standing on all fours and snarling directly at the camera with twin rows of razor-sharp teeth stained with the blood. Its snout was wolf-like, but abnormally long, and with two reptilian-like slits for nasal passages running the length of either side of its nose. As unsettling as the image was, it was the creature's eyes that really gripped Harker.

They were cat-like with yellow pupils, and the eye-sockets were sunk deep into the animal's head.

'What the hell is that thing?' Harker gagged, as Chloe raised her hand to her mouth in bewilderment.

'Short answer is they don't know.' Brulet replied, unable to tear his gaze from the terrifying image.

'What's the long answer then?' Chloe managed from behind her still raised hand.

'There has been widespread speculation, as you would expect. Everything from a new and undiscovered species of animal to aliens, but the main news networks have settled on something far more disturbing.' Brulet turned to face the flabbergasted expressions infront of him. 'They're referring to it as a demon and, given events recently at the Vatican and everything else that is happening around the world, it's a concept that is rapidly growing in support.'

Harker was already rubbing his face with both hands. *Demons!* This whole conversation, like everything else today, was becoming far too surreal for him. 'Have they caught one of them yet?' he asked.

'No,' Brulet replied flatly. 'That's because, shortly after they appeared, the entire area disappeared into a hole in the ground. Almost like a sinkhole, in fact, and from the sound of it not to dissimilar to what you witnessed at Pripyat.'

As Harker and Chloe were still reeling from this fantastical explanation, Brulet hit them with another incredible disclosure.

'And it didn't just happen in Spain,' he continued. 'The same thing has happened in three other towns – in Brazil, Africa and India.'

'Were they the same... demons?' Harker asked, almost having to force the ridiculous word from his mouth.

'Yes, they were, but I was unable to get any visual recordings before the networks all went down.'

'Which networks are we talking about here?' Harker felt a sensation of dread creeping into his chest.

'Literally all of them. TV, the internet and the mobile networks stopped working just shortly after reports of these animals started appearing on the news,' Brulet answered gravely. 'The only lines of communication still working are the radio, some of the landlines, and the military satellites.'

'That's impossible,' Harker protested finding the enormity of what he as being told difficult to comprehend. 'The entire satellite network would have needed to be put out of commission.'

'Apparently not,' Brulet was already shaking his head almost in despair. 'I am not even sure we can make it anywhere safely in this jet because presumably air-traffic control is down as well, but Captain Jones has some ideas for resolving that problem.'

Jones took a step forward as all eyes turned to him. 'We can still fly, though our inflight mapping system is down, so it's not ideal and it does present some dangers, but I can still do so the old way with maps and with directional frequencies which haven't been affected so far.'

'Thank you, Captain. I know we can count on you,' Brulet said approvingly, and then he used the remote to turn off the TV. 'Well, then,' he continued drily, and sitting back in his seat with arms folded, 'regrettably it seems that our journey is at an end.'

The Grand Master's unusually defeatist comment had Harker frowning. 'What! You're just giving up just like that?'

'In case you hadn't noticed, Alex, the whole world is going to hell... literally,' Brulet replied grimly. 'What exactly would you have me do?'

'Anything you can,' Harker urged in a frustrated tone that had Brulet shaking his head in exasperation.

'Alex, what is going on around the world right now is far bigger than anything the Templars – or any government, for that matter – can have any control over. This isn't some kind of mystery to be solved or a puzzle to be deciphered.' Brulet pointed towards the oval window right next to him with the fading light outside. 'What is happening out there is out of our hands... it's out of anybody's hands.'

The look of disbelief on Harker's face at Brulet's apparent lack of resolve had the Grand Master stammering as he continued to justify what he was saying. 'All over the world, destruction is occurring at a rate that seems to be gaining in momentum with every passing hour, and now these hellish creatures keep appearing all over the place.' He let out a frustrated sigh. 'And meanwhile, that odious little shit McCray has apparently got in his possession the one individual with any chance of thwarting the prophecy that has been set in motion. And McCray could be anywhere on the planet, so far as we know. So you tell me, what should I... what *can* I do about it?'

Brulet's total lack of a game plan left Harker feeling immensely troubled. In all the time he had known the Templar's Grand Master, he had never witnessed the man so much at a loss. Sebastian Brulet was a man who always had options, no matter what the circumstances, and yet here he seemed almost unwilling to even try to look for any kind of solution to the problems at hand.

Harker stared blankly at Brulet and, with each passing second an increasingly uncomfortable wedge of silence began to form between them, until eventually it was Chloe who intervened.

'So what do we do now?'

Brulet turned his attention to her. 'There is a place where all Templars are directed to go in the event of a catastrophe befalling the organisation. This is not the kind of catastrophe I envisaged when I commissioned it to be built, but it is nevertheless a safe place to go.' The questioning expression on Harker's face pushed him to explain further. 'We had it built back in the Fifties, when a nuclear war seemed highly possible. It contains the resources necessary for anyone needing to stay below ground for a prolonged period of time, and it is there that any Templar will now retreat to... those of them who can make it. Anyone else we find along the way who is in need of sanctuary will of course be allowed to join us. I suggest we go there and... wait this out.'

'Wait *what* out, Sebastian?' Harker demanded aggressively. 'This is the end of the world!'

Brulet offered him a conciliatory nod. 'Maybe and, when we are needed, the Templars will be there ready to fight the battle to end all battles at the right hand of God against the forces of hell, but that day is not today.'

Harker put his head in his hands and massaged his forehead as he was suddenly overcome with a terrible sense of foreboding. Here it was in his lifetime, a day that all religious scriptures had been warning of since the dawn of religious enlightenment, and he had to meet it head-on as an ex-priest who had hung up his dog collar and lost his faith. *Un-Fucking-Believable.*

He was still pondering that fact when something else occurred to him. 'Sebastian, you said that all other Templars know of this meeting point, didn't you?'

'Yes, I did,' Brulet replied. 'All Templars are given the location of the sanctuary upon their initiation.'

'All?' Harker questioned.

'I am aware I never disclosed it to you, Alex, but honestly I never thought you would need it,' Brulet replied sympathetically. 'But, yes, all Templars are made aware of it.'

'Then isn't it possible that the Magi have a similar procedure?'

'It's possible,' Brulet replied, unsure of what Harker was leading up to. 'It's very likely in fact and, considering the Magi elite have done a vanishing act in recent weeks, I would guess they are either there already, or, on their way their way even as we speak, including McCray and the child.'

'So any of the Magi would likely know of the location of their sanctuary or convening place, right?'

'Sorry, Alex, but I'm not following you. What?'

'But they would, though?' Harker interrupted eagerly.

'Yes… maybe,' Brulet conceded, 'but only Magi members, and maybe some of the organisation's high level associates. Why?'

'Then let's find one of the Magi and get them to disclose that location.'

Harker's suggestion was greeted all round with looks of bewilderment, except from Shroder who began rubbing his hands together thoughtfully. 'There's Lusic Bekhit – we could try him.'

'What!' Harker gasped 'I didn't think anyone knew where he was?'

'He only resurfaced a few days ago, around the time this all started,' Shroder explained. 'Sebastian asked me to keep my ears to the ground, so I put in a terrorist check with the NSA and, when they picked up his name on a phone call, I was alerted and traced the landline.'

Brulet was already holding his hands up defensively as Harker glared at him mistrustfully once again. 'I only found out a few hours ago, when I contacted Michael for help with the trip to Chernobyl, but I doubt he knows anything.'

'Why?' Harker asked, encouraged by a potential lead.

'Because it is highly likely the Magi want him silenced just as much as we do, given his failed service to them. The Magi are not of the forgiving type, as you know.'

'Still,' Harker pressed, 'it's a possibility.'

'Am I missing something?' Chloe interrupted and becoming increasingly frustrated. 'Who exactly is this Lusic Bekhit?'

'Lusic Bekhit was once a Templar,' Brulet explained, grimacing as if he had a foul taste in his mouth. 'But he then turned out to be a mole working for the Magi.'

'He tried to kill me at thirty thousand feet and make it look like a plane crash.' Harker said indignantly, still angered by the notion that Bekhit had so far got off scot free.

'How?' Chloe looked shocked to learn of yet another person who had tried to murder Harker.

'Ask me another time. It's a long story,' he replied gently. He turned his attention back to Brulet. 'Shouldn't we at least try and discover what he knows?'

An awkward silence spread through the cabin as Brulet considered the idea, but before he could make his decision it was Shroder who offered a solution.

'I'll go,' he said, getting to his feet. 'Jones and I can take the other jet. Besides, with my credentials it will be a lot easier for me to reach his location, given the current climate.'

Brulet remained silent for a few moments, fingers interlaced and raised to his lips, before dropping both hands to his chest and eyeing Harker sternly. 'This idea of yours is pretty thin, Alex. It is wafer-like in fact. Bekhit would be considered by them to be no more than a low-level associate, if not a potential enemy. What we would really need in order to put your theory to a test is an actual member of the Magi, and as of this moment we don't know the whereabouts of a single one.'

The look that appeared on Harker's face made the Grand Master lean forward, his chin raised inquisitively. 'Do you know any Magi, Alex?'

Harker gave a shrewd smile and glanced at Chloe and Shroder before returning his eyes to the questioning gaze of Brulet. 'Yes,' he replied confidently, 'I know one.'

Chapter 32

'And I told you, Mr Harker, you're not getting in without special permission from the Home Office and that's that.'

Harker slammed his fist down on the front desk in frustration, eyeing the reception guard with contempt as Chloe nudged him aside and attempted to influence the man's decision with her own credentials.

'My name is Doctor Chloe Stanton and I am the chief of staff at Blackwater psychiatric facility. I need to impress upon you how important it is that you allow us access right now.'

'Listen, love,' the young guard replied sarcastically, clearly annoyed by Chloe's lame attempt to outrank him, 'I don't care if you're the Surgeon General, you're not getting in without Home Office approval.'

'But we *do* have approval,' Harker replied, becoming weary of having to explain himself, 'direct from the Home Office.'

The guard was already shaking his head. 'And I've told you that all our telephones are down.' He pulled a Samsung cell-phone from his trouser pocket and waved it in front of him. 'Even our mobiles aren't working and, without being able to confirm what you're saying, I'm not letting you in. End of conversation, understand?'

Harker glanced towards Chloe in the hope that she might have another suggestion, but the blank expression he received convinced him to stay silent. He turned back to face the uncompromising stare of the guard, and let out an irritated sigh. It had taken over four hours to fly back to the UK and Brulet had even managed to get a call through to a contact in the Home Office by piggybacking of a military satellite, but now here they were getting stopped in their tracks at the last hurdle. Harker was still racking his brains for a solution to the dilemma when another older guard appeared from one of the offices behind.

'It's all right, John, I'll take it from here,' the newcomer said with a reassuring pat on the man's shoulder. 'Why don't you go brew up a cuppa for us?'

'Yes, sir.' The younger guard shot Harker a look of irritation before disappearing through one of the side doors, leaving the three of them alone at the reception desk.

'My name is Peter Holcroft and I'm the senior officer here.'

'Thank you, Mr Holcroft. My name is…'

Officer Holcroft raised his hand between them stopping Harker mid-sentence. 'Professor Harker, right? I know who you are. And you're Doctor Stanton?' he briefly turned his attention to Chloe.

'Yes. Call me Chloe, please.'

'Very well then, Chloe, Professor Harker. If you'd like to follow me.'

Holcroft made his way from behind the reception desk over to a large steel security door, where he waved up at the surveillance camera above. Within seconds the door clicked open with a buzzing sound and he headed inside, followed by Harker and Chloe. They then headed along a series of short white-painted corridors to another door, where the officer repeated the procedure. It was only after the second door closed behind them that Holcroft began to speak again. 'Welcome to Wakefield Prison,' he announced, his outstretched hand gesturing towards a series of barred doors that led on to the cell wings beyond. 'Or the monster mansion, as the press have dubbed us.'

'Monster mansion?' Harker queried, and unaware of the prison's nickname.

'Professor, we house here some of the most prolific sex offenders in the UK: Categories A and B. If you've read about them in the papers, then chances are they've spent time here.' Holcroft moved away from the checkpoint, pulled a key from his pocket and unlocked one of the nearby holding rooms. 'Paedophiles, rapists and murderers with a five-year minimum sentence, all the way up to life imprisonment.' He swung open the sturdy door and motioned them inside, towards a metal table and set of chairs which were all bolted securely to the floor. Behind them Holcroft re-locked the door and slipped the key back into his pocket before turning to face Harker and Chloe, who had already taken their seats. 'We have or have had everyone here, from the child killers Ian Huntley, Roy Whiting and Mark Bridger to the notorious Charles Bronson, although he goes by another name these days.' Officer Holcroft took a step towards the table and folded his arms ostentatiously. 'And now you're here to see one of our newest arrivals… how come?'

Holcroft's increasingly aggressive demeanour had little impact on Harker. After all, the man had a right to be curious even if he wouldn't be getting any answers. 'With respect, Officer Holcroft, that is between myself and the Home Office. I'm just glad that you received the call before the phones went down.'

Holcroft kept his arms folded and lent towards them with a determined glint in his eye. 'I never received a phone call from the Home Office – or anyone else for that matter.'

The ominous way he was staring at them made Harker wary, but he continued to maintain an air of diplomacy as he asked the only question left open to him. 'Then why let us in?'

'Because I recognised you at reception and, considering everything else that is going on, I wasn't about to let this opportunity pass without speaking with you.'

'What do you mean?' Harker replied as Chloe shot him a concerned glance.

Holcroft plonked himself on the table top, pulled a newspaper out from under his arm and tapped on it heedfully. 'Over the past few days the entire planet appears to be going to pot. There have been earthquakes, chemical attacks… and that outbreak in Jerusalem.' Holcroft now began tapping more rapidly with his finger on the newspaper, his jaw muscles visibly tightening. 'And then these wolf-type creatures – demons – whatever you want to call them, are flashed across every news channel in the country just before all the TV stations pack up along with our mobiles and now some of the landlines.'

'Oh that,' Harker replied, almost sounding as if he were making light of these dramatic events.

'Yes… *that*,' Holcroft replied, his nostrils flaring, 'this prison's been out of contact for the past seven hours and when I made a trip to our local constabulary, they were just as much in the dark as we are… Half the prison guards didn't even show up for work this morning and there are reports on the radio of food riots breaking out all over the country. So when I saw you here today, I thought I would get some answers from you. Because, Professor,' Holcroft continued loudly, 'I have a wife and two daughters who are at this moment sat at home and scared shitless by the chaos that is already gripping this great country. So I ask you, what the hell is going on?'

'I understand your worry but with respect, Officer, why do you think I would know anything about it?' Harker replied as calmly and courteously as possible given that the officer's knuckles had turned white as his grip on the newspapers became ever tighter.

'Take a guess, Professor.' Holcroft threw the tabloid down on the table top so Harker could read the front-page headline. *Harker now spotted in Jerusalem as all hell breaks loose…*

As he gazed down at the front page, Harker began to feel a tightness in his stomach. The main picture showed a clear image of himself and Chloe racing out of the Temple Mount as fires throughout the city lit up the sky in the background. Beneath it were two smaller pictures: one showing the pair of them surrounded by bodies on the steps of Notre Dame Cathedral, and next to it a picture of just Harker himself at Vatican City four months earlier.

He skipped to the related pages inside only to discover that the main article was even more alarming than the suggestive nature of the photos on the front page and he began to read it aloud for Chloe's benefit.

'For almost five months now wild accusations have surrounded the Catholic Church regarding Pope Adrian VII's admission to world leaders that the second coming of Christ was upon us. Many, including this newspaper, have found the idea of Jesus Christ being reborn as frankly offensive and opportunist. The Church has, of course, denied these allegations even if the disappearance of the then Pope seemed to suggest to many that there was some substance to the rumours. For many others, though, Pope Adrian's vanishing act suggests a more plausible reason in the form of him suffering a complete mental break-down, which had the Church running around in circles to keep such knowledge from entering the public domain. Whichever side of the fence you're thinking you might have landed on, recent world events might give you cause to revisit your initial opinion. The past few days have seen incidents of disaster that would be better suited within the pages of the King James Bible rather than any of the major news channels. Starting with apparent chemical attacks at places of worship throughout the world, then the earthquake at Vatican City during the new Pope's speech, which is thought to have taken the lives of tens of thousands, and most recently the horrific outbreak in the city of Jerusalem.

'These terrible events, all with religious overtones, have incredibly been eclipsed by the torrent of cataclysmic earthquakes, tsunamis, tidal waves and violent storms that have rocked every continent of the world. At the moment of writing there is hardly a single country that has not been affected by them in some way, many have been no less than apocalyptic. Recent reports coming in are almost too fantastical to quote but I have it on unquestionable authority that unknown creatures have been seen attacking ordinary people just before some of the latest earthquakes. So are we truly witnessing the beginning of the end, or is humanity merely reaping what it has sown in a series of coincidences arising out of a global-warming meltdown? It is said that only one man may know for sure since he has direct links to several of these events, and in recent months has become the centre for conspiracy theorists worldwide.

'Professor Alex Harker is the individual in question and there follows a special feature aimed at disclosing what we know and fear about this elusive Cambridge don and his connection with the terrifying events that are now enveloping our lives. Natural cataclysm or approaching apocalypse: decide for yourself.'

Harker groaned as he flicked through the following pages which provided a disturbing timeline of the events to date and how they regularly connected to a one Alex Harker.

'How did they get these pictures?' Chloe gasped as she pulled the newspaper closer to her.

'With a camera most likely,' Harker replied sarcastically, burying his head in his hands as Chloe shot him an unamused glance and then returned to her inspection of the paper.

'So, Professor, I ask you again,' Officer Holcroft reclaimed Harker's attention, 'what the hell is going on?'

Harker paused before replying, preoccupied with the idea that the world's media might be focused on him. That he had made it back into the UK without being instantly detained was perhaps due to the fact that most lines of communications had gone down. In a world that had consigned pen and paper to the fate of the dodo, and replaced them with an invisible electronic cloud it wasn't surprising that life should slow down to a snail's pace if suddenly deprived of such tools.

'It's all true,' Harker announced flatly, even as Chloe eyed him with surprise. 'And the second coming has happened, and everything else that is happening revolves around that.'

'Alex!' Chloe yelled in protest, and Officer Holcroft gave a blank stare at Harker's candour.

'I should tell you I'm an atheist,' Holcroft finally revealed.

'Then I should tell you that it doesn't matter,' Harker replied coldly. 'What does matter is that unless I speak soon with your new arrival here, things are going to get much – much worse. If you want to get dramatic about it, you might say the world's salvation is now in your hands Officer Holcroft, and yours alone.'

Holcroft seemed to loosen up under Harker's direct approach, and he unfolded his arms, and nervously bit his lip. 'My wife is religious, however, and she thinks this really could be it.'

'Well, Officer Holcroft, what do you yourself think?'

The man remained silent as he pondered this question and a full sixty seconds passed which seemed like an eternity. Harker should have been feeling uncomfortable as the prison officer's stare continued to bore into him, but he wasn't because there is a time during any negotiation when all that needs to be said has been said, and all that is left is to wait patiently, and the first person to speak is usually the one who loses. Thankfully it was Holcroft who broke first, and he picked the newspaper up and placed it back under his arm. 'OK, you can see him,' he announced simply, and made his way over to the door and unlocked it. 'But if I sense for a moment that you're bullshitting me, then I promise you this... I'll dump both of you in the cell alongside him and throw away the key.'

Chapter 33

The streets of Hamburg were remarkably quiet for the time of night as Shroder made his way down Elbchaussee Road in the black Lexus LS four-door. Of course this emptiness was hardly surprising considering the papers had been full of talk regarding the possible implementation of a countrywide curfew. Even the heavily used river Elbe running parallel to the road he was on seemed dulled by the lack of container ships that usually dotted its cold dark waters.

Shroder turned right on to a narrow residential street and then pulled up outside a modern-looking apartment block with plush balconies offering a pleasant view of the river. 'There it is.' he muttered to himself, looking up at a corner residence on the first floor.

He switched off the engine, wound down his window and waved over to a man sitting in a navy-blue opal Corsa parked up on the opposite side of the road. In acknowledgement the Corsa's engine fired up and then slowly drove over, stopping only when the two cars' windows were aligned. The window whirred down to reveal a man in his thirties with slicked-back blond hair tied in a ponytail and with a thin moustache hanging from his top lip. 'There's a buzzer system for access but the security camera appears to have had a malfunction,' the man explained in a German accent and with a knowing wink. 'Your man has been inside there since we spoke. He's had a few visitors but they left just minutes ago… Don't worry, I have their registration number if you need it. Since then it has been all quiet on the Western Front.'

The insider joke made Shroder smile and he nodded. 'Thanks, Karl, I owe you one.'

'I know,' the other replied. 'You can buy me a drink once the world has decided to cool down a bit. So how do you want to handle this?'

'Given the limitations on time, I think a direct approach would be best,' Shroder decided, and he pulled the Browning from his side holster and released the safety catch.

'The direct approach it is, then,' Karl replied, pulling out his Beretta 71 Jaguar from an inside jacket pocket.

'Thanks for the offer, Karl, but I need to do this on my own.'

'You sure?'

'I'm sure.'

Karl paused for a moment and then, once satisfied there was no room for second thoughts, he replaced the gun in his pocket. 'OK, good luck.' He gave a friendly nod, wound up his window and drove away, leaving Shroder alone with only the gun and his thoughts to keep him company. The German intelligence agent was a good friend and a good man to have at one's side, but the Bekhit issue was going to require some personal attention that could cause any number of moral dilemmas for an honest agent like Karl. No, Shroder had to handle this alone.

He exited the Lexus and made his way along the short residential path leading to the apartment block's main entrance, with his gun now concealed in its holster. It was a cold night and the only interest in his movements came from a black cat sitting up on one of the balconies which, after a quick glance down at Shroder, resumed the far more important task of self-grooming.

Shroder reached the entrance door and studied the eight illumi-nated buzzers on the wall beside it, noting the names and then finally settling on one residing on the top floor. He pressed the bell and waited.

'Hello.'

'Hello, I have a special delivery for Mr Koch,' Shroder replied in flawless German.

'You have the wrong number. He's on the second floor.'

'I know but he is not answering. Can you buzz me in so I can leave it in the reception? And if you would be good enough to let him know it's there, I'd appreciate it?'

There was a slight hesitation and then the door buzzed open.

'Leave it next to the post boxes. I'll inform him.'

'Many thanks.' Shroder replied. He pushed open the glass door and headed into the reception lobby, then past a row of silver-coloured post boxes, towards the stairwell in the corner. Speedily he made his way up the steps to the first-floor landing and then on down an empty hallway to the corner apartment. Once satisfied there were no obvious sounds of movement coming from the other two apartments on the same floor, Shroder stepped to one side so as to avoid being seen through the spyhole. He then pulled out his Glock and carefully lowered his head against the surface of the door. Hearing no sound from within he pulled back to the side again, extending his arm to administer three firm knocks. He waited for a response before knocking again, but still nothing.

The agent readied himself, took a step back and, with one powerful kick, slammed the sole of his foot against the door, sending it flying open in a puff of splinters. He then rushed inside with his handgun aimed in front of him.

The apartment was small and, even though it was dark, he could make out a kitchen to his left which opened into a main sitting room. He carefully pushed the door shut behind him before continuing. There was still no sign of anyone being alerted to his forced entry and he now skirted the nearby wall and quietly moved deeper into the residence with only the glow of the street lights outside shining through the windows to light the way.

Off to the right he found an empty bedroom and adjoining bathroom, and it was not until he peered into the sitting room that he caught sight of a shadowy figure in the middle it. With his gun aimed, Shroder felt along the side of the wall with his free hand. Upon encountering a switch, he pressed it and the single bulb in the ceiling lit up the room.

Lusic Bekhit sat right in the centre of the room, the sofa and a wooden coffee table having been pushed up against the far wall. Tied to a chair, he bore all the hallmarks of a broken man: figuratively and literally. His chin drooped against his chest and bubbles of spittle had formed between his split lips before dribbling down on to his green polo shirt, as he struggled to breathe against the tight strands of rope securing him. Dark bruises and bloody cut marks ran across both his cheeks where he had been punched repeatedly, and his nose had been broken at its base, leaving a deep, painful-looking gash.

Shroder set about checking that the rest of the apartment was clear before he returned to the living room and knelt down beside the Templar turncoat.

'Lusic?' Shroder said loudly, tapping the man's cheek lightly as one would to awaken a sleeping drunk. 'Can you hear me?'

Bekhit's head bobbed up slightly in recognition of his name. 'Who are you?' he croaked, emitting fresh droplets of blood on to his shirt.

'My name is not important but we share a friend in common.' Shroder leant forward and whispered into Bekhit's ear: 'Sebastian Brulet.'

Bekhit's eyes widened in dismay and he let out an incredulous grunt. 'So it was your man they saw outside there in the Corsa.'

Shroder gave a slow nod and then pulled away from Bekhit's bloodied face. 'Who are they?' he asked, gesturing back towards the front door. 'And are they coming back?'

'They are… they were my Magi contacts, and I don't know if they are coming back,' Bekhit gasped and winced at the pain he was in. 'They did this to me.'

'Why?'

'Because, after all I've done for them, they still don't trust me.'

'Not trust you?' Shroder replied sarcastically. 'I can't imagine why not.'

'Maybe because they are a paranoid lot,' Bekhit said with a forced smile, 'and when they saw there was someone outside keeping an eye on this place, I'm guessing that clinched it.'

'Did they realise it was us?' Shroder demanded.

'No,' Bekhit mumbled, shaking his head. 'But they saw that someone was after me and that was enough to make up their minds… You must find this amusing?'

The suggestion had Shroder shaking his head. 'No Lusic, believe it or not, I've never enjoyed seeing anyone in pain.' He then lifted Bekhit's chin up to face him. 'Even a nasty little shit like you.'

Bekhit managed a short pathetic snort of laughter and Shroder let go of his chin. 'So, apart from that whole betrayal thing, why are you after me?'

'We're looking for the child,' Shroder replied seriously, 'and an explanation as to why the Magi want him.'

Bekhit took a moment before letting out a pained sigh. 'Why the hell do you think? Take a look outside. It's a fucking mess out there.' He nodded towards the window. 'The Magi believe unequivocally in the three Secrets of Fatima and in the prophecy… and, judging by what's happening around the world, I'd say they are absolutely correct in that assumption, wouldn't you?'

Shroder said nothing as he continued to stare in silence.

'As far as I know, only Wilcox has the whole picture and, without knowing what that is, the other Magi are likely to be just as much in the dark as I am.'

'Wilcox is dead,' Shroder informed him bluntly.

News of the Magi leader's death had Bekhit shaking his head in despair. 'Then I don't know what to tell you except that the child holds the answer and has them all fighting amongst themselves.'

'You better have something more for me than that,' Shroder growled, and Bekhit immediately began licking his lips nervously, obviously wanting to appease this would-be saviour.

'They offered me a safe passage to join the others, but instead of a pick-up all I got was a brutal interrogation.'

'Passage to where?' Shroder yelled impatiently.

'I don't know, but they were supposed to have made all the travel arrangements, and the only thing I do know is that I was to be on the last flight out.' Bekhit suddenly broke down into tears at the futility of what he was disclosing, as Shroder looked on with little sympathy as the fellow wallowed in his own self-pity.

'All right, Lusic, we'll take care of you.' Shroder said finally in a comforting voice. 'You may have forgotten but we're not murderers, and neither do we condemn people to death unless it remains the only choice. We're nothing like your new friends.' He reached over and began to loosen Bekhit's bonds. 'Besides, you may still be of some help to us.'

Shroder undid the last of the knots, allowing the broken wretch an opportunity to rub at the rope marks discolouring his chest, then he made his way over to the balcony window and peeped outside for any sign that they were being watched. Behind him, Bekhit sucked in a deep stabilising breath and then shakily got to his feet. But no sooner had he done so a beeping sound began emitting from the chair. Shroder spun around to see a green light flashing from underneath the seat and, without a second thought, he grabbed the large wooden coffee table resting against the wall next to him and raised it in front of his face and body just as an explosion ripped through the apartment. The table took the force of the blast and propelled Shroder backwards, crashing through the glass window, over the balcony's steel railings and out into the night air. He tumbled down on to the grass embankment below with a heavy wallop and then rolled on to a nearby pavement as the charred table top landed with a thud just metres away from him.

Shroder managed to catch a glimpse of a fireball, as it swelled up into the air like a flaming balloon, and he instinctively tried to get back up on to his feet, but his muscles wouldn't allow it. He knew he was hurt but how badly was anyone's guess, and he instead lay there and looked back up at the fiery inferno that had been Lusic's apartment while he tried to catch his breath. He wasn't sure how long had passed but eventually a woman appeared, standing above him. She took off her jacket and placed it over him. Shroder's first thought was that he was dead and that he was being covered up, but he then realised the helpful passer-by was only trying to keep him warm and, safe in that knowledge, he allowed his mind to drift.

'Are you all right,' she mouthed. Shroder couldn't hear a thing because his ears were ringing from the deafening blast of the explosion, but as he caught his breath he muttered a single word – one that he could feel his lips uttering but couldn't hear his voice saying it. It was a single pointless and futile word but he spoke it nonetheless.

'Shit.'

Chapter 34

The fluorescent strip-lights flickered alarmingly overhead as Harker followed Officer Holcroft down the white-walled corridor towards the high-security unit within Wakefield prison. 'They've been doing that all day. Problems with the power grid, I think,' Holcroft commented, pointing towards the malfunctioning bulbs. 'No reason to worry, though. The prison has back-up generators so that we can maintain our security-checkpoint integrity at all times.'

Holcroft's assurance went a small way to allaying Harker's unease after his near trouser-ruining experience at Blackwater insane asylum. Visiting two high-security facilities within forty-eight hours was not an excursion he ever planned to repeat, although at least this time a guard would accompany him throughout. Officer Holcroft had flatly insisted upon remaining at his side during the visit, and it was not a demand that Harker had any problem complying with. Holcroft had also requested that Chloe remain in the waiting room because, as the officer had put it, the presence of an attractive woman was only likely to excite some of the other residents in the specialist unit.

'Are these prisoners kept on suicide watch?' Harker asked, as they reached the final security door with its sign stipulating to 'Cardboard Furniture Only'.

'Either suicide watch or death threats from other prisoners,' Holcroft replied as he guided his master key into the door lock. 'But in your man's case it's for the protection of the other prisoners. He's got a bit of a temper, this one.'

'Yes, I remember.'

'Ahh, so you've had dealings with him before?' Holcroft concluded, with a hint of concern in his voice.

'A few times in fact,' Harker admitted, 'but I'm glad to have some bars between us this time around.'

Holcroft offered an understanding nod before unlocking the sturdy-looking door mechanism and then turning his full attention back to Harker. 'Then I should warn you straight away we don't have bars in these cells.'

'What!' Harker barked.

'All the cells have thick Perspex walls.'

Holcroft's statement had numerous and unsettling images bombarding Harker's mind. 'Like something out of *The Silence of the Lambs*.' Harker replied tersely and he felt his pulse begin to quicken at the thought.

'Similar,' Holcroft concurred, 'but we had them installed years before that movie came out. Interesting footnote though: the first one was built for the murderer Robert Maudsley who bashed his cellmate's skull in and ate pieces of his brain with a plastic fork. I heard that the character of Hannibal Lector was in part based on our own infamous resident. Art imitating life. Funny really.'

'Hilarious,' Harker replied.

'Don't worry, Professor.' Holcroft offered him with a calming smile. 'You would need a wrecking ball to get through the Perspex, and your man might be big but he's not that big.'

Holcroft turned the key and pulled open the door to reveal a corridor running the length of the short wing, fitted with a shiny grey lino flooring leading to a dead end, and with a row of eight cells on the left-hand side. The entire front of each cell was made up of two thick Perspex panels firmly held in place by a metal frame, with a door cut into the Perspex, and a black metal access box embedded in its centre, evidently used for handcuffing the occupants before the door was opened.

'The prisoner in the first cell is heavily medicated at the moment, so you won't get any distraction from him,' Holcroft murmured before motioning to the cell next to it. 'Your man's in the second cell and he already knows you're coming.'

Holcroft closed the door and then locked it behind them both with a clunk. 'I'll stay right here,' he said, gesturing for Harker to make his way over to the cell indicated.

So this was the 'monster mansion' wherein the most depraved and dangerous ended up, Harker reflected and all of them under one roof. But worst of the lot were those in the same corridor he was now standing in. He felt an uncomfortable twinge of nerves pass through him and he realised that his earlier jaunt to Blackwater had made more of an impact upon his psyche than he cared to admit. Harker took a measured breath and took his first steps towards the second cell and, inside it, the man who had been so hell-bent on trying to kill him during their last encounter.

The patient occupying the first cell was, as Holcroft had assured him, sound asleep on a safety-concrete slab bed and snoring away, and Harker continued on past the inmate towards the dividing wall.

As the next cell came into view, Harker was met by a pair of familiar, piercing amber eyes that aroused in him an unpleasant feeling of alarm despite the Perspex wall between them.

Drazia Heldon, the Magi hitman, sat motionless on his concrete slab, the killer's massive seven-foot frame rigid while he watched Harker halt a couple of feet short of the panel. The hulking giant's oversized hands gripped his muscular thighs as he stared at Harker with those hauntingly predatory eyes.

'Professor Harker,' Heldon rasped in his thick Serbian accent, 'what an unpleasant surprise.'

Harker had forgotten how intimidating the mere size of this man was and he found himself struggling to force any words at all from his lips. 'Hello, Heldon, it's been a while.'

'Not long enough,' Drazia replied through gritted teeth as he eyed his visitor up and down. 'And looking in such good shape, too.' He shook his oversized head slowly from side to side, then stood up and approached to within mere inches of the Perspex, moving with all the grace of a fairy-tale ogre. 'How disappointing that is,' he added gruffly as his hot breath fogged the glass. 'But I am glad at least you're still alive.'

The last comment drew a puzzled look from Harker. 'That's kind of you,' he said, fighting the urge to take a step back from the screen.

'Not really,' Heldon growled. 'It's just I would hate to think that someone else had got to you before I did.'

This menacing remark surprisingly had the opposite effect on Harker who felt oddly bolstered by how genuinely annoyed Heldon seemed to be at having missed the opportunity to kill him.

Harker scanned the edge of the cell's transparent panel with his eyes before returning the killer's icy stare. 'I don't think you're going to get a second chance from in there... do you?'

The sarcastic comment made Heldon's eyes blaze with anger and he slammed his bulging fists against the Perspex, causing the whole double pane to shake vigorously. This time Harker cautiously took the step backwards that he had previously denied himself. His retreat was met with an ominous grin from the enormous assassin.

'Maybe,' Heldon snarled, revealing chipped yellow teeth, 'but it's good to see you've not lost your fear of me.'

Harker offered the behemoth a respectful nod and his submissive gesture appeared to pacify the Magi's ego as well as his temper. 'I got lucky the last time we met and, if I'm honest, I think somehow you wanted to let me go,' he declared, continuing to appease the Serbian's ego. Heldon might possess the physical strength of an elephant but he had not been equally blessed in the intelligence department, and it was this weakness that Harker was now hoping to capitalise on. 'But now I am in a position to return the favour.'

'Let you go?' Heldon frowned. 'Why would I have done that?'

'Because even though you were invited to join the ranks of the Magi, they never treated you as an equal and I think that you were getting tired of them barking orders for you like you were some lapdog.'

'Bullshit,' Heldon scowled, 'I was always treated as an equal.'

'Really!' Harker replied seriously. 'Then tell me why it is that, after all these months and with all the connections the Magi possess, you are still rotting in a jail cell awaiting trial? This is the second prison you've been sent to, and no rescue has even been attempted.' Harker watched Heldon's scowl begin to evaporate as he contemplated the notion. 'I thought that no Magi was ever left behind... dead or alive, no matter what the cost. And yet here you are being left to rot even as the Magi begin their preparations for the end of the world, with the Christ child at their side, in a plan that I have no doubt you were aware of from the beginning.'

Harker knew that he was taking a huge gamble on this dumb brute being entrusted with his master's grandiose plan, but realised it was one he had to take.

'What would you know about it?' Heldon growled.

'I know that it's already happening, right now... out there even as we speak. And they're not going to let you become part of it.'

Heldon stared at him intently for a few moments, then his expression of puzzlement began to fade and he turned and lumbered back to his concrete bed. 'Why are you here, Harker?' he wheezed, sitting down.

'Because I can offer you something you want,' Harker replied. 'Something that has been on your mind ever since you realised your old masters aren't coming to the rescue.'

Harker's words piqued the oaf's curiosity and he tilted his head upwards. 'What's that?'

'Revenge, Drazia,' he suggested and took a step closer to the cell. 'Revenge against the people that let you down when you most needed their help. And in turn I want you now to help me take down the Magi.'

Drazia Heldon stared up at him with eyes wide at this mention of the one word that held any real currency for him – *Revenge* – and his fists began to clench tightly.

As Harker watched the giant struggle to order his thoughts, he thought back to his conversation with Brulet on the flight over. Harker had not known that Heldon had a condition: one that, when not medicated, quickly brought about mind-freeze and confusion. 'Get him off his medication and he should become more pliable for you, but be warned,' Brulet had added, 'it will also make him highly unpredictable, so choose carefully what you say, and when.' It was pure luck that Heldon had not received his daily meds, due to the prevailing chaos outside, as explained to Harker by Officer Holcroft on their way over. That was just the stroke of luck that Harker needed and, as he watched the murderous brute tussle with his particular sense of reasoning, he pushed further his efforts to confuse the man's rationale further. 'I can get you out of this place today, Drazia, and together we can exact revenge. But all I need to know is the location of the Magi gathering point. The place where you are all supposed to meet? The place where we must head next… I have a plane waiting and all I need is for you to tell me where to go.'

'Bullshit,' the giant hissed. 'They'd never let me out of this place.'

'Under normal circumstances you would be right Drazia,' Harker replied, 'but what is happening outside is far from normal and the Home Office has agreed for you to be released into my custody – and that you will be granted clemency for your past actions if, and only if, you help me find the Magi base of operations.'

Heldon stared at him blankly. Even though he was clearly not fully convinced, he was certainly entertaining the idea.

'You will of course remain under armed guard at all times. But if you keep your side of the bargain, then you will be free of this cell forever. That's unless you decide to kill again and then, of course, you'll be hunted down, but that is your choice to make.'

The casual mentioning of killing and actually having choice in the matter garnered a flash of excitement in Heldon's eyes, but it was immediately replaced with one of anguish. He rubbed at his temples as his eyes began to flutter, the familiar pain of his condition causing a throbbing in his head.

The Class 1 form of chiari malformation was a genetic disorder and in the simplest terms meant the patient's brain was quite literally too big for the skull and, without regular treatment, would cause blinding headaches. The chances were that the same genes responsible for Heldon's abnormal size were the likely reason for this condition, and in most cases the illness would bring about an early death unless major surgery was performed. For Heldon, unfortunately, surgery had never been an option and the best he could look forward to was a lifetime of medication and the increasingly psychopathic tendencies that had manifested in him from an early age. Perfect Magi cannon fodder, and also the perfect candidate to be manipulated so long as he was off his medication. By the way the giant was clutching at his head in pain he was without doubt in the danger zone right at that moment.

'This is your only chance for revenge on those who betrayed you.' Harker coaxed softly, fully aware of the disorder that was tearing through the killer's head.

'I have been betrayed,' he began to mutter in his usual deep monotone. 'They should… They should have never left me here…'

'That's right Drazia, they shouldn't have,' Harker cajoled tenderly, not wanting to sound in anyway dominating and risk the killer's naturally defensive nature bubbling to the surface. 'But I don't need to tell you what you already know.'

Heldon closed his eyes and rubbed at them with his thick fingers, then massaged the back of his neck before his eyes fluttered open once again. 'My head hurts,' he whined gazing at Harker with none of the malice displayed earlier. 'I need my medication.'

'I'll have some waiting for you on the plane, Drazia. Just tell me where we are going and I'll get you aboard quickly and then you can take your revenge.'

The calmness of the moment was suddenly broken by a bumping sound in one of the cells further along and for a moment the giant was distracted by it, turning his head towards the source.

'Don't worry about that, Drazia,' Harker urged, not wanting Heldon to wake from his hazy state. 'Tell me where we need to go, and then we can get the revenge that you deserve.'

Harker's mention of revenge brought Heldon's focus back on to him, and the killer began to nod slowly, his eyes still glazed.

'Caracas,' he muttered, the pain in his head clearly becoming increasingly debilitating. 'When the time is near I must go to Caracas and head for the base of the hill in Macuira National Park.' The sentence was delivered so mechanically that it sounded as if the assassin had been hypnotised into remembering it.

'Then let's go to Caracas and meet with the others,' Harker suggested, still in the same soft tone so as to soothe the killer's muddled state of mind. 'Is there anything else we should know before we leave here? Anything else that might help us once we get there?'

Further along the corridor the same bumping started again, but louder this time as one of the occupants continued to engage in whatever activity he was up to and Harker made the mistake of allowing himself to become momentarily distracted. The interruption was all that was needed to break Heldon from his daze, and to have the killer now staring at him menacingly again. The fiery hatred was back with a vengeance as the killer jumped to his feet and lunged forward, slamming both his fists against the Perspex screen – sending Harker flinching backwards.

'You're trying to trick me, you piece of shit,' Heldon raged as spittle flew from his lips on to the transparent partition. 'You won't get anything from me except a slow death.'

Harker lent in towards the Perspex barrier and eyed the Magi assassin with contempt. 'Caracas? Thank you, Heldon, you've been most helpful. I couldn't have known it without you.'

Heldon stood back wide-eyed as he realised what he had just divulged and then the giant let out an almighty roar and began pounding his huge fists against the divider, again and again, as Harker offered him a grateful wave of the hand.

'Enjoy your new home you homicidal maniac,' Harker yelled. 'You belong here.' He was about to turn away and head back to the exit when suddenly a thin crack appeared in the Perspex, directly under one of Heldon's fists. The fissure began to spread outwards even as Holcroft began pulling Harker towards the door behind them. It was abruptly flung open and three burly prison guards burst in and surrounded the second cell with Tasers drawn.

'Calm down, Drazia,' the lead guard bellowed as Holcroft hustled Harker through the open security doorway, then slammed it shut behind them.

'Time for your visit's up,' Holcroft announced grimly and he began leading Harker back to the main exit, with the sound of Heldon's heavy blows still vibrating through the steel security door behind them. 'Caracas,' he questioned, 'does it help?'

'Yes, it does,' Harker replied, hugely glad to be out of the Magi killer's intimidating presence. 'But I won't know in what way until I get there.'

Holcroft came to an abrupt halt and he grabbed Harker by the shoulder. 'Do you really think you can stop all this?' the officer demanded with an air of uncertainty.

Harker could see the real fear in the other man's eyes and he quashed his own feelings of doubt, because in truth he was not sure of the answer. 'I hope so,' was all he could offer.

Holcroft stared at him for a further few seconds before giving a nod. 'I hope so, too. Well, then, you'd better get your bloody arse in gear then hadn't you, Professor? Oh, and do me a favour,' the prison officer added. 'Don't ever come back here.'

The obvious sincerity in Holcroft's voice made Harker laugh. 'You have my word,' he replied firmly before continuing towards the security door. 'I just hope there's a *here* to come back to.'

Chapter 35

'All UK citizens are reminded that as of this evening a curfew will be in effect between the hours of 6 p.m. and 8 a.m., and will remain in place until martial law has been rescinded. Citizens are further reminded that any persons found outside their residence between these hours face arrest and detention by Her Majesty's armed forces. Please tune into channel 118.56FM for more information on how best to prepare for these temporary restrictions. In other news, the Home Office was unable say when normal communication services will resume. In a speech earlier today the Home Secretary declared that everything possible was being done to restore the satellite networks, and urged all members of the public to remain patient and pay close attention to the radio stations for updates as they become available... In a further appeal for calm, Britain's most senior police officer Sir Richard Mitchell-Smith, the commissioner of the Metropolitan Police, has voiced his concern over the use of lethal force by soldiers from the Scots Guard, which saw thirteen people injured and two dead while disbanding rioters in Glasgow city centre earlier today. The Commissioner said that the majority of British citizens were law-abiding people and that it was essential that lethal force be used only as a last resort. His comments come as fresh accounts of rioting have been reported in Manchester, Birmingham, Leeds...'

Harker switched off the radio and stepped out of the rented silver Ford Mondeo and made his way over to join Chloe, who stood waiting for him at the bottom of the Gulf Stream 450's entrance steps.

'Anything new?' she asked, brushing windswept hair from her face.

'Nothing we didn't already know,' he replied. 'I just wanted to make sure.'

The trip back to Leeds International airport from Wakefield Prison had been a swift one given they had driven through the centre of the city itself and experienced first-hand the bedlam playing out on its streets. It wasn't, to Harker's mind, rioting just to cause damage but rather rioting through desperation. In a bid to stock up on essentials, the supermarkets had been ferociously cleaned out and they had passed hundreds of people with filled-up shopping trolleys, all making their way home before the curfew came into effect. The setting up of temporary checkpoints by the army seemed to be making matters even worse, by causing an already nervous population to become even more panicky. Harker had been extremely relieved to get back on to the motorway and out of the city, even if it meant having to go on a detour so as to avoid the worst affected areas of the city.

'Deprive a society of three meals a day and you'll have a revolution,' Harker noted and quoting the famous saying as they watched the city's inhabitants scrambling to get home. But, in the modern context it seemed more relevant to say: 'Deprive a society of anything for a day and you'll get pretty much the same result.'

Arriving at the airport had not proved a problem but if they had needed to approach by the main entrance, where heavy queues were brought to a standstill, instead of a private side entrance, it would have been another matter altogether. The military had, of course, been present at the entry checkpoint and as Harker now made his way over to the waiting Gulf Stream, the sight of hordes of people packed into the concourses beyond made him thank God he had access to a private jet.

'Quick as you can,' Brulet called out to them as he waited just inside the jet's passenger door urgently waving both Harker and Chloe inside. 'If we don't get airborne right now we are likely to get grounded, along with all the other flights.' The Grand Master stepped back into the cabin, allowing the new arrivals to join him inside. 'Was Heldon any help to you?' he asked, closing the airtight door behind them.

'Caracas,' Harker replied, as Chloe chose a seat. 'We have to head to Caracas and then to the Macuira National Park.'

'Venezuela!' Brulet looked highly sceptical. 'And you're prepared to believe him?'

'Yes, I am,' Harker replied and this was received immediately with an accepting nod from Brulet who turned towards the internal cockpit door where the two pilots were awaiting instructions.

'Can we make it to Caracas, Venezuela?' he asked.

The senior pilot frowned and then nodded his head. 'We can but we'll need to refuel mid-route.'

'Good, then make the necessary arrangements.'

The pilot began pulling maps from a black leather briefcase resting on the floor next to him, then instructed his co-pilot to begin the aircraft's start-up procedures. Meanwhile Harker took a seat next to Chloe, who was staring out the window with a vacant expression on her face.

'I can't believe it,' she said, settling back into her seat. 'Great Britain hasn't seen any form of martial law since the early 1900s and even then that was only in Liverpool.' This historical titbit drew a look of surprise from Harker and he raised his eyebrows. 'I saw a documentary about it on the History channel,' she explained with an embarrassed shrug of her shoulders. 'What can I say except I don't get out much.'

Harker tilted his head at this telling admission and he let out an amused laugh. 'If we ever get through this, those quiet nights in are going seem fairly boring.'

'Or possibly more appealing,' she replied, and then squinted at him sternly. 'And what do you mean *if* we get through this?'

Harker smiled once again. 'I meant to say *when* we get through this.'

'That's better,' she murmured as Brulet sat down opposite and secured his seat belt. Meanwhile the engines powered up and the aircraft's wheels began to roll forward.

'The pilot reckons our best bet is to refuel at Lajes airport, on the island of Terceira in the Azores, and then head directly from there to Caracas,' Brulet informed them. 'It should take around four or five hours, which will give us more than ample time for you to tell me exactly what the butcher of Racak managed to convince you of?'

'The butcher of Racak?' Chloe perked up at the mention of such a gruesome designation.

'Yes,' Harker said, interrupting the conversation but feeling a need to explain to Chloe some of the details he had previously and deliberately left out. 'Drazia Heldon had an extremely disturbing history long before he was recruited by the Magi. He took part in the campaign of ethnic cleansing that occurred during the Yugoslavian war in the late '90's.'

'He sounds like a lovely fellow,' Chloe gasped.

'Indeed,' Harker replied, 'and what's even more lovely is that his preferred method of execution was crushing his victims with a large wooden hammer.' Harker paused there as what he had to say next was chilling even for him. 'Which was usually after he had first raped them... men, women and children alike... The Bosnian government is pushing to have him extradited for war crimes, and that's the reason he's being held at Wakefield.'

Chloe looked sobered by the thought and she folded her arms tightly. 'Fascinating... I would have liked to interview him.'

Her comment caught Harker off guard. Throughout all of this he had forgotten that she was a clinical psychologist used to working with the very worst of the worst. 'Well, maybe once we've made it through all this, you'll get your chance to,' he suggested.

'It's a nice sentiment, Alex,' Brulet said wearily, 'I only hope it is justified.'

Brulet's reaction brought a look of disbelief from Harker. 'What do you mean? We now know where the child is.'

'You mean we *think* we know where the child is,' Brulet corrected, 'and even if we do find him, how exactly does one go about bringing a halt to an impending apocalypse.'

The question was one that had been hovering at the back of Harker's mind since the chaos in Jerusalem, and he still didn't have an answer. Gratefully it was Chloe who broke the following silence with a question that any psychologist might raise.

'You know what's preoccupying my thoughts,' she declared as Harker and Brulet both focused on her with interest. 'Given what a monster Drazia Heldon clearly is I can only imagine what kind of people would hire someone like that.'

'What kind of person indeed,' Brulet replied, 'but don't waste time letting your imagination run wild,' he settled back in his seat with a very grave expression, 'because if Alex is right, you are going to have the chance to witness them first-hand... and, once you have, I can assure you will wish you never had.'

Chapter 36

Red and blue police lights flickered across the growing crowd pressed up against the police barriers, wanting a glimpse of the extraordinary event that had taken place on such an ordinary-looking road. Inside the cordon, Michael Shroder was perched on a gurney at the back of an ambulance with a blanket wrapped around his shoulders, watching a team of firemen as they doused the still smouldering, burnt-out apartment with a fire hose. On the grass further along, a black plastic sheet covered the charred body of Lusic Bekhit, who had been launched out of the apartment window by the blast and landed in one of the many flower beds surrounding the communal garden below. His corpse had been so badly burnt in the explosion that it was now unrecognisable and had been the first thing covered up upon the emergency service's arrival.

Shroder winced at the pain in his ribs but dismissed it immediately. The medic had already informed him how lucky he was to have escaped with only minor bruising and with no sign of breaks or fractures. But Shroder knew differently: luck had nothing to do with it. If he had not acted when he did, he would now be lying alongside Bekhit and covered by his own personal black bin-liner. Still there was something far more painful than any injuries he had sustained, which was the death of Lusic Bekhit and with it any hope of tracing the child, and he could only pray that Brulet and Harker were having more luck with that brute Drazia Heldon. Shroder was still brooding on his failure when the satellite phone in his jacket pocket began to buzz, causing him to recoil as its vibrations rippled through his midsection. He pulled it out and held it to his ear just as one of the medics appeared and motioned for him to move further back into the ambulance.

'Hello,' Shroder answered, as the medic joined him inside and closed the doors.

'Michael, it's me,' the voice said, and Shroder recognised it immediately as Karl, his contact who had been keeping Bekhit's apartment under surveillance. 'I am sorry,' Karl continued. 'Looks like they made me.'

Shroder wanted to scream down the phone at him but he didn't. He knew how professional the man was, and how sometimes these types of operations that were thrown together at the last moment went spectacularly wrong – as it had done tonight. 'It's not your fault, Karl, and the people we're dealing with are extremely well trained. The blame is all mine for dropping it into your lap at such short notice.' Shroder paused for a moment as the ambulance jerked forward on beginning its trip back to base. 'I'm heading to the hospital to get checked out. I should be there for an hour or so.'

'You may want to hold off on that.'

'Why?' Shroder replied and now resisting the medic's attempt to lie him out flat on the gurney.

'I've got a location on the car of those visitors to Bekhit's apartment, if you want it?'

'I want it,' Shroder grunted.

'It's at the airbus facility just across the river from you.'

'Good job. I'll call you right back.'

The line went dead, but Shroder was already banging on the metal partition separating him from the driver. 'Stop the car!'

The ambulance came to an abrupt halt, and Shroder began moving towards the doors even as the paramedic beside him raised a warning hand and shook his head.

'I can't let you do that, sir. You need to be checked out at the hospital.'

It was Shroder who was now shaking his head. 'What I need is to get out of this ambulance right now,' he insisted, retrieving the credentials from his pocket before waving them in front of the unhappy-looking paramedic. 'Do you understand me?'

The man took one look and with a defeated sigh turned to the doors and pushed them open, allowing Shroder out on to the road whereupon, without pause, the ambulance disappeared off into the night.

Well then Bekhit, Shroder thought to himself, *it looks like you might have been of some use to me after all.*

Chapter 37

With a puff of black smoke from its wheels, the Gulf Stream touched down at Lajes airport in Terceira and taxied over to one of the vacant parking bays on the far side of the runway. The aircraft had hardly come to a complete stop before Harker had opened the cabin door and was making his way down the steps and onto the tarmac. He was closely followed by Chloe and Brulet who spent a few moments stretching to loosen the stiffness in their muscles induced by having to sit in one position during the journey. The Gulf Stream 450 was one of the most spacious and comfortable airplanes in its class, but not being able to stand fully upright for such a prolonged period meant that most passengers were just as excited at simply being able to exit the aircraft as they were at reaching their destination.

'We should be ready to go in about another fifteen minutes,' Brulet announced, pointing out a cylindrical grey refuelling truck that was rumbling down one of the taxiways towards them. 'I'll stay here with the plane but if you want to stretch your legs, now is the time to do it. Just don't go far.' he warned, sounding like a watchful father. 'This base serves as a military outpost for the Portuguese air force, as well as for a detachment of the US air force, and last thing we need now is either of you being arrested for trespassing.'

'Noted,' Harker acknowledged, grateful for the warning. He had never visited the Azores before and was glad to have the chance even if it was just a short stop-over. The Azores is comprised of a small group of islands and although the main tourist spot was the larger island of São Miguel ninety miles to the west, the landscape here was nonetheless just as beautiful, affording a view of lush green vegetation surrounding the mountain towering at the island's centre. What was more impressive to Harker, though, was the fleet of American military aircraft that made up the 65 Airbase wing currently parked up at the other side of the airfield. The row of F-15 Eagles, complemented by three A-10 Thunderbolt IIs, was a remarkable sight to behold but even these were put to shame by the two gigantic Boeing C-17 Globe-masters at the far end. With a wingspan of fifty-two metres, these majestic leviathans were used to transport anything from a company of soldiers to an M1 Abrams main battle tank with six supporting armoured security vehicles, and Harker found himself rooted to the spot as he took in the magnificent sight.

'What is it with men and machines?' Chloe grumbled, as she joined him in surveying the spectacle.

'What is it with psychiatrists and crazy people?' Harker replied, receiving a look of astonishment from Doctor Stanton, whose mouth had dropped wide open.

'That's not all we do, Alex,' she replied with an amused smile. 'It's a bit more scientific than that, I assure you.'

'So is finding a way to lift 265 tonnes into the air and then land it safely,' he replied, pointing out the two parked-up C-17s.

His response had Chloe rolling her eyes teasingly, and then they both stood in silence and watched as a small passenger jet throttled up its engines, took off down the runaway and passed them before effortlessly lifting up into the evening sky.

'Alex,' Chloe asked, and ending this peaceful moment between them, 'what are we doing here?'

Her question had Harker looking confused and he offered the obvious answer. 'Well, at the moment we're refuelling.'

'No,' Chloe shook her head, 'I mean going to Caracas to find this child. What on earth do we do when we find him, and how is that in any way going to stop all the mayhem going on at the moment?'

It was a question that Harker was surprised she had not asked up until now, and the real problem for him was that he didn't have an answer. 'Chloe, I would be lying to you if I said I knew, because during the past few days everything I have ever believed in has been thrown into question.'

'That's a fair answer but it still doesn't explain what finding the child is going achieve,' Chloe continued.

'Honestly I don't know,' he said, raising his hands in the air despair-ingly. 'Maybe everything awful will just stop and we'll go back to the way it was… Maybe God will ride down to earth on an angelic chariot of fire and declare war upon evil throughout the world… Maybe nothing will happen at all… I just don't know.' He almost yelled the last words, frustrated by his own feeble lack of insight. 'But ever since visiting Chernobyl I've had this strange feeling that finding the child will solve everything. I can't explain how but there it is.' He gave a deep sigh. 'Besides what else can we do? This is it, Chloe, our only lead – and we have to follow it through to its conclusion.'

She watched him blankly as he now returned his attention to the fleet of military aircraft. 'Well, thank you, Alex, that has certainly cleared things up for me.'

Harker snapped his head around to face her, and was met with a friendly smile and he immediately started laughing. 'Clear as mud...'

'Mud is right,' she echoed. 'So you're not pinning everything on the fourth Secret any more... do you think there ever was one?'

'I don't think so, and I would wager that Marcus Eckard's imagination got the better of him.' Harker gave a shake of his head and now noticed how glum she appeared again. 'Look, Chloe,' he said pleasantly and without any bitterness whatsoever, 'I have no idea what we're going to find in Caracas, and if you want to bow out now, I wouldn't blame you in the least.' He reached inside his jacket, pulled out his wallet and picked out his Lloyds credit card, then held it out towards her between his two fingers. 'Why not stay here on the island until this whole thing has hopefully blown over. It's on me'

Without a pause, Chloe plucked the card from his fingers and dropped it back into his top pocket. 'That's very kind of you to offer, Alex, but you and I are in this until the end. And, anyway, I don't think this is going to just blow over, do you?'

'No, I don't,' Harker conceded with a shake of his head, 'and I can't tell you how glad I am to hear you say that.'

The remark made her smile and she reached over and squeezed his forearm. 'Because despite how pushy I've been, deep down you want me with you on this trip, don't you?'

Harker stared at her silently for a few moments before patting his top pocket and the credit card snugly tucked away inside it. 'Actually it's because this credit card's maxed out... so it's totally useless... Phew.' He started to laugh.

'You cheeky bastard,' she exclaimed but still retained her smile. 'Maybe I should catch a lift home with them,' – pointing over to the military jets – 'or not.' The smile had disappeared and was replaced with a look of surprise.

Harker himself turned towards the row of F-15 Eagles to see a bunch of flight engineers busily scrambling around underneath them in a flurry of organised chaos, while to the side of them a number of masked pilots dressed in grey flight suits began entering their respective cockpits.

Harker and Chloe watched in curiosity as, one by one, the cockpit visors closed and the jets began taxiing towards the far end of the runway.

'What do they know that we don't?' Harker managed just as a vibration rumbled beneath their feet. They looked at each other apprehensively as they felt another tremor, stronger this time, and from the military side of the runway the sounds of sirens began to wail. From inside the hangars a number of army trucks filled with personnel poured out on to the side road, then began heading towards the airport's main entrance at high speed, each with its own siren blaring loudly.

'Alex!' Chloe yelled as she directed Harker's attention to what looked like a spray of red neon being spat out from the side of the mountain in the distance, followed by a massive explosion sending the top portion of it away in massive plume of rock and dust. This was followed by a deafening explosion that had both of them clasping their ears in pain. As Harker peered though squinting eyes, he could make out a line of distortion on the ground hurtling towards them, and he instinctively threw his arms around Chloe protectively. Before he could say anything, the shockwave hit and sent them both up into the air before landing them back onto the hard tarmac, with Harker taking the brunt of the impact. They looked up and watched, as in the distance, the island's central mountain began to spit red-hot lava from a jagged opening created by the initial blast, sending liquid fire seeping down its side and towards the forests below.

Harker pulled himself and Chloe to their feet even as more F-15 Eagles roared towards the end of the runway and took their place in the queue.

'We have to go,' he shouted over the rumbling of both the fiery volcano and the jets now flying past them and up in the air. 'Don't let go,' he yelled and gripped tightly on to Chloe's hand as she struggled to maintain her balance over the tremors that continued to shake the ground underneath them. Harker only just managed to keep his own balance as he stumbled towards the Gulf Stream with his arm around her waist, to find Brulet ordering the fuel truck to disengage its nozzle. The operator, though, was having none of it and was already running in the opposite direction, so Brulet staggered over to the fuel hose and uncoupled the safety valve leaving them free to leave.

'Let's go,' Brulet shouted, before heading inside the aircraft which was already starting up its engines.

It was only sixty metres to the jet but the ground was shaking so violently that Harker found it difficult to navigate the black tarmac, which was beginning to tear apart in places. Spurred on at the thought of being left behind, he grabbed Chloe and lifted her up onto his shoulder – and just ran. He came close to tripping over twice but at each instance managed to regain his balance, and twenty seconds later they had reached the entrance hatch and he was hauling himself and her into the cabin even as the jet began to move.

'They're aboard,' Brulet shouted loudly to the pilots and in response the engines began to power up further.

Harker heaved the door shut and took to the seat next to Chloe, who was already buckling herself in.

'Where the hell did that volcano come from?' she cried out in disbelief, her eyes fixed on the window as they taxied towards the end of the runway, to join a shortening line of waiting F-15s.

'That's what the Azores are,' Harker explained, also captivated by the terrifying sight of a thick stream of lava making its way now through the forest towards them while igniting everything it got close to in a burst of flames. 'There are four stratovolcanoes on this island alone, but none has been active for centuries.'

'That doesn't look inactive to me,' snapped Chloe, focusing her attention now on the dark clouds of ejected material that went billowing upwards into the red evening sky as well as heading down towards them.

'God, it's moving fast,' Harker yelled, the cloud of debris getting closer with every passing second. He then turned his attention to the last few F-15's throttling up, even as another roared past them and up into the air. 'We're not going to make it,' he yelled. 'If all that dust hits our engines, we're not going anywhere.'

But Brulet was already ahead of him, barking orders to the pilot before Harker had even finished speaking. 'Get on that runway *now*,' Brulet instructed, pointing to the tight space intervening between the F-15 currently taking off and the last one readying itself directly behind.

Without hesitation, the pilot jammed his feet down hard on to the right rudder. The aircraft reacted immediately and careened off the taxi-way and headed straight across a narrow strip of grass, nearly clipping the wing of the departing F-15 Eagle.

The Gulf Stream's engines were already being pushed to full throttle before it had even properly lined up with the runway. The momentum of this lifted the aircraft up onto only two wheels, so the dipped wing came within inches of making contact with the tarmac, before the elevated wheel dropped back down again with a hefty thump. A collective sigh of relief ran through the cabin as the Gulf Stream now hurtled towards the end of the runway, even as the immense ash cloud reached the airfield's perimeter. The jet lifted off the ground and sped upwards just as the peripheral buildings below were enveloped in a thick black mass of noxious gases and displaced earth that continued to unload devastation upon everything in its path.

'Did the last jet make it?' Harker shouted anxiously, straining to see out through the side window and back towards the cloud of dust that had covered the runway. His question was answered with a thunderous boom from two glowing Pratt and Whitney F100 engines that zipped past them at high speed. The F-15 then dipped its wings from left to right in friendly acknowledgment that their queue-jumping had been warranted and acceptable. Either that or the pilot was severely pissed off and considering now shooting them down. Either way all the planes had made it safely off the ground, which was more than could be said for some of the ground staff.

'Bloody hell, that was close.' Chloe groaned.

'I'll say,' Harker replied before turning to Brulet, who still looked extremely concerned and was already shouting up towards the cockpit. 'Did we get enough fuel?'

The pilot glanced back at him with a deep frown and nodded his head slowly. 'I think so, yes. Just as long as we don't encounter a strong headwind which will mean burning up more fuel getting there. In which case it's going to be close.'

Brulet said nothing but he shot Harker a concerned glance.

'Have faith, Sebastian.' Harker ordered before glancing at Chloe reassuringly. 'Our luck's held out so far… we'll make it. Everything is going to be fine.'

Chapter 38

'This is going to be tight,' the pilot yelled, as another streak of blue lightning ripped through the air just metres off their right wing, followed by a monstrous clap of thunder which had both men clasping their hands around the ear mics.

Harker looked over to see Chloe clutching desperately on to her armrest with white knuckles, whereas Brulet looked oddly at ease despite the incessant turbulence, and was talking into his satellite phone. This extreme thunderstorm had flared up within minutes and, even though San José airport was only thirty miles away, the pilots had been considering re-routing to a closer destination. Ordinarily that would not have presented a problem but since the closer airfields had all been closed due to adverse weather conditions, this left San José as the only option. Their problems had been further compounded by the fuel issue, since the high winds generated by the thunderstorm had slowed down the aircraft's speed, thus draining more of their precious liquid. This meant that they would be making their final approach solely on fumes, which is never good even in perfect weather conditions, let alone during a thunderstorm like this one.

'A helicopter will be waiting for us at San José to transport us to Mancuria National Park,' Brulet shouted out over another clap of thunder as he put away the satellite phone. 'That is of course, if we ever make it to San José.'

Harker and Chloe glanced at each other with concern as Brulet sprouted a mocking smile. 'Seriously, like you said, it's going to be fine,' he continued, before turning his head to the rain-lashed window and enjoying, as best he could under the circumstances, the impressive lighting show outside.

Harker failed to see the humour of the comment and sat back in his seat, his muscles noticeably tenser with every fresh crack of thunder. Since having to make an emergency landing on Lake Bracciano months earlier as a result of Lusic Bekhit's treachery, he had found his love affair with aviation considerably diminished. He still enjoyed flying, of course, and nothing would ever change that, but these days it was only when the skies were clear and not amidst the life-risking conditions they were now facing.

'We'll be making our approach in the next few minutes,' the pilot informed them loudly, then paused as yet another lightning bolt lit up the cabin's interior in a bluish hue, while the whole aircraft bucked mid-air as they entered another pocket of heavy turbulence. 'Make sure you're strapped in tightly.'

His last instruction was met with blank expressions from Harker and Chloe, who had both tightened their belts to the point of suffocation upon hearing the first clap of thunder. The man waved a hand reassuringly and turned back to the windscreen, and the rain across it, as he continued his struggle to keep the Gulf Stream straight and level.

'Try not to let this get to you, Chloe,' Harker yelled to her. 'We'll be on the ground soon enough and you'll have a great story to tell your grandkids.'

His attempt to put a bright spin on this nightmare trip was met with an unamused glare. 'I wasn't actually planning on having any kids,' Chloe called back, 'and even if I do, I'd rather have made up the story than experience it for real.'

Outside the window next to them one of the turbines, without warning, now suddenly began to wind down before stopping altogether, offering an eerie calm on the right hand side of the aircraft. 'Oh, come on,' Harker muttered to himself in disbelief as the pilot now throttled up the remaining engine in an effort to compensate.

'Everybody hold on. We're coming into land,' he announced. As the aircraft's nose dipped, Harker spotted something that overshadowed his anxiety with a huge sense of relief. Through the cockpit window he could see two rows of landing lights looming out of the darkness ahead, and the jet descended until it was within just fifty metres of the black and shiny rain-swept runway. It was then that all hell broke loose.

An alarm started wailing from the cockpit just as the left-side engine cut out in a high-pitched wind-down. Within seconds all that could be heard was a whistle of wind and the rain crashing down against the plane's exterior.

'This is going to be tough,' was all the pilot had time to say before the Gulf Stream touched down with such a force that the front wheel buckled. The whole aircraft then smacked forward onto its nose with a metallic crunch and began to slow amid a shower of sparks as the aluminium frame scraped across the tarmac.

Sparks could be seen flaring up past the windows and for a moment Harker found himself obsessing over just one thought: the fuel tanks. His sudden feeling of dread was immediately replaced with the sense of being an idiot when he remembered that there was no fuel left in the tanks, which was the reason they were scraping along the runway in the first place.

The aircraft came to an undignified halt halfway down the runway and within moments the pilot was throwing open the external door and waving them outside. It was a gesture that was totally unnecessary because Harker and Chloe were already hurling themselves towards the entrance and out into the cold and the surprisingly refreshing torrent of rain pouring from overhead. Behind them, Brulet made a rather more dignified exit, followed by the two pilots who immediately began inspecting the damage.

The entire underside of the nose was crumpled and worn away after the weight of the aircraft had left black scorch marks running behind it for half the length of the runway, and the fuselage had cracks behind the door where the pressure had snapped the frame. All in all, and considering the impact with which they had touched down, the damage wasn't that bad, but it was a safe bet that the aircraft wouldn't be flying again any time soon, if ever.

'Good landing, gentlemen,' Brulet said, congratulating each pilot in turn with a pat on their back. 'I trust I can leave it to you to make the necessary arrangements to get her somewhere safe?'

'Of course, sir,' the lead pilot answered, and the two of them began making their way towards the fire truck and back-up vehicles that were already approaching from the far side of the runway.

Brulet turned his attention instead to a silver van which had emerged from one of the hangars and was just now pulling up along-side Harker and Chloe. The driver's door swung open and out jumped a young man with dark skin, cropped hair and wearing a red boiler suit. 'Is everyone OK?' he asked in English, but with a heavy Columbian accent.

'A little shaken up but we're fine thank you,' Harker replied.

'Mr Brulet, is it?'

Harker shook his head and gestured over to Brulet, who had already pulled open the van's side door and was directing Chloe inside, before turning his attention to the driver.

'We need to reach the heliport as soon as possible,' he explained, gesturing for Harker to get inside as well.

'Of course, sir. I will take you there immediately.' The driver glanced over at the buckled Gulf Stream. 'Nice landing,' he muttered to himself.

Brulet waited until Harker had got in the van before joining him, sliding the side door shut as their guide hopped into the driver's seat.

'You must be paying serious money to persuade a helicopter pilot to fly in this weather,' the young man said, as he started up the engine and headed for a back road running the length of the airport. 'There were three crashes yesterday and another one today – not counting your own.'

'Are you saying this storm has been raging for two days non-stop?' Harker asked in surprise. 'Is that normal?'

'There's nothing normal about it. One second it's a beautifully clear day and the next it's turned like this.' The driver pointed to the dark swirling of clouds above and the continuous lighting strikes emerging from them. 'It's the worst storm I've ever seen and I've lived here all my life. It's even got the airport radar system going haywire.' The driver took a right at one end of the hangar and turned in the direction of the main entrance, heading past a green helipad sign pointing straight ahead. 'San José is on the edge of this storm but it's reported to extend all the way to the north coast, which is one hundred and fifty miles away if you can believe that.' The driver shook his head in disbelief. 'You really are lucky to have made it down in one piece, Mr Brulet.'

'Then you should know that we are heading next to Macuira National Park.' Brulet explained.

The young man's eyed widened, clearly stunned at learning their next destination. 'You know that will take you right into the centre of the storm,' he gasped.

'I know.' Brulet glanced back at Harker. 'Let us hope our luck holds, shall we?' He lowered his black-lensed sunglasses onto the bridge of his nose, so Harker could now see the adventurous glint in his star-crossed pupils. 'Well, then, my friend… once more into the breach.'

Chapter 39

The single-file sixty or so passengers stood patiently next to the Boeing 747, as a set of white boarding steps was rolled into place directly underneath the aircraft's entrance. The group consisted of men, women and children, all neatly dressed and carrying a modest selection of briefcases and carry-on bags. They waited there silently on the wet tarmac of Finkenwerder airport, as they had been doing so since being dropped off by a procession of grey Scania coaches which had arrived ten minutes earlier. Located in the south-western part of Hamburg, with a single runway overlooking the river Elbe, this private airfield was part of the Airbus plant and housed the Airbus A380 major component-assembly factory. The facility was also regularly used for freight, test and delivery flights... but not today.

At the head of the queue a man wearing a flight jacket and blue nylon trousers climbed to the top of the steps and pulled open the door before beckoning to the first in line to join him. The passengers gradually began to ascend the steps and head into the aircraft, each of them focused on getting to their seat, and totally oblivious to the man crouching behind a nearby freight container, watching them closely.

Michael Shroder poked his head around a corner of the large metal crate and considered his next move, as the line of passengers began to shorten. The car containing Bekhit's unwelcome visitors had originally been spotted arriving here by a local policeman who had quickly responded to the alert placed on their registration number. The airport was less than half a mile away across the river Elbe, and could actually be seen from Bekhit's now burnt-out apartment block. But, with no boat available, it had taken Shroder almost twenty minutes to make his way back over the Billhorner causeway and continue on to the Airbus facility. Fortunately, he had reached it just in time to witness the coaches arrive, and had managed to take cover behind the cargo crate he was currently huddling against.

'Are you people all Magi?' he whispered quietly to himself. Having expected to find only the two men and the car they were driving, this mixed group of travellers was vexing to him. That there were so many different faces and many of them were children, which only added complications to the plan he had devised on his way over.

Slipping on the Airbus security cap he had commandeered from one of the security guards, Shroder made his way over to the Boeing 747 as casually as his bruised chest would allow. He had made it to within metres of the last person standing in line, when a man in a dark blue, expensive-looking Armani suit appeared from behind the boarding stairs and interposed himself between Shroder and the final passengers.

'What do you want?' he asked, eyeing Shroder with suspicion.

'We had a report of an intruder on site,' Shroder replied. 'I have some men skirting the perimeter. Have you seen anyone?'

The smart-suited man shook his head, taking a moment to glance around the otherwise empty airstrip. 'No, nothing.'

'Good,' Shroder replied. 'It may have been a false flag but we need to check around, OK?'

Reluctantly the man offered a nod of his head. 'Very well, you may carry on.'

'Thank you.' Shroder replied before looking directly over the man's shoulder with a deliberate look of inquiry. 'Who is that?'

The man had barely turned his head to investigate when Shroder pulled out his Browning and dug it firmly into the man's chest. 'You move, I shoot, understand?'

The suit turned to face Shroder and, even though his body had visibly tensed, the man nodded submissively as beyond him the line of people continued to shuffle forwards, unaware of the activity going on right behind them.

'What's your destination?' Shroder demanded but the man stayed silent, and instead he looked over his interrogator's shoulder with the same kind of interest that Shroder had expressed moments earlier. 'Oh, please,' Shroder voiced with disdain. 'You must think I'm an idiot.'

'Then an idiot you must be,' a voice whispered from behind him and Shroder felt the muzzle of a gun pressing into his back. He swivelled his head far enough to see another man, dressed just as smartly as the first, fixing him with a cold and icy expression. 'Put the gun down,' the newcomer ordered fiercely.

Shroder glanced towards his own hostage, then back at the latest arrival. 'Well, isn't this a pickle,' he remarked with a smile.

The newcomer took a step closer and pressed the gun deeper into Shroder's back. 'Not really,' he gestured towards Shroder's hostage. 'You may kill him if you wish, but I will certainly kill you.'

Shroder took a moment to think this, before bobbing his head in compliance. 'Then I suppose *now* would be a good time to drop my gun wouldn't it?'

The armed man was already grinning when the three of them were suddenly lit up by a dazzling white spotlight directed somewhere far overhead. Then a booming metallic voice cut through the night air: 'Lay your weapons at your feet and get down on the ground.' At the same time half a dozen black sedans, with flashing lights, appeared on the runway and began closing in on them at high speed.

With the man behind him completely stunned by the spotlights, Shroder spun around fully and knocked the gun from his hand, then punched him hard in the face dropping him to the floor. This, though wasn't to be the case with the first man, who kicked Shroder in the back sending him crashing to the ground, before taking off past the remaining passengers who had all obediently dropped to their knees with hands held high.

Shroder leapt back to his feet and turned to see the nearest sedan speed past him and clip the escapee with one side of its bonnet, sending him flying off balance and skidding face-first into the unyielding tarmac with a painful sounding crunch.

Shroder trained his gun on the remaining suit, who was still streched out on the floor, as the other vehicles came to a halt in a semi-circle around the foot of the boarding stairs, hemming in the crouching passengers. Meanwhile another vehicle pulled in front of the Boeing's front wheel, just in case the pilot got any stupid ideas. From two of the sedans jumped out an assault team wearing balaclavas and they immediately headed up into the aircraft leaving one member behind to handcuff the man Shroder had initially knocked to the ground.

Shroder holstered his gun and listened out for any weapon fire inside the aircraft but all he could hear were muffled screams amid offerings of surrender. It was clear that the passengers had no desire to engage in a firefight, for which Shroder was relieved because it meant more survivors to question.

'So much for your waiting,' a voice called out to him, and Shroder turned around to see his friend, the German intelligence officer, Karl making his way over.

'I couldn't afford to wait longer,' he replied with a relieved smile, retrieving the bulky satellite phone from his pocket and holding it out in front of him, 'anyway, I knew you were listening in.'

Karl shot him a cold look, pulled out his own satellite phone and turned it off. 'Maybe so, Michael, but lucky for you we got here in time.'

'You've never let me down before.'

Karl grunted despairingly as Shroder made his way over to the same cuffed man whose ribs he had stuck his gun into and who was starting to wake up from the knockout blow.

'I need a room where I can speak with him in private.'

'There's the factory hangar over there,' Karl pointed to a large building on the far side of the runway. 'The whole place is empty at this time of night, so there must be an empty room you can use.'

Shroder knelt down and brought his lips close to the prisoner's ear. 'A friend of mine once told me that you Magi are tough bastards, and incapable of cracking,' he whispered grimly. 'Let's put that to the test, shall we?'

Chapter 40

The Bell 430 helicopter was buffeted wildly as another clap of thunder crackled overhead out of the swollen black rain clouds that hung from the heavens like morose charcoal-coloured drapes. Inside, Harker clutched at his tanned-leather seat grimly as he continually bumped around due to the turbulance. The beautiful sleek furnishings and plush walnut interior meant little when contemplating one's own fate. His uneasy demeanour was nothing compared to that of Chloe, who had been freaking out ever since the rocky take-off from San José airport.

'These things crash, Alex,' she exclaimed desperately. 'We should land right now and hike the rest of the way.'

'That's not going to happen, Chloe,' he replied, pointing through the window to the dense woodland below. 'There's nowhere to land and, besides, we would never make it past the wildlife.'

'Wildlife?' she echoed, finally distracted by something other than her own impending death.

'Yes.' Harker said sternly. 'There are bears, snakes, even mountain lions in that forest below us. We would be picked off one by one.' Of course that could be a lie because in reality he had no idea. For all he knew, there could be a settlement of brightly coloured and highly territorial Care Bears living among those trees but, nonetheless, his answer appeared to distract her and she became far more quietly preoccupied with staring out the window at the dark woodland below rather than worrying about the tin can they were being rattled around in. 'Don't worry we'll be there soon,' Harker said reassuringly to the back of Chloe's head, her now silent distraction allowing him to concentrate on his own fears.

Since taking off, Harker had been keeping an eye on the pilot's demeanour. If the fellow looked calm, then he felt calm too, but, as he stared up towards the cockpit, he could swear the young man looked nervous as hell.

He glanced over at Brulet, whose eyes were also keenly fixed upon the young pilot and obviously just as concerned at the uneasy glances being thrown in their direction. 'Anything you need to share?' Brulet called out above the ear-numbing growl of thunder outside.

The pilot shifted in his seat so as to face them as best as he could, and it was only then that they both could see he was looking not so much nervous as panicked. 'We're close to the mountain now but I think we need to turn back,' he yelled, as more of a plea than a suggestion. 'This storm's getting too heavy.'

'How far are we now from the base of the mountain?' Brulet shouted back, not wanting the pilot's anxiety to rub off on Chloe, who was now also listening intently.

'We're almost there but the storm is becoming too violent.' The pilot glanced back out at the heavy rain cascading down the cockpit windscreen. 'I'm struggling now to just keep her in the air. I'm sorry but we need to turn back to San José. This is becoming too much of a risk.'

He focused his attention on the control panel, leaving Harker and Brulet unsure of what to do next. The genuine fear in the young pilot's eyes said it all but if they turned back now who knew how long it would take them to get back here.

Brulet raised his hand from the armrest and pulled back his sleeve to reveal the arm-sword neatly strapped to his forearm. He then shrugged his shoulders as if inviting Harker to decide whether this was the only viable course of action left open to them. Harker stared back blankly. Forcing someone at knifepoint to continue on a course towards potential oblivion was not a scenario he had ever contemplated, but then he had never been faced with attempting to prevent the end of the world. He was still wrestling with the dilemma when the decision was plucked out of his hands, as a thick bolt of lightning struck and consumed the helicopter momentarily, lighting up the interior like a camera flash before plunging them back into darkness. The strike caused the entire fuselage to rock violently and Harker was slammed back against the cabin wall and, as he struggled to pull himself upright, he could hear the whine of the helicopter's engines begin to falter.

'Didn't we just go through this on the jet?' Brulet yelled, as Harker thrust his face against the window in time to see a jagged bolt of lightning reach down and strike a tall conifer a long way down below them, which then burst into blistering flames sending a scattering of fiery ash to the ground below.

Harker reeled back in his chair at the realisation of how close they were to the ground and, as the rotors began to slow even further, his body was frozen under the increasing feeling of freefall. His safety belt tightened as his whole frame rose off the seat, and he turned his head to see the silhouettes of Chloe and Brulet being levitated in the same manner.

Amidst the roar of the failing engines, Harker could hear the pilot yelling something but the only words he caught was 'Brace' and 'Emergency'. It was enough, however, to know what was coming next. He let his whole body slacken, which is not a natural instinct when you are hurtling towards the ground at unknown speed, but surprisingly it felt like the most natural thing in the world. During a collision the worst thing a person can do is tense up, because tightened muscles offer more resistance to the force of the impact. When you drop a rod of glass onto a tiled floor it shatters, but when you do the same thing with a length of rubber nothing happens. This was the analogy quoted by Harker's driving instructor many years back when discussing how best to survive an accident. At the time the logic of it, or even why a driving instructor would discuss the factors of car crash during a driving lesson, had not been fully clear to him. But suddenly it was beginning to make sense.

Nonetheless in the moments of freefall he now found some solace in this titbit of information and it was a concept that he now clung to.

Just relax and let the helicopter itself do the crashing he thought, keen to share the advice with his companions. 'Try to relax,' he yelled warningly amid one of Chloe's uncontrollable screams. For a moment there was silence, before she erupted again and louder this time.

The out-of-control sensation of being in freefall seemed to go on for minutes, and Harker was still fighting any urge to tense up when the high-pitched whine of the engines re-engaging, back up to full throttle, shrieked throughout the cabin. He was forced back deep into his seat as the rotors began to slow their descent and he felt a welcome feeling of relief overcome him. Sadly it was short-lived as, seconds later, a tremendous impact rippled through the aircraft from the floor upwards, when the Bell 430's undercarriage hit the ground with such force that the two landing wheels were instantly crushed and the tail cone snapped clean off. The machine bounced upward as the rotors continued to spin on full throttle, dragging the entire fuselage down onto one side and starting the spinning rotors digging into the ground, until they splintered asunder sending large fragments of twisted metal in all directions.

Inside the wreck, it was near pitch dark but after a minute or so the vibrations began to soften and the only sign of life was faint groaning barely audible over the heavy pattering of rain against the cabin's exterior and a weighty clicking sound as the revolving rotors outside continued to scrape against the ground.

Harker groggily fumbled with his seat belt, which was digging painfully into his waist, since his seat was now tilted at 90 degrees to the floor. The impact itself had been hard but nothing as bad as one would expect of a helicopter crash, which was no doubt due to that last-minute recovery of the engines. *That and damn good flying by the pilot.* Harker attempted to raise his head but winced immediately, since the force of the fuselage being wrenched on to its side had flicked his head violently to one side, causing a nasty whiplash. Apart from that he seemed remarkably unscathed.

'Chloe,' he croaked, 'are you OK?'

'I'm still here,' she replied immediately and, after a pause, 'I'm still in one piece… I think?'

Harker gave a sigh of relief and slumped slightly on detecting a hint of humour.

'And I am fine too.' Brulet joined in, whereupon Harker swivelled his bruised neck to catch sight of the dark profile of the Grand Master grappling with his seat belt. There followed a series of metallic clicks as the locking mechanism released, then a thud as Brulet's body collapsed to the floor. He then stood up and slowly reached over to Chloe and, after a moment of rooting for her seat belt in the dark, released her as well and gently eased her down.

'We're lucky to be alive. So take it easy,' he advised as Chloe immediately attempted to push herself upright using the side of the cabin – formerly the floor – for support. 'You'll probably have a concussion… that was one serious knock.'

The Grand Master took a moment to steady his own shaky legs, then leant over to Harker who was still hanging from his seat as outside one of the helicopter's landing lights began flashing and in doing so it lit up both their faces in a bright coloured orange. 'Are you alive, Alex?'

Harker managed a gentle nod. 'The amount of pain I'm feeling in my neck would suggest so, yes, Sebastian.'

Brulet offered a thankful smile. 'Good; it's when you can't feel anything at all that one needs to worry. Now let's get you down.' He reached over and prepared to release Harker's seat belt. 'Hold on to my shoulders.' In one swift motion he released the belt lock and grabbed on to Harker as he tumbled loose, managing to bear the weight of the man until he had regained his balance.

'Thanks,' Harker said shakily.

'You two get outside.' Brulet gestured to the still seemingly intact sliding entrance door that was now directly above them. 'I'll go check on the pilot.'

In the minutes since the crash, Harker had not even considered the man who had managed to get them down safely. 'I'll help you,' he replied, but Brulet nudged him back towards Chloe.

'No, I'll do it. You get her out of here.'

Without argument, Harker reached up for the entrance door and pulled at the handle. Much to his relief it released with a click and slid back easily on its rollers, allowing a shower of rainfall to pour in on them. The cold shower was invigorating for Harker, who grabbed the rim of the opening and pulled himself up, using the protruding seat as a footstool.

The air was warm in contrast to the cool rain and, even with the spinning rotary hub behind him now slowing to a halt, he took a moment to relish the refreshing droplets against his face, before reaching down and helping Chloe up to join him outside on top of the fuselage.

Despite swirling dark storm clouds overhead, which appeared to be warring violently amongst themselves, the full moon was still visible, casting a welcome silvery light over the surrounding area. The pilot had managed to come down on a large piece of open land, cut into the surrounding forest, and leading up to a small mountain range covered in thick foliage. Metal fences had been constructed around its exterior, encompassing a large portion of forest, which ran way up to the mountain slope and then across its steep incline creating a large enclosed area of land. At the base of the mountain, a few hundred metres away from their position, Harker could also make out the dark outline of a building with a single light glowing on top of it and the sight provided him with a small measure of comfort.

Harker carefully climbed down across the helicopter's underbelly, making sure to avoid the jutting-out metal spikes that had been the

293

landing gears, then he assisted Chloe in joining him before he led her clear of the wrecked aircraft. It was not until they reached a safe distance that Harker realised just how fortunate they had been. Due to the rain, the sparsely vegetated sandy area they had ended up in was muddy as hell, providing some cushioning on landing but it was obvious now that it was the pilot's actions that had saved them. For the helicopter had plunged cockpit-first into the ground, thus taking most of the impact, then fallen back on to its base and then ended up on to its side. The whole front of it was crushed, having taken the brunt of the impact, and there was no doubt in Harker's mind that it was this that had saved them from receiving far more serious injuries. The damage to the cockpit looked regrettably severe so it seemed unlikely that the pilot could have survived. This assessment was confirmed when Brulet appeared alone from the entrance hatch moments later. As he navigated his way to the ground, then began making his way towards them, Harker could only wonder if the young pilot had crashed that way deliberately in a last-ditch attempt to save his passengers, or whether it had just been the luck of the draw. Either way they owed the man their lives... someone whose name Harker didn't even know.

'The pilot?' Harker yelled over to Brulet, as he approached them.

'No, I am afraid not.' Brulet was shaking his head sadly.

The three of them took a moment to survey the torn and broken remains of downed helicopter, with its orange and white navigation lights still flashing, before it was Brulet himself who broke the respectful silence.

'I hope this is the place, Alex,' he said, with a tinge of desperation in his voice, 'because we're not going anywhere else for the time being.' No sooner had he finished his sentence when a piercing howl penetrated the rain-swept night sky with such a ferocity that they all instinctively huddled closer to each other and stared in the direction it had come from. Near the edge of the forest, on the far side of the clearing, a pair of yellow eyes glinted amidst the downpour and the large body behind them started to sway impatiently from side to side in the gloom. Something dark. Something large. More pairs of eyes now appeared – and with them an increase in movement.

Harker felt an uncomfortable chill ripple through him as the multiple pairs of yellow eyes began to move ever nearer, gaining in speed, and as the darkened shapes broke out from the murkiness of the forest, the silver moonlight revealed the shadows to be a mass of individual bodies, each covered in a thick coat of matted fur. Behind the snarls were exposed glints of white teeth, and all the while they kept moving faster and faster.

'I think that answers your question, Sebastian,' Harker whispered even as he began to take a step backwards, pulling Chloe and Brulet each by the arm. 'Now *run*.'

Chapter 41

'Keep going,' Harker shouted as Chloe stumbled on a clump of thick weeds and was immediately hauled back onto her feet by Harker and Brulet before she could hit the ground. She regained her balance and kicked off her single remaining leather-heeled shoe mid-step while remaining on course and still heading for the single source of light and the darkened building underneath it, about sixty metres ahead.

Harker glanced back towards the flashing lights of the downed helicopter and the number of hunched-over black silhouettes that were rapidly catching them up. The deep snarling had now dissolved into a heavy panting as these creatures increased their speed, sending up sprays of water at every step as their paws connected with the sodden ground.

'Those things are too quick,' Harker cursed, glancing back at the ghostly pack of beasts that were gaining on them fast. At their current speed they would close the gap well before anyone reached the building up ahead. They had no more than fifty metres to go, but their wraithlike pursuers were quickly closing the gap. 'We're not going to make it,' Harker called out, having already decided what he would have to do next. 'You two keep going,' he yelled, 'and I'll distract them for as long as I can.'

This generous offer of self-sacrifice was met with a disapproving growl from Brulet, who reached into his side pocket and retrieved an orange plastic flare gun he had scavenged from the helicopter. 'Noble offer, Alex,' Brulet puffed, continuing to sprint, 'but I thought this thing might come in handy.'

Brulet aimed the gun at the lead creature and squeezed the trigger. A brilliant white shower of sparks shot out from the barrel and launched a fiery distress flare right into the middle of the pack, sending the animals scattering in all directions.

Harker glanced back in time to see the flare light up one of the animals clearly, as a section of its thick fur erupted in a ball of flame, revealing the beast's true form. The image lasted only for a moment, but it was enough. These were identical to the 'Demons' described in the news report. The oddly elongated jawline and double row of teeth, the yellow eyes and thick black fur were unmistakable, but they looked so much bigger than on the news footage – indeed comparable in size to a small grizzly bear, only less bulky.

Brulet's fiery blast had done its job and the pack was still regrouping as the three of them reached the building, but the sight that greeted them immediately dispelled any hope of safety. The structure was no more than a barn with two window frames on either side, boarded up with a few rotting planks nailed across them and a rickety double wooden door in the middle.

'Inside.' Brulet barked and swung the door open. It grated against its rusty hinges before he slammed it shut behind them.

'That's not going to hold,' Harker yelled and both he and Brulet immediately began to search the dark interior as Chloe leapt to one of the windows and peered out between the nailed planks, acting as a lookout.

The inside of the place consisted of one large empty room containing rows of wooden stalls and what looked like milking equipment, but with not a cow in sight, while off to the left a small entrance led into an adjoining room.

'There,' Harker directed before sprinting over to a worn-looking wooden desk pressed up against the nearest stall. 'Give me a hand with this.'

He and Brulet shimmied the weighty piece of furniture over to the barn's entrance, then jammed it up against both doors just as one of the creatures collided with them on the other side with such force that the impact almost knocked both men to the floor.

'They're coming,' Chloe cried out, never taking her eyes off the crack at the window.

'They're already here,' Harker shouted back to her as another blow against the door rocked him back on his heels. 'Check all the stalls,' he called out, using all the strength he could muster to hold the wooden desk in place. 'Find anything we can use as a weapon.'

'There's another room back there,' Brulet added, as he too struggled to keep the hefty piece of furniture in place. 'Take a look... and hurry.'

Without hesitation, Chloe sprinted deeper into the building, heading first towards the nearest milking stall. But, without shoes and with sodden tights, she slid across the dusty floor slabs and crashed into the partition with a thump. She hauled herself back up and began to scour the stalls one by one, but all she could find there was mere dust, mud and spoiled hay. There was nothing at all that could be used as a weapon except for a pathetic-looking three-legged milking stool which she reluctantly decided could be used as a club. The very thought brought a nervous gulp to her throat, for the 'club' would be hard pressed to keep a disgruntled guinea pig at bay, let alone a razor-fanged 250-pound monster! Chloe had begrudgingly reached over to pick it up when something glinting on the wall above it caught her eye. It was difficult to see clearly because of the shadows, but also because it was covered in rust. A single farming tool – or more accurately a gardening-tool, hung from the wall. The spade was hardly an item worthy of space in an armoury, but at least it was a step up from the milking stool.

Chloe yanked it off the wall and rushed back to the others who were still wrestling desperately to hold the desk in place, as the beasts outside ramped up their assault on the barn's door.

'This is all I could find,' she panted, presenting the rusty implement to view, whereupon Harker glanced over at the unimpressive weapon and offered her the most grateful look he could manage.

'It'll have to do,' he yelled, grabbing for the spade. 'Now check the other room.'

Chloe hurried towards the rear and approached the side door, skidding again on the dusty floor. 'What I'd give for a pair of trainers,' she muttered furiously, then quickly surveyed the dark room beyond, with only patches of moonlight shining through a series of small high-up windows to illuminate its interior. Sadly, it contained nothing more than a series of cubicles but she quickly peered into each one in turn to discover nothing more than several filthy, blocked and broken toilets.

'It's only a washroom, a dead end.' she yelled and was already searching the ceiling for any sign of an air vent when the sound of splintering wood echoed from the main barn. She immediately leapt back to the doorway, to be met by a sight that twisted her stomach like a grinder. The entire lower section of barn door had broken away, and one of the beasts was already inside and lunging at Brulet, while Harker kept bashing at the opening with his rusty spade in an attempt to keep the others from following.

Brulet dodged the beast's initial lunge with the skill of a matador, sending the creature leaping past him to collide with the concrete floor behind. Meanwhile he flicked his arm out, thus clicking his attached arm-sword into place and brought the steel blade down firmly on to the animal's spine just below the neck. The strike was so fast that the beast had barely time to turn around before its legs buckled and it dropped to the floor without so much as a whimper.

'Sebastian!' Harker yelled a frantic warning as another of the beasts thrust its head through the opening and clamped its fangs around the mid-section of the spade with such force that the wooden handle snapped in two, leaving Harker holding nothing more than a jagged stick.

Brulet was at his side in an instant and the Grand Master began slamming the tip of his blade through the opening, again and again. High-pitched yelps could be heard even over the roar of the storm as the blade repeatedly hit its mark, driving the wounded recipient back into the blackness outside – but only to have another take its place in the continuing onslaught.

'We can't hold them off,' Harker yelled as the last section of stick was ripped from his hand, and he now began to kick out at the beast's muzzle with his shoes.

'Fall back,' Brulet ordered, while continuing to gouge at the snapping fangs thrust through the opening as Harker raced over to join Chloe, pushing her back into the washroom and readying the plywood door to be slammed shut.

A few metres away, Brulet inflicted a well-placed blow into the cheek of the leading beast, which emitted a deep howl of pain and it fell back and gave Brulet the opportunity for a gradual retreat, all the time swinging his arm blade from side to side as three more of the jet-black monsters forced their way through the gap and began to advance upon him slowly.

Harker was finally able to get a clear view of the creatures as a fourth now joined the pack, and he was struck by how they all moved with the dexterity of a big cat. The swagger at the hips and the side-turning of their heads as they growled at Brulet's swinging sword, was similar to the behaviour of a lion or a tiger, yet they resembled canines with those elongated snouts and with incisors akin to some devilish crossbreed dog sent from the very depths of hell itself.

'Close it now,' Brulet yelled as soon as he slid through the narrow gap, and Harker slammed the washroom door shut. Both men then pressed themselves up against its surface as a series of heavy thuds began to rock it from the other side.

'Look!' Chloe shouted with her eyes fixed on the door, pointing to the bulging cracks that were appearing on its surface and becoming thicker with every impact.

Harker watched helplessly as the middle of the door began to bend and splinter. Suddenly the idea of dying in that helicopter crash seemed remarkably pleasant compared to being ripped apart by all those razor-sharp teeth. He glanced at Brulet and Chloe, both looking equally helpless, and opened his mouth to say something reassuring. But nothing came out. What do you say when there is nothing to be said?

Harker was still searching for words when a high-pitched shriek echoed through the barn, silencing even the roars and growls on the other side of the door. At the same time the pounding ceased and the three of them visibly winced as the shrill wail continued throughout the barn. This continued for a few more moments, then it cut out as abruptly as it had begun. Harker and Brulet's eyes met in a look of confusion, but at no time did they take any pressure off the door they were still glued to.

Then, without warning, Brulet's whole body snapped to attention, becoming rigid, and his fists clenched tightly as he began to shake violently before dropping to the floor. In the dim light Harker instinctively began reaching down to his companion, then something struck his chest. As his body began to tense and his veins began to burn, he managed to glance down at the two metallic darts, each attached to slender wires, that had embedded themselves into his upper body. Unable to otherwise move, he fell to the floor and begun twitching uncontrollably as 50,000 volts electrified him. Up ahead two similar darts sent Chloe also crashing to the ground, to join her friends in the same undignified dance.

After a few more seconds the electric charge ceased and, with bleary eyes, Harker followed the wires back to the two men, wearing balaclavas and armoured vests, who had appeared from the secret hatch where the end toilet had stood and who now made their way towards them, each holding a stun gun. The nearest one lowered his Taser, unclipped a black Motorola walkie-talkie from his belt, and began to speak into it.

'They're now incapacitated, sir,' the man explained in a husky German accent. 'Do you want them all neutralised?'

There was a few moments of silence before the walkie-talkie crackled into life. 'No. Bring them inside.'

'Copy that,' the guard replied and he was just about to reach down and unhook the metal darts from Harker's chest when the Motorola crackled once more. 'But before you do… give them an extra shock.'

Chapter 42

'We've dosed your prisoner with sodium thiopental Mr Shroder, but its barely had any effect at all. If this doesn't work, we could try cutting. It's messy, and should be considered an option of last resort, but it will work. Everyone has their breaking point... *everyone.*'

Shroder returned the steely gaze of the GSG 9 captain with his poker face intact, not betraying the high level of unease he felt regarding the method now being proposed. GSG 9 was Germany's top counter-terrorist unit, dealing with everything from the airborne breach of an oil platform to hostage rescue. The elite unit had been set up after the 1973 Munich Olympics massacre, when eleven members of the Israeli team were taken hostage by the Palestinian terrorist group Black September. From start to finish the whole episode had not gone well, resulting in two of the hostages being murdered in their hotel rooms and the final nine dying in a botched rescue attempt by the German police. With all the hostages dead and the failed operation being played out on the world's media, it had been decided that a special elite unit was needed for any future such eventualities. That unit was designated as GSG 9 and although its recruits were chosen solely from active police officers, as was not the case for the majority of similar units around the world, they had proved themselves over the years to be among the best at what they did.

'I wasn't aware that the GSG were in the business of torture, Captain Müller,' Shroder remarked plainly, and without a shred of accusation in his tone.

'We're not,' Müller replied, 'but given that half of Europe is under martial law and thousands of lives have recently been lost, the Federal Ministry of the Interior has given me free rein to follow up any leads as I see fit,' the stocky captain then motioned to Karl, who stood watching the exchange with arms folded. 'And, according to our own intelligence officer working on the information you provided him, it is my understanding that these individuals may be central to those disastrous events. So, unless you have any other evidence explaining why the hell we were called in to arrest these people, I can only offer you the options I have at my disposal.'

'Thank you, Captain Müller,' Karl stepped in between the two men, realising the conversation was beginning to boil over, 'your co-operation is much appreciated. Could you give us a moment alone?'

Müller paused and then exited the room with a frustrated grunt.

'I think it's high time you gave me an explanation, Michael,' Karl said softly once they were alone. 'I organised this assault in good faith, and instead of the terrorists you promised me, I find we've just arrested a group of families who are simply taking a fucking holiday!'

Shroder turned away with his hands on his hips and paced away a few steps. He did this not out of frustration but to give himself some time to figure out how best to explain the situation without losing his friend's confidence. The thought of revealing his knowledge of the Magi and their seemingly supernatural bid to bring about the end of the world was laughable, and Karl would have him thrown into a padded cell. What he needed was the right mixture of fact and fiction – but mainly fact – to get Karl on-board. 'OK,' Shroder said, finally turning round with his face full of resolve. 'But I need you to keep an open mind here.'

'How open?'

'As open as you can manage.' Shroder replied, watching as the German intelligence officer's shoulders twitched and his hands dropped to his sides. At first he thought his friend was about to shake his head in disappointment but instead he focused on him with sincerity in his eyes.

'Yesterday I watched half of Vatican City disappear into a hole in the earth, and today I saw a news reporter getting mauled by something I can describe only as a monster from my worst childhood nightmares.' said Karl, moving closer to Shroder. 'At this very moment my wife is sitting at home having stocked our cupboards with every type of canned food known to man, and praying that she'll live to see another day. And she's not even religious! The internet and the TV stations are down and a quarter of our national police force failed to check in for work today, presumably so they could be at home with their families. Believe me when I tell you that at this point that my mind isn't just open… It is *gaping*.' Karl reached over and placed a hand on

Shroder's shoulder sympathetically. 'So how about you tell me what's really going on?'

Shroder took a moment to gauge the man before offering a compliant nod. 'There is a group – a small but very powerful group – that has been attempting to bring about the end of the world.' He felt his cheek muscles tense at the mere mention of such a notion but was immediately bolstered by Karl's stare which remained unflinching and resolute. 'And the people you've just arrested are, I think, the families of this group... and wherever they were heading is where we need to be.'

Karl removed his hand from Shroder's shoulder and his eyes wandered to the floor then back up again. 'Are we talking about 'the' end of the world here? Fire-and-brimstone kind of end?'

'Yes,' Shroder replied firmly, now devoid of any embarrassment. 'The Old Testament kind.'

'And the man that died tonight, what did he have to do with all this?' Karl questioned and referring to Lusic Bekhit.

'He was the whistle-blower. The man that managed to infiltrate this group and was killed for it.' Shroder lied because there was only so much he was going to reveal.

'Does this group have a name?'

'They call themselves the Magi and they are an influential consortium of religious zealots who I believe have set this whole crisis in motion.'

Karl suppressed a gulp and his eyes began to wander. He made his way over to the large single window overlooking the airbus factory floor, and focused his gaze on the group of people being detained by a squad of GSG 9 officers. He then rested his hands on the windowsill, exhaled a large sigh and shook his head. 'That is the craziest thing I've ever heard, Michael... especially coming from you.'

Shroder was already making his way over to the same window to further justify his case, when the German raised a hand towards him.

'What's crazier still is that I actually believe you.'

Shroder immediately unstiffened and the two men stood there in silence for a moment until Karl turned to face him with a look of renewed bewilderment.

'You really think this is happening, don't you?'

'I know what I've seen over the last few days and something is definitely happening... something bizarre and totally out of our hands. But, despite how either of us might feel regarding the religious element, there is one thing I am certain of and that is someone down there knows what's going on – and we need to find out, *now*.'

A few seconds passed before Karl gave a nod of his head. 'Fine, you can interrogate him. But, for the record, this is a terrorist investigation and there will be no mention of this discussion, or they'll have me locked up even before you are... Agreed?'

'Agreed,' Shroder replied, already heading for the door.

'Wait,' Karl called out after him. 'How the hell do you expect to persuade this man to talk? He's been on sodium thiopental for the last twenty minutes, and hasn't even told us his name!'

The question stopped Shroder short, and he turned back around. It was the same question he had been brooding on ever since the Magi group had been arrested, and the answer to it had his stomach churning ever since. It was one that had every moral scruple in his body screaming out in disgust, but the truth drug was proving useless so far, and Shroder suspected that Captain Müller's option of 'cutting' would have little effect either. Brulet had been right when he had stated that these Magi soldiers would rather die than disclose any information, so that left only one option no matter how much Shroder detested the thought of it.

'Well,' Karl badgered, 'what will you do?'

'I'm going to give him two options,' Shroder replied coldly, already getting himself into character. 'Either he tells us where they were heading,' the MI6 agent snarled, 'or I'm going to kill his entire family... right in front of his eyes.'

–

'Everybody out now,' Shroder yelled to the guard as two GSG 9 officers dragged a hooded and handcuffed woman into the room and sat her down directly opposite the same Magi soldier that had been knocked out on the airport tarmac earlier. Once the guard and both officers had left, Shroder closed the door behind them. He then approached the handcuffed suspect and slapped him sharply across the face.

'Don't feel like talking yet?' Shroder scowled.

'I have nothing to say,' the prisoner replied sluggishly as a result of the sodium thiopental still fresh in his system.

Shroder strode over to the female he had brought in and ripped off her hood to reveal a blonde-haired woman with a strip of duct tape over her mouth and black lines streaking her cheeks where tears had caused her eyeliner to run. Her gaze widened at the sight of the prisoner opposite, and she gurgled in distress behind the confines of the sticky tape. The male prisoner, on the other hand, continued to stare ahead blankly.

'How about now?' Shroder barked.

The man shook his head. 'She's not one of mine.'

Shroder reached into his back pocket and pulled out two German passports. He flipped them both open at the ID pages and held them out in front of him. 'That's strange because these documents say otherwise... Mr and Mrs Roth.'

Shroder slipped the black hood back over the head of the still gurgling 'Mrs Roth' then dropped both passports on the floor before turning back over to the man who was looking decidedly unimpressed. 'There's something I want you to see now,' Shroder declared, and he pulled Roth up by the collar and hustled him over to the far end of the room, then through a sliding door on to a metal walkway that looked down over the factory floor. Shroder slammed the prisoner against the metal railing before pulling out another passport from his inside pocket. He thrust the photo page into Roth's face, then pointed down towards a ten-year-old girl wearing a hooded red overcoat with appliqué bows on the pockets. The young girl huddled next to one of the female adults, seemingly oblivious to the two men up on the walkway staring down at her. 'And that is your little girl, Ada.' Shroder announced. 'She really is a lovely little thing, isn't she?'

Roth gazed down at the child with dull eyes, then looked back at Shroder and nodded listlessly. 'Yes she is,' he replied. 'So what?'

Shroder pushed the fellow along the walkway and back into the office where the hooded Mrs Roth was still gurgling away in terror, most likely unaware they had even left the room. He pushed the bound man back down on to the chair, then took a position directly between them. 'So what, Mr Roth, is that I am going to make you an offer,' Shroder explained in a cold and callous tone. 'You tell me where you were heading and I walk away.'

'And if I don't?' Roth replied with a sarcastic smirk at the answer he guessed would be forthcoming.

Shroder pulled the Browning handgun from his side holster and dangled it in front of him by the grip. 'Then I will kill your family one by one, starting with your wife here.'

His threat seemingly had little effect on the Magi soldier, whose lips curled cynically.

'You're not going to do that,' Roth stated smugly, with a sarcastic rolling of his eyes. 'The police don't kill women and children.'

Shroder moved in closer to his cuffed prisoner, knelt down beside him and began lightly tapping the barrel of the gun against his own thigh pensively. 'I know who you are, Roth... and I know what the Magi are.'

The mention of the Magi drew a flicker of surprise from Roth. 'What are the Magi?' he replied gruffly.

'Come now, Mr Roth there is no need to be coy. After all, we are all old acquaintances here.'

Roth was now looking confused as the MI6 agent continued.

'I know that your little group of power-hungry psychopaths has been responsible, in one way or another, for every disaster that has happened in the past few days, and for the hundreds of thousands of people that have already lost their lives, including women and children. So the question you have to ask yourself is not why would I kill your wife and child... but why I wouldn't?'

Shroder stood up again and stepped over to the other chair. He placed the muzzle of the gun against the side of Mrs Roth's head, whereupon she immediately tensed up. 'Do you really think that a couple more casualties is going to make the slightest bit of difference to me, seeing as we have already lost so many?'

Roth eyed him cautiously. 'I don't believe you,' he said and then slumped in his chair.

Shroder raised an eyebrow and cocked his pistol. 'Do you believe *this*?'

Without warning, and no doubt in response to sound of the gun cocking, Mrs Roth leapt from her seat and began running blindly past her husband and towards the open sliding door. She had just made it to the walkway beyond when a shot rang out and she dropped to the grating, with only her quivering legs still visible. Roth gawped in shock as Shroder, gun still raised, marched over to the fallen body and unloaded two more shots until her legs went still.

From down below, frightened screams echoed around the factory floor, which were joined by an enraged screech from Roth, who jumped to his feet only to be slammed back into his seat by Shroder, who forcefully jammed the still hot muzzle deep into the man's ribs.

'Do you feel like talking now or do I go and fetch your daughter?' he snarled with his eyes full of determination. 'It's your decision, Roth. Solely your choice.'

Tears began to form in Roth's eyes and he now trembled and hissed in anger.

'Well? What is it to be, Roth?' Shroder persisted. 'Your stubbornness has already caused the death of your wife. Do you want your daughter's blood on your hands as well? And I promise you she won't die so easily.'

Roth continued to struggle violently against his restraints as tears trickled down his cheeks, before, finally calming, he closed his eyes and nodded sombrely. 'Give me a map.'

Shroder pulled out an already prepared ordinance map of the world from his inside jacket pocket and unfolded it before placing it upon the grieving man's lap. He then stood back with the gun still raised. After a few seconds of examining it, Roth swivelled his hand towards the map as best as his handcuffs would allow and pointed to a particular area. 'This is the airfield we were flying to, and where we are all instructed to meet.'

Shroder retrieved the map and studied the location. 'Why? What's there?'

'I don't know,' Roth replied, shaking his head miserably. 'We all received word to pack what we could and head for that location with our families immediately. The details for the flight were sent on to us shortly afterwards, but as to why there I have no idea.'

'Who sent those orders?' Shroder demanded with his gun still raised in a threatening manner.

'McCray,' Roth replied, bitterly now. 'Donald McCray.'

'I thought John Wilcox, our wonderful ex-Pope was head of the Magi?' Shroder was fully aware of the change in leadership but wanted to hear it from this Magi underling's own mouth.

Roth shook his head. 'He was until recently but something brought about a change. What, I don't know, but McCray is now the official Prime, meaning I follow his orders regardless.' He gazed up at Shroder, his eyes brimming with hatred. 'Did you enjoy killing my woman?' he rasped. 'Did it make you feel good?'

Shroder placed the Browning back in its holster and shook his head. 'I wouldn't know,' he replied drily, 'but I'm sure your "brothers" would know more about that type of activity than I do.' He looked over at

Mrs Roth's lifeless body and smiled grimly. 'Thank you, Mrs Roth, we're good to go.'

Roth watched in astonishment as the corpse got to its feet, pulled off the cuffs and removed the bag from its head, to reveal the smiling face of a woman with short black hair.

'Mr Roth, this is Officer Jung... and this,' Shroder pointed towards the office door, 'is Mrs Roth.'

The door swung open to reveal Karl standing with the cuffed Mrs Roth at his side, wearing an oversized boiler suit and still gagged with a piece of silver duct tape.

'I thought you were going to come back in off the balcony before I could get her clothes on in time,' Officer Jung announced, as Roth sat fuming over the trick that had been played.

'Thank you, Officer Jung, you have been extremely helpful,' Shroder acknowledged, as the policewoman made her way out of the room, taking Mrs Roth and Karl with her. 'As have you been, Mr Roth,' Shroder said, turning his attention back to the prisoner, before pulling out his weapon to reveal the blank cartridges inside. 'Killing innocent women and children!' he scoffed with disgust. 'What do you take me for? A Magi?!'

Chapter 43

'I said wake up,' the masked man shouted before delivering a firm kick to Harker's ribs. 'It's time to go.'

Harker prised open his heavy eyelids and stared up at a blurry image of the same masked man he had seen earlier, whilst on the business end of his Taser. The intense pain across his chest convinced him that his jailer must have already unleashed a few blows in bringing him round and, as the man raised his foot, ready to unleash another kick, Harker reached out and gripped the tip of his boot, pushing it away with what little strength he had.

'I'm awake.' Harker croaked, his throat tender and with that sensation of cottonmouth similar to the after-effects of an anaesthetic. 'Where am I?'

The guard seized the chain of Harker's handcuffs and roughly dragged him to his feet. 'I said let's walk not talk,' the man growled unyieldingly in a voice thickly tainted with a Russian accent that Harker recognised all too well.

'You're one of McCray's men, aren't you?'

The answer to this question was delivered in the form of a firm punch to his stomach, before he was hauled out of the room and into a brightly lit corridor outside. It took Harker a few moments to regain his footing, and he tried to shake off the pain in his ribs as the guard continued dragging him forwards. The bright light from the halogen bulbs overhead helped improve his hazy vision and by the time they had navigated a series of narrow passages and were approaching the end doorway, he could make out his surroundings clearly despite his head throbbing.

The guard paused at the grey metal entrance and firmly gripped Harker's cuffs as one would with a dog's choke chain, before knocking firmly upon the door. They waited in silence for a few moments and Harker was sure he could hear a low-level mumble of conversation on the other side, which then went quiet before a voice called out. 'Come in.'

The guard opened the door with a gentleness that had eluded his actions up until that point, and firmly shoved Harker inside.

The room was dark and, as the door closed behind him and the light from the corridor outside was cut off, Harker found himself in pitch-blackness. The air was warm, though, and a low level hum or buzzing sound was the only thing he could detect here. Wherever *here* was.

'Hello?' Harker attempted, his voice wavering ever so slightly at such unnerving surroundings. It is one thing to gaze into the darkness inside your own bedroom, secure in the knowledge that you are the only one there, but when one knows one is not alone and is being watched, a person will tend to give into their baser instincts. It's all about the feeling of the hunter... and being hunted. Thankfully for Harker, it was his usual inherent sense of logic and the understanding of why we feel the way we do that immediately put him back at ease, and any fearful thoughts soon melted away.

'If this is a bad time, I can always come back... I'm free same time next Thursday?'

The silence continued, and Harker was preparing to deliver another flippant remark when all around him the glow of a lighting system began to brighten. His first impression was that he was in a cave, but as the darkness faded, he realised it was more than just that. The room wasn't that big, maybe twenty-five metres in length and only half as wide, but the walls were composed of bare rock with an uneven surface. The ceiling was the same and so low that Harker could have touched it with an outstretched arm and a small jump. Indeed a cave would have been an apt description but for the shiny black marble tiles covering the floor and the glowing up-lighters set into the walls. The enclosed space was void of any furnishings and otherwise empty except for a single individual standing motionless at the far end of the room. With arms folded across his chest, he fixed Harker with a cold unemotional stare. It was the same stare Harker had seen previously at the Blackwater insane asylum just before Nurse Decker had taken a bullet to the head.

'Captain McCray,' Harker voiced challengingly, 'I was wondering when we would meet again.'

McCray remained motionless, arms still crossed and his stare unflinching. 'Of course you were,' the assassin replied flatly, and without any hint of sarcasm. 'I, on the other hand, knew exactly when we would meet, and I have done so since our first encounter.'

'Really,' Harker responded and he frowned in disbelief. 'I doubt you ever expected me to find your little cave – or whatever this place is.'

McCray shook his head from side to side. 'On the contrary, Professor Harker, I was counting on it.'

This response was perplexing and Harker got the feeling he was being toyed with, which caused him to dismiss any further peripheral questions and to focus instead on what he most needed to know. 'First thing's first, McCray,' he said with an air of confident authority. 'Where are those two people I arrived with?' He had been about to mention Brulet by name but, considering the Magi's hatred of the Templars, he now thought better of it. It was just possible that they did not know who they had captured, but that was a hope that was immediately dashed.

'Ahh, yes, the woman I had expected to see. But to bring to my door the Grand Master himself, the infamous Sebastian Brulet, now that was a surprise – and a most welcome one.'

'Are they alive?' Harker asked, ignoring McCray's apparent satisfaction.

'Yes, there're alive. Would you care to see them?'

'I would care very much.'

'Very well,' McCray replied cordially and he reached back to the wall behind him to press a silver button. Within seconds a portion of the wall slid back to reveal the inside of a well-lit elevator. McCray entered first and waited for his guest to join him. Harker approached and then stopped cautiously to inspect the confined space he was being asked to enter.

'I almost forgot,' McCray gave a faint smile, 'you're not a fan of enclosed spaces, are you.'

Harker shot the assassin a mistrustful glance. 'It's not the enclosed space I'm wary of.'

This drew a contemptuous nod from McCray, who lent back against one side of the elevator, allowing maximum room for his guest. 'Professor, you may or may not believe this but I have no particular wish to see you come to any harm.'

'Really?' Harker replied, finally taking his place in the elevator. 'I could have sworn you've been trying to kill me ever since we first met at Blackwater.'

McCray pressed a button on the panel and the doors slid shut before the elevator began to descend. 'Yes, of course, from your point of view it must have seemed like that but, believe me, if I had wanted you dead you would be.'

Before Harker could reply McCray continued. 'But I must warn you that if you try anything foolish in here, I will be forced to rethink my attitude.' The assassin surveyed Harker with glazed eyes. 'My training would enable me to take your life without even breaking a sweat. So, please, nothing rash.'

'Oh, I've seen what your training can do,' Harker replied with distaste.

'Good,' McCray replied. 'Then why don't we enjoy this ride in peace and quiet.'

The uncomfortable silence only lasted thirty seconds before Harker felt compelled to voice one of the many question swirling around his head since waking up. 'So where are we exactly?'

McCray seemed happy to reply. 'We are still in Caracas. We are now just deeper. Construction of this facility began back in the early 1960s when the Soviet Union was attempting to build a secret silo that could give them first-strike capabilities against the US.'

This casual remark about something so incredible drew a disbelieving gasp from Harker. 'What! Venezuela would never have agreed to that. It would have made the whole country a prime target during a nuclear war.'

'I never said they completed it. I just said they tried… besides, the Venezuelan Government never knew about it. On the contrary, they thought it was part of a project to protect the National Park above us. It was run by the KGB and directly overseen by Khrushchev himself. Of course, when the whole Cuban missile crisis thing happened, the project was called off and all the work they had done was sealed up. But when the Magi learned of its existence in the Seventies, they decided to pick up where Soviets had left off… all covertly of course.'

This startling revelation was almost as mind-blowing as anything Harker had learnt over the past few days. 'You're telling me that an entire underground facility was built here, and no one else even knows about it? How could you even keep that a secret?'

'A lot of money, a lot of bribes and most of all a lot of fatal accidents happening to anyone that got even a whiff of what was going on. This facility has been the jewel in the Magi's crown for many years.'

'So you have taken control of the Magi?' Harker was grasping for any shred of information he could find.

'No, that particular institution has had its time in the sun.'

McCray's answer was baffling and Harker let out a sigh of frustration. 'So what is this place, then?'

'This, Professor, is sanctuary for the devout. For the true believers.'

'Sanctuary from what?'

Harker's question drew a look of wide-eyed surprise from McCray, who leaned in closer. 'What do you think? From the impending apocalypse of course. The world is about to be reshaped by God's own will, and there is no stopping that.'

Harker eyed the assassin blankly and this was immediately seized upon by McCray, whose expression was now displaying an uncharacteristic fervour of emotion.

'After everything you have seen in the last few days, do you doubt it?'

Harker's mind began to fog over and suddenly became awash with doubt and confusion. The things he had seen: the destruction of the Vatican, the panic throughout the world, the 'demons' rising up to tear people apart only to then disappear back into the earth whence they came. A heavy sweat was now forming across his brow and he gulped deeply, the fluttering in his chest curiously dropping down to his stomach, and he felt his knees go weak as he struggled to hold himself upright. Up until that moment, he had been sure that he would find some type of down-to-earth answer for all those cataclysmic events happening across the world, and that his own profound sense of logic in all things would be rewarded. But, as he stared into the stern gaze of McCray, all he found was belief and conviction, and for a moment Harker thought he was going to throw up. 'But those animals we encountered up top, you're telling me they just *happened* to be in the same place as you, and attacking this… sanctuary?'

McCray placed his hand on his shoulder and squeezed it. 'Those things are not attacking us. They are protecting us.'

'What?'

'We are God's chosen ones, Professor – we who followed His prophecy and would serve to protect those blessed with the belief,' McCray was now yelling with spittle dribbling from his lips, his eyes piercing and unrelenting as those only found in a true believer, 'and

314

the faith and the courage to do what must be done, no matter what the cost.'

Harker's head was aching and he could taste bile in his throat as McCray continued.

'He is all things and he loves mankind above all else but He is a vengeful god and He will spite and destroy those that do not believe in His word… the true word… the only word, just as the Old Testament teaches us.'

Everything that had happened over the last few days, the deaths, the cataclysms, the world beginning to fall into chaos, it all suddenly began to descend upon Harker like a lead weight, crushing the last ounce of doubt from his very being, and he felt his mind and body begin to fold as he finally gave in to the possible truth of what he is being told. 'This… this is really happening, isn't it?' Harker muttered. 'The end of the world?'

McCray looked towards the door even as the elevator came to an abrupt halt, and he reached out and grabbed Harker by the lapels. 'Are you prepared to meet your maker, Alex Harker? And to be judged for your eternal soul.'

The elevator doors slid apart to reveal nothing but pitch blackness and Harker was unceremoniously thrown into it, landing roughly on the floor. Behind him the light from the elevator vanished as the doors closed with a clank, and once again he found himself immersed in complete blackness. The intense nausea he felt forced him to lurch forward and retch but nothing came out, and he shivered for a few moments, with his forehead pressed against the cold surface underneath him. His head was now spinning and, as he attempted to pick himself up by resting on his hands, they slid away under a film of sweat, which sent him crashing back on to the floor. Shrugging off the shock of it, Harker wiped off his damp palms on his jacket sleeves, and slowly manoeuvred himself until he was standing upright, his shaking legs still causing him to sway back and forth. He struggled to contain the intense feeling of nausea that came and went in wave after wave when a sudden realisation sent a wave of panic surging through his body. It wasn't nausea he was feeling, but fear: a terrifying, uncontrollable sensation of total fear causing goose pimples to tingle across his body.

Harker gulped deeply and began to wrestle with an overpowering and irrational desire to burst into tears and simply collapse in a heap. He was still fighting this urge when, out in the blackness in front of him, something growled. His whole body then went rigid as the growl became a voice. A deep bellowing voice piercing his eardrums like hot pins, and making him clasp both hands on to the side of his head.

'Haaaarker... Alex Haaaarker,' the voice boomed as he desperately tried to maintain some semblance of sanity.

'You belong to me now,' the voice continued coldly. 'Welcome to hell.'

Chapter 44

Harker tightened the grip on his shins, pulling them closer to his chest in the foetal position, and then buried his face into his knees as he lay hunched in a ball on the cold hard floor. The feeling of dread that gripped him had reduced his mind to an empty morass where his thoughts remained locked into revolving around every worry, every nightmare he had ever had, and all wrapped up in an inescapable ball of self-doubt and despair. Despair over what exactly he couldn't be sure, but this gut-wrenching feeling of spiralling hopelessness was so pervasive, so penetrating that he struggled to even contemplate moving, as if his muscles had become locked in the same invisible bindings that were also constricting his mind. How long had it been now since the voice had spoken? Seconds, minutes, even hours? He couldn't tell, and at that moment he didn't care, because the misery he felt overrode every ounce of free will in his body. Then a single thought pushed itself through the hellish dark blackness of his mind, forcing its way to the surface. And he prised open his mouth and pushed it out with a straining breath. 'God forgive me. Help me… Please.'

The words had barely left his mouth when bright light cascaded all around him in a brilliant, blinding sea of white, and he recoiled, wincing in pain, as its rays washed over his contorted body. Harker kept his eyes shut until the glow through his eyelids appeared to dim slightly and then, with a nervous shake of his head, he began to open them. Slowly at first, his eyelashes parted, still quivering in response to the light, then wider and wider until he could make out a single shadowy figure in front of him. As his full sight returned, the blurriness began to disperse and he found himself gazing at a dazzling pair of white smiling teeth. Everything else within his line of vision remained black as if looking at a photographic negative, then in an instant all the colours flushed back into view. And Harker found himself staring directly into the face of a man, a face he knew... and tears of despair or relief, he wasn't sure which, began to trickle down his sweat-smeared cheeks.

John Wilcox stood glaring down at him with contempt, his twisted smile an unsettling mix of loathing and joy all rolled into one. 'I knew I could make a believer out of you once again, Alex Harker.'

'What?' Harker managed to splutter, fighting against the tears in his eyes.

'McCray claimed you wouldn't break, but I just knew you would,' Wilcox replied, gesturing to his left.

Harker turned his head stiffly to see McCray himself leaning against the rear wall with his arms folded casually. 'I have been known to be wrong... from time to time,' he conceded.

Harker awkwardly returned his gaze to Wilcox as painful spasms rippled through his entire frame. The ex-Pope looked different somehow, his nose thinner and cheekbones higher, but it was unmistakably him. 'What have you done to me?'

'Oh, don't worry, my little lamb,' Wilcox replied, clearly taking great enjoyment from the pain Harker was in. 'It's nothing that cannot be reversed. Doctor, if you would.'

Appearing to Harker's right, a man in a smart white jumper knelt beside him and pressed a needle into Harker's arm, before injecting him with a small amount of clear fluid.

'It should only take a few seconds now to flush out the toxin,' the medic stated casually, before withdrawing.

'Thank you, Doctor,' Wilcox offered politely. 'I will call when we need you again.'

A pensive silence descended amongst them until the man had disappeared through one of the security doors behind. Then it was Wilcox who spoke first, with a glint in his eye. 'Feeling better?'

The heavy sweats afflicting Harker's body were already beginning to ease and that suffocating sense of fear began to subside. He began to feel the haze lifting as his rational thoughts now returned, and with them the same barrage of questions that had filled his head prior to that nightmarish elevator ride down into hell.

'What the hell was that stuff?' Harker sputtered, wiping the remaining sweat from his brow.

'Oh, just a little something we cooked up,' Wilcox explained. 'Its actual name is full of abbreviations and scientific symbols, but for your simple mind let us call it liquid fear. It renders the recipient a jabbering wreck and highly susceptible to any ideas one might impose upon them. I had it injected into you whilst you were unconscious.'

Harker pulled himself to his feet, grasping the nearby table for support, and he took a deep breath as the last vestiges of nausea and dizziness deserted him. 'I thought you were dead... and what happened to your face?' He panted, feeling the urge to take a swing at Wilcox who was within reaching distance. But, sensing Harker's rising anger, McCray appeared at his side and then stood next to Wilcox with a cautionary expression on his face.

'No foolishness remember, Professor,' the assassin barked, then pulled aside to let Wilcox lean closer towards him.

'Reports of my death have been greatly exaggerated... as they were intended to be. And as for the new look,' Wilcox ran a finger across his cheek, 'well, as you know, the old one had become far too well known.'

'Of course,' Harker replied with a hint of sarcasm, 'and I suppose you personally are responsible for everything that has happened over the past few days... Although how and why I have no idea.'

Wilcox pulled his head back with a puzzled look. 'In point of fact it is you yourself that bears the responsibility for everything that has happened recently, whether you realise it or not.'

'Me?' Harker almost choked at the idea, and he glanced over at McCray who immediately stiffened as if preparing to subdue their guest if needed.

Wilcox slowly nodded before he placed his hands behind his back and began to pace back and forth in his typically arrogant manner. 'Let me tell you a story that begins with the appointment of a man to the highest position in Christendom. A man selected as pontiff of Rome, who would go on to dazzle the world with undeniable truth that the Second Coming had occurred and that Jesus Christ once more walked among us, and that under his supreme guidance a new world could rise from the ashes of a religion that, having become so corrupted and watered down, barely resembled the greatness it once was. And then this glorious notion of a second golden age was halted in its tracks, when this great man's vision was brought to a halt as he stepped in a piece of shit that ruined his shoes.' Wilcox stopped his pacing and glared over in Harker's direction. 'You are the piece of shit, by the way, and the shoe was mine.'

'Yes, I guessed that.' Harker said, rolling his eyes.

'Of course you did. It's fairly obvious,' Wilcox replied and then resumed his slow pacing. 'But let us imagine for a moment that you never stuck your greasy little hands into my affairs and instead follow the journey that this great man had planned to its natural conclusion, shall we?'

'You know that speaking about oneself in the third person is usually considered the trait of a problem mind, don't you?' Harker interjected with a smile.

'If you interrupt me once more, I shall ask Mr McCray here to slowly cut out your tongue, understand?'

Harker simply nodded his head while taking a measure of satisfaction from Wilcox's momentary loss of temper, then the ex-Pope continued with his account of all the things that should have occurred.

'As I was saying before you rudely interrupted me, while the world at large fretted and debated the validity of this Second Coming, and they argued amongst themselves, the Pope would have ultimately revealed the existence of a prophecy, the true nature of which had been shielded from the public for over seventy years. Namely the three Secrets of Fatima... the true Secrets of Fatima that until that moment had never been acknowledged by the Church. These Secrets would foretell a series of events including the Second Coming of Christ, which would either culminate in saving the world as we know it or else in its total destruction. These Secrets would identify places around the planet where such cataclysms or miracles would occur, and reveal that a single man of greatness – and he alone – would be responsible for halting the approaching doom.'

He paused thoughtfully, then continued. 'The first miracle would occur in France, inside the great Notre Dame Cathedral where a terrible event would occur, at the same time, coincidently, where that great man – myself, the Pope – would be visiting. And, as a terrible plague of death took hold of the faithful, it would be the Pope alone that was left standing after having vanquished the evil that sought to take hold and destroy his flock. With much reverence and fanfare, the Pope then would have to make his way to the Temple Mount in Jerusalem, after being visited during a prayer by God Himself. And once again, as the forces of evil sought to eliminate the Holy Land, it would be his arrival there that once again halted the spread of this scourge of Satan that sought to take hold of a world that had fallen into such degeneracy. By now news of the devastation resulting from these tragedies and the miracles the Pope had performed in response would have circled the globe, and much of the bickering surrounding the cause of these events would be silenced and agreed upon. And then further so after reports of vicious animals appearing and disappearing around the earth and, under the onslaught of earthquakes and tidal waves, the still faithful would look to the only man who seemed able to quell these cataclysms that sought to destroy everything good.'

At this point he gave a smile of triumph. 'And then, during a truly remarkable speech delivered from the Vatican, the Pope would perform a type of cleansing ceremony, and instantly the cataclysms would halt. Then humanity would know the truth that the words of the Bible were not just cautionary tales but instead a reality of the planet we inhabit. A reality in which a higher power *does* exist and that dark forces do seek to control the weak, and that only by showing the faith in the Church, and the Pope who had saved them, could such forces be held at bay.'

Wilcox paused and allowed himself to revel in the idea, before resuming his pacing back and forth. 'Of course, there would still be many Doubting Thomases who would initially refuse to believe that these events did not stem from more natural explanations. But faith is a potent force and when a person is shown a miracle that they can experience for themselves and that they are part of, and not just listening to a story then something remarkable takes place. The belief can solidify into something unbreakable and unshakeable, until finally it becomes irrefutable. I once told you that people want, no they *need* to believe in something. Something bigger than themselves. And it is this very ideal that transforms into hope and is one of the most basic needs of the human spirit. Take away hope and you have little to keep you going, to push you into getting up in the morning or putting one foot in front of the other. The Second Coming was destined to strengthen this belief and to set them on the right course once again. But this series of cataclysmic events was meant to take it a step further. Any doubts would therefore be cast away and any uncertainties resolved, forcing those willing to accept one truth above all others.'

Wilcox paused and turned to face Harker, his eyes glazed with self-assurance. 'That I and all those that follow me are humanity's only salvation. And indeed that I am their saviour and, for all intents and purposes, I am their god.'

An uncomfortable gulp rippled down Harker's throat as he took in this display of complete insanity but he managed to remain quiet and motionless. For all the while he was under the watchful eye of McCray, who had produced a silver flick knife from his pocket halfway through Wilcox's rant, and was now tapping it menacingly against his palm.

'That was,' Wilcox continued, his face contorting in anger, 'until you turned up with you Templar amigos and took it upon yourselves to murder my brothers and destroy our carefully crafted plans. You robbed me of the chance to unite the believers of the world under my leadership and, in doing so, made me redundant even in the eyes of the Magi council. At first, I will admit, I was at a loss and at my lowest ebb... but, as is so often the case, success can rise from the ashes of failure and evolve into a far greater victory. A victory that is gaining in momentum even as we speak. You see Alex, your destruction of our plan to bring Christ back to the Earth – and thus all that would follow – gave me an idea that could change the world far more irrevocably than I ever considered possible. And to think that without your intervention none of this would have become a reality, for why focus on changing the world around you when instead it can be rebuilt in your image. Why not start over with a blank slate and dispose of the useless and rebuild only with those that are worthy. Just as during the Dark Ages, when the Church set about rewriting history and eliminating books, ideas and even people that did not conform to their new way of thinking, we will now proceed to do likewise, just on a more industrial scale – and you have been the instigator.'

He paused briefly to reflect. 'In the past four months, since you destroyed our plan and stole the child from us, your reputation has been surrounded by conspiracy and speculation that you were part of it, and indeed seeking to withhold any knowledge of the Second Coming and all that it entails. Further still that you have been in collusion with the Church to withhold these details, for whatever reason. And, as you well know, this scent of conspiracy or even treachery – however you wish to describe it – has been following you through the media ever since. So I decided to capitalise upon this. Instead of myself, as Pope, discovering and averting further cataclysmic events, I saw no better way to convince an already sceptical public than by having you, the conspiratorialists' poster boy, now unveiling the Secrets of Fatima... Secrets that didn't foretell the biblical terror of things to come, and how this could be prevented, but just declaring that it was happening regardless, and that the only action left to humankind was to prepare for it.'

At this point Wilcox began to smile menacingly. 'Simply put, I needed a harbinger of doom whom people would likely believe and the individual perfectly suited for the job was you Professor Alex Harker. And I must congratulate you on doing an excellent job. So far hundreds of millions around the world now believe that we are under attack from some supernatural force foretold in the Book of Revelations and this has become fused, at some level or other, in the minds of believers everywhere.'

With an arrogant smile Wilcox made his way past the still vigilant McCray towards a closed door at the end of the room. There he stopped, turning back to face Harker who remained dutifully tight-lipped even if the expression on his face was one of bewilderment. 'Christians call it Armageddon, Muslims call it eschatology, whilst Hindus refer to it as the Age of Kali. But my brethren and I know it by a different name.' Wilcox grasped the door handle and swung it open, motioning for Harker to join him there, which he did with McCray dutifully at his side. 'The word is HAARP.'

Harker followed him through the steel door and emitted a gasp at the sight that greeted him as the ex-Pope raised his arm and gestured flamboyantly across the large room ahead.

'And the angels will play their harps and the disbelievers of the world will shudder at the approaching dawn, as the righteous cry aloud in exultation of the heavenly things now to come.'

The room contained rows of work stations spaciously arranged open-plan next to one another. Each desk was equipped with a state of the art computer and various monitors, all facing a gigantic LED screen mounted on the far wall. A digital representation of the Earth's land masses was displayed on it surrounded by numerous split screens full of numbers and data, the meaning of which Harker had no idea. It reminded him of images he had seen of the Houston control centre, except that here only ten or so people manned the various desks, all of them intently focused on their own portion of the room. Not one of them even batted an eyelid at Harker's entrance.

'You know what the Kardashev scale is?' Wilcox continued, not even waiting for Harker to reply. 'It is a method of measuring any civil-isation's level of technological advancement. It's a theory devised by a Soviet astronomer which demonstrates how technologically advanced a civilisation has become, and how it measures up to the rest of the cosmos compared to other space-faring cultures. As I said it is, of

course, just a theory because we don't yet know of any other civilisa-
tions other than our own but, the theory is based on the amount of
usable energy a civilisation has at its disposal. Regarding the Kardashev
scale, there are three stages, and to keep things simple I will explain it
in terms your feeble little mind can comprehend. Stage one indicates a
civilisation that has the technological ability to control all the available
energy produced by its own planet. Stage two is the ability to control
and use the energy produced by its own sun and solar system, not
unlike, say the mythology of *Star Trek*. And, finally, stage three is where
a civilisation is able to harness the energy potential of its own galaxy
much akin to say the *Star Wars* universe, using the same analogy. Now,
of course, stages two and three will remain out of human reach for
thousands if not hundreds of thousands of years yet stage one is another
matter altogether. It was the famous and much lamented astrologer
Carl Sagan who believed we may only be one hundred years away, or
less, from reaching a stage-one type civilisation, in that our developed
technology would then allow us to harness all the Earth's energy for
our own needs.' Wilcox turned back to face Harker, who was still
in the depths of confusion as to the relevance of anything the Magi
leader was now explaining. 'Now, Alex. I can see you're wondering
what this has got to do with anything. Am I correct?'

Harker remained silent but offered a perplexed nod much to the
satisfaction of Wilcox, his arrogance never deserting him.

'Well, one of the major milestones for reaching this first stage is to
control the very engine that governs our world. It is an engine that,
for all intents and purpose, is invisible to the naked eye, and the only
glimpses we see of it are via its consequences. It is this engine that,
through technology, we are now able to control.'

Finally, Harker realised what Wilcox's long-winded, riddle-like
explanation was referring to, and a deep sense of foreboding overcame
him as the word slipped from his lips. 'Weather? You're talking about
the weather?'

An unpleasant smile appeared on Wilcox's face, and his eyes lit up
at the somewhat nervous tone in Harker's voice. 'That is exactly what
I am talking about.'

'But that's not possible,' Harker argued. 'People would already
know about it.'

'People *do* know about it,' Wilcox contradicted, still smiling.
'They're just not the type of people who would pass it on to a wider
public.'

Harker bowed his head and mulled over the fantastic proposition being laid out before him. It would explain some of the cataclysmic events during the past few days but surely it was the stuff of science fiction. Wasn't it? 'How?' Harker stammered looking back up at Wilcox with keen interest.

'Ever heard of Nikoli Tesla, one of the fathers of electricity? Well, what you may not know is that upon his death all of his patents and ideas were confiscated by the FBI, most of which were then stored away in the bowels of their archives. There they gathered dust until in the early Nineties some of these ideas were revisited. After the fall of the Soviet Union, the military still had a huge amount of government money at their fingertips and, with the loss of its main adversary, some of the cash was pumped into ideas that had not been seen to be as important to America's defence from the red menace. Amongst many other clandestine projects, they began to sift through much older ideas, and one of these was a theory put forward by the great man Tesla himself. The idea was passed on to a research-and-development company buried within the military industrial complex which was one of the Magi's considerable number of subsidiaries, and thus HAARP was born. It stands for High Frequency Active Auroral Research Programme, and essentially it is composed of just a series of transmitters and antennae which produce, at any a single moment, 3.6 megawatts of power which is then aimed at a specific spot located on the outer edge of the atmosphere. This in turn superheats the surrounding area and then, acting not unlike a mirror, the energy is focused back down on to a predetermined section of the Earth.'

Wilcox began to smile mischievously. 'And it is then that remarkable things begin to happen: tremors, minor earthquakes, as well as major air distortion which can culminate in storms, even tornados. Now that was just one facility originally, so we decided to build four more of them around the globe, giving us total coverage. And, when combined, we realised that the signal strength only magnified the effect: one you have witnessed first-hand back at Chernobyl and at the Vatican. And it is from this very station where you stand now that we can link up all five facilities with devastating effect.'

He drew a deep breath, folding his arms. 'Why just believe in God's wrath, when you can actually create it? Now, I won't pretend that this has been easy. Over the past few decades it has demanded substantial financial, political and military resources from the Magi, and has proved a monumental challenge to keep it firmly in our hands and away from the general public but our most important ally has been the project itself. For all intents and purposes this is, and the government has been persuaded to this fact, an instrument dedicated solely to the understanding of the stratosphere and that any military application is non-existent. Also it helped immensely that we funded the operation privately, without the kind of scrutiny that a government-funded project would entail. The facilities themselves have of course entered the public domain, and all one would have to do is check on Google to see that they exist. But only a few crackpot conspiracy theorists have ever guessed at HAARP's true purpose, and those have either been dealt with or discredited, without too many problems. You know yourself that for the majority of sane people on this earth, reality is what you read or see in the media and if you mention the word conspiracy it only serves to fuel further the disengagement and disbelief in such notions. In fact, we have done such a good job of hiding HAARP's true nature that as of 2014, and in the eyes of the world, the whole operation has officially been cancelled due to budget cuts. And like that, voilà, it disappeared from public view... until now.'

Harker was already shaking his head. 'Let's just say, for argument's sake, that I believe you...'

'For argument's sake?' Wilcox huffed, his mood quickly turning to anger. 'Then how else would you explain all those events going on at the moment?'

This stifled Harker's bravado, since clearly Wilcox was right. After all if it wasn't this HAARP device causing the mayhem, then indeed the alternative option was far more terrifying. 'OK, let's say you telling me the truth, then how the hell do you explain all those people at Notre Dame dropping dead around me while I myself was untouched, or how Jerusalem erupted into chaos like it did, or the fact that those unknown animals appeared when they did?'

'Demons!' Wilcox corrected with a smirk.

'Fine, demons or whatever you care to call them,' Harker replied, already suspecting the answer due to Wilcox's casual tone. After all, everything else began to pale into insignificance following that explanation of the cataclysms he had witnessed.

'Ahh, now that is a lot simpler to explain,' Wilcox replied, clearly taking relish in being able to reveal his tricks. 'What you witnessed at the cathedral is something our research department was working on for the military for some time. The military wanted to develop a nerve agent that could be released over an enemy population, and that would turn the infected into a military asset. Ergo the person transforms into a weapon of chaos before dying without leaving any trace of the agent that caused it. The technology is known as a *limiter*. The agent is released and, instead of killing the host immediately, it serves to temporarily block certain neural pathways to the brain, causing panic and heightening aggression as well as a haemorrhaging to the eyes and other basic physical changes to the skin and gums, etc. In layman's terms the host is turned mad and goes after anything that moves, causing more casualties. The body can only function then for a limited amount of time, until oxygen restriction to the brain brings about clinical death. The real genius, though, is that after death the agent bursts on a microscopic level and dissolves in the body, leaving no identifiable trace whatsoever. Complete deniability. As far as our contract with the military went, they were told that we couldn't get it to work and therefore funding was stopped. Of course, our Magi subsidiaries continued with the project, and perfected it as you witnessed for yourself. The agent used in the Jerusalem operation was a slightly different strain, and in fact the chemical you yourself were just recently infected with was an offshoot of that same research.'

Harker's stomach churned sickeningly at the total lack of respect for life being shown here, for Wilcox seemed to take so much pride in these twisted achievements.

'Don't go soft on me now, Alex,' Wilcox chided. 'There's so much more to tell you. Now the fires erupting in Jerusalem were easy. We had some teams set up firebombs just an hour before you arrived, and others that would release the chemical agent around the city. The wind did the rest.' A satisfied smile appeared on Wilcox's lips. 'Even I have to admit it did look remarkable on the news reports. Hell, it almost made me a believer.'

'Remarkable!' Harker yelled. 'Thousands of people died horribly and Jerusalem was left looking like a war zone.'

'Well, no change there,' Wilcox quipped and waved his hand dismissively as if swatting a fly. 'You know, it is true what they say: kill a few thousand and you're a mass murderer, but kill a few million and you're a conqueror. And I plan to become the most significant conqueror in human history, because kill a few billion and you become a god.'

Harker was staggered at the man's sheer lunacy and lust for power, but he set aside the series of insults he wanted to hurl at the sick bastard and instead focused on a question that was still nagging him. 'So why wasn't I affected by this agent?'

'Good question but a boring answer. Remember that Secret you unearthed in Notre Dame? Well, the sealed vial that you broke open contained the agent which then spread throughout the cathedral, but the paper it was printed upon was doused in the antidote. By just touching the paper, it was absorbed into your skin and blood, making you impervious and apparently miraculously untouched. And I am guessing that your lady friend must have inadvertently touched the paper as well, or she would have died along with all the rest.'

Harker thought back to that moment in Notre Dame when Chloe had snatched the parchment off him to read for herself. Her determination, it seemed, had saved her life even though from the outset Harker had been sure it might instead get her killed.

'You know I myself should have been the one to have miraculously survived that outbreak.' Wilcox griped. 'Imagine how it would have looked when I, the Pope, had walked out of that cathedral alive, as if having vanquished the very evil that had sought to kill *everyone*.' He shook his head in frustration. 'Damn, that would have looked impressive. Still, you got the job done I suppose and managed to spread the fear of what was to come, without even being aware of it. As for the demons you asked about, those nasty-looking devils were spliced in our test labs from an assortment of different animal genetic codes. Incidentally those were the same labs in which we created the cloned copy of Jesus Christ, using some of the same techniques.'

Wilcox took a moment to reach over and gently tap McCray on the shoulder. 'Of course I could not have got to where we are now without the help of this man. Contrary to your belief that he was banished from the Magi before taking over leadership of the Skoptsy, nothing could be further from the truth. I had specially asked McCray to initiate contact with that vile cult many years ago, in the hopes of using them as scapegoats if ever the need arose. But instead they proved far more successful in convincing you to pursue this trail of breadcrumbs. No... McCray has always remained a valued member of the Magi, even if he needed to deceive the Council into believing otherwise, and so his loyalty to me will be rewarded tenfold in years to come.'

'So where is the child, and what of Marcus Eckard and the actual Secrets... And what about the fourth Secret?' Harker demanded, realising that every answer Wilcox gave him only created further questions.

'The Child?' Wilcox was looking confused himself. 'I have absolutely no idea. That treacherous witch Claire Dwyer was supposed to bring him to me but, lo and behold, she turns up with only the mother.'

'What? You don't have him?'

'I've already said I didn't,' Wilcox snapped angrily, 'God knows where she put him, and frankly I couldn't give shit!'

Harker was totally flabbergasted, for if the Magi didn't have the child, then who did? 'That doesn't bother you?'

'No, why should it?' Wilcox said, looking sincere. 'That child's usefulness came to an end the moment you screwed up my original plans, and the only reason I tried to retrieve it in the first place was to appease some of the Council and to initially give me some continued leverage over them. As for Eckard and the Secrets, they are hardly worth mentioning,' Wilcox sneered, 'but I am happy to enlighten you further. When the Magi learnt that a council had been set up by the Pope to investigate the Secrets of Fatima, over thirty years ago, we decided to take a gander for ourselves. Through Eckard, we were able to get a look at them but they seemed pretty useless... that is until the Pope insisted they be locked away and because, after that, the only person ever permitted to know what they contained was the ruling Pope. And since all of those have passed away except me, eventually I alone knew what was written in them. I could therefore have made up anything I wanted, and no one else would have been any the wiser.'

'Except Marcus Eckard?'

'Yes,' Wilcox sneered, 'I will admit he did pose a problem at first, but after we threatened to kill his wife and child he went along with us and gave the box to Bishop Canard at Notre Dame... Of course it was empty but good old Canard kept his word and never opened it, so a few months ago we had someone sneak in and put the vial containing the agent into the box without him even knowing. Then it was ready for you to 'discover'. The idiot never even considered that there might be two keys to that precious little box of his.'

'And Eckard?'

'Marcus Eckard was a loose end and we did try a number of chemical treatments on him to make him more... docile. But I'm afraid we did not get the result we had hoped for, as you saw for yourself, so we had to kill his entire family and make him take the blame. Still, he proved his worth by helping to suck you into all this. The poor bastard didn't even know that he was helping us... as for the precious fourth Secret he spoke of, there never was one. His ruined mind just made it up. But I knew that having such a mysterious thing to chase after would only help in getting you on board.'

'So this whole elaborate plan has been about control and nothing more,' Harker growled, sickened by the flippant and callous description of murder after murder.

'This isn't just about control, Professor,' Wilcox hissed at his belit-tling of the project, 'or about subjugation for that matter. This is about manipulating a worldwide populace into wishing to be controlled and protected. The Romans once managed it through sheer bloody force, whereas the British Empire added global trade and a 'fair' justice system to its repertoire, thus making it far more palatable to the masses. The Magi will do it through *choice* however, and the people of the world will *choose* it, and we the Magi will implement it.'

This madcap idea already had Harker shaking his head. 'If you really believe that billions of people are suddenly going to willingly enslave themselves to the Magi, then you really are insane. More importantly, you can't truly expect that all the governments of the world, with all their military power, are simply going to relinquish their authority to an ex-Pope with a Napoleon complex... Really?'

'I am far too tall to suffer from a Napoleon complex... but yes, that is precisely what I expect,' Wilcox declared. 'That is why, beginning in the next few hours, HAARP will begin pulverising government infrastructure around the world – only nuclear nations at first – and that will quickly be followed with the sanitising of less important countries.'

'You'll start World War Three!' Harker shouted loudly and as if Wilcox was going deaf.

'I don't think so,' the Magi Prime replied confidently. 'Who would they attack... Heaven itself?'

Harker's mouth was already open ready to respond, but Wilcox directed a finger at him before he could make a sound. 'Yes, there will no doubt be some vengeful individuals on both sides, but you forget that in the last few hours we have been targeting the majority of the world's military satellites through HAARP. Most of their communications and many of their guidance systems are as of now inoperative. I will concede that there may still be instances of nuclear strikes, but frankly this will only serve to help in our goal of thinning down population numbers. But you miss the point, Alex. My plan for a new world is not something that will occur overnight, over a few months or even a year. Completion of our goal will take decades, maybe even a century, but all the while under the carefully planned guidance of the Magi. You forget that the period called the Dark Ages lasted from five to eight centuries, depending on how you define it. That is a full eight centuries to transform the world and set it on a course for a new world order. But I believe, with the technology at our fingertips, we can achieve it in less than one.'

Harker now felt a sense of deep emptiness and, even though the mammoth task of culling the world's population was an impossibility to his mind, it was the trying to do so that concerned him most. 'Even after everything you're taking about – weather-induced cataclysms, the chaos of a world stripped of its economy and industry, Christ even a nuclear war – there will still be billions of people who survive. And, over time, they will restore their own communities and political systems, and there is no way you can ever hope to control that many people... ever.'

A look of stubborn determination crossed Wilcox's face, and Harker was surprised to find the man nodding in agreement.

'You are right, which is why we could never leave the task solely to the mechanisms I have so far described.'

Mechanisms? This cold word to describe the annihilation of billions of human lives rattled around Harker's head painfully, as Wilcox went on to describe his plans further, and with an increased zeal.

'Firstly, starvation alone will wipe out hundreds of millions, if not billions, during the months that follow. Since the inception of mass food production after the Second World War, the population of the globe has doubled in size. Take away that same process and people will begin to drop like flies. For a short while inevitably the world will be in the grip of a truly Darwinian society: the law of the wild where only the strongest and those most suited to survive will flourish. But still that won't be enough, which is why further strategies will be needed. For that reason, we had to formulate what I consider our most effective method of ensuring that what is left is ripe to be picked and used for the foundation of a new society. Even now, large sections of the media are beginning to succumb to the idea that the events of Notre Dame and Jerusalem are akin to a Biblical plague. As society begins to crumble around them, the news that the media have been delivering to people will turn into one of fear and desperation, and then into the need for a belief in salvation.

'That belief will ultimately, on some level, manifest itself as a reality... one that the Magi will be happy to provide. Those exotic nerve agents that we have already unleashed are but the tip of the iceberg, since they derive from something far greater than that which I have already mentioned. You see, the mother source of those strains has not only been engineered to contain a time limit of effectiveness, but it is also able to target specific genes within the DNA of every living creature. It is able to target people of a select genetic strain, whilst at the same time proving harmless to others. Of course, everyone will become infected by this agent as it spreads throughout the world, carried by the global wind patterns, but only those specially chosen will be affected by it.'

Harker immediately thought back to the storage disk the Templars had found at Father Strasser's wretched apartment. The hundreds of thousands of names on it and the one connecting factor they all possessed. A renewed sense of excitement and shock fizzled through him: excitement because of the connection he had made and shock because of the awful truth it revealed.

'Christians.' He whispered from his lips. 'Devout Christians.'

Wilcox's raised his eyebrows, clearly surprised by Harker's informed understanding of the end process the Magi leader had been about to reveal. 'Yes, exactly. Well done.' Wilcox clapped his hands in congratulation of the man he hated so much. 'How on earth did you figure that out?'

'We found a list at your man Strasser's apartment, containing thousands of names, and they appeared to have just one thing in common: all were church-goers and Christians.'

'Not just Christians,' Wilcox corrected, 'but devout Christians and true believers. We have blood samples from each person on the list allowing us access to their own individual genetic breakdown. With this information we can ensure that our manufactured disease will only target the undesirables and not our chosen faithful.'

'That's impossible,' Harker protested defiantly. 'Firstly, how could you obtain blood samples from all of those people? Secondly, it would take years to decipher the genetic codes from so many people!'

Wilcox stepped closer and thrust his face towards him. 'Oh ye of little faith... firstly, almost everyone in the Western world has had blood taken at some stage in his or her life, and the Magi made sure that when someone on the list gave or had blood taken it was scooped up for our own files. Don't forget that the Magi organisation has its fingers in many areas of industry including the health sector. Secondly, we have, so far, genetically mapped only about fifty-five percent of the donors, but that is not information we need right at this moment. As I have already explained this entire process will take years to play out, and it is during that same time that our scientists will complete the task. This facility has eighty separate levels, and is not only self-sustainable but also has every conceivable piece of medical equipment needed for the project, including numerous backups. We could stay down here for generations if need be whilst above us it all else goes to hell... with a little help from us, of course.' He smiled coldly.

'It all sounds like a pretty messy endeavour,' Harker remarked, hoping to annoy this little Hitler standing before him.

'This is not and never was going to be clean-cut in any way. You cannot aim to remove ninety-nine percent of the world's popula- tion without numerous setbacks, unintended casualties and unforeseen mistakes. Such mishaps are bound to happen. But given a long enough time-scale, with the technology needed, the foresight to prepare for such instances and most of all the sheer will to see it through to the end, I can assure you all this will come to pass. And it begins now.'

With that announcement, Wilcox returned his attention to the display screen and raised his head proudly. 'The dawn of a new world begins today, and with it a new God.'

Under the watchful eye of McCray, Harker calmly made his way over and stood at Wilcox's side. 'I called you insane earlier, Wilcox, but I was wrong. What I should have said is that you are the devil incarnate.'

A twisted smile crossed Wilcox's lips, as he leant over and whispered into Harker's ear, 'Maybe so, Alex... but even hell has its heroes.'

Chapter 45

'Where are my friends?' Harker demanded for the third time. 'Or are have they already become part of your intended 'collateral damage' alongside the rest of civilisation?'

Harker's yelling provoked a wicked smile from Wilcox, who was taking great satisfaction from this. 'Calm yourself, Professor.' He glanced over to one of the guards standing in the corner of the control room and clicked his fingers. The man disappeared through a side door, then reappeared just moments later with a hooded figure which he dragged over to where Wilcox was standing. The guard whisked off the hood to reveal the furious glare of Chloe Stanton, with a piece of silver tape fastened across her mouth. Her eyes widened in relief on seeing Harker, before Wilcox firmly ripped away the tape.

'Now, now, Doctor Stanton. No more outbursts or I will be forced to silence you again,' he warned before glancing over at Harker. 'She's a feisty one, this assistant of yours.'

'I'm not his assistant,' Chloe protested through gritted teeth. 'I'm his partner and I demand to know why you've kidnapped us.'

Harker smiled at this correction as to Chloe's position. After all she had already been through, she was sticking to her guns and refusing to budge in regards to her role in all of this.

'Partner it is, then.' Wilcox sighed, slapping the piece of tape back across her mouth. 'But let's have you as a silent partner, shall we.'

He pushed her away into McCray's waiting hands who secured her as she fumed silently underneath the gag. 'Now, why don't we see how your other friend is doing.' Wilcox clapped his hands and turned to address the people still working at their desks. 'Gentlemen, would you please leave the room and allow us some privacy.'

Without hesitation the group of staff made their way out through the side doors until only the four of them remained. 'My team is made up of members of all the Magi families, plus a few specialists we had to 'convince' into joining us. They are all well trained and will never question an order.' Wilcox said proudly, before shooting Chloe a sarcastic glance. 'You could learn a thing or two from them.'

He then reached over and took control of the keyboard at the work station in front of him, tapping at it until the large central screen went black. A few seconds later, it clicked on to night-vision display, with footage from a security camera set high up in the corner of some darkened room about the size of a squash court. Harker noticed the room was completely empty except for a single individual patiently squatting in one of the corners, with his forearms resting on his knees.

'Sebastian,' Harker murmured as the camera zoomed in from above, giving him a clearer image of the Templar Grand Master. A few cuts and bruises on the man's cheek suggested his captors had not been as easy on him as they had been with Chloe, and a ripped jacket and torn white shirt confirmed this. 'What have you done to him?' Harker demanded and riled that his friend had been roughed up.

'Nothing really! Only a bit of rough and tumble getting him into his cell.' Wilcox gave a mischievous smile. 'Nothing *yet* anyway.' He gestured to McCray who reached for his walkie-talkie and mumbled something unintelligible into it. 'Sebastian Brulet. Grand Master of the Knights Templar.' Wilcox continued, licking his lips. 'Let's now see if that sanctimonious title is fully justified, shall we?'

–

Brulet flinched and covered his eyes as above him spotlights burst into life illuminating the room in a blinding light. Without those obligatory sunglasses to shield his sensitive eyes from the glare, he became adrift in his surroundings. The effect was made worse by the dazzling white paint covering the walls, making it difficult even to discern where the walls met the floor.

Brulet remained motionless with both hands cradling his eyes, cocooned in that haze of white light, waiting for his vision to acclimatise as best it could. He was still waiting when in front of him a portion of the wall slid away to reveal a darkened entrance. At first this dark patch in the wall seemed a welcome relief, alleviating the sense of complete disorientation, but this comfort was quickly swept away as a sinister growl rumbled from somewhere inside the opening.

The now familiar shaggy outline of the beast he had encountered earlier steadily padded into the room and halted, as the door slid shut behind it. The fact that the creature ignored the moving door, told Brulet that it was at ease with its surroundings. This plainly was the animal's familiar territory and that knowledge served to heighten Brulet's unease. He instinctively shook his arm, only to realise his arm-sword had been removed. He cursed his own foolishness: of course the weapon had been taken, it would have given him a chance and the Magi were not known for their sense of fair play.

As Brulet pondered the options open to him, the beast lowered its head and began to slowly make its way around the edge of the room, heading towards him. That it remained so close to the walls suggested the animal was being cautious. But, as it got closer, it stopped and then jumped a bit closer, forcing Brulet to move in the other direction. This creature wasn't wary at all but just taking its time. Savouring the inevitable outcome like a cat playing with a mouse. Once again it made a small jump, emitting a low clicking growl. It was enjoying this.

Brulet slowly moved backwards until his shoulders were pressed against the wall, but with no sudden moves that might encourage the creature to pounce.

His options were few but he did have one thing to his advantage, and that was the colour of the animal's coat. Its jet-black fur provided his still-struggling vision with something to latch on to. This, at the very least, meant that any move the animal made could be calculated somewhat in advance.

The beast made another leap forward but this time it was further. And as Brulet continued his cautious withdrawal, he desperately sought to formulate a plan. This stalking game would not last for much longer before the animal became bored and decided to end things in a flurry of gnashing teeth and ripping claws. Regardless of who walked out of here alive, the conclusion to this standoff would have to come fast and quick and, with no way out, Brulet decided upon the only option left to him.

It is an odd thing that when someone is confronted with a hopeless situation, an idea that in the normal light of day would seem rather pathetic can suddenly gain tremendous merit. In the human mind, hope springs eternal, and the instinct for survival is so strong that odds and probabilities fade into significance when faced with one's own fate. It was this very instinct that now impelled Brulet's thinking as he reached down to his belt buckle and unfastened it. He slipped it loose from around his waist and began feeding it tightly into the palm of his hand, section by section, not wanting to reveal its true length for fear that the beast might see it as a threat. Unfortunately, the beast was not that stupid and even though it had no idea what its prey intended, it did suspect something. It lowered its head and after a quivering of its rear legs, it pounced forwards. The brief pause before the pounce allowed Brulet just enough time to press one shoe against the wall and launch himself sideways, just missing the animal's outstretched claws. He rolled once across the floor using the same momentum to leap upright as the creature's body thudded into the wall. He then swiftly retreated into the opposite corner, and again pressed his shoe against the wall, with the belt now unfurled as the beast turned and began to advance, the near miss only having excited it further.

In Brulet's mind there was no way the animal would miss a second time, and would expect him to jump out of reach, so the only way to cause confusion in the beast's mind was to bait it into making a mistake by doing something it would not expect.

With the ends of his belt clasped in either hand and one foot still firmly pinioned where the wall met the floor, he lowered his head and widened his eyes as far as he could before emitting the most ferocious snarl followed by the deepest growl he could manage, while revealing as much of his teeth as possible.

This display of defiance caught the creature off-guard and it hesitated for just a fraction of a second before unleashing an almighty roar. It hunched up as Brulet watched intently for that tell-tale quiver of its back legs and, in a perfect moment of timing, he launched himself sideways just as the animal leapt towards him. One of its claws caught Brulet's shin before its head slammed into the wall with a painful-sounding crack.

The beast dropped to the floor, stunned, and without hesitation Brulet dove on to its back, slinging the belt buckle around its throat and into his other waiting palm. The animal was still recovering as Brulet slid the other end of the belt through the buckle and, with all his strength, yanked it upwards until the metal point of the buckle caught in the last hole on the belt, constricting the leather tightly around the creature's throat.

Brulet then leapt off its back and then watched from a safe distance as the beast writhed against the strip of leather compressing its wind-pipe emitting a series of wheezing, hissing noises as it struggled to breathe. The animal lurched to its feet and tried to claw at the tight-ened noose with its hind legs, merely causing it to fall back to the floor. As it did so, Brulet launched himself into the air and brought both feet back down together squarely on the stricken creature's skull with all his weight. He felt a crack ripple under the soles of his shoes as a part of its skull gave way, and then jumped back out of the way of the flailing claws, which were already beginning to go limp.

Brulet watched as the beast's body sagged and expelled a strange burbling noise as it struggled to breath under pressure of the belt still tightly wrapped around its neck. The blow had not killed it outright, but it was clearly not going anywhere any time soon.

Satisfied the enemy had been incapacitated, Brulet raised his arms to fill his lungs, but then he recoiled at the sharp pain across his chest. He looked down to see a line of blood running just below his ribs, that was now becoming thicker and thicker. He pulled up his shirt to view the source of his discomfort and discovered the creature had caught him with a claw, ripping a nasty wound right across his stomach. He could not tell if it had pierced any organs but his strength was beginning to dwindle and he fell back on to the seat of his trousers, trying desperately to steady himself. He was still trying to catch his breath when the door opposite him once again slid open to reveal the now familiar, gloomy, entrance. Without further thought, Brulet pulled himself to his feet, still tenderly clasping the wound across his stomach.

He waited anxiously for another one of those creatures to appear, and racked his mind for another strategy. But due to the wound he had sustained, and just like the creature throttled by the belt, he was not going anywhere.

A few seconds passed and then a figure appeared out of the gloom. 'Not bad,' McCray remarked with genuine sincerity in his voice. 'From one solider to another, not bad at all.'

A metallic voice interrupted and Brulet gazed up at a meshed speaker built into the wall. 'Enough of the pleasantries,' John Wilcox's voice crackled. 'Fetch him here to me.'

'Come on, let's go.' McCray strode over and hauled Brulet fully upright. 'OK?'

Despite the severe pain of his injuries, a smile crept across Brulet's face. Wilcox had sounded furious, no doubt severely irked by the thorn in his side that was Brulet's survival of the organised death trap.

'I'm fine,' Brulet replied loudly, so that Wilcox would hear over the intercom. 'Just dandy.'

Chapter 46

'The hero returns,' Wilcox hailed him sarcastically, as Brulet entered the command centre accompanied by McCray. 'What a show you put on for us, Mr Brulet. You really are quite the performer, aren't you?'

'That depends on your definition of entertainment,' Brulet replied scathingly, aware of Harker and Chloe, who still had tape strapped across her mouth, 'but, given your warped mentality, I would probably have to agree.'

Brulet ignored the glowering look on Wilcox's face and turned his attention to Harker. 'Glad to see you alive, Alex.'

'The feeling's mutual, Sebastian,' he replied, hugely relieved to see him standing there. 'Wilcox has been enlightening us all about his plans to make himself immortal.'

'Yes, he took great pleasure in telling me about it earlier,' Brulet declared. 'He's quite the genius.'

The mention of that word had Wilcox smiling happily. 'That's quite a compliment coming from a Grand Master.'

'Not really,' Brulet snapped. 'Hitler was a genius too, but he was a depraved and evil genius... just like you.'

'Quite,' Wilcox replied, but the smile on his face faded.

Harker now gestured to the bloody wound on Brulet's stomach. 'Are you OK?'

'I'll live.' Brulet next glanced over at Chloe and her restrictive strip of silver tape. 'Still uneasy around women, I see,' he commented, with a shake of his head, 'I had always heard that about you, Wilcox.'

The comment clearly riled their host, whose nose wrinkled in irritation. 'As if you know anything about me,' he snorted, before reaching over to rip away the tape from her lips.

'Well, you know what they say,' Brulet continued calmly. 'If you've met one psychopathic and narcissistic egomaniac, you've met them all.'

'Is that true?' Wilcox marvelled ironically. 'Then you'll undoubtedly know what I am about to do next, won't you? Mr McCray, would you call the staff back in, please, and get someone to stem the flow of our guest's bleeding. I don't want him dying on me just yet.'

McCray disappeared through one of the doors and returned moments later with a procession of support staff, who quickly resumed their positions at the work stations.

The doctor who had injected Harker earlier also appeared and made his way over to Brulet with an impressive looking first aid-box and began attending to the Templar's stomach applying a large cotton pad which was then held in place with medical tape. 'Now let us get started,' Wilcox continued, indicating a gruff-looking man in his fifties sitting at one of the work stations at the far end of the room. 'Mr Samprey, if you would now be so good as to bring up our first location.'

The man immediately began issuing instructions to his team, whereupon the main view screen in front of them began to flicker back into life. On the screen appeared an image that was all too familiar. It immediately elicited an uncomfortable groan from Harker, who then shot Wilcox a despising glare.

The live image of Westminster Abbey was most likely taken from a surveillance camera high up on a building opposite, as it looked down directly over the impressive cathedral and the scores of people flowing inside through the main entrance.

'Fear and ignorance,' Wilcox mused, 'the staple diet of any religion wishing to fill its pews. Unfortunately for the sheep already inside, their prayers will not be answered today.'

'John, you can't,' Harker protested. 'There must hundreds in there. They're just scared and looking for reassurance.'

'Well, they won't be getting it and besides this is not about them. This is about everyone else. People must have their hopes in the existing Church shattered if we are ever to rebuild a new belief in the coming years. I thought the destruction of St Peter's Basilica would have made that obvious.'

This statement left Harker stunned, if not surprised, and he continued staring coldly at Wilcox in silence.

'I will admit that I chose this next location, in the heart of London, for your benefit, Alex. But don't feel guilty, because I would have got around to Westminster eventually.'

He pointed a finger at the screen and wagged it. 'Gentlemen, if you would.'

Even as the technicians tapped away at their keyboards, Harker was already lurching towards Wilcox in a fury but he was stopped almost immediately by McCray, who rammed his forearm across Harker's chest to stop him getting any closer.

'You're mad,' Brulet hissed, tensing impotently against his handcuffs.

The frustration in his voice received only a dismissive grunt. 'What you consider insanity I call vision,' the Magi leader declared sanctimoniously. 'It takes a great man to conceive a vision but it takes an exceptional man to implement it. Now watch as that vision becomes reality.'

Behind them one of the technicians began counting from ten, as another recited the necessary checks.

'Ten, nine...'

'All HAARP facilities online and location locked on.'

'... eight, seven...'

'Power surge beginning and receptors at maximum.'

'... six, five, four...'

'Generators purged and clear for release.'

'... three, two, one. Payload is away.'

Harker stared at the screen as a momentary flash of light lit up the sky above Westminster Cathedral. Then the image began to shake... the two stone towers of the west entrance were the first to go, crumbling into jagged blocks that crashed down onto the pavement in a cloud of dust, and right on top of the crowds queuing up to gain entrance. Next the main roof began to wobble as vibrations rippled across its tiles, whereupon the stonework gave way and collapsed in on itself. The main front entrance was next, tumbling down onto those who now fled the collapsing structure and the magnificent stained-glass windows shattered into pieces, sending further misery down onto the frightened people below. Most of them had already disappeared from sight due to the falling debris and the dust clouds rolling out in all directions.

'That's enough. We do not want to destroy it completely,' Wilcox decided even as the southerly wall began to wobble. 'Like many other shrines to come, this husk of former glory must serve as a visual reminder: a testament to the power that the new order wields in years to come.' Wilcox leaned closer to Harker, his expression full of spite. 'Stings, doesn't it, to see so many lives snuffed out in such a seemingly senseless tragedy? Now you know the pain you yourself caused me when you killed my brothers.'

The fact that Harker had not actually been responsible for the deaths of Wilcox's siblings seemed immaterial at that moment. It would obviously have been futile to try and change this psychopath's mind and as he watched this vision of destruction flicker into darkness, Harker felt a deep sense of total despair. Maybe it was the sight of so many people losing their lives, or maybe it was because he was so utterly powerless to do anything about it, but either way he felt totally drained of energy and uttered the only thought that came to mind. 'You'll burn for this, Wilcox. I don't know how or when, but you will burn.'

The man raised his eyebrows sarcastically as he reached over and tapped Harker on the chest. 'Naturally I disagree, but if I am going to burn for that event, then I am undoubtedly going to roast for this next one.'

Wilcox turned his attention back to Mr Samprey who was still hunched over his computer screen. 'Next location, please, quick as you can.'

Once more the main screen lit up, displaying a satellite image of the Vatican City in its entirety.

'Now this is one landmark the world can really do without,' Wilcox rasped, rubbing his hands together. 'St Peter's was a good start but I'd feel better if this whole place was gone entirely.'

'What happened to leaving husks to serve as visual reminders?' Brulet asked flatly.

'The ruins of so many other Catholic churches around the globe will serve that purpose adequately, but as for the Vatican…' Wilcox replied pensively. 'It is too much of a symbol… evoking too much history to be left standing. There must be no beacons of hope left if the Magi are to seize the reins of world power. There is a fine line between symbols of despair and those of hope. Take the cross upon which Jesus Christ died: it should have been an icon for pain and suppression but instead it became one of hope and belief.' Wilcox shook his head vigorously from side to side. 'No, the Vatican City must disappear. Out of sight and out of mind, it is the only way.'

The dark logic initially drew a disheartened sigh from Brulet, but he was then visually overcome by an air of serene calm. 'John,' he began, in all but a whisper but somehow maintaining an air of authority, despite being handcuffed. 'Our two organisations have been at war with each other for a millennium. We have fought at every stage in the evolution of the Catholic Church. The Magi have always sought to control and the Templars to protect the religion we hold so dear but, despite the bloodshed and loss on both sides and the inescapable differences of our creeds, there is one thing that has always united us.'

'And that is?' Wilcox replied and looking extremely curious.

'We both believe in God's divine plan, through religion, to lead people to a better and more just world. Our only real difference is that you people believe it must be done through control and subjugation, whereas we believe it should be achieved through the will, belief and peaceful intentions of the people that serve Him.' Brulet gazed at Wilcox, with eyes that pleaded for understanding. 'But to destroy religion itself, and all it stands for, goes against everything our ancestors aimed to achieve. Please don't do this… for their sakes as well as ours.'

John Wilcox slumped back against the console and any malice or loathing for his arch-nemesis evaporated, and a contemplative expression began to surface. He looked down to the floor for a moment before returning to face Brulet's imploring stare. 'You're right,' he replied. 'My ancestors and yours have always shared that particular ideology that you refer to and, in many ways, we are similar beings you and I. But, I, unlike my ancestors, decided to pose myself a question that neither side had even considered before, let alone dared ask.'

'And that is?' Brulet inquired apprehensively.

'It is so simple, so base, so obvious a question that I doubt it has ever even entered your indoctrinated mind, Sebastian,' Wilcox replied.

'Well?' Brulet urged, 'what is it?'

Wilcox raised his hands as if impatient at the lack of vision being displayed. 'Does God actually exist?'

The question left both Brulet and Harker staring at each other in amazement, but it was Chloe who spoke first.

'Hold on, I thought your Order's entire history was based on what you believe to be God's chosen path. Doesn't the whole purpose of the Magi rest on the belief that you are doing His work?'

'For my ancestors, yes and without question, and for a long time I also was unwavering in that same belief but I have come to realise that in order for any civilisation to thrive, it must evolve, and that applies to religion and belief and is it not fair to say that God is a creation of man? There were the gods of Egypt then the gods of Rome and finally the one God of Christianity. Human thinking has evolved so as to believe in a higher power, and that somehow our lives are part of something greater, but that doesn't necessarily make it true.'

Wilcox raised his head confidently displaying all the arrogance of a dictator. 'God is merely a figment of the human mind needed to justify our own miserable existence and, in this evolved and technological world of science we now live in, people look for other beliefs to satisfy that logic. There are more atheists than ever, and the numbers are growing with evolution replacing religion.' A contemptuous scowl appeared on Wilcox's face and he shook his clenched fist. 'Well, if they want a world of Darwinism, I intend to give it to them – and only then will they realise the true horror of its reality. With civilisation in tatters and primal survival instincts gripping those who manage to survive the coming apocalypse, they will realise just how wrong they were. Billions dead, the world in chaos and only the truly faithful left standing but leaderless. Rape and murder will become the daily norm.' Wilcox wagged a finger at Harker, with true wrath in his eyes. 'Only then will the survivors seek a light to guide them out of the nightmare that the world has become... and the Magi will be there to offer it to them.'

'That's pure insanity, John,' Brulet protested wildly.

'I already told him that,' Harker intervened quickly, much to the anger of Wilcox whose lip began to curl.

'Enough,' he spat, pointing to the screen and the image of Vatican City. 'Mr Samprey, would you please erase that vile place off the face of the earth immediately.'

The technician began to run through his ten-second checklist, while Brulet struggled futilely against his handcuffs and McCray continued to restrain Harker and Chloe.

'There's an easy answer to the question of whether God exists,' Wilcox continued, turning to face Harker with a look of determination 'If he was really up there, then I wouldn't be able to do what I am about to do now, would I?'

'Ten, nine...' Samprey called out.

'All HAARP facilities online and location locked on.'

'... eight, seven...'

'Power surge beginning and receptors at maximum.'

'... six, five, four...'

'Generators purged and clear for release.'

'... three, two...'

Mr Samprey's voice tailed off and Wilcox immediately swung around to see what the holdup was about. 'Why have you stopped?'

Samprey spent a few seconds staring at his monitor before looking up in a panic. 'The other four HAARP facilities have gone down, sir... total loss of power. They're not even registering.'

'What!' Wilcox shouted. 'How the hell is that possible?'

'I don't know, sir, but the only one registering power is ours.'

'Then proceed with that one.'

'We don't have enough power, sir. The best we could manage is an earthquake, but without the other facilities there's no way we could produce the seismic activity needed to...'

'Then you'd better find out why those other facilities have gone offline,' Wilcox screamed, now seething.

Samprey quickly bowed his head towards the console, searching for answers, but it was McCray who now offered the cause. 'Sir, you need to see this.'

Wilcox turned to see the man pointing at one of the computer screens. He then pressed at its keypad, bringing up the image onto the main screen.

The sight drew a gasp of shock from Wilcox and a sigh of relief from Harker, who almost laughed out loud. Eight Chinook helicopters hovered over the wreckage of their own downed helicopter, as lines dropped to the ground and a horde of soldiers in military gear abseiled to the ground. The markings on the aircraft were a mix of British, US, Chinese and Russian, and in the background he could make out Apache helicopters approaching in the distance as, overhead, two Harrier jump jets skimmed in and out of view of the surveillance camera.

'How the fu...!' Wilcox raged, his words fading in despair, as Brulet locked eyes with Harker and silently mouthed the word 'Shroder.'

Harker could already felt the excitement bubbling inside him though it was swiftly dampened by the realisation that even though Wilcox's plan was now ruined and the world was saved, their own fate was still hanging very much in the balance.

'Sir, we are compromised,' McCray declared firmly and he grasped Wilcox's forearm. 'We have to go now.'

Wilcox shrugged off the man's grip and continued to stare blankly at the screen. It seemed an age before he turned again to address the entire room. 'Everyone leave now,' he ordered curtly.

The instruction fell upon deaf ears as the technicians hesitated, not knowing exactly what to do next, or where to go for that matter.

'I said *get out*,' Wilcox roared with an intensity that finally broke the stillness, and suddenly all the technicians began to clear the room in a rush. Wilcox then returned his attention to the screen showing the soldiers now pouring towards the surveillance camera and the barn's doorway.

'We won't have long before they discover how to gain entry.' McCray pushed his way to Wilcox's side. 'We have to evacuate everyone now, before they do so.'

Wilcox turned to face McCray, his face ashen white and his lips twisted in a scowl. 'Forget them... they mean nothing.'

This response caught McCray off guard and his eyes widened in surprise. 'Sir, these are our people,' he argued. 'We have to get them to safety.'

'They have failed me and so I shall fail them too... fuck them.'

As the two men stared at each other, one in defiance and the other in shock, Harker was already reaching for a keyboard at the nearest workstation. He grasped it in both hands and raised it over his head, ready to strike, but as he did so the connector cables fell back to the desk with a click. McCray spun around to investigate the noise just as Harker brought the keyboard's edge down hard across the bridge of his nose, sending him down on to one knee, clasping his nose in pain. The assassin barely had time to look up again, before Harker had dropped the now shattered keyboard and proceeded to deliver two sharp punches to the face of the already dazed McCray, dropping him face first onto the shiny tiled floor with an unhealthy thud. There he remained motionless, the force of the impact rendering him seemingly unconscious.

Before Harker had even landed his second blow, Brulet was already rushing Wilcox. But the Magi leader spun off to the left, sending Brulet flying past him, like a matador sidestepping a bull, and in one motion he slid his arm around Brulet's neck and flicked his forearm, engaging an arm-sword which popped out and clicked into place, the blade pressed firmly against Brulet's throat.

'That's far enough,' Wilcox snarled as Harker edged closer. 'Or else I slit his throat.'

Harker halted as somewhere on the floor behind him, McCray began to murmur but his return to consciousness was cut short when Chloe briskly pushed a large 42⊠ Apple work monitor off the table and sent it crashing down on to McCray's head, silencing any further sounds from the already wounded man.

'That's enough,' Wilcox demanded weakly, his complexion growing paler by the second. 'That's enough.'

Chloe now stepped over to join Harker and both sides fell silent as each of them weighed up their options.

'It's over, John,' Harker said finally. 'Why don't you put away the blade? Haven't enough people died already?'

The statement appeared only to inflame Wilcox's anger further, and he hugged the sword tighter to Brulet's throat. 'Who the hell are you to give me orders, Professor? *I* say when it is over.'

Wilcox stumbled over to Samprey's empty work desk, dragging Brulet in tow, and began to tap at a keyboard with his free hand. 'During my life I have encountered every type of person imaginable: the good, the bad, liars, cheats, psychopaths, murderers; men of action, men with the determination, motivation and ambition to pursue their goals regardless of the cost.' He continued to work at the keyboard, all the while maintaining the pressure of the blade against Brulet's throat. 'From its inception, many of these unyielding individuals have graced the ranks of the Magi with a passion to enter its world and learn its secrets, and yet you – a man of no real conviction – have in such a short time sought at every opportunity to stick your vile little nose into it.' Wilcox finished the typing and now turned his full attention to Harker. 'You, Alex Harker, are one of the most irritating, interfering, snooping, prying and meddlesome little shits it has ever been my misfortune to encounter... Well, then, you want in? So be it.'

Wilcox shuffled his hostage across the big room until he was again next to the main display screen. 'You might not have been around for the creation of the Magi Order... but you will be here for its end.'

The main view screen once again flickered into life but gone was the image of the Vatican, and it instead it had been replaced with an overhead shot of their present location showing the military helicopters that had already landed, and the increasing number of troops that were now crowding the barn's entrance.

'The last remaining HAARP facility – Our facility here – will now unleash one final show of force… upon us.'

The floor underneath them was already starting to vibrate and although Wilcox's voice sounded defiant, his face was filled with fear. His lips had turned downwards and Harker could see tears forming in the Magi lord's eyes.

'You might have won this battle, but I shall still be the one to win the war. Only I will be the one to choose my fate, and I take great relish and satisfaction in also determining yours. I sentence you all to death, and among you the Grand Master of the Templars. A fitting end to a war between us that has played out since history was first recorded.' Wilcox seemed suddenly gripped by the notion and a smile spread across his lips. 'Yes, I see it now,' he continued as if trying to convince himself. 'Maybe it is and always has been my destiny to destroy and rid the world of the blight that is Sebastian Brulet.'

As Wilcox became entranced by the concept of such a destiny he loosened his grip of the sword and Brulet immediately took full advantage of the slip. He flew his hands upwards so the chain connecting his handcuffs came in-between the blade and his neck and then flung his head backwards slamming it hard into Wilcox's face who fell back stunned. Before Wilcox could recover, Brulet spun around him and pressed the arm-sword back towards the Magi prime's own neck using the handcuff chain for leverage which slid the razor-sharp blade deep into Wilcox's throat effortlessly. The whole move was, as always with Brulet, executed so quickly that Harker barely had time to react.

'Thank you for the offer, John,' Brulet declared sardonically, standing back as Wilcox struggled to dislodge the sword buried firmly in his neck, 'but I am afraid we have to decline.'

As blood began pouring from his lips, the Magi chief's legs began to wobble, but instead of dropping to the floor, he slowly descended on to his knees and then slowly slid on to his back like a man choosing to do so rather than being forced to. A lungful of air hissed in its escape from the deep cut in his windpipe, followed by a sickening gurgling as Wilcox began choking on his own blood. During this entire time the dying man's eyes remained locked on only one person – the one he blamed for everything that had gone wrong.

Harker stared back, as the venomous hatred in those eyes continued to linger until it faded into a blank expression when Wilcox succumbed to his fatal wounds.

If a moment of silence might have been on the cards, it was not one that could be afforded as the vibrations in the floor began to increase in number.

'We need to go,' Brulet yelled, pulling Harker roughly away from the grisly sight of Wilcox's corpse. 'The tremors are getting worse.'

With Brulet in the lead and Chloe next, they rushed back into the other room and towards the same elevator to hell that Harker had arrived in. Brulet was already hammering the call button even as Harker reached them.

'It's coming,' Brulet called out above the rumble of rock scraping overhead. He gestured to the red digital display above the sliding doors. 'Shouldn't be long.'

The next few seconds seemed amongst the longest Harker had ever experienced and he tried his best to remain calm, which is difficult when the whole room was shaking and cracks were appearing in the walls all around. The only thing they had going for them was that, with only one of the HAARP facilities online the effects of the assault were taking longer. But, even then, by the time the elevator doors opened, chunks of rock were already falling from the ceiling above. All three of them leapt into the waiting carriage and Chloe began tapping on the *ground floor* button furiously.

The elevator doors had closed to within a few inches when a hand thrust through the gap and grabbed Brulet by the hair. The doors then reopened to reveal the face of a vengeful-looking McCray, who heaved Brulet back out into the room and sending him flying to the floor. Harker instantly threw a punch which landed squarely on the assassin's back, but it seemed to have little effect and the killer retaliated with a punch to Harker's face that had him tumbling back against the elevator's rear wall. Chloe also began landing blows, but she was easily fended off with a single jab to the stomach.

McCray now moved over towards Brulet, who by this time was back on his feet, and the two men confronted each other. Brulet's initial expression was that of an angry glare, but in a single moment it morphed into one of calmness, as a large chunk of rock dropped off the wall behind him, sprinkling fragments all around them. The Grand Master glanced over at Harker, who was already picking himself up, and gave a meaningful nod of his head as McCray moved in closer, not in the least interested now in the elevator's other two occupants. 'You're a good friend, Alex,' Brulet yelled, 'but I am afraid it is time for us to part ways.'

'I'm not going to lose you, Sebastian.' Harker yelled back, steadying himself as the elevator began to shake.

Brulet pulled a silver chain from around his neck and threw it past McCray into Harker's waiting palm. 'And you never will,' he replied as McCray now raised his hands in front of him ready to fight. 'Now, for the love of God, go.'

Harker could feel Chloe pulling at his waist, doing her utmost to restrain him, but there was no way he was abandoning the Templar down here. His muscles were already tensing in readiness to launch himself at McCray when another block of rock fell from the ceiling right in front of the elevator, forcing him back a step.

Beyond the rubble, it was now McCray who was doing the shouting. 'All I have ever wanted to do was to face a Grand Master,' he said before tossing over a silver handcuff key to Brulet who in turn swiftly unlocked the restraints and let them drop to the floor. 'We don't have long, so let's see what you've got, Templar.'

As the doors began to close, the two men warily circled one another, and Harker watched with a bizarre sense of pride. He watched as the opponents squared up to each other, and then a confident smile appeared on Brulet's face. The two men began moving towards each other even as the room continued to crumble around them... before the elevator doors closed for good.

Chapter 47

'I said, get everyone back on the birds, *now* Captain!' Colonel Rackman ordered firmly. 'This whole area is going to give way.'

The young captain hesitated, continuing to stare intently at his superior with a look of respectful defiance. 'Sir, we haven't had time to search the area yet. There could still be people here.'

'Maybe so, but we won't be much use to them if the ground gives way under our feet, will we? I want everyone back in the air now... that's an order.'

Without hesitation the British army captain offered a swift nod then hurried back towards the barn, issuing the fall-back orders into his shoulder radio. Within seconds a stream of uniformed soldiers appeared at the barn's door and began quickly making their way back to the waiting helicopters.

'Shit,' Rackman muttered as yet another tremor rippled underfoot, causing the old barn to shift on its foundations sending out puffs of dust from its stressed joints and appearing to wheeze for its dying breaths. *Where the hell were they?* This rescue-and-recovery operation was turning into a search-and-destroy, and no one had even fired a shot!

Rackman waited for the last soldier to pass her before turning and following him onto the waiting helicopter still grounded. Meanwhile the other helicopters of the US, Russian and Chinese units were rising into the air and began to put some distance between themselves and the mountain.

'Let's go.' Rackman ordered and she slid into the passenger seat, twirling a finger above her head.

The helicopter's engine began to wail as the rotors speeded up, lifting them into the air. Rackman looked down as parts of the ground in front of the barn started to crack and heave, the undulations hitting the barn which shuddered with each successive wave. The building was already beginning to collapse, parts of the roof giving way and falling inside the building, when two figures raced out through the open doors and came to an abrupt halt as they were hit by another ripple of moving earth, throwing them over the crest and back down onto the ground. The man had already noticed the helicopter overhead and was waving frantically with one hand as he helped the woman to her feet.

'Get us back down there,' Rackman yelled, pointing to the two figures below.

The pilot began to descend as the two individuals began running forward, jumping across cracks in the earth that were widening with every passing second. The helicopter touched down with a bump and Colonel Rackman was already out and on the ground as in the distance, the barn completely fell apart, its struts giving way and the roof folding in on itself.

Rackman continued watching as the two figures ran closer, but another swelling of the earth rose up in-between so that for a moment they disappeared from view. As the rampart of earth subsided again, they both hurdled the crest to land safely on the other side and then continued sprinting frantically.

Rackman waited until her new passengers had entered the Chinook through the side door before herself jumping back inside. 'Get us out of here,' she yelled and, with a roar of the rotors, the helicopter was up in the air and heading away.

Now airborne, the colonel turned in her seat and stared back at the late arrivals standing next to the window and, surrounded by soldiers all relieved to off the ground. She reached over and offered her hand. 'Professor Harker?'

Harker grasped the colonel's hand and shook it gratefully. 'Yes, and this is…'

'Doctor Chloe Stanton,' Rackman supplied, offering a welcoming nod. 'Yes I know.'

'How did you find us?' Harker asked.

'Michael Shroder. Your friend is a resourceful man.'

'That he is,' Harker replied, 'but how did he do it?'

'There'll be time for that later, Professor,' Rackman declared firmly. 'But I was told there would be three of you?'

The question drew an expression of regret from the both of them. 'He didn't make it.'

'I am sorry,' Rackman replied with a look of consolation, but not one to suggest she knew the significance of the man they had lost. 'OK, we're heading back to base.'

Harker and Chloe stared out at the scarred landscape below, just in time to see a bright flash illuminate the clouds with a yellowish hue before the entire area of ground collapsed in on itself in one violent spasm. Clouds of dust swirled into the air until only a black mass of debris was visible at its core, the remnants of the vast base now destroyed underneath.

'He may have made it,' Chloe yelled hopefully, struggling to be heard over the din of the helicopter's engines.

This wishful thinking was lost on Harker as he watched even more earth collapsing in on itself. Sebastian Brulet was the man who had saved his life on more than one occasion, and had never asked for a single thing in return except Harker's discretion in everything revealed to him about the shadowy world that the Templars and the Magi inhabited. The Grand Master of the Templars had now given his life to ensure both he and Chloe survived and, in a much more important way, the world at large. Harker found himself recalling to the last image he had of his friend facing up to McCray, and the smile he had worn. A smile not born out of courage or of confidence in facing his adversary but in knowing that Harker and Chloe would both escape, and more importantly that the world at large had been spared the nightmare conclusion of Wilcox's insane plan.

This thought brought to his mind something that Harker had forgotten about during the confusion of their escape from the base and he now reached into his pocket and retrieved the object Brulet had thrown to him just before the elevator doors closed. He raised his closed fist to his face, not wanting anyone else to see what it contained and then slowly released his fingers to reveal the metal object nestling in the palm of his hand. The silver medallion was worn and its once circular edges were dented with abrasions as a result of its age, but Harker recognised it immediately. There was an image carved into the surface and, even though he knew what would be on the other side, he took his time in slowly turning it over to view the second engraved image. On one side appeared the familiar image of two medieval knights riding on the same horse with the words 'SIGILLUM MILITUM' stamped around the edges, while on the reverse side the words 'CHRISTI DE TEMPLO' encircled the image of a temple.

'Seal of the soldiers of Christ and the Temple,' Harker muttered to himself and for some reason the very saying of those words added a sudden emotional connection to the seal resting in his palm. Those two riders on the horse were the unmistakable emblem of the Order of the Knights Templar, but the image of the temple was less familiar. It depicted the Church of the Holy Sepulchre located in Jerusalem and it was said by many to be the final resting place of Jesus Christ himself, as well as of his crucifixion and resurrection. To Harker it was a case of *take your pick*. What was fact, though, was that the same emblem had been originally carried by the first Grand Master of the Templars Hughes de Payens, but only copies of the fabled item had ever been discovered and presumably the original artefact had been lost somewhere in the mists of history... *until now*. With no other way of passing this symbolic artefact on to his natural successor, Brulet had entrusted it to Harker. But not so much because he deserved the honour, as much as Harker would have liked to believe, but rather because down below amongst the tumbling rock and the certainty of his death, who else was he going to pass it on to?

Harker slipped the emblem back into his coat pocket as the helicopter raced onwards, and an optimism raised his spirits confident in the knowledge that Brulet's last unspoken request would be fulfilled.

It was Chloe, huddling next to him, who awoke him from these thoughts. 'You once told me how Sebastian always managed to defy the odds,' she suggested consolingly. 'You claimed he had nine lives like a cat.'

'Yes, I did,' he replied, as the sense of loss he had felt moments earlier returned to him, and he continued to stare out at the dark billowing dust clouds now in the distance. 'But I think he just used up his last one.'

Chapter 48

The flames of blue-tinted torches flickered in the evening air, lighting up the narrow path on which a modest procession of people slowly made their way towards Kirkliston parish church. The mood was sombre but not sad, and each of the arriving guests was met by a well-dressed man in a smart Yves Saint Laurent black suit, white shirt and thin black tie. He accepted each of the guest's small white invitation cards with a gracious nod, before quietly reading out their names, and then allowing them inside the small stone chapel encircled by its own cemetery, containing a number of weathered headstones arranged in rows. Built in the heart of the village of Kirkliston, and about ten miles from Edinburgh, the twelfth-century parish church sat atop an ancient burial ground, with its elevation allowing a view of the small village surrounding it. The light was fading as the dusk drew in, but the outlines of surrounding buildings were still visible and provided a pleasant, calming atmosphere to the solemn event taking place inside. It was a sight that the latest guests to arrive were taking in as they reached the greeter and handed him their invitations.

'Professor Harker and Doctor Stanton,' he announced and passed the cards back to them. 'You are most welcome. Please enter and be seated.'

Harker gave a respectful nod and politely waited for Chloe to head inside first.

The interior of the church was modest but impressive in its own right. A small flight of steps led up to a stone pulpit, and behind this a large organ sprouted darkened metal pipes leading up towards the ceiling, providing a striking addition to the small building. The most remarkable feature, though, was an additional gallery raised up above the rows of pews on the ground floor, giving the feeling of an old courthouse minus the dock and officials, of course.

'May I see your invitations, please?' asked a man identically dressed to the one outside.

'Of course,' Harker replied passing them over.

The man studied the invitations for a moment before pointing them in the direction of an empty pew about five rows back from the front. 'Just over there. The service will begin shortly.'

'Thank you,' Harker replied. He and Chloe made their way down the aisle and took their seats as more guests arrived.

'This place is very small,' Chloe whispered quietly into Harker's ear.

'Yes, it is,' Harker said, 'does that worry you?'

'Not at all. It's lovely. I just expected something more grandiose for the funeral of a Grand Master of the Knights Templars.'

'Quiet, inconspicuous and off the radar... sounds just like the Templars to me,' he declared. 'Besides we're only ten miles from Rosslyn chapel, which is something of a centrepiece in Templar lore. This whole area was overseen by the Templars when they first came to Scotland, so it fits with tradition. Anyway, surely a smaller venue makes it harder for the Magi to discover.'

This mention of the Magi made Chloe take a deep breath, then she shook her head. 'If there even are any Magi left... It's been quite a trip, Professor. Death, mayhem and destruction, you really know how to show a girl a good time.'

Her playful remark made Harker smile. 'Well, that's the problem you face when you invite yourself to someone else's party. You never know what reception you're going to get.'

They both fell silent as an elderly couple sat down in the pew behind them, giving Harker an opportunity to settle back and reminisce about the events that had led to this night. It had been quite a trip all right, and the past few weeks since the destruction of the Magi's base had proved just as eventful.

Both he and Chloe had first been transported to a US aircraft carrier, the *Ronald Reagan*, which was anchored just off the shores of Caracas, and this served as a forward base for the joint British and US helicopter party that had them picked them up. They had spent six hours holed up in one of the cabins under armed guard, and with only a tatty-looking chessboard to occupy them. Ten games later, most of them lost to Chloe much to the detriment of Harker's ego, they had been met by an American who simply described himself as a member of the security services. Without discussion they'd been placed on a twin-engine Grumman C-2 Greyhound and flown directly back to the United Kingdom, where they had been greeted by two men offering MI6 credentials. Blindfolded and handcuffed, they were then driven to a warehouse somewhere in London, and been 'requested' to sign forms which guaranteed their silence under the Official Secrets Act. Without further ado, both he and Chloe had then been blindfolded again and dumped in the middle of Camden Town, right in front of the Dublin Castle pub. And that, as baffling as it seemed, was that. No interrogation, no threats – not even a goodbye. They had simply been dropped back into the ordinary world once more along with everyone else amid the chaos of destruction Wilcox had left in his wake.

They had spent an hour or so in the pub casually drinking and discussing the whirlwind that was their past few days, whilst all the while looking over their shoulders for any suspicious-looking characters who might be keeping an eye on them. Shortly afterwards Chloe had headed back to try and salvage her job at Blackwater, who strangely welcomed her back with open arms, and Harker resumed his teaching position at Cambridge University. Upon arrival he was nagged incessantly by Dean Lercher about his whereabouts during the crisis, and Harker stuck to the story that he had been caught up in the chaos of world events just like everyone else. Reluctantly the Dean had finally let the subject go and besides he had plenty to deal with. Although Cambridge had been largely unaffected by the pandemonium created by HAARP, many of its students had ties to places that were, and the University had been closed down until communications such as phone lines and the TV networks could be restored.

The one bright light amidst the gloom had been the funeral of Pope Gregory XVII – or Salvatore Vincenzo to his friends – who was already being considered for canonisation, a process usually taking far, far longer than just a few weeks after death. What was really unexpected, though, was how all places of worship of all religions, every faith and creed, had seen a huge rise in attendance and thus defying Wilcox's hopes for a dark future. Would it last? Probably not, but the sense of world community had never been stronger and almost all governments had made an unprecedented show of unity and solidarity, by working with each other much more closely than in the past. Would it last? Again probably not but it did offer hope to the masses, and a world without hope, as Wilcox had claimed fervently, was a world not worth living in. Harker found it odd to think that the very actions the Magi had hoped would destroy humanity were in fact bringing it closer together and that, in a world where so much devastation had taken place, there was something positive to be gained from the nightmare that had been the three Secrets of Fatima.

Martial law had now ceased to be enforced, even if the army was still a visible presence on the streets, although it was now mainly involved in clean-up jobs and in helping to rebuild the worst affected areas of the country, including the remains of what was once Westminster Abbey. Speculation had run rife throughout the newspapers and TV networks after they came back online, posting everything from a mass solar event to global warming as the cause for such destruction, but it wasn't until a story broke in the *Sunday Times* that things began to become interesting. A journalist had been sent a package containing documents relating to HAARP and its various facilities around the globe. This had also been accompanied by a letter stating that the technology involved was of such importance that everyone should henceforth be aware of its existence, for to keep such devices secret could have dire consequences for the whole planet. The letter had been printed in its entirety, but it was not so much the contents that caught Harker's interest but rather the initials of the sender, which appeared at the end: S.B.

Harker was certain Brulet could not have written the letter himself, because there was no way the Grand Master could have survived, but in his mind the disclosure must have come from the Templars, and his initials had been used to honour the leader they had lost. Harker guessed that the various governments involved in the clean-up had initially decided to keep the wonder weapon to themselves, but after a week of silence the Templars had decided to ensure complete transparency regarding the technology involved. HAARP needed to be controlled by governments, there was no doubt, but only so long as the public were aware of it. Then those in charge could be held to account and the press would keep an ever-vigilant eye on its progress, even if it was from a distance.

Despite this startling revelation, there were many other things to consider still up for grabs. The film shots of the hellish beasts had already been dismissed as fakes: computer-generated images created by hackers wanting to contribute more chaos in a climate of fear. And the fact that the virus had turned so many into raving lunatics had been widely ascribed to gas mains erupting during the seismic activity and warping the minds of those who inhaled the fumes. It was a terrible cover story and the newspapers were having none of it but no doubt, in the weeks and months to come, more plausible explanations would surface from some branch of the government. Harker was sure that, rightly or wrongly, those individuals high up the chain of military command would surely be unwilling to publicly acknowledge a virus that targets a specific person for death based solely on their DNA. It would be considered far too valuable… wouldn't it?

Harker found himself lying awake late at night still preoccupied with thoughts of the Templars, Sebastian and Michael Shroder, whom he had not encountered since Chernobyl. Was it the MI6 agent who had arranged for Chloe and himself to have such a quick and easy escape from the prying eyes of the security services and from further involvement in the whole affair? But there was one question that burned brighter in his mind than all else. One that superseded all others as far as he was concerned, and the main reason he had allowed himself to be drawn further and deeper into Wilcox's insane web of deceit. *Where was the Christ child?* This was the one loose end, and the most important that continued to tug at Harker's conscience and his very soul, with a terrible dread of what the fate of that small child might have been.

A few weeks later a hand-delivered letter had appeared through his door, inviting him to the funeral of Sebastian Brulet in the small parish of Kirkliston, just outside Edinburgh. Chloe had received the same invite and now, two days later, they were about to pay their last respects to the man who had not only saved their lives but arguably the lives of six and a half billion others. It was with such thoughts that Harker was now engrossed, and so much so that he hardly noticed the man wearing a long black overcoat who sat down next to him, and it was not until the other spoke that Harker awoke from his ruminations.

'Hello, Alex.'

Harker spun to his left to find Michael Shroder gazing at him with a friendly smile.

'So you got the invite, then?' the MI6 agent surmised, offering a subtle wave of greeting to Chloe, who had now also taken note of his presence. 'I trust your trip back to the UK was as uneventful as I had hoped.'

'So it *was* you,' Harker replied, glad to find at least one of his loose ends wrapped up. 'Thank you, Michael.'

Shroder nodded. 'You're welcome but I can't take all the credit. Our friends played a significant role, and anyway your further involvement would have only opened a can of worms which many people wish to remain closed.'

The two men sat in silence for a moment until finally Harker voiced the only question that really mattered to him. 'What about the child?'

Shroder said nothing but instead reached over to pick up the hymn sheet laying next to him, then gestured to the priest, who was now making his way up into the pulpit. 'Let's enjoy the service, shall we.'

The ceremony lasted about forty minutes, during which a number people stood up to offer short yet pertinent eulogies to the man they had all known. Words such as *honourable*, *brave*, *decent* and *caring* were used again and again, but nothing to suggest these speakers had any idea of their dead friend's ties to the Knights Templar, or the extent to which he had been involved in recent events. Afterwards the congregation was ushered outside to a grave waiting in the far corner of the cemetery, where the final send-off would take place. Harker, Chloe and Shroder stood and watched as the shiny walnut-wood coffin was gently lowered into the ground and shortly afterwards the small crowd began to disperse.

'So, tell me again what is it you wanted to know?' Shroder asked sympathetically.

'What about the child?'

Shroder motioned to a tall man standing with his back to them, wearing a dark navy overcoat, and shaking hands with the remaining guests. 'There's someone I think you should meet,' he said. 'I'm sorry Chloe, but this invitation is for Alex and for Alex alone.' Shroder gestured to the man who was now standing on his own, and with a nod to Chloe Harker cautiously made his way over. He was within metres of reaching him when a somewhat familiar voice stopped him in his tracks.

'Professor Alex Harker, at last we meet.'

The man then turned around and Harker was immediately struck by his similarity to Brulet. Silver hair poked out from underneath a navy trilby and a pair of dark-lensed aviator glasses reflected the flickering of the burning torches lining the cemetery walls. He offered a glove-covered hand to Harker. 'My name is Tristan Brulet,' he said 'Sebastian was my brother.'

Harker took the hand and shook it warmly. 'You remind me of him very much, if you don't mind me saying so.'

'Not at all,' Brulet replied, releasing his grip and with one finger lowering his glasses to reveal the same cross-shaped pupils that had made his brother so distinctive. 'As you see, we share many similarities. Come, let us talk.'

Harker walked at his side as he was led over to the perimeter of the cemetery, waiting silently for his host to speak first.

'The Templars thank you, as do I, for your help during the past few days. Your service has been exemplary and it is not something that will be forgotten. But, before we go any further, I must ask you a question. My brother, how did he die?'

Harker was already opening his mouth to reply when Brulet continued. 'I know where he was, and for what reasons, but what exactly happened?'

Harker paused for a moment, because he had not actually witnessed Sebastian's death with his own eyes but he understood what this brother was getting at. 'A Magi assassin named McCray tried to prevent us leaving the facility, and your brother decided that was not going to happen. The truth is, Mr Brulet, he died while saving our lives, and I will always be in his debt not only as a protector to me but as a friend.'

Tristan Brulet stared out towards the twinkling lights of the village, and then lowered his head. 'A hero to the end – I would have expected nothing less of him.'

It was said with such obvious sorrow that Harker was unsure what to say next, but the small object in his pocket gave him pause for thought. He reached in and retrieved it before offering it to the grieving brother. 'I think this belongs to you.'

Brulet looked down at the silver Grand Master's emblem, then gently plucked it from Harker fingers. 'This has been in my family a very long time, and I thank you for it.' He studied it for a few more moments before popping it into an inside pocket, then turning his attention back to Harker. 'You had my brother's trust and now you have mine.'

'Thank you, that means a great deal,' Harker declared. 'So, what now for the Templars?'

'I am not sure, to be honest,' Brulet replied matter-of-factly. 'With the last of the Magi bloodline gone, I am unsure of what role, if any, the

361

Templars have left to play. We will of course use our financial resources to help in the rebuilding of the Vatican, albeit from a distance, but other than that our purpose for the future remains unclear.'

Harker appreciated the honesty of the man's words and he moved closer to him. 'I am sure that, under your leadership, a new course will be set. But there is something else I have to ask.'

'The question of the child, I assume?' Brulet answered.

'Yes,' Harker was not surprised in the least that Tristan Brulet possessed the same power of intuition as his brother.

The man reached into his pocket and pulled out a white envelope bearing a red wax seal whose image was identical to that on one side of the Grand Master's emblem: the Knights Templars riding on the same horse. He passed it over to Harker who, respectfully took his time to open it. After cracking the seal, he carefully extracted the folded letter inside, and began to read the handwritten message.

> *Dear Alex,*
>
> *If you are reading this letter it means that for whatever reason I have not managed to reach the conclusion of our journey alongside you. It is an unsettling business, whilst I am still alive, to be writing a letter for you to read after my death, so allow me to get straight to the point. I would firstly like to repeat my apologies for keeping you in the dark regarding Claire Dwyer's association with the Templars. You should know that from the outset her trust in you was absolute, and it was my decision and mine alone to hide her true role from you. Initially, you were an unknown quantity to me but had I been aware then of the man I now know you to be, things surely would have been different. Then, again, maybe not, for you are a worthy archaeologist and truly honourable man, but frankly you are a terrible actor. So the Magi would very likely have recognised this fact, and I fear I might have put you in even more danger than you were already involved in. Regardless, you should know now that Claire had been a member of our Order long before those events that caused our paths to cross. At the time I write this, I do not know if she has survived or not. I can only pray that she is with you now. If not, then you need only know that she was one of my most trusted colleagues, and I am eternally grateful for the sacrifices she has made. Who knows, maybe we are together both watching over as you read these words.*

Harker stopped for a moment and he found himself glancing up at the star-lit sky, before continuing.

> *I shall entrust this letter to Mr Shroder who will pass it on to my brother, Tristan, with instructions to give it to you. My brother and I are similar in many ways, and I have total confidence that he will make a worthy Grand Master of the Knights Templar. He is by nature a more cautious fellow than perhaps I was, but feel secure in the knowledge that the trust and friendship you and I enjoyed shall be extended to you by him. Remember that you are now part of a brotherhood that transcends both leadership and time. You are a Templar and the link you share with those in its service can and never shall be broken.*
>
> *As for any other questions that you undoubtedly may have, I can only refer you to Tristan. As Grand Master it is now up to him to judge whether those questions should be answered.*
>
> *I wish you a long and prosperous life, Professor Harker and that all your hopes and wishes see fruition. I know you will uphold the beliefs and aspirations that have made us close friends in such a short amount of time. I leave you therefore with one last piece of advice. Some secrets have the power to warp a person's sensibilities, and in doing so transform them into the very thing they most deplore. Be wary of this, my friend, and never allow yourself to veer aside from the path of what you know to be right.*
>
> *Yours respectfully and always,*
>
> *Sebastian Brulet*

A grateful tingling feeling ran through Harker as he slid the letter back into its envelope. He thought back to Lusic Bekhit, the Templar betrayer, and how the man had been swayed to serve the Magi. Harker had not even found time to ask Shroder whether he had tracked down the turncoat, but that was a question for another occasion.

It was Tristan Brulet who now pulled him away from such contemplations by offering him a small piece of lined notepad paper, which Harker took in his fingers and read in silence.

'You should take a trip to that address,' Brulet explained. 'No one else apart from you and me know of it, and I would be more than happy to accompany you there tomorrow morning if it is suitable?'

'I would like that very much,' Harker said and he glanced back at Chloe, who was deep in conversation with Shroder. 'But may I bring Doctor Stanton along with us?'

Brulet nodded. 'If you feel you can trust her, then the decision is yours.'

'I do,' Harker replied.

'Good. I will have a driver pick you both up tomorrow. Someone will be in touch.'

After shaking hands, Harker offered a final respectful nod and then made his way back to Chloe and Shroder.

'Everything all right here?' he asked.

'Everything's grand,' Shroder replied. 'Doctor Stanton and I were just discussing the finer points of…"spook work", as she puts it.'

'So what happened, Alex?'

Before Harker could answer her, Shroder was already making a move.

'I am sure you two will have a lot to talk about but I must say goodbye.' The MI6 agent shook both of their hands. 'I'm needed back in London as there's still a lot to be done.' He then handed Harker a business card. 'My number is on there, so maybe we can catch up for a drink sometime and chew the fat?'

'I look forward to it,' Harker replied, putting the card in his pocket. 'And thank you for everything. I was sure that I'd be sweating it out in some interrogation room for the next few years at least.'

'Oh, please, we only do that to our enemies.' Shroder shot Chloe a quick smile. 'Be good, Doctor Stanton.'

'And yourself, Mr Spy,' she whispered after him as the man made his way back along the path to the church gate and the car park beyond.

'So, who was he and what did he say?' Chloe asked eagerly.

Harker pulled out the note with a single address scribbled on to. 'Do you fancy taking a trip?'

She stared at him cautiously. 'That depends on how dangerous it is.'

'Don't worry, it's not anywhere that will be hazardous to our health,' he replied. He glanced back towards Brulet, who was still gazing thoughtfully up at the starry night. 'I bloody hope not, anyway.'

Chapter 49

The bright midday sun radiated its warmth down from the clear blue sky, flooding the quaint Cotswold village of Moreton-in-Marsh in a rosy cheer, as the grey Audi A4 pulled up outside a honey-coloured sandstone building just off the main high street.

'This is it,' Tristan Brulet gestured to the house with a light-green wooden door. He turned around to face Chloe who had taken the back seat during the journey from the local airfield. 'I must ask that you wait here for us, Doctor Stanton.'

Chloe gave an understanding smile. Having only been invited by Harker to accompany them, she was not in the position to demand anything, and she knew it.

He now turned his attention to Harker, who was already undoing his seat belt. 'Let's go.'

They had flown in by private jet arriving at Membury airfield, near Swindon, where they had been met by a driver with a rental car. Oddly, Brulet had requested the driver to wait with the plane, and instead asked Harker to then drive the fifty-minute journey into the Cotswolds. They had done so in near total silence but it had not been in any way uncomfortable, and the muted atmosphere had served to amplify the sense of anticipation over what might lie at their final destination. As Harker stared up at the impressive but modest house, he had to admit to a feeling of disappointment. He was hoping to find himself visiting a Templar lair, or even one of their vaults, and the less impressive sight of this rural building did not quite meet those expectations.

'Come on, follow me,' Brulet urged softly, and Harker followed him up a short stone path to the green door, on which he knocked three times.

There was a brief wait and then with the muffled scuffling of shoes before the door unclicked open to reveal a man in his mid-thirties wearing a tan cashmere jumper and dark green jeans.

'Mr Denton,' the young man addressed Brulet, before shaking his hand. 'I hope you didn't have trouble finding us. The back roads can be confusing.'

The fact that Brulet was obviously using an alias should not have surprised Harker, but nonetheless the reference did catch him off guard. He paused for a moment shaking the man's hand, too.

'And you must be Mr Harker?' the man said retrieving his hand. 'I'm David Evans and it's a pleasure to meet you. Please come in.'

Harker followed them into a hallway and waited for their host to close the door, before leading them into the kitchen.

'This is my wife, Abigail,' Evans explained, putting his arm around an attractive woman with black hair, who offered them both a welcoming smile.

'It's a pleasure to see you again Mr Denton, and good to finally meet you Mr Harker.'

'Please, call me Alex.' Harker replied and shaking her hand.

'I was just telling Alex, that now the papers have been signed and approved, he is as of this moment your point of contact and representative for all and any future issues. Congratulations to the both of you. It is official.'

Harker watched in confusion as the couple erupted in excitement and began hugging each other. The moment proved so powerful that Abigail was fighting back the tears.

'That is the best news we could have hoped for. Thank you for everything Mr Denton. And Alex...' David said and he wrapped his arms around Harker and gave him a tremendous hug, 'I look forward to knowing you.'

To say Harker was somewhat bewildered, was like saying the Pope was somewhat Catholic, and he just hoped his expression did not betray what he was feeling. Who the hell were these people? 'I feel the same way and look forward to getting to know you to.'

Harker caught the amused smile on Brulet's face from the corner of his eye. Mr Denton was unquestionably finding Harker's confusion highly amusing.

'So, Abigail, may we take a look?' Brulet inquired and was met with an excited nod. With a wave of her hand she ushered them through to a spacious lounge next door. And as Harker entered the room, every question was instantly answered and he gasped.

The glinting brown of eyes of a contented young child stared up at him and he blinked as a smile formed across his tiny lips, waving his arms up and down in excitement.

Harker watched as Abigail scooped the child up in her arms, then made her way over towards them.

'Here's the little man,' she announced proudly and placed the excited infant into Harker's arms. 'He has so much energy and such a wonderful temperament. Hardly cries at all.'

'Except when he's hungry or has a dirty nappy that needs changing.' David joined in, smiling as enthusiastically as his wife.

Harker stared down at the small child and only two words came to mind: *Thank God*. How the infant came to be here, though, was a complete mystery, and it was Brulet who filled in the minutiae.

'I am sorry that your original case worker Claire Dwyer could not continue at the adoption agency, but she has taken a new position as head of our Irish office. Nevertheless she sends her regards and is happy that Alex will take over.'

'We understand,' David replied, 'but please offer her our thanks for making the adoption process so quick.'

The couple gazed lovingly down at their new charge as Tristan Brulet stiffened and prepared to leave. 'If you have any questions, feel free to call us night or day.'

It was Abigail who looked up and realised their guests were about to leave. 'Would you like a cup of tea or anything?'

'No, thank you. We have a meeting in London later this afternoon but we appreciate the offer. As I said when we spoke earlier, I just wanted to make the introductions. No doubt Alex will be in touch again very soon.'

Harker pulled himself away from the penetrating gaze of the small child in their arms. 'Yes, I'll certainly be in touch and I am very happy with what I've seen here,' he replied, feeding into the role. 'I tend to have a somewhat hands-off approach once we feel happy with the new parents, but I'll drop by from time to time and can be contacted through the agency if the need arises.'

David skipped ahead of Brulet who was already making his way for the front door and opening it. 'We look forward to seeing you soon.'

Harker took one final look at the child in Abigail's arms, and then made his way down the path to join Brulet, who was already waiting on the pavement. He gave a final wave, before the door closed behind them.

'Happy, now?' Brulet enquired.

'Yes, I reckon so,' Harker replied, then shook his head at what he had just learnt. 'So am I right in saying the child was never in danger?'

'None whatsoever. We never had any intention of letting that child anywhere near John Wilcox and his not so merry band of men.'

'And how about the loss of Templar lives in the war against the Magi?' Harker asked, 'was all that made up?'

'I am afraid that much is very true, but only because it was decided that the Magi had crossed the line, with their grandiose plans with their cloning of the child and their attempted hijacking of the papacy and the Templar council voted that the time had come for end game.' Brulet explained with a saddened smile. 'Little did we know back then that the Magi were planning an end game of their own.'

'And how about the adoption agency? Just a front?'

'No. Quite the contrary.' Brulet said, shaking his head. 'The Templars are involved in and fund many charitable organisations and adoption agencies in conjunction with government departments and the Church.'

'And Claire? How did she meet with them if she disappeared at the same time the child's mother died?' Harker asked, with a splinter of mistrust building in his voice.

'She never did meet them, but the woman the Evans's were referring to, one of our operatives, used her name. It seemed the decent thing to do in honouring her sacrifice for the child's survival and her dedication to the Templars.' Brulet reached over and squeezed Harker's shoulder warmly. 'It is only when we forget the people we lose do they truly cease to be part of our lives.'

In a strange yet pragmatic way the answer made sense to Harker and even though he found himself in total agreement with the Grand Master, there was still something he found perplexing. 'So, why on earth did your brother let me think the child was in danger? Why not tell me everything from the outset?'

Tristan Brulet eyed him in silence for a few moments, as if grappling for the right words. 'That is a decision both Sebastian and I tussled with for some time and, if I am being honest it is something I wasn't going to tell you. But after meeting you last night and, the way in which you have proved yourself throughout this whole fiasco, I decided to revisit my earlier conclusion.'

He reached into his pocket and pulled out a small piece of paper that he held up in front of him. 'Because of this.'

Harker stared at it for a moment before he realised it was a fragment of parchment, and furthermore identical to the type on which the Secrets of Fatima had been written. 'The fourth Secret!' He gasped. 'So there really *were four*?'

'Yes,' Brulet replied, still firmly holding the scrap between his forefingers. 'The Magi were not the only ones to receive word of the Fatima prophecies and we sought to acquire them too. Unfortunately, we were only able to lay hands on the fourth and final one, before the Magi had swooped in and discovered the contents of the other three for themselves. As you may already know, the Magi therefore never had any idea that a fourth Secret even existed, and that was a blessing made possible by just one man.'

'Marcus Eckard.'

Brulet offerd a slow nod. 'Yes, the late Marcus Eckard, who managed to withhold it from them despite the terrible tortures they inflicted upon him. He could see for himself how important this final part of the prophecy was, and at great personal detriment he kept it to himself and out of the Magi's clutches. It is because of the fourth Secret, and this alone, that you were so readily invited into the Templar ranks.'

The Templar Grand Master raised the piece of parchment and began to read it aloud. 'There will be many who seek to pervert the truth of this prophecy I have been entrusted with, and to that end much credence must be given to the one who will thwart such attempts. For, as revealed to me from the virgin's own lips, it will be an angel who will hark the truth from the heavens, and it is in that harker that we must trust.'

Harker felt his whole body tingle as Brulet passed the fourth Secret over to him.

'My brother and I debated the true meaning of this for many years and we could never reach a conclusion that satisfied us both… That is until we met you. Since that time Sebastian was convinced that your role in the rebirth of the Christ child and a resolution to the destruction described by the three Secrets was essential. It is this reason you were, will and are given so much trust in this matter, and it is a belief that has been proved right, time and time again. It is also the reason that I entrust the protection of the child's identity to you alone. Your judgement is final and exceeds even mine.'

Brulet waited as Harker read through the note for himself before continuing with his explanation for his brother's secretive reasoning. 'I am not sure what would have happened if the Magi had retrieved all four Secrets, but when you did enter their radar I am sure they would have handled things a little differently. I can only imagine the force they would have unleashed to ensure your demise.'

Harker was stunned with everything becoming a little too surreal and his hands shook slightly at the thought. There were just too many coincidences to be… well a coincidence, and he thought back to his encounter with Marcus Eckard at Blackwater insane asylum and the patient's curious reaction when Harker had introduced himself. 'Harker, Harker, Harker. That name sounds familiar, have we met?' Had the deranged man recognised him from the beginning? Had it been the reason that Eckard had been so forthcoming in his knowledge of the subject and so eager to disclose it? 'So why not tell me. It could have helped to know how involved I was.' Harker asked and still reeling from the apparent connection being made between the prophecy and himself.

Brulet offered a light pat on his shoulder. 'It is for that very reason that it was kept from you. The knowledge of this fact could have influenced your thinking and ultimately your decisions, and who knows where that would have led. Sebastian believed, as do I, that it was imperative that you be left to decide your actions organically, as it were and without intervention for fear of changing the destiny of the prophecy itself. It was also the reason he decided to keep you in the dark regarding the child's safety, so as to ensure you maintained the resolve we knew you would need.'

Brulet could see that Harker was looking irked at the idea of having the child used as a carrot, to keep him pushing forward, and he immediately set about rectifying it. 'Alex, if you had known the child was safe and sound, would you ever have been convinced to go to meet with Marcus Eckard in the first place?'

Harker thought about it for a moment before, with a sigh, he shook his head. 'No,' he replied, 'probably not.'

'Then it appears that Sebastian was correct in insisting upon it.' Brulet continued softly. 'You must remember at that stage, none of

370

us knew anything about the Skoptsy or how exactly the Magi would approach you.'

Harker expelled a deep breath, his mind buzzing with ordered confusion. He offered the parchment back to Brulet, who refused it with his palm raised.

'You keep it… as a memento. Besides, it is now useless to anyone.' With that Brulet turned around and began walking away. 'I'll be in touch, oh, and you can keep the rental for as long as you need it, just return it when you're done.'

'Where are you going?' Harker called out, a bit shocked at how rapidly the Grand Master was making his departure.

'There are a few friends living in this village I would like to visit,' Brulet replied, 'I spent part of my youth growing up here you know.'

With that Brulet continued along the pavement and Harker waited until he disappeared around a corner before heading over to the waiting Audi. As he got close, Chloe opened the door and got out to meet him.

'Where has he gone?' she asked, her face full of curiosity.

'He had to leave,' Harker replied. 'Friends to meet, apparently.'

'Oh, that seems rather abrupt.'

'Well, as I keep saying, the Templars aren't the norm.'

She was already nodding. 'That's the truth. After all, aren't you yourself a Templar?'

'Yes I am.' Harker smiled.

'So, are you going to tell me what happened then?'

Harker thought about it for a moment, then something Chloe had said to him a few weeks earlier came to mind. 'You once made me a proposition to sleep with me… Does that still stand?'

Chloe looked shocked for a moment and then she crossed her arms defiantly and leant back on her waist. 'If I remember accurately, we thought the world was coming to an end.'

'True but…'

'But nothing.' She said with a smile. 'Are you telling me I have to sleep with you to find out what happened back there?'

'No. Of course not.' Harker replied and looking offended. 'Still, it couldn't hurt your chances.'

They both burst out into laughter and Chloe slid her arm between Harker's.

'Come on, let's go,' Harker said, and leading them both towards the centre of the village. 'I saw a bar at the top of the street. How about we start there?'

–

The sun was just setting on the sleepy village of Moreton-in-Marsh when someone knocked on the Evans house's green door. Wearing a dark suit and shiny brown brogues, the caller waited patiently until the door swung open.

'Mr Evans?' The man displayed a wide smile.

'Yes, can I help?'

'Mr Denton said you would be expecting me.'

David Evans immediately nodded and waved the man inside. 'Oh, yes, he said you would be popping by. My wife Abigail is out at the moment, but she'll be back soon. Please, come in.'

The visitor followed his host into the lounge and over to the cot the child was lying in.

'Here he is,' Evans said as the man knelt down to gaze down at the sleeping infant. 'Mr Denton warned us that you always like to do a final check on any new parents.'

'That's true.' The man pulled aside a long wisp of white hair which had fallen across his forehead and tucked it behind his ear. 'It is something of a tradition for me.'

David watched him delicately brush a finger against the baby's cheek and then pull the blanket up higher as if to keep the child warm. 'We met one of your staff, Alex Harker, and I'm told he's a good man.'

'Yes, he is,' the visitor replied, now standing up. 'He's one of our best.' He turned to face Evans directly. 'I would appreciate it if you didn't mention to him that I came here though?' The man knowingly tapped his nose upon which rested a dark pair of Ray-Ban sunglasses. 'I wouldn't want him to think I was treading on his toes.'

'I understand completely,' Evans replied and he examined the other man's face keenly. 'I hope you don't mind me saying so, but your resemblance to Mr Denton is quite remarkable.'

'Not at all,' the man smiled politely, 'It is a family business.'

'Ahhh, I see. That makes sense... So is everything OK, then?'

The man stared at Mr Evans blankly for a moment, then he nodded gently. 'Everything is just fine,' he declared. 'In fact, it couldn't be better.'

Acknowledgements

A special thanks as always to my editor, Peter Lavery, for his patience and continued guidance throughout the writing of this book. I owe you my friend.

My thanks to Tamsyn Curry whose hard work and copy editing skills have made my life as a writer so much easier.

The Harker Chronicles